T0305014

DEEP BLACK

DEEP BLACK

Miles Cameron

Arcana Imperii: Book Two

First published in Great Britain in 2024 by Gollancz
an imprint of The Orion Publishing Group Ltd
Carmelite House, 50 Victoria Embankment
London EC4Y 0DZ

An Hachette UK Company

1 3 5 7 9 10 8 6 4 2

A CIP catalogue record for this book is
available from the British Library.

ISBN (HB) 978 1 399 61503 7
ISBN (eBook) 978 1 399 61506 8
ISBN (audio) 978 1 399 61507 5

Typeset at The Spartan Press Ltd,
Lymington, Hants

Printed and bound in Great Britain by Clays Ltd,
Elcograf S.p.A.

www.gollancz.co.uk

For Sarah Jane Watt, who takes her coffee black

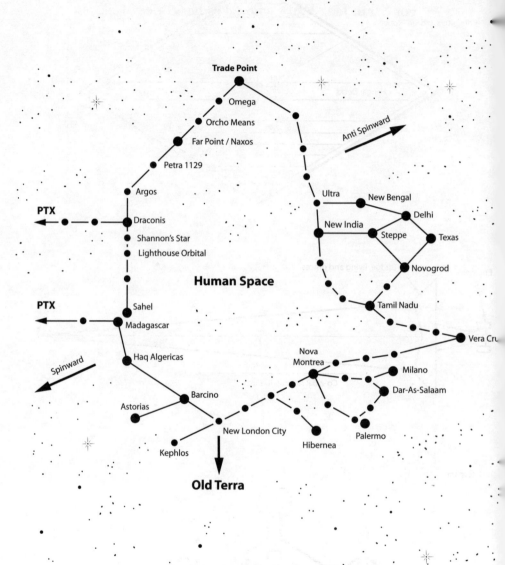

Trade Point

Omega

Orcho Means

Far Point / Naxos

Petra 1129

Argos

PTX ← Draconis

Shannon's Star

Lighthouse Orbital

Human Space

Ultra

New Bengal

Delhi

New India

Steppe

Texas

Novogrod

Sahel

PTX ←

Madagascar

Tamil Nadu

Vera Cru

Spinward

Haq Algericas

Nova
Montrea

Milano

Dar-As-Salaam

Barcino

Astorias

Palermo

New London City

Kephlos

Hibernea

Anti Spinward →

Old Terra

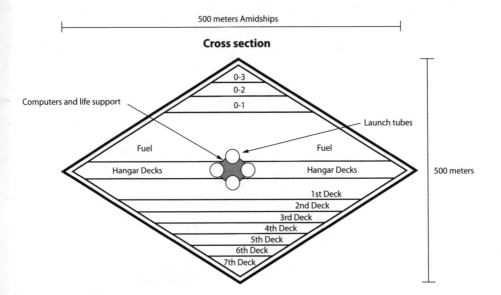

500 meters Amidships

Cross section

0-3
0-2
0-1

Computers and life support

Launch tubes

Fuel

Fuel

Hangar Decks

Hangar Decks

1st Deck
2nd Deck
3rd Deck
4th Deck
5th Deck
6th Deck
7th Deck

500 meters

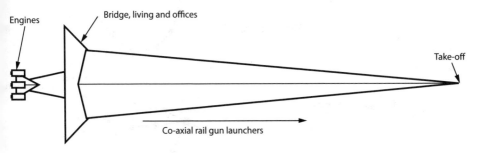

Engines

Bridge, living and offices

Take-off

Co-axial rail gun launchers

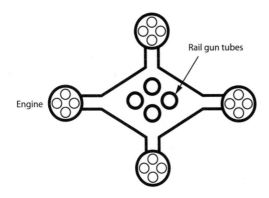

Stern

Rail gun tubes

Engine

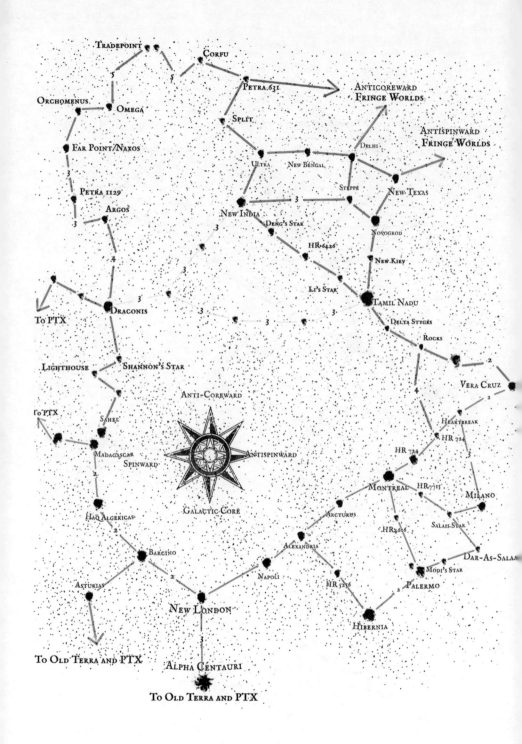

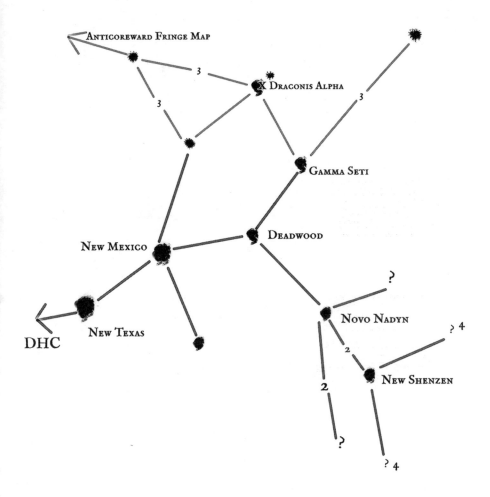

ANTICOREWARD FRINGE MAP

X DRACONIS ALPHA

3

3

3

GAMMA SETI

DEADWOOD

NEW MEXICO

?

NOVO NADYN

DHC

NEW TEXAS

? 4

2

NEW SHENZEN

2

?

? 4

I

'Come in,' Truekner said.

The commander was sitting on his rack, back against the screened bulkhead and padded with a piece of nano-fluff that had to have been salvaged from another acceleration couch. Truekner was old – right at the limit of what most people tolerated before they went to rejuv. He had creases where his jaw met his neck, crow's feet around his eyes even when he wasn't smiling, and most of his hair was grey. He wore a flightsuit and his feet were bare, which struck Marca Nbaro as faintly embarrassing, and intimate, which she knew was ridiculous.

She stepped over the knee-knocker of the hatch. Truekner's stateroom was big enough that it had an airtight hatch and separate interior compartments. It was formidably neat; there wasn't even an abandoned T-shirt. On the main screen, there was a picture of a dog – a big dog – frolicking in an endless loop.

Nbaro cleared her throat. 'Personnel reports and commendations,' she said.

Truekner gave her a thin smile. 'Perfect.' But then he shrugged off whatever remark he'd been ready to make and sat up. 'Grab a seat, Nbaro. Give me a quick walk through, so I can sign 'em off fast.'

It was seven ship-days since the largest space battle in human history. It was twenty-two hours since humans had first managed to communicate directly with the Starfish, the aliens who controlled the xenoglas trade – the first real contact in two hundred years.

And the skipper had pulled Nbaro back to the ship and required her to stay and finish the paperwork, which Nbaro thought was a funny phrase because none of it was on paper. But the Directorate of Human Corporations, a four-hundred-year-old trading combine that maintained a loose control of about half of Human Space, maintained 'the Service', and the Service had traditions that went back to wet navies, sailing ships, and ... paper. She'd spent her life learning them on sims, and a year trying to make them work for real, and still the age of it all daunted her.

Truekner gave her a slightly cynical smile. 'Yes, Nbaro, through war and plague and alien contact, we still need to file our reports and nominate our people for medals. And while I have you, did you post that material readiness survey I gave you two weeks ago?'

She had to think about it. The material readiness survey had been completed before the battle, and thus seemed to have been done in a different age, so long ago she could scarcely remember the tedium. 'Yes, sir,' she said at last. 'Filed and approved by Morosini.' Morosini was the ship's AI, which manifested as a courtly but difficult man in the scarlet clothes of a bygone era.

He nodded. 'Nice. Good. I missed that. OK, let's see the reports.'

She'd posted the 'material readiness survey' – which was really a report of cleanliness and stock in the squadron spaces – just before the battle; or rather, between the first big fight and the second ...

It was hard to keep track.

Time had dilated for everyone on board DHCS *Athens*.

Their voyage had been dogged by violence almost from the first; indeed, one of Nbaro's first memories aboard was the full alert that the Doje, Eli Sagoyewatha, had ordered when the Greatship *New York* had been reported destroyed – the first of the DHC's huge trading ships ever to be destroyed. That had happened while they were in initial refuelling and workup, before they'd loaded cargo and launched. What had followed was sometimes hard to sequence: an attempt to get a nuke aboard; a second attempt, that had succeeded in getting boarders and hackers aboard; a complex plot to take or destroy the ship while corroding the command AI, Morosini; a simultaneous fight with two apparent PTX Q-ships in dock at Sahel, and then what was, in effect, a single space battle that lasted, in ship-time, for months – seconds of combat conducted by computers, interspersed with trade missions and thousands of hours of watching space for enemy signals. All culminating in the Battle of Trade Point, as everyone called it: a three- or even four-sided fight that the *Athens* had won decisively.

So far.

She pointed her tab at the skipper's screens and thumbed her first display.

'Petty Officer Tresa Indra. Star of Honour posthumous.'

Truekner read the display, nodding along, and saying aloud, 'In the highest traditions of the Service...' He made a face. 'Service has given out sixteen Stars of Honour in three hundred years,' he said. 'How many have you got in that pile?'

She frowned. 'Just Indra and Zeynep Suliemani, sir. Indra spotted the alien ship under fire, located it, and notified the ship. Without her we'd all be dead. Suliemani gave her life ejecting her crew when the PTX tried to ambush us.'

'And Lance Ko from Flight Five, and Naisha Qaqqaq from Engineering – she might even live to receive hers. And you, Lieutenant. Yours went off after the boarding action at Sahel.

There might be more – not for nothing does the Master call this "the ship of heroes". Five Stars of Honour from one ship.'

Nbaro nodded. 'Yes, sir.'

He gave an odd roll of his head that was like 'yes' and 'no' combined into a single motion. 'Well, let's run it up the flagpole. I'm happy to do anything I can for Indra's family, and for Suleimani's. Bits of ribbon are free.' He smiled. 'And of course, the Star comes with a promotion and a pay bonus that any family might want.'

'Promotion?' she asked.

Truekner smiled. 'You hadn't worked that out?' He shrugged. 'And in Indra's case, she'll get a patrician's cargo allotment, which will be worth a kingdom after this trip.' The smile transformed into a grin. 'I mean, if we make it home alive. We're on even money in the senior officers' mess.'

'Even money?' Nbaro asked. 'I mean, who pays off in a bet like that?'

Truekner sighed. 'Oh, Nbaro, we old people have our little jokes, and we just hope you young folks will play along.'

'Yes, sir,' Nbaro said.

She thumbed the next display item: Lieutenant Suleimani's Star of Honour.

'Nicely worded. Ever read Owen's "Dulce et Decorum Est" about war in the Age of Chaos, Nbaro?'

'Can't say that I have, sir.' She was slightly chagrined, as Age of Chaos literature was one of the very few things the Orphanage had provided.

'Eh.' He leaned back, all his smiles gone. 'I think about Suliemani's courage – punching her crew out, knowing she'd die alone. In hard vacuum. Owen had it right, and I'm a little sick of heroism this shift. Tab me the rest and I'll read 'em when I'm … ready.'

'Yes, sir.'

4

'Got the personnel reports?'

'Yes, sir. Here's Eyre's. Sir, technically he should receive "not observed" because . . .' Nbaro waved a hand ineffectively.

'Because he was a petty officer for most of the reporting period,' the skipper said, 'and was only promoted midshipper a month before we got to Trade Point.' He made that funny yes/no motion with his head again. 'They can come and court-martial me. We'll write him an officer report so that the battle goes on his permanent record as an officer.' He looked up.

'Do you realise that those of us who were here will probably get favourable promotion tracks for the rest of our careers?' He looked unimpressed with himself and his career; his smile was as close to cynical as she'd ever seen on him.

'"We few, we happy few"?' Nbaro asked. Truekner liked allusions to ancient literature, and she *did* know some.

'We band of sisters, brothers and 'gynes,' Truekner said. 'Yep, like that.'

'If we make it home at all,' she said.

'Touché,' Truekner said. 'Did you write your own?'

Nbaro hesitated. 'No, sir.'

He shook his head. 'Go and write it. Now. Tell me what a glow-in-the-dark wonder you are. Seriously. I'm up to my arse in crap right now. Do that, and you can go back to chatting with Starfish.'

She had been on the team that had broken the code of the Starfish language. In a way. And the team leader . . .

She clamped down on that thought. 'Any idea what's up next, skipper?'

Truekner was already sitting back into his neurofoam cushions. 'You have a closer relationship with Pisani and Morosini than I do,' he said. 'And if they whisper in your ear, *Lieutenant*, I'd appreciate a heads-up.'

He opened his tab and put a hologram in the air. Then he

put on music: a wailing male voice with a guitar. She heard the word 'Strange'. The singer sounded insane.

'The Doors,' Truekner said.

'I'll close them,' she said, and backed out. *Skipper is definitely in a mood.*

'It's a band,' he insisted as the hatchway closed.

'Does your boss make you write your own personnel report?' Marca asked Thea Drake, her room-mate and best friend. Thea was also back from the Trade Point asteroid. She, too, was doing 'paperwork'.

'Captain Hughes has us all write our own,' Thea said. She was tall and blonde and pale, and pretty much the physical antithesis of Nbaro. She leaned over, her arm around her friend. 'It's not a punishment, you barbarous orphan. It's a reward.'

Nbaro made a sound like a growl. 'Mostly I'm just afraid that I'll never, ever get back to Trade Point.'

'I hear that, sister,' Drake said. 'Every half-hour is like a spike in my dreams.'

They'd had to come back; they needed everything from hot showers to fresh EVA suits and more oxygen bottles. The battle had almost totally destroyed the human side of the Trade Point station; now it was barely habitable and there were only four pressurised spaces left. The *Athens* had taken heavy damage in her first fight, more damage in her second fight, and had been down two reactors and a number of other critical systems while she was coaxed through the Battle of Trade Point, and Nbaro was convinced that only her immense size had kept her from catastrophic damage. A 30 mm depleted uranium slug from a PTX cruiser had to work very hard to find something critical in a ten-kilometre hull. The new aliens and their energy weapons were something else again.

She had these moments all too often, where some idle thought would provoke an almost tangible memory of the battle – one of the battles – and she'd find herself standing in a passageway, looking blank.

Like now. Except she was looking at the display of space in front of the bow, as shown on her cabin in-screen. It was a live video feed of the repair work to the station, forty thousand kilometres away. Due to the lack of 'right-side-up' in three-dimensional space, the repair crews and sleds around the trade station looked upside down from her perspective. Half of Engineering was out there, including her friend Naisha Qaqqaq, who was second in command of the station repair effort while the rest of Engineering was working on the damage to *Athens*.

Out there, doing things...

'We need to trade our gold,' Drake continued.

Nbaro leaned against the locker that held her very meagre wardrobe and managed a smile. 'I think we can trust Dorcas to trade for us,' she said.

Drake gave her *that look*: a mix of frustration and resolve that said her will was indomitable. 'I want to be there to trade my gold,' she said.

Nbaro straightened up. 'Hey, me too—'

'I want to tell my grandchildren that I went eye to eye with the Starfish and negotiated...'

Nbaro, who knew more than most humans about the anatomy of the deep hydrogen-ocean dwelling aliens, couldn't help but laugh.

'Fine!' Drake spat. 'Eye to tentacle receptor!'

'I'm sure if Dorcas was here he'd insist they be called rhinophores, unless you mean the cer—' She didn't get the word *cerata* out completely before both of them were laughing. Nbaro was in love with Dorcas, or thought that the lust-tinged constant desire to see him might be love, but she also enjoyed mocking him, both in person and with Thea Drake.

7

When their laughter subsided, Nbaro made herself sit down, conjure her holoscreen, and begin inputting her own evaluation. After fifteen minutes, Thea put her arm around Nbaro's neck, leaned in close like a lover, and said, 'You suck at self-praise. Go and lie down. I've got this.'

'It's all there,' Nbaro said, but she left the stateroom's one tiny seat and climbed into her acceleration couch.

'Yeah,' Drake said. 'I especially like the bullet point, "Served during Trade Point conflict, securing station from enemy boarders." Very evocative.' Drake snorted so hard that she had to wipe her nose.

Drake sat down and spoke quietly to Morosini – everyone's secretary and translator – and then went back over her work with a light pen.

'There,' she said. 'Hero with a capital *H*. Your only short-coming is that you didn't die. If you were dead, I'd say they'd make you Doje.'

Marca dropped down off her rack and looked at the evaluation on Morosini's gleaming holo-display. The words PROMOTE IMMEDIATELY in capitals caught her eye, and then farther down the screen, *Under direct enemy fire, rescued...* 'Hey! "Captured and extracted an enemy alien while under hostile fire" isn't even true. I captured it *after* the firefight.'

Drake grinned. 'The battle was still going on, right? Ships were still shooting at each other?'

'Thousands of kilometres away, maybe...' Nbaro shot back.

'Perfect. And what was their target?'

'Thea, I think you are stretching—'

'Sweetie, this is how we get to be captains. Modesty is for civilians.' Thea Drake, the scion of a hundred generations of patrician officers, leaned in and toggled the 'send' button on the holo-display before Nbaro could stop her.

Nbaro made herself pause, be calm, and smile. The Nbaros

had as many generations of officers as the Drakes – but her parents had died when she was a girl, and hadn't passed on the ruthless self-confidence that seemed to cling to Thea Drake like the finest glas armour.

But she knew that the other woman was right: modesty didn't lead to promotion.

'Listen, love,' Thea said. 'I'm sure when you were eating rust and rotten rat soup at your barbarous Orphanage, they told you all to be modest and keep your head down, but this is an evaluation that will, in time, be read by every commanding officer you serve under, and every officer who sits on your review boards.'

Nbaro nodded. 'Truekner said that those of us who fought at Trade Point could probably coast on it for the rest of our careers,' she said.

Thea grinned. 'My point exactly. You need to ensure they can never forget what you did. Never. Ever.'

Nbaro shrugged. 'It seems like an odd way to spend our time after being heroes – writing about it.'

Drake met her shrug and raised the ante with her own. 'No matter what happens,' she said, 'all the documentation needs to be filed.'

Fifteen minutes later the final copy, signed and sealed digitally by Truekner, entered her personnel record with four of Drake's flamboyant lines of praise underlined and the words 'ready for immediate promotion' added a second time, at the bottom.

Appended was a note that said 'Lt Nbaro is released for spaceflight operations.' She had a message on her tab from Qaqqaq asking her to review a sim on weld inspection, and a long list of stores she was to bring back. *Typical.*

Marca punched the air and let out a whoop. But it turned out that she had seven hours before she was due to take a flight to dock with the Trade Point asteroid, so she walked down to the aft wardroom, ate a very quick meal, fetched a cherry pie to trade for a helmet bag of cookies, and, when the cookies were secured, flew a mission in the sim for a ship's pinnace. Then she reviewed Qaqqaq's sim on weld inspection and took a nap. Sleep was almost as valuable as food. On waking, she moved briskly about the ship, gathering Qaqqaq's list of necessities, most of which were spare parts for things Nbaro didn't understand at all.

It was her third flight on the command deck of the pinnace, the smallest spaceship by Service definition, because it carried an engine capable of navigating between stars. In fact, the pinnaces were mostly engine; they could be crewed by as few as three people, or even just one in a crisis, and almost everything was automated. She had a cargo payload of sixty thousand litres of fresh water, fifty tonnes of carbon-fibre sheets and bags of fibre-crete, a sort of nano-powered epoxy that substituted for concrete in deep space construction. She was 'under instruction' with a lieutenant commander from Flight One, Fuju Han, a tall, thin, handsome man who looked ridiculously young and boyish for his rank, and who looked vaguely familiar; perhaps they had shared a martial arts class somewhere out in the dark. The only dark wrinkle was that Doros McDonald, a red-headed lieutenant from Flight One, had apparently not been chosen for a place on the pinnace, and there had been some cold looks.

Which Nbaro thought of as normal. Orphanage normal.

Han favoured her with a small smile. 'I'm writing evals,' he said. 'You take her.'

The pinnace didn't launch from the launch tube rails. Instead, she docked against the upper hull, which created a completely different launch sequence, new undocking procedures, and a whole series of possible errors she had to avoid. She was very cautious in her launch, sneaking the pinnace out of the clamps with micro-thrusts until she was sure that she wasn't going to hit any antennas in her ascent from the dock.

Han glanced up, smiled, scanned the screens and went back to whatever he was doing on his tab.

She took that for approval, however mild, and allowed the onboard sub-AI to feed more power to a more aggressive flight path. In seconds they were accelerating at a smooth 1 *g* away from the *Athens* and aiming at the shining white pinpoint that the HUD identified as Trade Point. She checked the whole course against the sub-AI's course from habit, put a warning on her tab for five minutes before turnover and breaking burn, and slid her command seat back from the instruments.

Han looked up. 'Looking good,' he said, somewhat automatically.

She smiled, hoping to get him to talk.

He went back to his tab.

She sighed and went to hers. People were shy around her since her first brush with shipboard fame, and it was only getting worse, and no amount of coaching from the socially talented Thea was going to save her. And regardless, she still had plenty of work to do. She missed Suliemani, and Truekner had given her Suleimani's personnel to handle: fifteen spaceflight techs and as many fitters and data systems techs. All of the squadron personnel were divided up among the officers, but until recently Nbaro had been too junior, and now she discovered that taking endless onboard classes was *not* the greatest timewaster in the service.

She was sure that she could hear the skipper's voice telling her that *'taking care of your people is never a waste of time'*, and she winced at her own thoughts, but what she wanted more than anything was...

Was...

What in a hundred hells do I want?

She stared at space. All she had ever wanted, through nine hellish years in the State Orphanage, was to be a spacer. Now she had her dream, and it was her everyday life. It didn't lack for excitement or fulfilment, and yet...

And yet...

I put so much into getting here, she thought. *Now where do I go?*

And part of that was about seeing Horatio Dorcas. Who wanted to marry her. *Maybe.*

And I definitely want him. But what happens then? Babies? A home? A life in politics? Dorcas won't ship out again, so...

A life apart? With me out for five years a cruise, and him at home...?

And I'm just borrowing trouble, as Thea would no doubt tell me. We're at least two years from home in the middle of a long shoot-out. Why worry now?

Because we've been apart three days and I fear he might have moved on? Really?

Because I'm an idiot.

And she was resolutely trying not to think of the neural lace she'd discovered she had. With all of the consequent doubts and paranoia of her Orphanage upbringing.

Morosini put that thing in me as soon as I came on board, damn it all. What does that mean? It means they never trusted me. It means they always knew I was a fake...

God, if Morosini knew all along... what the hell does that make me?

She slowed the racing spaceplane of her thoughts, lowered her eyes to her tab, and went to work on Spacer Patel and his poor exam scores. Exemplary performance reviews, excellent under pressure, bad test results.

Yeah, I think I know you. OK, make time to chat with Patel.

'What was the alien like?' Han asked.

She looked up. 'Huh?' she asked, or something equally unintelligible. Then she managed a smile, her best new reaction that was almost natural. She knew she'd done some backsliding since the space battle. *Do not snarl at your superiors, there's a dear.*

'The Starfish...'

Han managed a smile of his own, which only served to make him seem younger. 'I meant the other aliens. The bugs.'

'Bugs?' she asked. She hadn't heard them called bugs.

'Did it have... eyes?' Han asked.

She thought back to her brief glance inside its faceplate – if the term 'faceplate' could be applied.

'It had something,' she said. She shrugged. 'I felt... something.'

'I hear we're going to interrogate it?' Han said.

'Above my pay grade, sir.' She put a smile at the end, a carefully chosen reaction to show that, in this case, she was aware that it was above both of their pay grades. Another of Thea's little tactics.

'I hope they stick it to that thing.' He nodded at her. 'Pretty impressive, Lieutenant, got to say. I was... happy you were assigned to me this flight.'

She nodded. 'I'm sure anyone would have done the same,' she said, aware how banal and lame the comment sounded.

'No way.' He frowned. 'I'd like to think I might have rescued the Marine, but damn, I'd just have shot the bug.' He glanced at her. 'My best friend was sent off into the Deep Black...' He paused. 'You know about the second pinnace?'

'I know we used to have two,' Nbaro said carefully. This was a matter of ship-wide speculation, which Han had to know.

'Davies took number one, way back, right after Sahel.' Han made a face. 'I thought she'd be back in a week or two. Now I'm afraid the Bubbles got her.' He looked at Nbaro. 'We're not supposed to talk about it.'

Nbaro hoped she did a better job of keeping a secret than Han. She murmured something diplomatic and went back to her tab.

'What do you think the Master will do now?' Han asked. Rather pointedly, he said, 'Everyone says you have his ear.'

She wasn't sure why this comment bothered her, as it was occasionally true. 'I really don't know, sir.'

'Call me Fuju,' Han said.

She smiled. 'Call me Marca. I had very limited access to the Master. It's just scuttlebutt that I know what's going on.'

Han smiled, as if he knew a secret. 'Sure,' he said. But his smile seemed genuine, and he let her get back to work.

About forty minutes out from Trade Point, he cleared his throat. 'I know you are an excellent pilot,' he said, 'but do you mind if I take the docking?'

'Sir?' she asked.

'The dock is a shambles and there's all kinds of stuff to hit, and the automated systems don't have it all logged yet.'

'Sure,' she said.

'You sit in the co-pilot's seat and watch. There's a trick to it.'

There definitely was a trick to it: a combination of a well-located automated camera that could be locked on to a docking target, and the understanding of how to guide that camera into the docking ring. It *had* been in the sim, but Han didn't use the school solution, and her appreciation of him went up several notches. In effect, instead of 'landing', he backed in, never changing the ship's orientation in order to keep the main engines on a deceleration burn. It was fancy and elegant and simple.

'Nice,' she said. And she meant it. His good piloting cut straight through her foul mood.

Han beamed.

People like to be complimented. Remember that when you talk to Patel.

The trade station had changed so much that she didn't even know where to find the crew quarters. *Changed* wasn't really fair; *completely rebuilt* was closer, and there were derricks and frames extending in three dimensions from the asteroid that was the basis for the station, and every EVA-qualified spacer who wasn't repairing the *Athens* was here, working as fast as safety, fatigue and materials allowed.

Nbaro was staying; she moved her bag off the pinnace, waved farewell to the handsome Han and heard multiple dings as her tab accepted a dozen messages and comm requests. She wanted to open the PERSONAL from Dorcas, but the WORK SCHED said she had a fifteen-minute walk to an EVA, working on structural integrity with Qaqqaq.

'Ma'am?' someone commed.

She was standing in the airlock, frozen by the weight of message traffic. But she knew his voice immediately: Marine Wilson Akunje.

She turned, touched helmets. 'Mister Akunje,' she said with real pleasure.

'Gunny thought that you, being an officer, would get lost. Sent me ta take you to your quarters, like. Ma'am.' He smiled.

She grinned. 'Gunny has me pegged. How's he doing?'

'Still clamshelled.' *Clamshell* was an ancient term for a sailor bound for the brig, but the new medical units actually looked like giant clams and the term had migrated. Wilson smiled. 'But the clamshell is here, aboard the station, and he's givin' orders like he ain't got nothin' else to think about, like.' Akunje pushed a button on a lift – a brand-new, matt-black carbon-fibre lift.

'Nothin' outside is pressurised yet,' he said. 'Saves time.'

The lift slid to a stop and its double doors opened on another airlock. This one was active, and once the elevator was locked out, atmosphere began to push in. Her helmet read amber, then green, and Akunje winked at her.

'You can pop your helmet, ma'am,' he said.

'But Gunny has you lot in full kit all duty, right?'

'Yes'm.' Akunje's shrug could be read right through his EVA suit and battle armour.

She nodded. 'Well, I'm just a squid,' she said, and popped her visor. The air was good: cool, fresh, the sign of clean filters and brand-new components.

There was carpeting on the 'floor', and artificial gravity.

'Wow,' she said. 'I love what you've done with the place.' Last time she'd been aboard, there had been no carpeting and, in many places, no walls. The precise railgun holes in the passageway were gone, but the space still conjured a moment of terror; she'd stood helpless, right here, while an alien starship targeted this corridor. Only luck had kept her alive.

But she kept walking. In some strange way, it helped steady her. After all, she was genuinely the hero of the station fight. She really had been an effective officer. Whatever Morosini thought of her when she came aboard, she was clear about that.

Right? Truekner isn't a game-player. He wouldn't blow smoke...

They clomped down the passageway, passed through a common messing area where a dozen off-duty spacers and officers looked up, and people she knew waved and greeted her warmly; then they were in a berthing corridor that ran at what would have been, planet-side, a ridiculous angle, but artificial gravity made it possible to turn and walk 'up' as as easily as turning a corner.

'B1601,' Akunje said. 'Enjoy, ma'am. Welcome back.'

She grinned. 'Good to be back. I have an EVA in ten minutes.'

He laughed. 'Yeah, we're understaffed. To say the least. I gotta run. *Ciao!*'

She tossed her bags into the tiny stateroom – it was basically a rack and a locker, more like a cylinder than a room – and dogged the hatch closed.

'Wait up!' she called. 'I'm with Qaqqaq on structural integrity,' she added.

16

'I can get you there.' Akunje consulted his tab, mounted on his left wrist. *'Hakuna matata.'*

She followed him back through messing, and into the same airlock and elevator, re-sealing her helmet as they moved along. This time, they went past the dock and up into the unfinished rigging above the docks – the mess of girders and cables she'd watched Han avoid in his landing.

There were at least ten spacers working here, and their speed was incredible; carbon-fibre panels were assembled so fast that she could watch an arm of the station grow as if it was some Earth-side plant in a speeded-up video.

Akunje's voice spoke in her helmet, even as he turned back into the lift.

'See you around, ma'am!'

Almost simultaneously, Nbaro heard Qaqqaq say, 'See, the conquering hero comes!' The shortest of the suited figures released a girder, flipped, and dived towards her with the grace of a porpoise or a seal. Qaqqaq's landing was so perfect, so poised, that the two ended up helmet to helmet, almost in an embrace.

They touched helmets.

'Now, if I say to go inside…' Qaqqaq said, not entirely joking.

'Yes, ma'am,' Nbaro agreed.

'You're on weld-inspection for a bit,' Qaqqaq said, as if this was small talk. 'I'll check you out on construction later. I hear you're staying around?'

'A week at least,' she said.

Qaqqaq kept her helmet touching Nbaro's. 'I know you have other stuff to do,' she said. 'But any waking minute you have spare, you're a lowly construction tech. I'm desperate for bodies with EVA quals.'

'You make it sound so appealing,' Nbaro said, but in truth, she was delighted to be 'outside'. It always got her: the reality of the universe around her. Days, even weeks could go by when she was in the ship and didn't even think about...

...the expanse. Out here, far from the two stars, and on a station arm projecting into the void from an asteroid, she could look at infinity in every direction – up, down, everywhere. It just went on and on, being infinite *everywhere*.

Here in the Trade Point system, it was stranger than most: the lone asteroid that had clearly been moved to the balance point between two distant stars; the two asteroid belts – or rather, moon belts – around the stars in a complex and balanced chain of orbits.

It looked artificial. In fact, it looked more artificial to the naked eye than it did on the various charts and 3D representations.

And then beyond the bright points of the two stars, there was...

Space. The deep black absence of light was beautiful, and so was the vast brilliance of the infinite pinpoints of light created by all the stars. The moon belts gave the scene depth, and mystery, but the starfield gave it majesty, and the Horsehead Nebula on her Spinward horizon gave it awe.

'Are you space-sick?' Qaqqaq asked.

'No, Naisha,' Nbaro said. 'I'm in awe of the universe.'

'Fair,' Qaqqaq said. 'But functionally similar. Myself, I try not to look up.'

'Wherever up is,' Nbaro quipped. 'Take me to my welds.'

There followed a brief refresher course in weld inspection. As Nbaro had *just* watched the vid, it felt mildly patronising, but she was experienced enough in space operations to know this was a vital job and needed her full attention, and that there was all too often a gap between vid instruction and ground reality.

The next six hours passed in a blur of welds and QR codes. Each weld she inspected received a code burned into the girder by her inspection laser, listing the date and time of inspection, and with her name.

She was very careful. But the welds were all good despite being done in haste; this was a veteran crew. She was floating, tethered, by a six-way junction weld when her tab chimed.

'Shift's done, Marca. You can come in now.' Qaqqaq sounded amused.

Nbaro finished her inspection of the sixth weld, stamped it, tabbed the result into the ship's memory, pulled herself back to the assembly and then jumped for a handhold and again for the lift platform, proud of her hard-won zero-*g* skills. When she'd first come to the *Athens*, even a jump up a lift-well had been a risk.

Qaqqaq and two other spacers held the lift for her and they filled it, the four of them pressed against one another for the ride down.

'Airlock,' the lift said into their helmets. They packed into the lock, and it cycled. Nbaro was surprised to see the others pop their visors as soon as the lights showed amber, and suspected familiarity bred contempt, even for hard vacuum.

'When do we get to the gun turrets?' a spacer asked. She was young, shaved nearly bald, and almost as short as Qaqqaq.

The engineering officer smiled. 'Rosta, our protection is the *Athens*. If the Bubbles come back, we're not going to fight them off with a couple of small railguns.'

The male spacer looked sour. 'Understood, ma'am, but I'd feel better if we had guns.'

'Nine more days at this rate and we'll put in a railgun turret,' Qaqqaq said. But she sounded ... doubtful. As if she knew something.

When the two spacers turned into their berthing area, Nbaro glanced at Qaqqaq. 'So we're here at least nine more days?'

Qaqqaq shrugged. 'I thought you'd tell me?' she said. 'I stink. I'd kill for a fewkin' shower.'

Nbaro knew that the station had water reserve issues. Part of her cargo in the pinnace had been sixty thousand litres of fresh water. 'Sonic?'

'Sure, honey, but sonic never makes me feel clean.' Qaqqaq stopped at a hatchway. 'This is me.'

'Good to be back.'

'Good to have you. Get some sleep.' It was a slightly pointed remark, and the Terran-born woman smirked as she waved.

Nbaro couldn't see what all that was aimed at. But she gave Qaqqaq a wave and clomped up the corridor, through messing, and then up to her own tiny cylinder, where there was *just* room to get off her armour and her splendid, high-tech EVA suit, which was technically both the property of the Special Services and a piece of evidence in the web they were building on the conspiracy to take or destroy the ship. She was honest enough with herself to admit that she never planned to give it back.

She loved her EVA suit and her armour enough to spend fifteen minutes cleaning them; the suit had a self-renewing inner surface that claimed to be self-cleaning, but she'd noticed that in high perspiration areas it needed a little help. And the xenoglas armour was virtually indestructible, but she liked to wipe it until it shone.

She was sitting on her tiny rack, cleaning her gauntlets and thinking about food, when her tab chimed and so did her hatch

'Nbaro, are you hiding?' came a voice.

It was Dorcas.

Nbaro was naked; Dorcas was her fiancé; he was also her commanding officer on the away team for diplomatic interaction with the Starfish: all that went through her mind in a quarter of a second, and she simultaneously blushed deeply and put a palm firmly against the hatch.

'I'll be out in five minutes,' she said.

'I'll be in the mess,' Dorcas said. One of the best things about him was his essential straightforwardness; he didn't get angry over little things. He wouldn't mind being kept waiting; he'd just download some esoteric journal.

She pulled on a flightsuit and zipped it up, found soft boots and pulled them on, ran her fingers through her hair and opened her hatch. He wasn't leaning there waiting for her; he was, as he'd said, sitting in the mess with his tab set to holo-project.

'What are you reading?' she asked.

'"Heating Freezes Electrons in Twisted Bilayer Graphene",' Dorcas answered.

'Graphene?' she asked, despite knowing that she didn't need to understand anything he was reading.

'Graphene is a single layer of carbon atoms in which the atoms form a hexagonal lattice.' He smiled.

'Do they? Is that stuff real?'

'Your carbon-fibre construction sheets are layers of graphenes with electron bonds that—'

She leaned over the table and kissed him.

He paused for a moment. 'I believe you are trying to tell me that's enough about graphenes.'

'For the moment,' she admitted. 'Although the concept is interesting… Damn it! I haven't seen you in days.'

Dorcas smiled. 'As you see, I have not changed. Nor have you.'

'How are the Starfish?' she asked.

He made a face, licking the inside of his cheek with his tongue so that his cheek bulged out. She'd seen him do it before, and she still didn't know exactly what it meant.

'How *are* the Starfish?' he asked her back. 'If only I knew. I can only translate things that I essentially already understand. Then we search a three-dimensional logic grid for the chemical response, take a day to work it out, fail, succeed, and then we can work on the next component, only to arrive at "it's cold".'

'But there's a world of meaning in "it's cold",' she said.

'If only "it's cold" was the meaning we'd picked up. I was making an example... You're so literal.'

'This from you?' she asked.

He smiled in self-knowledge. 'One of the great patrician families feared this contact so much that they were willing to engage in piracy and assassination to prevent it, and look – we're not learning anything.'

She'd never heard him sounding bitter. It wasn't in his approach.

'You expected immediate success?' she asked.

He shrugged.

'Wow, I'm not the only one who's an idiot,' she said.

He looked up, then sat back, considering her. He nodded as if he'd come to a decision. 'It's good to have you back.'

She managed to say, 'I missed you,' and he grinned his natural, full-pleasure grin.

People like to be complimented and missed. Got it.

As if they'd mutually agreed that this ended round one, they both rose and went to the food dispensers. Everything was pre-packaged for free-fall eating, in bulbs: curries with rice, orzo pasta with ground meat, a spicy dish with eggplant for vegetarians. Marca took a bulb of each and extra rice, and made delighted sounds as she chewed through the curry.

'It is the highest testament to the depraved quality of the food at your Orphanage that you vacuum up our zero-*g* fare with such enjoyment,' he said.

She shrugged, because her mouth was full.

Naisha Qaqqaq appeared, her hair wrapped in a towel, grabbed food bulbs and sat with them, and then they were joined by several of her shipmates from her last tour at the station. Nbaro opened her helmet bag and shared the cookies, to everyone's delight.

Nbaro's eyes kept meeting Dorcas's, and then they'd both look away, and finally Qaqqaq leaned over and murmured 'get a room.'

Nbaro made a little moue of feigned surprise. And tried not to look at Dorcas. And that set the tone for the next days, because the two of them followed rules, and the rules said they couldn't be together until he was no longer her commanding officer. Qaqqaq thought they were crazy, and said so. But Nbaro put her head down and worked, because that was how she dealt with most problems. And because her experiences at the Orphanage made her...

...hesitant.

2

It was remarkable, and a little sad, how quickly her tours of duty beyond the air/ammonia lock into the Starfish half of the station went from heart-pounding alien encounters to dull routine visits. It had been extensively rebuilt since the battle, with xenoglas partitions and a huge drain tank that allowed the human side to flush the ammonia out of the lock faster, and then refill it. The result was to make her feel a little as if she was in an aquarium, with the ammonia holding tank behind her, so that all four walls of the observation deck were xenoglas and it was always cold. She didn't mind.

She'd sit watching the monitors, and a little tool that was meant to measure vibration in water for fishermen on Sahel. She'd epoxied it to the xenoglas partition that effortlessly restrained the high-pressure liquid ammonia atmosphere in which the Starfish lived, and it gave her a few seconds' warning when a Starfish was coming to visit. For this innovation, she received the plaudits of the rest of the language team, but all it really served to do was to take the edge off each encounter. The little tool would flash its tiny red LED, and she'd look up to see the ammonia swirl with some sort of sediment that showed in the low lighting, and then, like the monsters they were, the Starfish would appear – usually just one, but sometimes two.

They *were* star-shaped, like two Terran starfish joined at the centre, back-to-back, with five radial arms on each half. The arms were covered in short tentacles called 'cerata' by Dorcas, and various other names by the rest of the team. They waved and flowed in a very non-mammalian manner that left most observers queasy, and the ten arms could tie themselves in what appeared to be knots, so that two or three of them looked... very frightening. One of the Starfish had cerata that were much more elaborate – almost feathery – and they had dubbed it *Feather Dancer*. Dorcas thought it might be the most advanced in age, but they had no evidence one way or another. It never seemed to be alone.

Regardless, each watch, she'd sit waiting for a Starfish to appear, and if one did, she'd trigger preset greeting routines in their model starfish robot, and a greeting would be exchanged. And then the Starfish would have one of their robot sleds move a cargo into their trade airlock. On the advice of a Cargo officer, usually Don Jha from Large Cargo, she'd stack gold ingots in the DHC trade lock. Both airlocks had transparent hatches made of xenoglas, so that all parties could watch the exchange. The DHC representative would pile gold bars – sometimes refined aluminum or steel or copper, but mostly gold – until the operator felt the exchange was fair, and the lock door would be closed with some formality. Then the Starfish representative would either open their side and take the metal, or remove some of the xenoglas panels.

What was perhaps most surprising was that the exact amounts traded seemed to vary from day to day, and even from trade to trade, as if the apparent value of the glas fluctuated. Nbaro wanted to talk to Thea about it, and what that suggested about the Starfish as economists, but she was working too hard; two four-hour shifts at the trade locks, and then at least one four-hour shift on a construction team rebuilding the Trade Point station. Whole days passed when she only saw Dorcas for a moment; they never seemed to have a watch together, which she assumed was deliberate.

She ran all the language tests that she dared. Dorcas would send her word lists, each with a chemical compound as a modifier; the great breakthrough of the last four weeks had been the realisation that the Starfish communicated both by chemical pheromone analogue *and* by sound. Dorcas had a lab in the secure section of the station and he was always tinkering...

The language structure matched nothing human, but that didn't surprise them. Dorcas was searching for verbs, for actions, and found a key word in *move/swim*. Progress was glacial, because the Starfish rarely wanted to talk. Don Jha was the first to get Feather Dancer to participate in a point and name session and got the all-important 'I' and 'You' described, and then something that they hoped was 'here' and 'there', but which might have been 'airlock' and 'ammonia'.

'We'd need fifty years,' Nbaro said to Jha.

The Cargo officer smiled. 'You know, this isn't my job, but I love it. I never expected to do anything this ... fun. It's like a giant puzzle.'

Nbaro was glad someone enjoyed it. She was too impatient, and the Starfish all too often swam away as soon as the robot went beyond a simple greeting.

She did begin a notebook cataloguing any individual traits she could detect – size, colour, and so forth – only to have them proved unreliable when she saw one of the larger Starfish both shrink and change colour as another arrived.

But Jha liked the idea, and had others of his own. He spotted the damaged cerata on the Starfish they'd christened *Bentnick* and the frayed arm ends on another, as if it was old and worn. That one became *Granny*. Nbaro *thought* that she could tell the difference between younger and elder, and she suspected that the young were required to shrink in the presence of the old – but these were guesses.

Jha worked on correlations between prices paid and the Starfish who were present. It was not immediately fruitful, but it was part of the game, and the xenoglas continued to move across the airlock barrier and into the holds of the *Athens*.

In her other shifts, Nbaro learned to do a little welding, and how to build structures on the steel girders with epoxied carbon-fibre panels. It was fun to watch the station grow, and the evening of day four was punctuated by widespread celebrations as the new habitat area was opened to the crew, including a vast water recycler and forty showerheads.

'Fuck, there's going to be an orgy,' Qaqqaq said, but in fact what happened was more like a warm water fight, followed by a meal.

Nbaro's day five began well, as Gunny Drun was released from his medical shell and moved to a powered chair. He was groggy, but his sense of humour was still there, and he gave Nbaro a thumbs up as he rolled by.

She took a shower, because she could, and then went on to her duty at the trade locks.

Dorcas was there.

'Hello,' he said.

She smiled. 'Hi,' she said, suddenly a little shy.

He took both her hands and kissed her, and she responded…

'Let's not make love in a glass box,' she said.

Dorcas was flushed and breathing hard, and she laughed because he was usually so controlled. She reached out, planning to *at least* kiss him again, when Feather Dancer's elaborate fronds stirred the sediment under the lights and she realised that her little vibration monitor was flashing.

'Damn,' she said.

Dorcas snorted a laugh, and began to manipulate the robot starfish on the other side of the hatch.

'Don't we have a Cargo officer today?' she asked.

Dorcas shook his head. 'Today we trade for our own little cartel,' he said. 'I arranged it.'

'Of course you did.' Horatio Dorcas, in addition to having a neural lace and an incredibly high security clearance, was also from one of the richest patrician families in the whole of the Directorate of Human Corporations. He had access to power that Nbaro couldn't even imagine. So he'd arranged that they could make private trades with the Starfish. It was absolutely legal; the DHC service was a commercial organisation, not a navy, and every spacer was allowed to trade. At least technically.

'That's our gold?' she asked, looking at the grav sled with its cargo of dull yellow ingots.

'And some copper,' he said. 'And with a little help from Thea, I have added a few dozen kilos of phosphor and silicon bronze, an alloy that I suspect will prove durable in liquid ammonia.'

'Neat,' Nbaro said. 'No one's tried that before?'

'Everyone is incredibly secretive about trade here,' he said. 'I have access to most records, and even I know virtually nothing about what has been tried with the Starfish.'

'Well, at least we have Feather Dancer,' she said.

'If it's actually senior. For all I know, it's thought to be from a lesser race and has no power to trade. I'm sure you've noted that it is never alone?'

'You are full of good cheer,' she quipped.

Feather Dancer was interacting with Dorcas's robot while a larger Starfish observed from the shadows of their side of the air/ammonia lock, invisible except for the occasional flash of a tentacle in the murk of their gigantic bay. Nbaro flashed on a memory of being in that huge area with Dorcas, and the endless darkness that ate light.

Feather Dancer drifted forward towards the robot, and they exchanged greetings, and then Dorcas tried his new pheromone/audio phrase.

The Starfish answered. Nbaro saw the spike on the receptors as they took in the response's chemical component, and then she saw the audio input register as a set of green waves on the monitor.

It was a mixture of ammonia perfumes and whale song. Dorcas glowed with satisfaction.

'What's it mean?' she asked. Feather Dancer had been joined by the second Starfish, and their cargo robot rolled into their side of the lock and began to unload stacks of xenoglas plate.

'Are you and Jha still keeping a descriptions book?' Dorcas asked.

She nodded over her shoulder, watching the stack of xenoglas plates grow.

'Can you make a note of the second Starfish, please? I mean, if you feel that...'

'I think what I'm feeling right now is greed.' Nbaro tore her eyes away from the stack of xenoglas.

'Hmmm,' Dorcas said.

'Easy for you, rich boy,' she snapped.

'Hmmm?' Dorcas was still studying the readouts on the monitor from the language bot they'd planted on the other side. 'I think I've isolated "move/swim",' he said, breathless with excitement.

He hasn't heard a word. Right.

Nbaro hadn't done this before without someone directing her. But she had her own notions, and she watched the alien robot-forklift, which looked remarkably like a slightly rounder, duller-finished version of their own forklift, as it manoeuvred a stack of plates and placed them on the deck of the trade lock. A precise scale, installed hundreds of years before, measured the weight of the plates. Her tab deducted the weight of the light material the Starfish used between the plates.

A big parcel: about 160 kilos. Not by any means the largest offer, but the biggest in their five days of trading so far.

She looked at yesterday's offers, both accepted and rejected, and deliberately lowballed the lowest accepted offer, putting down nine gold bars, and putting in four copper bars and one of the phosphor bronze bars as well.

'That's not enough,' Dorcas said. 'Put in at least another gold bar. What if they're offended?'

She looked at him. 'Can they be offended? Isn't that a human concept?'

'Touché, my young entrepreneur. Are you willing to risk it?' he asked.

She added one of their hard-earned gold bars, and left the trade lock.

Now the Starfish pressed up against their glas wall, its suckers and cerata clutching at the smooth glas in a manner that was almost obscene. But it gave Nbaro a great view of the larger Starfish's arm-ends: young; smooth. And its cerata were un-damaged, but on one arm it had a remarkable double cerata – two arms on one trunk.

She noted this, took a photo, and labelled it *Double*.

While Nbaro was busy with her observations, the Starfish triggered the trade lock without releasing their own.

Nbaro looked at Dorcas.

'It happens,' he said. 'I assume they want to examine the bronze.'

Sure enough Double swam into the trade lock, picked up the bronze bar in one of its manipulator cerata, and swam away with a curious undulation that only a creature with five sides could manage.

Suddenly there was a burst of audible whale song.

Dorcas was head-down over the language-bot monitor. 'Feather Dancer is communicating with the robot,' he said.

'It's as if they've just realised we can talk,' she said. 'It's been a week!'

Dorcas nodded, intent on his monitor. He tapped something, and she knew him well enough to know that he was using his neural lace to interface directly.

But after a long minute, he looked up. 'Imagine that every time you went to talk to a deaf friend, a light went on next to her head. How long would it take you to realise she was trying to use the light to communicate?'

'About thirty seconds,' Nbaro said.

Dorcas sighed. 'It's a hypothesis,' he admitted. 'Two minutes forty seconds and it is still communicating. Gods above, I have so many chemicals coming in, I can't even trace their delivery order. This is the longest transmission ever recorded, in hundreds of years.'

'Or in five days, depending on how you look at it,' she said. 'Where's that thing gone with our bronze? Eh?'

'Probably a lab,' Dorcas said.

'Right.'

'Three minutes twenty and still singing,' Dorcas said.

'No doubt complaining about the temperature,' Nbaro said.

Dorcas looked at her. 'What?'

She shrugged. 'I was really just talking shite.' She pointed at the murky liquid ammonia. 'But Feather Dancer is all in a tizzy. Look at the way its fronds are moving. Surely some of that 3D posturing is part of their language.'

'Shit.' Dorcas rarely swore, and when he did, it was effective. 'Shit,' he repeated. 'I didn't consider that placing the robot here would keep the speaker closer to us. We need to get a camera on that.'

Nbaro had a neural lace of her own; she just didn't really know how to use it. But she did have a friend…

She accessed Morosini. The ship's almost all-powerful AI had twinned part of himself into the station.

'You called?'

'Can you get a camera on the Starfish? Without making it obvious?'

Morosini chuckled. *'Yes.'*

'Give me the feed?'

In real time, her inserts allowed her to overlay the camera images – almost 3D – and an additional instrument was clearly watching Feather Dancer in another spectrum. *Infrared?* she wondered.

'Pass to Dorcas.'

'You really need to learn to do this for yourself.'

'But you're so good at it,' she said, and Morosini was gone.

I didn't ask for your neural lace, either, she thought. The neural lace made her uneasy every time she used it; it made her think dark thoughts about surveillance and the Orphanage.

Dorcas shook his head in obvious frustration. 'I'm standing under a waterfall of fascinating data and I don't understand *anything*,' he said.

Feather Dancer's gesticulations were calming, and its song lowered in intensity.

'What's the propagation of sound in liquid ammonia like?' Nbaro asked.

'About sixteen hundred metres per second at this temperature and pressure,' he said. 'Why? Oh, right. Feather Dancer isn't being private. It's communicating to their whole station.'

'And us.'

'Morosini?'

'How may I help you?'

'Is there anything happening in real space that might prompt ... alarm? From the Starfish?'

'*No.*'

Nbaro had time to sigh and then Morosini said, '*Yes.*'

The red lights flashed, and outside the trade lock, the scream of alarm sirens could be heard.

'Battle stations,' Nbaro said. Then she contacted Morosini. 'What's happening?'

'*Unknown spaceship has dropped into the system. It is moving very fast. The* Athens *has gone to full alert.*'

Nbaro looked at the readout that Morosini helpfully provided her. It was almost exactly like seeing a screen in Space Operations, her usual post when she wasn't flying. The object's velocity was terrible: above 0.6 *c*.

She read the tag on the UnID object twice before that registered.

Dorcas shook his head. 'I can read most data,' he said. 'What am I seeing here?'

'Are you looking at the main Space Ops board on your neural lace?' Nbaro asked.

'For all the good it's doing me, yes,' Dorcas said.

Nbaro nodded. Unless you made regular use of the 3D displays, they were very difficult to read, packed with information in the form of notes and colours and a vast array of symbols.

'Every object that appears on the sensors and is tracked, every object that is known or presumed to be a ship or even an important object, is classified in two ways. Once by colour—' She interrupted herself. 'Look for the newest contact.'

'Ah,' he said. 'If you were better at using your neural lace ...' He paused. 'Whatever it may be, it is moving very fast indeed.'

She nodded. 'Yes,' she said, with something in the pit of her stomach rolling over. She started to speak and then hesitated.

Dorcas glanced at her. 'Don't stop now,' he said. 'Tell me

how all this works. It can't be more complicated than Greek or Hebrew.'

It was so rare for her to know more than Dorcas that she was tempted to lecture. She held herself back. 'See the different colours? Red means hostile, green is neutral, and blue is friendly. This object is orange-brown, the colour for "unidentified".'

'It has a number.'

'Sure.' She was looking directly at the 3D board herself, marvelling at the direct interface with her neural lace. She wondered, idly, if she could share with Dorcas.

'Anyway, every object has an alphanumeric tag,' she said, and then, somewhat pedantically, 'The format is usually letter, letter, number, number, number.'

'Like your Flight Six shuttles. Alpha Foxtrot 6–0–7.'

'Exactly,' she said, and then, relishing the moment, 'You are really quite intelligent.'

Dorcas grunted.

'Some objects get a special symbol,' she said. 'Look, the fast-mover just got tagged as a ship …' She paused. The ID went red somewhere in her optic nerve and the UnID transformed into 'PTX/Hostile' with a ship symbol and a number. DD 3–9–7.

Heavy Cruiser, Juniper Class. We tangled with her and her escorts.

'Hells,' she said. 'They're already dead.'

The ship was going so fast that it couldn't possibly have the fuel to slow down.

Dorcas grunted again, and then said, '普天下 Pǔ Tiān Xià. They tried to follow us.' PTX – or, as it was actually known to its trillions of citizens, 普天下 Pǔ Tiān Xià – was from the other Human sphere, stretching away from Old Terra in its own direction, with its own traditions of space flight – and of government. Relations between the Directorate of Human Corporations and 普天下 Pǔ Tiān Xià had never devolved into open conflict, although it had come close several times, and in

34

the last six months the *Athens* had had repeated clashes with a trio of PTX heavy cruisers. But the evidence of the PTX officer they'd caught and interrogated seemed to indicate that they were not facing the whole empire by any means, but rather a faction – much like the DHC faction that had been trying to plant a nuke on the ship.

'Poor bastards,' Dorcas said. 'Dee Dee 3–9–7 is moving at almost 0.7 *c*. Then he said, 'And accelerating.'

Nbaro couldn't stop herself. 'Delta Delta 3–9–7, please,' she said.

'Right,' Dorcas said. 'Alphanumeric, like the spaceframes.'

DD 3–9–7 was moving so fast that Nbaro could watch it move relative to the whole system. DD 3–9–7's vector was a function of a missed jump, or a jump taken with too much mass or velocity already accrued, or perhaps just of damage. It was every spacer's nightmare. A missed jump, and then a relativistic eternity.

'Almost 0.7 *c*,' Dorcas added. 'I'd fly my ship into a star. Much faster than starving. And think of what you might observe before you burned up ...'

Nbaro found that her face was set and she had tears in her eyes, despite the fact that this was almost certainly the PTX faction who'd tried to kill their ship and had killed one of their stations.

After a long pause, Dorcas glanced at her. 'You think Feather Dancer was alarmed by the PTX ship?'

She nodded.

He raised an eyebrow. 'Feather Dancer started communicating over three minutes before the PTX ship dropped in system and hit our detection limit,' he said. 'It might be coincidence.'

'Or the Starfish might be able to detect incoming ships earlier than we can,' she said.

Dorcas raised an eyebrow. 'My professional reply would be that no one can detect an insertion before it occurs.'

'True. No one can make xenoglas, either,' Nbaro said in Thea's most sarcastic tone.

An hour passed, as the hyper-velocity ship streaked across the system. It travelled from its insertion point to somewhere above the Trade Point station in the high ecliptic – roughly the distance from Old Terra to the gas giant Jupiter – in seventy-four minutes. It didn't release anything: not torpedoes, nor beam weapons, nor escape pods.

Nbaro wanted to distract herself from the horrible human drama racing across the system; her mind kept throwing up rescue scenarios, and she was sure that every pilot was doing the same, but a speed of 0.6 c meant no one was able to catch them. They were already in a different time frame of reference.

'If any of them are alive,' Dorcas said. 'We don't even have a blue-shift transmission. Nothing. You'd think...'

Nbaro was staring at the trade lock, and the stacks of xenoglas plates. Thinking about the PTX ship and its doom. Her stomach felt heavy; her joy at trading with the Starfish was firmly quashed. 'We're fighting for that,' she said. 'For the glas.'

Dorcas smiled. 'A gross oversimplification.' He shrugged. 'Or perhaps not.'

'And we don't know how they make it!' she said.

He sat back, his full concentration on her. 'Marca, we're emerging from a scientific dark age. We barely struggled through, and no one has done serious science—'

'Serious science? We have computers and AIs and space-ships...'

'The technology of the twenty-third century! Nbaro, the article I was reading on graphenes was written in 2020! Listen to me. In the late twenty-first century, physics was on the edge of unifying all the forces, all the particles—'

'We have the Tanaka drive, don't we?' she asked.

'And we don't really know why it works. In fact, it's not too much less alien than xenoglas. That's why the graphenes—'

'You and your graphenes,' she said.

'There's a very interesting 'gyne at New Beijing Orbital who thinks that xenoglas is a stack of silicon molecular sheets analogous to graphene, held in place by…' He smiled. 'By magic. Nothing should allow silicon to line up like that.' He sent her tab an article; it pinged as it arrived. 'Doctor Ho is probably the leading expert on glas in Human space.'

Nbaro read the abstract while following the PTX ship on her inserts. At one level, she hated the neural lace and what it did to her belief in herself and her friend Morosini. But at another level, the thing was… like a magic spell. For learning, for piloting…

They're incredibly expensive. Why did Morosini put one in me?

'Feather Dancer's friend is coming back,' Dorcas said. He went back to the trance that indicated he was using his neural lace, and Nbaro wandered up behind him and put a hand on his neck.

'Battle stations alert is cancelled,' she said softly.

The smaller Starfish swam into view, placed the bronze ingot precisely where it had been lifted from and then swam to one side. It extended some sort of applicator, and made a mark.

'That has absolutely never happened before,' Dorcas said.

In fact, the mark was very precise: five parallel lines.

And a line, pointing to the bronze ingot.

'You're a genius,' Marca said.

'I know,' Dorcas said, modestly. 'And look, we're communicating.'

Nbaro felt inspired. It was the moment, the miracle of it all: the tension, the release; Dorcas, the aliens…

Nbaro opened one of the medical fridges they used to store the pheromonal analogue compounds, and took out the greeting chemical. When she opened her side of the trade lock, after the automated system emptied out the ammonia and flushed the system, she carried in five more bronze ingots and sprayed them lightly with the pheromonal analogue that went with the audible signal for 'Greeting', their first word.

'Oh, my,' Dorcas said. 'You really are very bright.'

'I'm told it's my best feature.' Nbaro dogged the trade lock closed and watched as it filled with cloudy, ice-cold liquid ammonia. She remained pressed to the glas as the larger Starfish swam in and appeared, after a pause, to embrace the ingots. The glas was cool under her fingers – cool and smooth. It should have been icy cold; in fact, her breath should have frozen to it.

'More whale song,' Dorcas reported unnecessarily. Pressed against the trade lock glas, she could feel it, even hear it. The larger one sang, a good twenty seconds, and Feather Dancer responded.

The hatch to the xenoglas unlocked; the trade was accepted.

Nbaro couldn't stop herself from giving a soft *whoop*, and then their robots were emptying the trade lock on their side, and it was their turn. Nbaro put in fifteen gold bars, the rest of their reserve, as well as four copper ingots and five more of Dorcas's bronze. She dusted the whole offering with the greeting pheromone analogue and shut the hatch, starting the trade process. 'So Doctor Ho, at New Beijing, thinks xenoglas is a silicon version of graphene with the atoms connected by forces we don't understand,' she said.

'Concise and accurate,' Dorcas said. They were both watching the smaller Starfish as it swam-walked around the ingots. The Trade Point tradition was that each species took a turn to initiate, putting out items for trade, waiting for an offer.

'Our consortium now owns one hundred and sixty kilos of xenoglas,' she said.

'Which may have almost any ascribed value by the time we get it home,' Dorcas said. 'Probably very high.'

'Unless we're killed,' Marca said.

'Right. But then we won't care, will we?'

'Excellent point.'

Dorcas began to kiss her where her shoulder met her neck. It was very pleasant and promised even better, and she was genuinely regretful when the dull metal forklift rolled into the alien side of the lock and began to place trays of glas.

'Are we being filmed?' she asked, suddenly pushing him away.

'Absolutely not.' Dorcas sounded offended. And then he stiffened. 'Ah. Yes, we are.' He looked at her. 'Ah. Morosini turned them all back on when you asked.'

He really was easy to like. And then the Starfish caught her attention.

'Damn,' she said. 'That looks like lots.'

'We're at about 240 kilos,' Dorcas said.

'And there's more coming...'

'Three hundred and forty-some kilos. It's not quite record-breaking, but it's a very good deal. Especially considering the relative value of the copper and bronze.' He looked at her. 'Do you want to send them back for more?'

She made a face. 'I think... No.' She raised a hand. 'Here's my logic. We engaged them emotionally, assuming we know they have emotions, by including the pheromone. But if we then ask for more, we look greedy and we forfeit the delicate compliment of the use of the greeting pheromone.'

'A human might think that way,' Dorcas said. 'I admit I might think that way – a pleasant perfume to go with something I already want, and then a feeling of mortification when it's clear I'm being gouged. But who knows?' He spread his hands.

'Worst case, it's an excellent deal,' she said.

'Absolutely true,' he agreed.

She released the lock on the far side to conclude the deal, and Feather Dancer waved all ten arms and seemed to gyrate.

'Was that a whoop?'

'Ask me in fifty years,' Dorcas said. 'And two long items of song, and the matching chem emissions. A red-letter day.'

'Except for the PTX ship,' Nbaro said.

They were both silent for a while.

'Now what?' she asked. 'We've done our trades. We aren't allowed to trade for other consortiums...'

'We can trade for the ship, but that's usually a Cargo officer's job.' Dorcas had his hands at her waist.

'If you lick my ear again, there will be trouble.'

'I am feeling amorous,' he said. 'I'm a simple creature. Success makes me amorous.'

'Nothing about you is simple, mister. And nothing makes me feel less amorous, as you put it, than the opportunity to be a zoo exhibit for two aliens.'

Dorcas looked up. 'I wasn't proposing...' he began, and blushed. He opened his mouth, but whatever he was going to say remained unsaid, because suddenly Feather Dancer was singing.

Dorcas froze.

'I'm recording it,' Nbaro said. 'Morosini is, rather.'

Dorcas had the immobility that came over him when he was interacting via his neural lace.

Instead of asking him, she tried finding him in the digital soup of the interactive dataworld. It wasn't hard; he glowed like a lamp.

He reached out and handed her a string of data: a comparison of the digital audio signal from the alien's first song and this song – nearly identical for a given value.

Morosini accepted the data comparison and issued a red-alert warning.

In the dataworld, where everything happened with ridiculous

speed, she understood without words that Dorcas and Morosini were assuming the Starfish did indeed have some early warning of ships dropping into real space, and as the song was the same …

'RUN SILENT,' came the command from the Master. 'RED ALERT.'

On her Space Ops feed, Marca watched every human ship in the system run for cover: shuttles and ferries ran to dock or hide in the shadow of asteroids; the remaining frigate powered down; the two Gunslinger heavy fighters turned off their engines and active radar and ladar and went dark. Her squadron mate, Thor Storkel, did the same; Storkel even turned off his internals of 7–0–4, relying on suit air for his crew.

The whole human expedition went silent and cold in perhaps five seconds, the fruit of a long voyage under threat and repeated drills.

The station turned off virtually everything that could be turned off. Turbines went down; the constant whisper of the air conditioners stopped, and the silence was chilling. She could see information in the dataworld, and beyond it, another layer – the real. But she couldn't hear anything but her own breathing, and Dorcas's, and the beat of her heart in her ears, and beyond, the terrible, eerie counterpoint of the Starfish's song.

Her heart was beating fast.

'What's happening?' she said aloud, and it was ridiculously loud.

'Crash-couch,' Dorcas said, rolling into one. There were four, and Nbaro allowed herself to fall back on another. They were inside the rock of the asteroid – one of the best armoured places on the station, or in the whole system, for that matter.

Dorcas had rigged a countdown in their shared dataworld display; it was based on the lag between the first whale song and the first appearance of the runaway PTX ship. She watched the numerals tick down.

The restraints of her crash-couch settled automatically over her, bending or straightening her limbs and neck to optimal positions, and then tightening down. The datasphere was thinning; she guessed that the *Athens* was no longer transmitting, and thus Morosini wasn't providing data updates. By comparison, his cousin, the station sub-AI, lacked both power and speed. She couldn't refresh her Space Ops feed for ten real-time seconds, and then it refreshed sluggishly and without any new data from most of the outlying repeaters.

The station just didn't have the command-and-control bandwidth. She wondered what the Starfish were doing. Feather Dancer and the smaller Starfish were gone.

Her mind was racing, and she had no data to feed it and the neural lace made her feel more ignorant. Not to mention the basic invasion of privacy. She hadn't even thought that part through...

The counter was down to 10, 9...

What the hell do I think is about to happen?

Dorcas said, 'I love you.'

So he's nervous, too.

She couldn't turn her head and...

The counter went to zero. She breathed, wondering if the circumstances required her to tell Dorcas that she loved him, and her damn Space Ops frame still wouldn't reset or refresh. It wasn't a good day to have a neural lace.

She put together the words 'I love you' with a little vid of the Starfish experiencing the pheromones she'd sprayed on the bronze, and pushed it at him in the datasphere.

He laughed aloud. Very satisfying, really.

And then her Space Ops frame refreshed, apparently off a deployed beacon.

BOGEY.

Another ship, this one at almost 0.4 c, the fastest it could go and *probably* decelerate in-system. It was broadcasting a wavefront of messages, and its insertion point showed a glowing starburst of Cherenkov radiation.

'Well, well,' Dorcas said. 'The Starfish have a way to see the ships as they come in, ahead of their light-speed wavefront. That's not possible. But it's obviously true.'

It was moving very fast, and Nbaro's information was badly lagged; it came in high above the ecliptic and well out from the station, so there was a delay between the sensors detecting it and their own antennas. Dorcas entered into her own calculation and inserted an answer – about eight minutes.

She ran the calculations. 'The Starfish knew eleven minutes before we did,' she said. 'Three minutes before our outermost sensor did. At least.'

Dorcas was glowing with calculations. 'If I didn't know it was impossible,' he said, 'I'd guess they had a form of FTL communication with an invisible sensor net three light minutes out from our own sensors and...' He shrugged. 'I think it's a good time to say "I have no idea".'

Nbaro had switched to a prediction plot on the bogey. It could be almost anything; if it was chasing the doomed PTX ship, it could even be one of theirs, except that their long-jump battlecruisers weren't intended to come to Trade Point.

'The new watch will be here in thirty minutes,' Dorcas said. 'Anything we should be cleaning up?'

Nbaro laughed. 'Shall I mop the trade lock, sir?' she asked sweetly.

The icon on her neural-laced digital model of a Space Ops repeater station turned bright red.

'PTX heavy cruiser, Juniper class,' she said. 'Another one.' Someone in Intel had a sensor picture and she saw it, fuzzy and dark, but it still had its long tail deployed from jump, and that confirmed its identity.

'Unencrypted SOS,' she said unnecessarily, reading the info off the same data that Dorcas could access. 'She's surrendering.'

'She's jumping into this system of her own free will and surrendering,' Dorcas said. 'That wasn't anyone's expected outcome.'

Suddenly, her data field was flooded with information. Morosini was back; the *Athens* was broadcasting again. All through the asteroid ring, ships moved; out in the open space nearer the station, shuttles and fighters lit their drives.

'This is all on an eight-minute delay,' she said. 'Space Ops believes they're seeing the cruiser taking in her tail. They're predicting she's going to flip and start decelerating.'

Dorcas was drawing lines in the air with his hands, as if he was some wizard from a holodrama.

'Same insertion point, give or take a few thousand kilometres,' he said. 'Same point of origin – ninety per cent chance. Did they have a spat, our friends from the Eternal Empire?'

Nbaro was full of useless energy, her veins coursing with adrenaline she couldn't use, her heart pumping more blood than she needed, her lungs drawing extra air to fight no battle.

'You are agitated,' Dorcas said.

'My squadron is deploying and I'm sitting here.'

'You can't do everything. A moment before, you were making everyone in our little cartel a fortune. How much adventure do you require in a day, Ms Nbaro?' Dorcas asked. 'What if I can't keep up?'

Marca grunted. Thea's instructions would have her make a snappy remark, but Dorcas was Dorcas – her friend, and probably her lover. 'I'm not good at sitting by and watching,' she admitted.

'I'd suggest that you avoid politics,' Dorcas said. 'Let's start shutting down.'

'The cruiser—'

'The *Athens* is not really going to be threatened by a single

PTX ship, no matter how well captained,' Dorcas said. 'In fact, I suspect that even now, some Flight One shuttles full of Marines are preparing to launch, and the *Athens* will no doubt stay hidden. It's not a crisis.'

'We're two years away from home in an alien system, and we're seven days from the biggest space battle in human history and ... you think this isn't a crisis?'

'No,' Dorcas said. Despite the pulsing red light of the general quarters alert, he began the process of leaving his acceleration couch. She considered the accuracy of his usual analysis and grunted again.

And then the little red light flashed, and she turned in time to see Feather Dancer re-emerge, alone, from the murk of the sea of ammonia in which the Starfish lived.

Feather Dancer went straight to the robot starfish and began what could only be described as a dance, along with a chemical fusillade.

But no sound.

'What the ...?' she said, and told the couch to let her off. She did not enjoy the feeling of the flexible fibre needles withdrawing from her flesh any more than she enjoyed the insertion, but it happened, and experience had taught her that wriggling only made it worse, and eventually raised a rash.

'Damnation!' Dorcas said. 'No audible component! Unprecedented!'

All ten Starfish arms waved, first in unison, and then in an incredible ten-beat rhythmic pattern.

'Please tell me we are filming this,' Nbaro asked Morosini.

'*Top priority*,' Morosini responded.

She stood behind Dorcas, and she could see the symbols for the chemicals he was detecting.

'If you have any insight, I'd be happy to hear it,' he said.

'Nothing,' Nbaro said.

Finally, Feather Dancer stopped. It was still for a long moment, and then gave a five-armed shrug. It was so like a human shrug that Nbaro gasped.

'Fire off the greeting,' she said.

'Without sound,' Dorcas agreed. He looked blank; he wasn't using the keyboard, but was accessing the robot via his lace, and she watched him in dataspace.

'Why no sound?' she asked.

'I think Feather Dancer just told us something it doesn't want the other Starfish to hear,' Dorcas replied.

The robot starfish waved its arms, a poor parody of a real Starfish. And then the chemicals were released.

Feather Dancer turned, locked the suction cups of five arms on the xenoglas wall, and knocked with one lower arm.

Knock knock knock.

Nbaro felt the hairs on the back of her neck prickle.

And then Feather Dancer turned and swam away.

'What the fuck did we just see?' she asked. 'Is it trying to defect?'

3

The next three days passed in a wave of complex drudgery. The squadron's command sub-AI demanded Nbaro's personnel reports via niggling little messages that went right through her filters and into her neural lace at inopportune times; the work on the station was back-breaking and constant, and she didn't draw another cargo watch with Dorcas. Every time she had a chance, she asked about Feather Dancer. But no one had seen the distinctive Starfish since their trade at the airlock.

The third day was enlivened by the arrival of a Flight Two shuttle – one of the senior officers' 'barges' reconfigured as a cargo pallet with engines, incapable of atmospheric flight. It brought them pallets of new material to construct – so much material that it filled the new pressurised warehouse space that they'd just finished building.

Good planning there, Morosini.

The cargo included Thea Drake, who shot out of the command module as if she intended to conquer the station, not just work there. She touched her helmet to Nbaro's and said, 'Anything fun? How's the sex?'

'I did our trade,' Nbaro said. 'I got—'

'You tabbed me about the trade. I mean Dorcas.'

'No,' Nbaro said.

'Do you need lessons or something?' Drake replied, and leapt away to land on the station's airlock platform.

Boredom and grinding work with Thea around were much better than boredom and grinding work without her. Thea was standing endless cargo watches to learn the trade with the Starfish, and she ended up spending more time with Dorcas than Nbaro had, but watch rotation had them all on the same shifts, and they developed a routine that was almost . . . fun. With Naisha Qaqqaq, they had four for meals and occasional games, although Qaqqaq usually did a quick workout and went straight to bed. At Thea's urging, Nbaro began to work out with Dorcas in the tiny fitness space, which was so intimate that . . .

There was some blushing. But Nbaro and Dorcas held to some sort of line, despite the constant teasing of their social peers that suggested that no one, from Qaqqaq to Gunny Drun, thought that they were celibate.

Nbaro found it all frustrating, and her answer to that frustration was to work harder. When she started to think too much about Dorcas, or certain aspects of Dorcas, she volunteered for yet more work, cataloguing and moving cargo coming from the *Athens*.

The cargo pallets contained some fascinating mechanisms, and four days after Thea's arrival, Nbaro raised Qaqqaq on her private comms.

'Are we building a shipyard?' she asked. The new portion of the station seemed to have huge beams, heavy derricks and a big metal-forming shop, and Nbaro knew the look of the 3D printers that she'd just bolted down to a spin-capable outer hull. In fact, they were building a whole spin-ring to generate gravity. It was also quite big. For the first time, she was involved in sinking bolts into the asteroid itself, and building what could only be described as foundations for further construction.

Qaqqaq made a clicking sound with her tongue. But after a moment, she said, 'Yes. I'm just guessing here, but I think the Master plans to build a new frigate.'

Every greatship carried two frigates. They weren't really warships; they were more like giant Electromagnetic Counter-Measures (ECM) drones with heavy-duty engines, designed to mimic the *Athens* in combat. Both of theirs had been destroyed.

'We carry a spare frigate?' Nbaro asked.

Qaqqaq jumped over, clicked home against the metal girder where Nbaro was standing, and touched her helmet to Nbaro's. 'I'm pretty sure,' she said in the utmost privacy. 'And I know they're breaking a bunch of new stuff out on the Hangar Deck of the *Athens*, so there's no room over there.' She smiled through their visors, and winked. 'But this isn't something to discuss. Do you know there's a big argument on the *Athens*?'

Nbaro leaned in slightly to keep their domed helmets together. 'No,' she said.

Qaqqaq's eyes were bright under her visor. This close, the gold tint barely hid her.

'Some of the command team want to run for home,' she said. 'Especially now we know where two of the PTX ships are.'

Nbaro initially thought, *That's what Aadavan wanted*, followed almost immediately by the realisation that it made some sense.

'Astrogation wants to continue on our course,' Qaqqaq said. 'My boss, Captain Dukas, also wants to. She says it's our duty.'

Which also makes sense.

'But the scuttlebutt is that Pisani wants to ...' Qaqqaq's dark eyes locked on Nbaro's. 'Do you know anything? Pisani talks to you.'

'Not lately,' Nbaro said, slightly miffed. 'Ask Dorcas. He knows everything.'

Qaqqaq's eyes shifted briefly. She was actually showing fear.

'What?' Nbaro asked. 'What's the gossip?'

'The cargo pilot says that Pisani wants to follow the aliens who jumped out. The bugs. The Bubbles, depending on who you are talking to.'

'What?' Nbaro asked.

Qaqqaq backed away and shook her head.

A sleep cycle and another work cycle later, and Nbaro was working against resistance bands while Dorcas, at her feet in the artificial gravity, was doing push-ups. He was literally between her legs . . .

She'd already used her growing neural-lace abilities to sweep for surveillance devices. The success of her sweep was not guaranteed, and she was all but certain that Morosini could overhear anything she heard or saw, which should have piqued her Orphanage paranoia but, so far, had not.

Because I trust the AI? Or because if he wants to watch me mate, he gets what he deserves?

Not the way to answer that one.

'There's a rumour that Pisani plans to follow the aliens,' she said.

Dorcas's body went up and down. 'Really?' he said. And then, 'Yes, I'm fairly certain he does.'

'Follow the aliens into unknown space?' she asked. 'With the only cargo of glas in four years? For what? Didn't someone tell me that we *just barely* won the fight here?'

'We won handily, after a tipping point was reached—'

'Spare me,' Nbaro snapped.

Sweat flowed. Her arms ached.

He rolled over and she shuffled back against the bulkhead to make room. She looked away.

'The Master has every right to decide on the course his ship takes, advised by Morosini and his officers,' Dorcas said.

'Thanks, dear, I had that lesson in DHC Law,' she said with bite.

Dorcas was a head taller than her, standing. His presence was almost overpowering, and she was watching him devour her with his eyes.

'We're funny,' she said.

'I agree,' Dorcas said.

'Everyone on this station assumes we're shagging the moment we come in here.'

Dorcas licked his lips. 'I am painfully aware of this fact,' he said.

Fuck it, she thought, and leaned forward.

His lips locked on hers, and one of his hands found a breast. It was a very, very good kiss, and it went on longer than she'd expected.

He broke off and smiled ruefully.

'I think we could just limit ourselves to that...' she said.

He half turned away, hiding his body's reaction, and he giggled, a sound he seldom made. 'I'm sweaty, I smell bad, it's hot in here and the air stinks, and this is *not* what I want for our... consummation.'

'Good God,' she said. 'Consummation? I will marry you just for your words, good sir.' Very deliberately, she leaned forward, brushed her lips hard against his, ran her tongue along his upper lip, and then turned and popped the hatch before anything else could happen.

Dorcas laughed. 'I cannot wait for my next workout.' As the hatch was open, most of the tiny habitable portion of the station heard him.

'What do *you* think?' she asked. 'About Pisani?'

He looked away. 'Tell you tomorrow,' he said.

*

Their attempts at secrecy were wasted, because by the time they were pulling bulbs of curry the next day after their working shifts, everyone on their rotation was talking about the three possible paths.

'It's obvious that we need to get home in the fastest possible way,' Commander Jha said. He was – at least technically – Drake's boss, and he was well thought of in Cargo. He had advanced degrees in economics, and he spent most of the meal laying out the cost of delaying their shipment of xenoglas to New London, in both financial and political terms.

Dorcas sat back and listened, and Nbaro suspected that his stillness bespoke disagreement.

'We can't afford risk at this point,' Jha said.

The mess was egalitarian; by custom, people who dined together could, up to a point, ignore rank. So Wilson Akunje waited until the commander was finished and shook his head.

'With respect, sir,' he said. 'Seems like bad tactics, going back the way we came.'

Jha glanced over at him. 'Why bad tactics?'

'Closer to PTX space. Right past places where we *know* they have agents in place. If we're pursued, we'll go right into the teeth of our pursuers. Just saying … we're trained to never go back on the same trail we go out.' Akunje smiled broadly. 'Maybe that's just Marine thinking.'

Qaqqaq moved her head as if she meant to speak, but then looked over at her engineering personnel and shook her head.

Jha nodded slowly, eyes slightly narrowed. 'I hadn't thought of it that way,' he admitted, and Nbaro liked him better for that. 'But I'm not sure that those factors can ever be balanced – the unknown versus the unknown.'

Akunje smiled his big smile again.

'I'm not a Marine, but I've done some hunting,' Jha said.

'Surely our ongoing course is the most predictable route? Why would they expect us to turn back?'

Akunje nodded, acknowledging his point.

A junior spacer from Engineering, Ramirez, shook her head. 'I hear the Master wants to jump off into the Deep Black,' she said. 'And that's just crazy.'

Jha glanced at her and smiled. 'I think that's just a rumour,' he said with smooth confidence.

Dorcas wriggled.

'Our cargo is too precious to risk,' Jha said, and that closed the conversation.

Out in the system, the second PTX starship struggled to decelerate, her drives showing real signs of damage: frequency variations that spoke of desperate patches and too much power for too long.

She noted that days had been added to her rota on the station; the extended assignment showed up on her tab with a note from Truekner that said simply 'not pleased'. That made her stomach churn. But she was very busy indeed.

From the station, in between watches and work shifts, Nbaro watched the dark green arrowhead on the Space Ops repeater, and watched the long, apparently slow curves as two big cargo shuttles and the pinnace reached out towards the distant ship and struggled to match velocities. Aside from station bridge watch-standers, she and Dorcas – with their neural laces and access to Morosini – were probably the only people aboard who could see the progress of the chase, and see how very close the outcome would be. She could only guess at the level of drama and the risk involved.

She was doing push-ups against the floor in a little over 1 g, and Dorcas was finished, wiping himself off with his T-shirt.

'We're cutting water rations tomorrow,' he said. 'It'll get even worse in here.'

'That's because most of our heavy lifters are chasing the PTX ship,' she said. 'I guess we'll have to wait for a big shipment.'

'We're going to cut food, too. Not hard, but people are going to notice it. Tomorrow's shipments are cargo for trade and a lot of building material.' Dorcas made a face. 'Morosini feels that we can manage for a few more days while he gets his little shipyard built.'

She rolled over. 'Why does Morosini like you better than me?'

He wasn't looking at her. 'I was asking some related questions,' he said, a little distantly. 'Are you planning on making a dozen more desirable postures first, or do I get to kiss you now?'

She rolled to her feet. 'You know, you're not really my commanding officer here,' she said.

'I really am.' He wasn't meeting her eye, and suddenly she realised that he was very serious.

She stopped. 'What does that mean?'

'It means that there's a lot happening,' he said. 'And ultimately…'

'Ultimately?' she asked. She didn't have *seductive* in her. She wasn't trying to vamp him. She just leaned against the other bulkhead and crossed her arms.

'Ultimately I'm in command here,' he said.

She swallowed. 'But Commander Jha…'

'No,' he said. 'Commander Jha, as a Cargo officer, can command this station, but ultimately—'

'You keep using that word, and I know you, and words. Does Jha know he's not in command?'

Dorcas gave a slightly bitter, fairly hesitant smile. She hadn't seen him like this in a while. 'No,' he said.

'Aha,' she said. 'What's happening?'

'I think this is *exactly* why I'm not supposed to be in love with someone to whom I may have to give orders.'

'Aha,' she said again. 'But you are, and here we are, and I'm not exactly a blabbermouth. So give.'

He still hesitated.

She considered drama but, like seduction, it wasn't her way. So she went for analysis instead. 'Pisani has taken a big risk with the pinnace and the cargo boats, and if the PTX drives keep fucking up, we're going to lose them all,' she guessed.

'You are so very intelligent,' he said.

'If this is supposed to be a secret, someone should keep it off the Space Ops repeater boards.'

'I don't think most people bother with the maths,' Dorcas replied. 'But every time those drives fluctuate, the PTX ship accelerates briefly. And our ships need to make that rendezvous or no one out there gets home. We've got the repair kits. And the fuel.'

'I guessed that,' she said.

'But the point of no return . . .'

She nodded. 'Is close?'

'Nine hours ago. The Master ordered them to keep going. It's done. Nbaro, he's determined to pull this off. It's part of his strategy . . .'

'They're *past* the point of no return?' she asked.

'If they don't catch the PTX ship, they're lost.' Dorcas sounded strained. But his head was still turned away.

'Why?' she asked. 'Why take that risk?' But in her heart, she knew the answer, because she still looked from time to time at the other ship: the Flying Dutchman that was headed out into the universe at 0.7 *c*. Because there were probably hundreds, even a thousand spacers aboard that ship, and whatever disagreement the DHC and PTX were having, out here, at the very edge of known space, humanity seemed a very strong bond indeed.

'What's she called?' Nbaro asked.

Dorcas turned. 'She's called 偷天換日 *Tou Tian Huan Ri*,' he said in his apparently excellent Mandarin. 'The *Stealthy Change*.'

'That's … quite a name.'

'Bit of a giveaway, if you ask me.' Dorcas looked at her, and smiled. 'A lot of people are deeply angry at Pisani over this, and I thought you might be one of them.'

'I'm not,' she said. 'No one should die out here.'

'Even after we shot each other up?' he asked.

'Which side are you on?' She wasn't used to him being so reticent. Or rather, he was always reticent, but she'd grown used to something more from him and this was like a relapse into an older and more correct, more withdrawn Dorcas.

She was tempted to press up against him and kiss him to break him loose of whatever he was worrying about, but …

Not seduction. Not even for that.

But something was definitely wrong, and it was more than Pisani's risk to save the *Stealthy Change*. Based on her very limited experience of relationships, it was something between them.

They left the workout box without so much as a kiss, and Nbaro buried herself in her fitness evaluations. And after that she had a four-hour rotation outside, working on what every spacer now openly called the dockyard.

Her officer's rank was of no value out there because she had so few work party qualifications, and she wasn't an engineer, so mostly she welded or inspected welds, and sometimes she joined the very junior spacers in just … pushing things. Moving mass. Otherwise, she was learning avionics at Qaqqaq's command, but today's work merely required her to guide a remarkably low-tech electric drill as it bored into the nickel- and iron-rich rock of the asteroid, pausing from time to time to cool the friction-heated bit and oil it. It was dull, repetitive, and demanded very little of her attention, leaving her far too much time to think about Dorcas, about Morosini; about the doomed PTX ship flying on at 0.7 *c* and the one that she hoped Pisani was going to rescue. She wondered how many of her squadron mates were strung out across the system as refuelling birds, trying to get the heavy shuttles all the way out...

And she thought about Sarah. Sarah, who had joined her in revolt, back at the Orphanage. Sarah, who'd paid the price, sold to a brothel. Sarah, who had found her a hacker to alter her record and get her aboard. *I wouldn't be here without Sarah. And I flew off and left her to it.*

Not very noble.

She usually locked all these thoughts away from herself, compartmented them so that she could... live. She wondered if allowing herself to... love... Dorcas was letting the demons free.

Somewhere in there, her attention slipped, and suddenly she realised that the drill had stopped. She worked it free...

I'm an idiot.

The bit was very hot, and vacuum wasn't a good place to cool it. And to her eye, it looked very slightly deformed.

An idiot.

However, she did the right thing: found the spares and popped the hot bit out of the drill. But it really was hot; the palm sensor in her hand-armour reacted, and the big tungsten bit shot away in near zero *g*, struck the shoulder of her EVA suit and bounced away into the rubble-strewn surface of the asteroid. By *good* luck, it stuck in the dust and didn't bounce back into space.

Very carefully, she put the new bit into the drill, remounted it, and put it back to drilling in its laser-registered hole. Then, after checking her tether, she released herself from the asteroid and moved cautiously along the surface on all fours. She could see the bit gleaming against the charcoal-grey dust, and she got a hand on it as she grabbed at a larger rock for support.

The rock moved. Dust rose, disturbed in the micro-gravity. She wondered idly how long it would take to settle again. A century?

There was something under the rock – an organic shape that had no business being in space. A *snake*. She flinched and immediately felt foolish.

She got a new handhold, and checked her tether automatically, and scooped the drill bit into a pouch at her waist.

The snake wasn't moving. That perception had been an artifact of her own weight shifting the rock. It was just a twist of something half-buried in the dust and rock...

She blinked. 'Morosini? Please record.'

'*Recording. You are aware that there are automated functions and control keys and breathing patterns...*'

She reached down and, with all the delicacy she could muster with her armoured hand, plucked the twist of material from the dust.

She completed her work, handed the drill over to another spacer, and found that almost everyone in the mess was glued to vid or holo as the *Athens* vehicles raced to catch the slower of the two fast-moving PTX ships.

She tabbed and marked the damaged bit and tottered off to her rack, painfully aware that Dorcas was on another watch, the little twist of material forgotten.

She was in the middle of her sleep cycle when Qaqqaq woke her via her tab. 'You'll want to see this,' she said.

After a glance at her comlog, she brought up her Space Ops repeater and watched it on the back of her eyelids through the neural lace. There was a seven-hour delay now on anything coming from the *Stealthy Change*, which gave her an odd feeling she'd had back aboard the *Athens*, when she watched events that she knew had already played out. It was like watching a sporting event when the game was already decided.

Somewhere out in space, millions of kilometres away, the master of the *Stealthy Change* and the trio of craft from the *Athens* trying to catch her had thrown the dice. They were close: all in comms, probably near real-time.

She lay in her crash-couch and watched the pinnace go to its maximum acceleration, and then exceed it. That would be Fuju Han, out there, going for it, risking his engines and his life.

I hate watching. I want to be there.

Han was an excellent pilot; she felt a strange resentment because she hadn't really liked him, and he'd impressed the crap out of her with his docking manoeuvre, and she'd felt a little...

The Space Ops repeater showed the *Stealthy Change* making a successful deceleration.

The two trailing shuttles were losing ground to the pinnace, and the PTX ship was *still* pulling away. Not by much.

The *Stealthy Change*'s drive vibrated. It was bad enough that the variation could be detected at a hundred million kilometres.

She wanted to turn it off, or close her eyes.

'Are you watching this?' Dorcas asked on the datalink.

'You know it,' she replied.

'I wish I could hold your hand,' Dorcas added.

It felt selfish to think it, but that one comment made her feel better.

On the repeater, the *Stealthy Change* seemed to wobble and flicker.

The pinnace...

...gained. It gained. She mentally ordered the screen to expand, and she ran a probably inaccurate mensuration and guessed at the distance between them and the probable run time.

59

The two ships were close, and the PTX ship was decelerating. It was also wobbling. Even at this incredible range, the sensors tracking it were showing some fluctuation, as if it was no longer moving in a straight line.

'It's going to explode,' she said aloud to her silent cabin.

Nbaro opened her eyes, blinking away tears and the awful reality, and thinking of Han and all the spacers...

'ALLLLLLLL RIGHT,' Dorcas sent through the datalink, with an image of a crowd applauding.

She blinked back into the Space Ops board.

The two dots had merged.

'He's going to try and dock,' Dorcas said.

'Morosini? Can I have the comms?'

Immediately she had a buzzing in her ears, and a low drone.

'Roger, *Tou Tian Huan Ri*, I am matching flight path and I have your automated landing sequence. Stand by for docking.' It was Han, and he sounded glacial.

Someone – *their equivalent of Lioness?* – spoke in Mandarin.

Han's comms beeped and he responded – in Mandarin.

'They've cut their engines,' Dorcas said hopefully.

Time passed like a spoon passing through jelly. There was no change on the repeaters, and nothing but silence on the comms...

Han's breaking thrusters at close range. The sound came through the comms link as a rapid pulsing, like machine gunfire.

RAT tatatatatatat.

Brak.

Brak ratatat.

BAM!

'Docked. Green and green.'

Nbaro could hear the cheers throughout the hab module, and she could feel them through the walls.

She was breathing hard, soaked in sweat, and the showers were turned off.

She was grinning from ear to ear.

Way to go, Han.

Argonauts. A ship of heroes.

4

Nbaro's alarm woke her from a deep sleep, and she clawed her way into a dirty flightsuit and her EVA rig on automatic before she realised that it was just an alarm, not a crisis. After a bulb of coffee and a tube of sweet sticky rice, she was ready to face another day assembling the new docking arm. Dorcas managed to pass her in the cargo bay access tube. He grabbed her hand and brushed her lips with his, and she felt immediately better about every aspect of life, which she found funny and faintly ridiculous.

'Hey,' she said.

'Later,' he apologised, and moved away.

'I have something to show you,' she said to his back.

Qaqqaq held a morning briefing for all the assembly crews in the pressurised hangar bay. Water was being rationed again; everyone smelled strongly of human being, and the acrid scent of bad coffee lay over all of them, along with the smell of drying epoxy and the artificial lubricant scent of spacecraft.

'...probably our last day on the docking arm,' Qaqqaq said. 'You folks have done first-rate work, and I appreciate it and so does the *Athens*. I'm sure everyone saw our pinnace rendezvous with the PTX ship last night. This morning, about 0400, both of the shuttles docked and started pumping them fuel, and my boss, Captain Dukas, went aboard with every spare part we could think to send.'

Nbaro thought that PTX engineering was renowned for its quality and inventiveness and wasn't sure what Dukas had to offer, nor could she imagine any parts from the *Athens* working on PTX engines, but … she kept her mouth shut.

'The shuttles will start back in two days. They're going to scoop one of the gas giants on the way, but in a week max, we'll have water and more food and all the things that make life worth living.' She smiled to indicate that that had been intended as a joke.

Most of the spacers managed a smile.

'OK, team, suit up. Today, I'll be leaving acting Ensign Hauser in charge of the docking arm, and I'll be taking all the team Charlie and Delta folks to start work assembling the frigate.'

Nbaro grinned at Hauser's faceplate. She didn't know them well, but the long-limbed 'gyne from one of the New London Orbitals had helped her with her two midshipper promotees in what seemed like the ancient days off Far Point, and Nbaro reckoned them a friend.

The young 'gyne managed to look both confused and humble even in a vac suit, but the midshippers were all rising to various challenges, and more than twenty of them had been promoted to ensign in the aftermath of the Battle of Trade Point.

But while she smiled at Hauser, Nbaro realised that Qaqqaq meant her to lead the team assembling the frigate. That meant she had a lot of responsibility in departments in which she had no training whatsoever, and after she got back into her EVA suit, she followed a dozen other spacers of every conceivable rank down a second access tube and along the docking arm that was, itself, still under construction. It was cramped, and there was the smell of burnt metal and welding, and it was very cold. Only two layers of specially treated plastics stood between them

63

and the airless void, and she already knew better than to allow any part of her to rest against the plastic wall.

Qaqqaq was crouched in the very narrow space at the end. Above her, upside down in zero *g*, two spacers were gliding a carbon-fibre panel into a pocket of girders that was shiny-wet with epoxy.

She looked back at the two work parties.

'So,' Qaqqaq said. 'We're going to build a starship right here, and what's even more fucked up, we're going to start building it while Alpha and Bravo teams build the docking cradle around us and Hauser completes the docking arm over our heads. Morosini estimates that by the time we're dealing with serious mass issues, the docking arm and part of the cradle will be complete. We still need to get another leg bolted down to the rock.'

While she spoke, she illustrated the whole plan in seven day/ night phases on a hologram projected in front of her face, and it repeated into everyone's systems for review.

'Lieutenant Nbaro, as she's a pilot, will take the avionics and bridge section. Marca, I am downloading you the specs and the connection diagrams. You get team Charlie.'

The other spacers smiled at her. Ramirez, who was a tiny, dark-complexioned woman, gave her a thumb's up. Luroy, a petty officer, also from Engineering, gave her a nod. He was big and fierce-looking, but she'd been gluing panels and pushing cargo with him for a week and she knew he was both funny and strong – and careful. And her friend Thea Drake just looked resigned.

Nbaro gathered her crew with a wave even as she used her new neural lace skills to review the various documents and the holographic production schedule.

'Well,' she said, 'I'm not in any way an engineer.'

Luroy grinned. It robbed his face of its habitual expression of dangerous rage, which she'd rapidly learned was just ... how he looked. 'Well, ma'am, we're all from Engineering, so we probably have that covered.'

Drake laughed. 'I'm from Cargo. I can only guarantee what comes *out* of the containers.'

Nbaro nodded. 'Yeah. Anyway... this looks like a three-dimensional puzzle, or maybe one of those model-building competitions they pushed on us at the Orphanage...'

Ramirez nodded. 'Yes'm. It's all coded shit. Ms Drake can check the codes, we can rattle it together and then you can test it. Not exactly rocket science.'

Luroy looked at her. 'It is, in fact, rocket science,' he said.

Ramirez made an obscene gesture, and Luroy scowled.

Nbaro had a moment of wondering if that obscene gesture constituted something of which she should take notice, but the moment passed and she took no action.

'Well, that's a plan made, then. I agree with Ramirez. Thea, you're going to watch the unload and check every crate and its assembly code, and coach the assembly teams. I'll test the components as they come on-line.' She smiled at Ramirez and the little woman beamed.

Everyone likes to be listened to. It was, in fact, exactly what Nbaro had intended to do, but it didn't hurt to share with Ramirez, who was the most junior, and wavered between enthusiasm and cynical fatigue.

She put a hand on Drake's arm as they both put their helmets on. She leaned in.

'Should I have said something to Ramirez?' she asked. 'She told Luroy to fuck himself. Not exactly...'

Drake winked, visible even through the reflective gold foil coating on her visor. 'They're shagging,' she said. 'Ramirez is a tough bird, she can take care of herself, and Luroy isn't delicate.'

'Oh,' Nbaro said. 'But he's her boss.'

Drake winked. 'It's the Deep Black,' she said. 'It's got its own rules. And anyway, honey, you ain't in a position to talk, are you?'

Drake kicked off and flew to the airlock hatch as if she had been born in zero *g*.

Nbaro sighed inwardly at the unfairness of it all – a familiar feeling from her Orphanage days – and made sure the magnets in her boots were activated before joining Drake in the tiny airlock.

A day passed. Nbaro glanced at the Space Ops repeater too often and noted that the *Stealthy Change* hadn't made any attempt to decelerate further since docking with the pinnace.

When it was time for her workout, she fetched the twist of material from her EVA suit external pocket; parts of it fell to a greasy black dust in her hand, but she managed to get the surviving third to the workout room.

Dorcas tried to kiss her, and she shouldered him away in the low gravity. 'Wait a minute,' she said.

Dorcas looked abashed.

'No, no,' she said. 'I'm a mess of hormones, just like you. Only I want you to look at this.'

Dorcas obediently took the little twist from her and sat back against the tiny compartment's bulkhead, a look of puzzlement on his face.

'This is carbon fibre,' he said. 'Very old carbon fibre.' He shook his head. 'So you kept some, after telling me it was immoral for me to keep some?'

She sighed, her hunch confirmed. 'I found it here.'

Dorcas became very still.

'You can access Morosini and watch me harvest it from the surface,' she said, and related the circumstance.

He looked at her, and finally blinked. Then he leaned forward, brushed her lips with his own, and stood. 'No workout today,' he said, his voice tight. 'I'm sorry. This is ... is ...'

He was rarely without words. He looked at her, clearly deeply troubled, and then shook his head. 'I need to get this in a vacuum bag as soon as possible. And then go out and see if there's more.'

And he was gone.

And Nbaro thought dark thoughts – because she could connect the dots as fast as he could. The aliens they called the Circles had been on Haqq and Far Point, at least. A hundred thousand years ago. And they'd had something very like xenoglas.

And they'd all died, or disappeared.

And now, it looked as if they'd been at Trade Point, too.

After she showered, Nbaro checked again and saw that one of the shuttles was breaking away and had taken a long, low-fuel path towards one of the outer gas giants beyond the asteroid belt.

'Get lots of readings,' she told the distant shuttle pilot. Whoever she was, she was bound inwards for a long, lonely flight in a cockpit with limited sanitation facilities. Nbaro's maths in her augmented head said that the shuttle was a week, at least, from refuelling in the atmosphere of the gas giant, and then would have a faster trip home after some fancy flying to avoid the strange debris ring and the plethora of moons.

The pace of the construction seemed to increase. Truekner, her skipper, came in person with two Flight Six spacecraft packed with cargo modules, including four matt-black packages that went into her avionics and astrogation schedule, but had no registered build codes.

She was happy to see Truekner, and the flight was long enough that he and his crews – her flight mates – stayed for a bulb of noodles and a cup of tea.

'I'm going to need you back soon,' he said. 'We've got a list of cargo for this station as long as my arm, and until the big lifters get back, we're transporting it, in hundreds of sorties. I've seen the sched. Are you required here?' He gave her one of his skipper looks: an apparently soft, understanding glance that hid a direct order.

'No, sir,' she said reluctantly, although she really, really wanted to make things … right? Better? … with Dorcas.

'When I send 6–0–2 over tomorrow, I want you to come back as co-pilot and leave Midder Eyre in your place to get some station time. Got that?'

'Yes, sir,' she said.

She hugged Guille and Storkel, gulped the rest of her too-sweet tea and went back to work. She tabbed Qaqqaq to inform her that she'd have to be replaced as a team leader, with a note that Luroy was doing some effective team leadership anyway.

The progress was incredible. Not only were the bridge and avionics systems mostly assembled, but the hull was assembling around the computers, so that it had already begun to look like a starship. Nbaro knew, as did everyone else on the crew, that it was a new design – something that Dukas and Morosini had created out of the parts available: part electronic warfare frigate and part pinnace, with actual deep-space engines and a massive computer, and a curious set of fittings that Nbaro knew had been machined out of printed titanium parts on the *Athens*. The ship also had a pair of massive clamps, and a hollow profile amidships, where she could see the new ship could take on various packages: an EW suite, a detection package, or just cargo. In fact, it could pick up a full-sized four-by-four metre packing container in those clamps.

Nbaro had already guessed what the increasing number of black boxes coming off the fabricators back on the *Athens* had to hold. As the spine of the little spaceship grew, she was

68

unsurprised to see that they received installation codes for the stern nacelles.

That evening was her last aboard the station, and she wished for a shower she couldn't take and went to the workout cubicle. Dorcas was already there.

'You know I'm leaving,' she said. It came out very differently from the way she'd meant to say it. It sounded accusatory, and not wistful.

Dorcas was using the resistance bands. 'I know.' He sounded … miserable.

'Hey,' she said. 'I like you, and everything.'

He smiled broadly at that.

She started to do push-ups.

Staring at the matt-black rubber of the floor, she said, 'You can tell me what's on your mind. I won't tell.'

She wasn't watching him; the only part she could see was his bare feet. He didn't smell bad, which was remarkable.

'I'm afraid,' he said simply.

She pushed off with her hands and stood. 'What are you afraid of?'

'Losing you,' he said.

She shook her head. 'Won't happen.' She was going to end the discussion altogether, but he turned his head away.

'I've volunteered to stay,' he said.

She was going to ignore that, except that something … 'Stay?' she asked.

'Here. On the station. Working with the Starfish, at least until the next ship comes.' Now he looked at her.

The workout cubicle was a box slightly more than two metres on a side. There was no place to run or hide. Everything in it was black, and the light came from three powerful sunlamps set into the ceiling – or at least, the wall that was 'above' when the station wheel was under spin, as it was now.

69

'You're going to stay,' she repeated.

'Yes,' he said miserably.

'Alone, in deep space, on this station.'

'Yes,' he said. 'It is my duty as I perceive it.'

She nodded.

'I know it appears that I prefer the Starfish to you—' he began.

'Spare me,' she said.

'I knew you'd be angry.'

'Shut up and stop patronising me,' she said. 'I'm not angry. If I'd thought it through, I'd have known this was coming.'

He looked puzzled. 'Am I so transparent?'

She shrugged. 'Truekner asked me to go back to the ship and I accepted that instantly. I was afraid you'd be mad, but my flight needs me. And you do not have to tell me, of all people, how important your work with the Starfish is.'

He flushed. As he was wearing short trunks and a barely existent tank top, the flush was visible over most of him. 'Oh, God, you *do* understand.'

Nbaro knew, without feeling around inside her head, that she wasn't actually all right with it: that some part of her had expected this and saw it as rejection; that another part had never believed that he loved her; a third part – a deeply injured part – had never expected any other outcome.

She felt all of that, but she also knew her man. And she knew how incredibly important actual communication with the aliens might be.

She knew she sounded calm to him, but the internal turmoil was real, and it wasn't going to go away. *Some men will do anything to avoid a relationship*, a bitter Nbaro thought, while another Nbaro believed that Dorcas was making a sacrifice, and a real one, and felt it.

'You won't be home until…' she began. 'Jesus, you're here until another greatship calls.' That was brave. He was brave.

He also *enjoyed* being by himself. With his friend Morosini, who would no doubt clone himself to stay.

All that, in two or three seconds of thought. And then, for another terrible second, she teetered on the edge.

Show my anger?

Or show my love?

She had both people in her.

Just walk out and quietly close the hatch. It's done.

Dorcas projected a data image of a man slipping away, a hand waving goodbye, and she reached out a digital hand and grasped his ghostly one.

She grabbed his shoulders as she had back on the orbital, so long ago it seemed like a lifetime – really, only a couple of months. She was smaller than he, and shorter, but she was a much better infighter, and she pushed his shoulders back against the bulkhead's matting, and put her mouth over his.

He put a hand on her bare waist, and then on her breast, and then under her workout shirt.

He broke away. 'There's cameras,' he said.

She had a flash of the chapel at the Orphanage, and then she looked straight into his eyes. 'If Morosini wants to watch…' she said, and she laughed into his mouth.

Dorcas grinned, and then he was fierce and she was fierce, and then…

…they were naked, and they'd overstayed their time in the cubicle.

'We are idiots,' Dorcas said.

'Hey, that's my line,' she said.

'Perhaps I'll grow more like you,' he said, fumbling with his shorts.

'So many reasons,' she murmured, not really ready to go back to non-sexual reality. She held him a moment longer, and his arms wrapped around her.

'I won't leave you out here,' she said. 'If I have to, I'll come get you myself.'

He kissed her.

Someone was pounding on the hatch, and they both flushed at the comments awaiting them from the next pair.

'I love you,' Dorcas said.

'Good,' Nbaro said. 'I needed to hear that.'

But as soon as she was alone, she felt her full reaction: the anger, the sense of betrayal, however unfair, and she thought, *I won't see him again. Not for a while.* Alongside another feeling – an alien feeling – of longing, and desire, and loss.

5

Seven hours later, Nbaro was in the pilot's seat of 6–0–2, landing in the well-lit stern of the *Athens*, and her world was both shaken, and searingly routine. Every time she took a bird to the station, she saw him; a week passed, as she carried black fabrication boxes and distilled water and food out, and sometimes people back. Flight Six flew round the clock, as if they were in combat; sometimes she'd hotseat a bird, taking the round trip, watching them refuel her from inside her cockpit and then tracking back to the railgun to be launched again. When she wasn't flying, she was working on her personnel reports, filing material readiness reports, and reviewing and updating her tactical briefings based on the ten thousand new things that had happened since Far Point. Some of her early slides on space tactics – the ones from her first lecture with Suleimani – made her wince; they'd come so far in those weeks. They now drilled to rapid launches and expected to go out behind a cloud of ablative dust – the use of Qaqqaq's passive sensors had changed the way tactical officers thought about detection – and when she had the time, which was effectively never, she took notes on what she'd observed with the Starfish. Clearly they had a detection system that was another degree of magnitude superior.

Nbaro had the whole stateroom to herself, because Drake

remained on the station, and she spent long hours there working on her various projects with a combination of direct digital interaction and neural lace. She might have limited her world to her stateroom and her cockpit, except that Captain Fraser from Astrogation was insistent that she return to her boarding party routine, and physical exercise seemed to help her sleep.

Dorcas loved her, but he was staying with his Starfish. Intellectually, she understood that he'd made the best choice for the human race and the DHC, but somewhere in her injured psyche she didn't like it at all, and she was...

Depressed. That's what she was. And it was easy to be depressed on board ship – easy to avoid others, easy to stay isolated – since she didn't have Drake dragging her to social occasions and making her eat with others.

Except that this is the person you decided not to be.

It definitely didn't help that she had to endure the hostile stares of Lieutenant McDonald and her friends from Flight One. Her second meal aboard, McDonald glared at her, and she reacted like an Orphanage survivor and not a service officer.

'See something you like?' she drawled. She was craving a fight.

McDonald's eyes flashed with anger. 'You get whatever you want,' she hissed. 'And if I'd been picked, I'd at least be out there. Han's flying almost alone!'

'Whatever I want?' Nbaro spat. 'What the *fuck* does that mean?'

Suddenly there was a hand on her arm. She flung it off, whirled, ready to fight.

It was Cortez. He was short and solid, and he stepped right past her, so that he physically stood between her and McDonald.

To Nbaro, he said, 'Let it go.'

Nbaro screwed up her face in an effort to make herself... be the person who walked away from this fight.

I'm an idiot.

McDonald snorted in contempt. 'Fucking patrician.'

Curiously, that didn't sting, at least in part because Nbaro had never seen herself as a patrician.

Cortez took her arm and dragged her through the hatch and into the passageway.

'You need to cool off,' he said. 'Jesu, sister. People think I'm a hothead.'

She was due to go to a boarding party training session, so she raised her hands in mock surrender. Cortez let her go, and she changed into her armour and sparred with people she knew, wrestled in zero *g*, and fought a couple of long bouts in the drop-shafts with Fraser and Locran and a big Marine she didn't know well.

Captain Fraser was having a bad evening; he was clearly very tired. She knew the look; a few days before jumps, he always looked frazzled. After she hit him for the third time in a row with a simple attack, she stepped back and opened her visor.

'Are we getting ready to jump?' she asked. Her own bluntness surprised her, but there it was. He had circles under his eyes. 'Sir?' she added, belatedly.

He glanced around, but they were effectively alone.

'It's more complicated than that' he said. 'I expect that you know more about it than me.' He managed an enigmatic smile.

Her puzzlement must have shown in her face. He shrugged. 'Sorry, Nbaro. I'm sure it will be clear in time.' He pulled his visor down and they both saluted. She gave it a little thought, and then was swept away in her work. Any spare moment was spent on managing her neural lace. The flood of data made her frustrated, and frustration fed anger and depression. Twice she tabbed Morosini for support and both times he answered laconically, directing her to vids and embedded instruction systems, without any of the more human interaction she loved in him.

That hurt, too.

She had nightmares of rejection; they came back to her like old friends.

Almighty, am I this weak?

Every trip to eat seemed like a return to the Orphanage: the hostile stares of the Flight One crew, and some others... so familiar. And Dorcas...

A week into Nbaro's self-isolation, Truekner ruined it by putting her back on the Space Ops watch standing rotation. She stood a watch with Musashi and found herself sharing her misadventures in construction on the station, to the amusement of everyone in Space Ops. Like a popular person.

It was ridiculous. The Space Ops crew enveloped her like a big embrace of teasing, joking, cynical, overworked... *family*.

Family.

That evening, she ate something pretending to be barbecued pork with Musashi in the more formal officer's mess when they went off watch, and then sparred with him for a while.

He is much, much better than I am, she thought, and then reveled in it, exploring his excellence, the apparent laziness of his crosses and parries, the stillness of his waiting guards, which offered her no real information as to his next movement, the precision of his cuts and thrusts, the depth of his deceptions.

'You are brilliant,' she said, when he left her blade deep in a counter and struck almost slowly across her wrists.

He smiled. 'When your name is Musashi, you have to work very hard,' he said. 'The expectations are terrifying.'

She laughed at that, and felt better. *Why?*

It wasn't all better, but three straight days with watches in Space Ops, one as Lioness, did something to crack her depression. It didn't just wash away, but the routine of the watch, and the pleasure she still took in a well-executed launch and recovery, and the routine excitement of handling the first of the big Flight

One shuttles to return aboard, went a long way to restoring her equilibrium.

It occurred to her that McDonald might be on edge because she wasn't out there with the rest of her Flight. It occurred to her to meet with McDonald and talk about their common ground, but she didn't.

She schemed a little, and arranged her part of the flight schedule so that she had her pilot rest layover at the station. As she flew in towards the rendezvous with the docking arm, she was not really shocked, but definitely amazed, to see how advanced the frigate-pinnace was. The whole hull looked to be closed and pressure-tight, and the starboard engine nacelle held a completed engine assembly.

She hugged Drake and tabbed Dorcas. Where are you?

She knew perfectly well he was on rest. She'd laid her snares carefully.

In my bunk, he replied.

Unlock your hatch and make room.

Two hours later her crew rest hadn't really been particularly restful, but she felt much better.

'How much longer do we have?' she asked him.

He smiled sheepishly. 'Three weeks? The *Stealthy Change* is making a grav-assist turn around the Beta Star and she'll start decelerating next week. If she decelerates at all.' He shrugged. 'Morosini seems confident.'

'He's sure not talking to me,' she said.

Dorcas shrugged. 'When the *Stealthy Change* is back and repaired, and the *Pericles*, our new pinnace, is spaceworthy, I believe the Master will feel he's as ready as he's ever going to be.' He rolled in the artificial gravity and looked at her. 'There's a great deal going on, Nbaro, and for once, you aren't at the centre of it. Morosini is running near his maximum capability – he doesn't have a lot of spare processing power for acting lieutenants.' He smiled to take the sting out. 'Remember – none of us, including me, is supposed to talk to him unless directed to do so. It's in your beloved ship's regs.'

She lay back, looking at his carbon-fibre overhead and thinking, *a person can get really tired of carbon fibre.*

'I got used to ... having him around.'

Dorcas looked conflicted.

Nbaro licked the tip of his nose. She had never known another person so intimately. Dorcas concealed many of his reactions, and yet, increasingly, she could read him. At the moment, he was naked.

But she didn't use seduction, and she knew from comments Truekner had made that learning to be a lieutenant instead of what Truekner called a 'special child' was part of her career path.

'Aye, aye, sir,' she purred.

'It's a very...' he began.

Nbaro's mind ran very fast, comparing the hesitancy of his reaction, the enigmatic smile of Captain Fraser, and all the other slight clues of the last week: newly minted Ensign Gorshokov looking as hollow-eyed as Fraser; Qaqqaq's rush to complete the frigate-pinnace.

She felt more enlivened by lovemaking, not less. The whole experience of sex was neither what she'd expected, nor remembered. She was alert and full of energy, and her brain ran along as if it was on rails. 'The Master isn't just waiting for the aliens to come back, is he?' she asked.

Dorcas eyed her steadily.

'I mean, you can tell that we're jumping out of here, and soon, from the behaviour of our astrogators,' she said. 'And since there's a rumour that the Master wants to follow the aliens, I'm going to guess that Astrogation is working round the clock on what we know of the Bubble entry vectors and what star systems lie beyond. Right? But even with my limited grasp of astro, I can't see that working. Can you? Seems to me we'd need to follow one, and follow pretty closely.'

Dorcas lay back. He was still naked, lying in the rack while she sat on the edge, getting dressed. 'Well,' he said, making a face. 'If you already know that, why are you asking me?'

'Because you are so poor at hiding your reactions,' she said. 'So, like I already asked, mister patrician, sir. How long do we have?'

Dorcas put a hand on her waist and pulled her, unresisting, back into an embrace. 'I can't tell you,' he said. 'But since you are so very intelligent, I'll bet you can guess.'

She chose to break away. 'So …' she said with real regret. 'So if they don't come back, we're leaving in three weeks, on plot and on time. But … the Master, and Morosini, and you, all think the Bubbles will come back. And then we jump out right behind them. How's that?'

'How often can you fly over like this?' Dorcas asked.

'As often as I can,' she said. 'I'm writing the flight schedule this week.' She leaned over, kissed him, and allowed herself to feel it: that precious thing.

Then she nibbled his lip, avoided his hands, and slipped away. 'Did you EVA and look at my carbon fibre?' she asked.

He nodded. 'Yes.'

'And?'

'Classified,' he said.

'I found it! You can tell me.'

'We know you did,' he said.

'We?'

'Let it go,' he replied.

And to her amazement, she did.

*

79

The *Stealthy Change* flew her slingshot with perfect accuracy, as one would expect from a professional military ship, and then, when she was inbound at slightly over 0.3 *c*, she rolled over and fired her engines, and there was no wobble. The Space Ops holotank, updating based on transmitted data eleven hours old, showed the PTX heavy cruiser decelerating smoothly from the first moments of her burn. Everyone in Space Ops cheered, so loudly Nbaro could hear them from the corridors and passageways.

Even though we were shooting at each other, she thought. But the fate of the other ship, now well out of the Trade Point system and deep in interstellar space, remained on the minds of every spacer. Bygones were not entirely bygones: every turret on the ship was manned; the ship itself remained on low power and snuggled up to an asteroid deep in the belt. No one trusted the PTX ship. But everyone was glad the *Stealthy Change* was alive and not dead, or running at relativistic speeds to the end of time.

Nbaro could run her own calculations through her lace: assuming current profile and no mechanical problems, the *Stealthy Change* was nine days out. The other ship was already gone; everyone called her the *Dutchman*, leaving the system for interstellar space at 0.7 *c*. They'd never communicated in any way; Nbaro and everyone she knew assumed they were already dead. It was just one of the many mysteries confronting them.

The *Pericles*, the new frigate-pinnace, was seven to ten days from completion.

She wondered about the aliens, the Starfish, and the conspiracy that probably still existed to destroy the *Athens*, and watched the time of her happiness tick away towards zero.

The *Athens* was beginning to move towards something like normal operations. Every spacer was keenly aware that they were very far from home, with alien ships around them and the threat of enemy action close. At the same time, every hole was patched;

all four reactors were online, and all four of the Tanaka drives were reported to be green and ready to go. And there were other developments. Down in the giant maw of the Hangar Deck, eight new spacecraft had been assembled, much smaller than the Flight Five birds – close-in defence fighters that could be crewed, or piloted by computer or flown remotely.

And now Nbaro could see why they'd had to build the *Pericles* on the rock: there were also replacement birds for losses in Flight Five and Six under construction. The Hangar Deck, usually an empty space where the crew could play sports, was a hive of activity, and there were so many crates of parts that it was difficult to thread a path between them. And the maintenance crews looked as tired as Nbaro felt.

She flew three consecutive sorties to the rock without seeing Thea or Dorcas, and then she had a shower and went to Space Ops without eating.

It was her second time in the Lioness chair in just a few days, and despite her fatigue she enjoyed it thoroughly – all the more because there was almost no in-system clutter, no flights that weren't her own, except the four Starfish vessels. She watched her scans and toggled her comms and was, in all ways, the Lord of Creation of her systems.

'One of the Starfish is showing a vector,' Banderas said from her console. 'Energy pulse. She's hot.'

Nbaro told her neural lace to show her, and there it was, complete with a 3D image inside her head in real time. Every time she did this, she wondered about the future of avionics: there was really no need for a bridge, or repeaters, or consoles, or screens, if everyone was laced. No one would even have to sit together. The crew could be almost anywhere and instantly...

She blinked it all away and concentrated on the Starfish ship. Not the *Behemoth*, which was their name for the huge Starfish ship that was a third longer than the *Athens* and much broader, but one of the smaller ships, each one of which was larger than the *Stealthy Change*.

She passed her note via lace to the Master and contacted Morosini.

'*I'm here,*' he said.

'I thought you weren't speaking to me,' she blurted.

Morosini raised a sculpted eyebrow and stroked his big cat. '*Not so. Or perhaps, not precisely so. You are Lioness – you have access. Regardless, we're all watching.*'

'Starfish Bravo Bravo 1–0–3 is leaving us,' Banderas predicted in real space.

Nbaro used her neural lace to contact Captain Fraser.

'Astrogation,' he said.

'Sir, are you seeing Starfish Bravo Bravo 1–0–3 on what appears to be a departure vector?'

'Innnteresssting,' Fraser said. 'Thanks, Marca. I've got it marked.'

Nbaro watched the outbound ship accelerate. A great many thoughts jumbled together in her head, and she had to fight to get the important one into the neural lace.

'Morosini, you know Dorcas hasn't seen Feather Dancer in two days,' she said. It seemed like a non sequitur, but her growing awareness of the speed at which the AI operated led her to hope Morosini understood the connection.

She was aware that, as an inexpert lace user, she was mouthing or even physically pronouncing the words. Banderas must have been wondering to whom Nbaro was speaking, and about what, but she was in the virtual environment with Morosini and, suddenly, with Pisani.

Morosini was reviewing a vid when Pisani interrupted.

'Nbaro,' he said politely, in virtual.

The three of them watched the Starfish ship, an experience which was less like watching and more like participating. Nbaro was actually one with the instruments of observation, and she realised, as a new user, that in time she wouldn't need the abstract representations of a 3D holographic map on her retinas, because she'd be able to read the raw sensor data for herself – or, at least, with a little boost from the AI. Her idea of the future bridge grew even less focused.

The Starfish ship continued to accelerate. It had a smooth and very rapid acceleration, the virtual opposite of the PTX ship's vibrating main engine nacelle and stuttering deceleration.

'Is that on purpose?' she thought, and her thought was transmitted to the other two.

'Interesting thought,' Pisani said. 'I assume we're recording everything?'

Morosini indicated they were.

'We haven't seen more than two Starfish ships at a time in this system in eighty years,' Pisani said. 'When the *Esperance* first found them, there was in-system traffic – a lot of little ships. Not any more. In fact, I've never seen one.'

'*I have recordings from the early days,*' Morosini said. '*There was traffic everywhere, especially by the Beta Star.*'

'Doesn't that strike you as odd?' Nbaro asked.

Pisani shook his head. 'Nbaro, everything about the Starfish is odd. They should never have lost a ship-to-ship duel with us. They should never have built Trade Point. They should be far more interested in communications, and now they send four ships, including this gigantic thing…?'

Nbaro tried to imagine what it would be like to be the Master, right then – with two species of aliens and hostile humans and a plot on his own ship, trade to conduct… responsibility after responsibility.

All that in a flash, while she watched the Starfish ship accelerate cleanly through 6 *g* and head for seven.

'Up to their usual seventeen gees?' she asked. 'Dorcas says he thinks it's their home world norm – the equivalent of one gee to us.'

Morosini gave off a mathematical amusement, '*I have some very interesting data from the shuttles that refuelled in the gas giants.*'

Nbaro saw the data: energy spikes, neutrino emissions, infrared.

'So they *do* have colonies in-system.'

'Colonies they make every attempt to hide from us,' Pisani said. 'Those transmissions were all on the dark side of the moons for our sensors out here.'

'*But some of them correlate with the* Esperance's *observations, over two hundred years ago,*' Morosini said.

Pisani grunted audibly. 'Figures,' he said. 'They run dark as soon as we come in-system.'

Morosini said, '*I am coming to believe that they run dark all the time. And have done so for eighty years. Maybe… Maybe they always have.*'

He seemed to leave her in virtual space with that statement.

Nbaro remained in virtual space for the rest of her watch, cycling in and out to chat with Banderas at her screen or Musashi on Tower, and then merging with the ship's systems to watch the space around her, playing with the figures from the shuttle fly-by, looking at the construction work on the base and on the frigate-pinnace. It became more and more immersive. She was easily overwhelmed, and she snapped at Banderas like an arsehat and had to apologise later. That was a real problem; the information overload was real, and eventually she had to leave virtual space entirely to focus on what she was doing in the real.

By the end of the watch, she realised that sense of being overwhelmed wasn't going away any time soon. But she handed over to Lieutenant Commander Dworkin from Avionics and stretched.

'How's our pet frigate coming?' Dworkin asked.

Nbaro smiled. 'I haven't been over in a couple of ship-days, but she's coming together nicely.'

'You assembled the avionics package?' he asked.

She shrugged. 'Four very competent people from Engineering assembled it, and someone smart built it all here...' She paused. 'That was you, wasn't it, sir?'

Dworkin's grin was very broad. 'Damn, a lowly lieutenant just called me smart,' he said. 'I may just replay that from time to time. Yeah, I designed the avionics, with a heavy load of help from our AI. That ship is...' He paused. 'You know all about it. But it was complicated, and I don't envy the eventual pilot-commander.'

She nodded. 'All the systems pasted together...'

'Morosini rewrote all the software, so it should be good, but the frigates have a bridge and the pinnace is fly-by-wire. You flew it, right?'

'Yes, sir,' she said. 'And Morosini has me doing more sims.' *Which I should be doing right now.*

Dworkin's eyebrows went up a fraction. 'Uh-huh. Well, Lieutenant, eat something sweet for me when you get to the mess. Doc just put me on a diet.' He looked at something on his tab. 'We had better train up some more watch-standers.'

She looked over his shoulder.

The space wing was spread very thin across the system. There weren't enough people to go around, and with Mpono now the ship's executive officer, they were at the edge of being seriously short-handed.

'I wondered why I had two watches in two days,' she said.

Musashi joined them as Cortez replaced him in Tower. 'At this rate, I expect to be Tower and Lioness at the same time,' he said. He inclined his head politely and headed forward.

Cortez gave her a long look. 'You OK?' he asked.

She was suddenly aware of how much Cortez liked her.

Actually liked her, not just wanted to get her flightsuit off. 'I had some bad days,' she admitted quietly. 'Better now.'

'Good,' Cortez said with a crisp nod. 'Shit happens.'

She grinned at him. 'Sure does.'

He answered her grin with one of his own, and then wiped it away and fell into the command couch.

She gave a sketchy wave-salute and headed for the mess, exactly as Dworkin had suggested. While she ate, Sabina, her sub-AI, whispered in her neural lace *and* her tab clicked with a message to see Commander Truekner, so she finished her pie and took an elevator forward to the squadron's space.

Truekner was in the tiny administration office with two of the squadron's admin spacers, signing the evaluations that they'd all spent two weeks writing. He signed with a physical pen, and with a flourish. He was wearing physical glasses; the whole scene was shockingly old-fashioned.

He looked up. 'Ah, Lieutenant Nbaro,' he said, with more relish than perhaps the situation warranted.

Uh-oh.

She automatically went to attention.

He raised an eyebrow. 'Morosini and I just had a spat about you.'

She winced. 'Sorry?'

He smiled, but it wasn't a happy smile. 'Morosini wants you to complete the little ship over there on the station. I want you here flying missions and in Space Ops. We all want you standing watches under instruction with the TAO. And while Morosini doesn't have the power to overrule me, he was very persuasive.'

She stood even straighter.

'What is it about this little monster ship, that only you can complete it?' he asked.

She shrugged. 'Sir, with due respect to Morosini, I was the least important member of my own assembly team.'

86

'That's what I thought,' he agreed. 'I'm all for getting you a little avionics experience for later in your career, but I need you flying right now.' He looked at the pile of evaluations. 'But you have all your reports filed, and I have to admit that the Orphanage served you well in one respect – you can write a report. When I read yours, I usually don't want to rip my veins open or breathe vacuum.'

He looked up over his curious antique glasses. 'Is this about Dorcas?' he asked.

'Dorcas?' she asked, and she knew that, despite her deep brown skin, she was visibly blushing.

'Ahem,' the skipper said, and waved to the two admin spacers, who rose from their acceleration couches and retreated beyond the partition, making small talk about coffee.

'Am I in trouble?' she asked.

Truekner took his glasses off and folded them, which she took as a bad sign. 'It depends. Did you ask Morosini to get you reassigned back to the station?' he asked.

She shook her head a little too hard. 'No, sir!'

He smiled warmly, and she realised how close to anger he'd been. 'Well, then,' he said. 'That's that.'

He put his glasses back on and knocked hard on the partition, and the two admin spacers reappeared as if by magic.

Truekner gave her a mild look. 'In some ways, Nbaro, you are as innocent as a lamb, and I'd like to keep you that way.'

'Yes, sir.'

'Nbaro, do you even know what a lamb is?'

'An edible Earth ruminant,' she said promptly.

'Was that you or the neural lace?' he asked.

She thought about it. 'Pretty sure that was the lace, sir. I don't think I'd heard of a lamb before a moment ago. But now I know what they look, smell and taste like, as well as the history of the phrase and the quasi-religious background to why lambs might be thought of as innocent...'

Truekner smiled. 'Perfect,' he said. 'You definitely needed to have the whole library of human knowledge at your beck and call. And please, do not tell me where the phrase *beck and call* originates.'

'No, sir.' *But I could, you know.*

'Seriously, Nbaro – here's the problem. Your lace gives you a power none of your peers has – and a direct line to the AI and the Master. People are starting to talk. You are the only lieutenant on the ship with a lace, and you're really just an acting midder.'

'Yes, sir.'

He shrugged. 'I'm sure you'll have my job someday, but I'd prefer it not be before the end of this cruise. What I mean is, I can't have you using your connection to Morosini to fix your love life.' He nodded. 'And to be perfectly frank, Nbaro, what you need is a long stretch of gut-wrenching normalcy, routine, and practice being a cog in the machine. I know that sounds terrible. But you need to work on...' He smiled. 'On not being a hero all the time.' He nodded again. 'I apologise for thinking you would go over my head to your friend the AI.'

Now she was definitely blushing. 'I would never—'

He nodded. 'Keep it that way. I'm sending you to Trade Point with a cargo of stuff for the *Pericles* tomorrow, and you'll stay and send Eyre back. Morosini wants you there until the damned little ship is completed.'

'Yes, sir.'

He nodded. 'I need you here, Nbaro. I've lost three veteran pilots and replaced two of them with half-trained midders. Build this weird space boat and get yourself back here.'

'Yes, sir,' she said.

'Also, the Master has posted the awards ceremony for eleven

days from now. You'll want to be there.' He winked. 'Of course, everyone on board is receiving something, so it'll take about four weeks to pin 'em all on. Oh, and I read your eval on Patel. You'll need to talk to him. We need him. *You* need him.'

'Yes, sir.'

'May I offer you some advice about Patel?' Truekner asked.

She finally smiled, in relief. 'Yes, sir.'

'Rohan Patel is a smart young man who has got along pretty well with a minimum of work here in the Service. And he has some form of test-taking anxiety which he avoids by avoiding tests. Now, suddenly, we need him to make petty officer, and he needs to work up the energy and enthusiasm to overcome his anxiety. Right?'

'Yes, sir,' she said. That was pretty much what she'd seen herself.

'And how are you going to do that, Ms Nbaro?'

'No idea, sir.'

Truekner pulled his glasses down on his nose, for all the world like a professor in an old vid. 'Ms Nbaro. You are, or shortly will be, the most heavily decorated midder in the history of the Service. You are physically attractive, fit, and a verified hero. I would think that you might *lead* and *inspire* young Patel with a few choice words and some solid encouragement.'

She swallowed, hard. 'Yes, sir?'

'Nbaro, while I want you to have about twenty-four months of mind-numbing boredom and routine operations during which a material readiness review is something to be looked forward to, I also believe that you are allowed to think of yourself as an inspiring hero. Got that?'

She laughed aloud.

'Good response, Nbaro. On your way.'

'Yes, sir.'

She was deeply happy to be going back to the station: happy to be able to talk to Dorcas, happy to...

It was all about Dorcas. And that was foolish. Very foolish. And bad for her career.

Got to talk to Patel first.

She went to her stateroom and picked up her combat gear, and then went forward to an exciting evening of boarding party drills, did her sims, slept, and walked to her spacecraft. She had a full load of cargo, including a small blue box that a spacer from Fabrication handed her in person, to transport in her helmet bag.

'For Mister Dorcas, deliver in person,' the spacer said.

'I'll probably see him,' she said with a smile. Part of her was pretending that she didn't particularly care; her best bra mocked her attempts at dissimulation.

I'm an idiot.

6

Nbaro docked 6–0–8, the new Flight Six spacecraft, against the small craft dock that was part of the new dockyard facility on the station. There was no sim for it, so she had to fly the whole landing. In fact, it was dead easy, with dedicated smart systems that functioned perfectly, but she managed to work up a good level of adrenaline over it, and she was pleased to hear the chime that signalled a good seal and air on the other side of the crew hatch.

She picked up her duffel in near zero g and wriggled out of the cockpit without using her hands, passing down the tube and rotating smoothly to grab the sides of the crew hatch. She checked the external lock alarm one more time: green. She opened the hatch, and there was a slight hiss and the smooth functioning of hydraulics, and she was station-side, with Thea Drake looking thinner and almost frail, and Dorcas...

Dorcas had come to meet her.

She had no trouble managing a smile.

Qaqqaq gave her perhaps twenty seconds to hug her friends, and then she was holding up her tab. Nbaro shot her the bill of lading, and Qaqqaq nodded.

'You brought all the secret stuff,' she said. 'And now you're going to install it.'

She mouthed *later* at Dorcas, kissed Thea Drake, and followed Qaqqaq to a dockside elevator that hadn't been there a week before.

'You know what you have aboard?' Qaqqaq asked.

Nbaro was having the very strange experience of having Morosini download that information via the neural lace, so that even as Qaqqaq spoke, her understanding awoke and then deepened. In a way, she had guessed as soon as she'd seen the black box components towards the frigate's stern. But there it was, all laid out: the latest in PTX technology. A jump-tail, complete with Relic-Particle Sensors (which she already had pegged as RPS units) and the quantum web that allowed a material computation of an immaterial problem, reading the Higgs Field...

'Did the PTX just hand us all this?'

Morosini sent her a cat's smile. *'We traded. We are, after all, traders.'*

'For saving their ship?'

'You do ask all the hard questions. But no. In exchange for their officer who was a prisoner aboard our ship. As Major Darkstar had surmised from interrogation, he was important, if antithetical to the faction now in control, which, I will tell you for nothing, I fervently hope represents the actual government of the Empire. But this is a problem for another day.'

In real time, she gulped.

'And of course,' Morosini went on casually, *'someone may have pointed out that we could simply take their ship.'*

Do not ever make an enemy of the AI, she noted, not for the first time.

And all this conveyed in an eyeblink. With blueprints, installation guides, plug-and-play instructions, software manuals, and a navigation sim.

A navigation sim.

92

'You are putting me on this ship?' she asked.

'*I thought that was obvious,*' Morosini said.

Shit. Truekner will have a cow, and I don't blame him.

'*Only occasionally. You will be Truekner's most of the time.*'

In real space, Qaqqaq was looking at her in the way that Nbaro herself looked at Dorcas when his face went slack.

'Yes,' she said to Qaqqaq. 'Yes, I know what I have aboard. I know how to install it and I know what to do when it's installed.'

Qaqqaq looked relieved. 'I'm putting in the power plants tomorrow, and then you can install...' She grinned. 'The secret shit.' She waved her arms. 'The other secret shit. This thing has more stealth technology than anything except the new battle-cruisers we came out with.'

Nbaro nodded. She was overwhelmed. 'I guess I'll start moving the palettes of secret shit down to construction bay four,' she said with forced cheer.

Qaqqaq shook her head, and put her helmet on. 'I want you to see her first. I'm guessing you're taking her out. I can't see any other reason why Morosini ordered you in. And I'm guessing I'm going to be your engineer.'

'Almighty,' Nbaro muttered. But she couldn't disagree.

The next hour was like walking through a dream of technology. The *Pericles* was seventy metres longer than the pinnace; a quick reference via neural lace showed her that this was the maximum size that could dock against the hull of the *Athens* in the cradle built for the pinnaces, and Nbaro suspected that even now, that cradle was being altered.

The ship lay against the asteroid, supported on the slim towers that Nbaro had helped plant, with umbilicals into the dockyard area and a tube that suggested that the crew compartment was under pressure, and a tent of hard plastic aft, where a work crew was welding in atmosphere. She was matt black, with no markings, the whole exterior a waffle weave of complex carbon-fibre shapes.

'Not capable of atmosphere,' Nbaro said.

'Eh.' Qaqqaq put her helmet against Nbaro's for ultimate privacy. 'Oh, she is. She's deceptive. Also long-jump capable, and almost invisible to radar, and good against ladar too.'

'With a tail,' Nbaro said.

The *Pericles* was two engines and a bridge. There really wasn't much more to it. Four bubbles set radially amidships held sensor packages and close-in weapons turrets, and Nbaro already knew that she had a light railgun running co-axially, but everything else aboard was either power, thrust, or computer. There were clamps in recessed positions between the two centreline stations, where she could take a standard cargo cube; even the ultimate in DHC design still had to take cargo. She smiled.

After touring the outer hull, Qaqqaq took her aboard.

'Almighty, my cockpit is bigger,' Nbaro said. It wasn't literally true, but for a ship that was almost two hundred metres long, the cockpit was tiny and the living spaces consisted of four staterooms, each of which was a two-metre cylinder with independent life-support and a storage locker. Each rack doubled as the emergency escape system.

'Lifeboats,' Qaqqaq said. 'Keep us alive for ten days.'

'Almighty.' Nbaro's too-fertile imagination pictured being trapped in the coffin for ten days, waiting, waiting...

She concentrated on the here and now, her stomach queasy from her vision of a long slow death.

Better a ball of fire, she thought.

The galley had four seats, a fold-down table, and a food unit.

'They're only sending us because we're the smallest officers aboard,' Nbaro said, hoping that humour would banish the nightmare.

Qaqqaq, whose Inuit heritage had kept her stocky and short, nodded. 'I said the same.'

It was all gleaming and new. The poly-fibre on the galley seats was unworn, untouched. Everything smelled faintly of construction epoxy and titanium welding.

Nbaro wanted to love it, but she was still overwhelmed at every level: overwhelmed by the information flow rate from the neural lace; overwhelmed to think that she would be responsible for this ship; overwhelmed because she didn't know how to say to Dorcas ... to say ...

Dorcas probably already knew that she was going to be on the *Pericles*.

Dorcas ... who had volunteered to stay behind ...

She blinked.

Then she did the mental equivalent of toggling off the neural lace. It was never fully off, but she could limit the input. Then she opened her faceplate. So did Qaqqaq.

She went forward into the cockpit and put a hand on the back of *her* acceleration couch. It was her own tiny bridge, and it reminded her of Space Ops after the reconstruction, and she was delighted to see that every instrument casing and every screen was edged in etched bronze; the acanthus leaves scrolled across it like an outburst of the Ancient World across the fertile ground of technology.

'It's beautiful.' Nbaro slithered into the command seat. 'Beautiful.'

'We have a week or less to get her to launch,' Qaqqaq said.

Nbaro smiled. 'Surely a craft named the *Pericles* should be a *him*?'

7

Stripping out of her EVA suit in the cramped confines of the riggers' shop on the station, Nbaro decided to find Dorcas immediately. It was her way: to attack things she feared.

Saves time.

For once, finding Dorcas was no harder than leaving the riggers' shop. He was in the corridor, his very tall form slightly bent in the confined space, looking a little like an ungainly predator in a cage.

But he smiled.

She answered with a smile, and didn't even have to think about it.

Thea Drake waved from behind Dorcas, and then dropped down a passageway towards the mess with no more communication than a broad wink.

Dorcas loomed. 'Thea says...' he began.

Nbaro popped up in the light gravity, kissed him, and then pulled him along.

He laughed, grabbed her in a gargantuan hug, and then pulled her the other way. 'This way, now. Dukas has moved the crew quarters to make more room for the dockyard...'

His hug almost made her weep. *Is this love?* she asked herself.

They went up a deck and along a passageway that included

a brief section of ice-cold plastic hardwrap and a construction crew installing the ubiquitous carbon-fibre panels. The smell of epoxy was everywhere.

She smiled at him again, her fondness overwhelming, her various anxieties and angers all suddenly unimportant. 'They just... moved? The crew quarters?'

He smiled back. 'You helped build the big swing-derrick for the dockyard,' he said. 'At some point, they cut the whole crew block free, swung it to here, and they're still reinstalling it.'

'You're not the only one staying behind,' she said. That trod very close to the dangerous territory, but it came out spontaneously.

'No,' he agreed. 'Maybe,' he added enigmatically.

The door to his crew compartment looked unfamiliar: new, black instead of the pale grey-green favoured in the first wave of construction. He tapped the palm plate with his hand and swung the door open, and she was shocked to see how much space he had.

'This is bigger than the bridge of the *Pericles*.' And then she realised that by saying that, she'd started them down the road to Armageddon.

Dorcas pulled his singlet off and looked at her with a set to his jaw that he often wore when he was solving a difficult problem. 'Thea said we should make love first,' he said, waving his singlet towards his rack. 'I believe her view is sound.'

Nbaro laughed. It was a good laugh, and totally genuine, as she could imagine the exact tone in which Thea would make the suggestion, and the serious consideration Dorcas would give it.

'Usually is,' she admitted, and unzipped her flightsuit.

'Now we have to face the music,' Nbaro said over her elbow. She was holding herself against Dorcas's rack, and he was embracing her; they were in microgravity, and sudden movement would fling them across the room. Artificial gravity would only be restored when the station's reconstruction was complete.

Dorcas laughed. 'I love you.'

She wasn't looking at him. She was looking at his matt-black carbon-fibre bulkhead, which seemed to glow in the soft, warm light of the LED strips.

'I think I love you, too,' she said. And then, trying for humour, 'I certainly ought to love you.'

Dorcas shrugged, something she felt rather than saw.

'How long have you known I was going to the *Pericles*?' she asked.

'Since Morosini made the decision,' he said. 'It was supposed to be Han.'

That went through her like an electric shock. 'What happened to Han?'

Dorcas pushed off, and in a very elegant movement, rolled over her, barely touching, and held himself on the other side, so that they were face to face. 'Everything we discuss here is absolutely privileged and secret,' he said.

'I know that, you ninny,' she said.

'People have called me a ninny since I went to school, and yet in your mouth I almost like it.' Dorcas flushed a little.

'Pisani and Morosini are trying to avoid...' he began, and stopped.

'Mutiny?' she asked.

'God save us. I hope not. But disquiet and panic and rumour.'

'There are plenty of rumours,' she said, and then felt foolish, because there were surveillance devices everywhere on the *Athens* and on the station, and Morosini would know everything that was said.

Dorcas nodded. 'There always are. Han was injured when an extremist faction attempted to seize the bridge of the *Stealthy*

Change five days ago. He took several bullets in the arms and chest, and he's not going to recover for weeks.'

'Almighty!' Nbaro spat. 'PTX barbarians!' She regretted her outburst as soon as she made it. Dorcas was patriotic but despised jingoism, and she saw his lip curl in distaste.

'Barbarians they most certainly are not,' he said pedantically. 'Their physics is better than ours.'

'Sorry,' she agreed. 'Han...' *I didn't like him because he was too handsome and too charming, and then he turned out to be a shit-hot pilot and a hero, and now I don't want him dead.*

Like Ko and Suleimani and Indra and Aadavan and...

She made her face relax, forced herself to smile at her lover. The man she loved.

Loved. *Stop fucking around, girlie.*

'Regardless,' he said, banishing his look of distaste, 'the *Pericles* was meant for Han. And now he's wounded. It will still be his when he recovers, but until then, she's probably yours. And while we're on full disclosure, I volunteered to stay behind *before* Morosini told me he was selecting you to command the *Pericles*.'

'Ahh,' she said.

'We will get home,' he said. 'But this is bigger than us. Marca...' He rolled her. In the very low gravity, they sank a little, slowly, to sit-float together on the edge of the rack. 'It's the Starfish. Morosini and I think they wiped out the Circles, a hundred thousand years ago. There are other ways to read the evidence, but that's the simplest explanation.'

'Oh,' she said. She *had* thought about it. She'd even considered the idea...

What a terrifying idea.

The Starfish are mass murderers.

'Why trade with us?' she asked.

'No idea,' he said. Words he seldom said. 'None of it makes sense, and I'm already tired of hearing experts say we cannot predict how aliens think. That's a cop-out – either they are rational beings, or not. Either way, what we lack is data, and the data is here, and out there.'

'Yes.'

'That little twist of fibre you found…'

'Yes?' she asked. 'I haven't told anyone.'

'You weren't the first to find some. One of the crews setting synthacrete found a few metres of the stuff, and we covered that up. But it matches. Now I have two samples with the… Remember the writing? The symbols along the woven edge?'

She looked at him fondly. 'Do you think I'd forget?'

He sighed. 'No one I'm working with is as intelligent as you, Nbaro. Except Qaqqaq, and I barely have her attention. Morosini is…'

Nbaro leaned towards him. 'What?'

He looked away. 'Sometimes I feel as if Morosini already suspected that the Starfish were behind the genocide,' he said softly, as if whispering would hide his thoughts from the implant in his head. Or hers.

It was like the moment when they'd ripped Sarah from Nbaro's arms and thrown her into the lift tube. Her world crashed. She wasn't sure about anything for a moment.

'Already knew?' she asked. 'Almighty, Dorcas—'

'I have to stay and talk to the Starfish. If they stay. Feather Dancer is gone…' He grabbed her hands, a curiously intimate gesture when they were both naked, and he kept her from floating away. 'I think that the Starfish are getting ready to leave. In a hurry.'

'What?' she asked. It was too much, too fast.

'We did something that spooked them. That, or they know something we don't. And they have stopped singing where I can hear them – as if…' He shook his head.

'If they leave…?'

'Then there's no reason for me to stay.' He nodded. 'Feather Dancer was our best communicator.'

'I know,' she said, mostly so he'd know she had kept up.

'I'm working on translating the long speech it made when the first PTX ship came in-system. Remember what you said?'

She used the straps to pull herself firmly back down onto the rack and relax her spine. 'No,' she admitted.

'You made a dark jest that it wanted to defect.' Dorcas looked at her, his eyes wide and bright and penetrating in the room's warm light. 'We have factions. Why wouldn't they? And they're very old, Marca. Smith's friend in Science has been working on their DNA analogue. Of course it's different, but it has many similarities, and one is that he thinks he can track the age of traits, or will be able to, in time. He thinks they've been sentient for ... well, for aeons. Millions of years. Perhaps hundreds of millions.'

That *didn't* rock her. 'Sure,' she said. *I guessed that when we started looking at chemicals as communications agents.*

'And you brought us a Bubble,' Dorcas went on.

'Who's us, now?' Nbaro asked.

Dorcas wriggled – a low-gravity shrug. In the process he lost his place on the rack, and floated free, and had to grab Nbaro's arm to pull himself back. 'Mostly Morosini and me,' he admitted. 'There are others – Agam, Qaqqaq ... you. Morosini has been ... affected by recent events. He's ... cautious.'

'Paranoid,' Nbaro said.

'Perhaps,' Dorcas said. 'Morosini is sufficiently self-aware to experience something like attachment disorder when he's betrayed. I have reason to know that he hand selected Aadavan – and Aadavan must have been working against him from the beginning. Maybe even was planted.'

Dorcas's hand, which had grabbed her arm, had begun to wander, apparently of its own accord. It was one of the most human and male reactions she'd ever seen in him. She smiled as he stroked her, casually, gracefully.

'Hey,' she said, taking control of his hand. 'So you're staying to talk to the Starfish, and to find out if we're trading with a race of mass murderers.'

'Yes,' he agreed. 'While you are going to jump off into the Deep Black.'

'The *Athens* is,' she said. But even as she said it, she knew that wasn't what he meant.

'I think that was Pisani's original intent,' Dorcas said. 'But now I think Morosini means to send the *Pericles*. Or he did until the PTX ships came in-system. I'm not sure what he intends now.'

'Almighty,' she said. It was a little like being kicked in the gut.

He looked at her, eyes bright, penetrating, loving. All at once. 'There's more. Morosini is ... uncharacteristically reticent about sharing this.' He was nervous – not a normal state for Dorcas. But he went on. 'The Bubble you took prisoner ... She speaks Italian. And Anglatin, and Mandarin.'

Nbaro was reeling.

'So her kind – the Hin, as they call themselves – have been in contact with the diaspora out to Anti-spinward.'

She crossed her arms over her chest, feeling, for the first time, naked. 'In contact long enough to learn our languages.' Then she said 'Hin,' testing the word, sounding it out. *That's what they call themselves. So we're talking to them.*

Dorcas put an arm around her. 'The prisoner has asked for you. Morosini believes that in Hin society, you have some relationship, as you captured her.'

'Almighty,' she muttered, for the sixth or seventh time. An instructor at the Orphanage had once commented to her class that people who used the same swear words over and over were unoriginal and unintelligent. *Or in a state of shock*, she thought.

She'd allowed herself to *almost* forget the eyes behind the face-plate. Had they been eyes? If so, there had been too many of them. Or was that her imagination?

'If...you can make contact with the Hin...' Dorcas said, and then went on with more confidence. 'Assuming that you make contact with the Hin, you will be in a position to support or deny anything I have learned from the Starfish.'

Nbaro was breathing hard, as if she'd been in a fight. Her heart was racing.

'Let me get this right,' she said. 'Morosini hasn't told me this yet, but he's sending me in an untried and experimental small craft to make contact with hostile aliens to corroborate our belief that the Starfish are genocidal.'

Dorcas raised an eyebrow. 'Well put.'

The challenge of it lit her like a lamp, while the terror of it threatened her equilibrium. 'Why doesn't he tell me himself?'

'I believe you are on "Full Privacy" in your neural net,' Dorcas said carefully.

I'm an idiot, she admitted privately.

His hand was roaming again, and all the nervous tension, the elation of the whole idea, the terror...

'And I'll leave it that way a little while longer,' she said, which was as close to seduction as she was ever likely to come.

Nbaro was still learning to enjoy sex; it was something she had to wrestle with, in that she found she looked forward to it, and yet had...issues with it. She didn't like the way it controlled her. And, on the other hand, she'd never imagined that it was so much fun. At the Orphanage, it had mostly been a protest: forbidden, and thus required.

Horatio Dorcas, for all his bookish ways, seemed to know how to please her, and seemed to enjoy pleasing her, and had no inhibitions that she could find; a massive change from her partners at the Orphanage.

And she couldn't stop her mind from whirling on its merry way, even when...

When...

Sabina *pinged* in her head.

'Battle stations!' Nbaro said, pushing Dorcas away. The gravity was almost non-existent, so he slammed into the overhead a little harder than she'd meant. But he was already moving for his black flightsuit, pushing off the overhead like a swimmer turning in a pool while she climbed down the acceleration couch.

Dorcas was not embarrassed by their nudity. He smiled at her, his bare feet tucked under a restraining strap as he wriggled into his underwear. 'Some day,' he said, 'we're going to make love with gravity and a bed.' He didn't seem worried by the alarm blaring from the loudspeaker. 'And time.'

She fastened her nicest bra, deep in her neural lace, looking at the ladar/radar overlays on her system repeater.

'The *Behemoth* is dropping her lines to the rock,' she said. 'Not sure why we're at battle stations.'

Dorcas had his flightsuit zipped up and was forcing his feet into boots. 'Someone's being cautious.'

Then both of them were still, reaching out into the data field.

There was no sign of a new intruder entering the Trade Point system. The *Stealthy Change* was still decelerating, and had just received a fuel load scooped by a Flight Two heavy shuttle. Lieutenant Commander Han was listed as returning from the *Stealthy Change* on that shuttle. She noted that he was stable and improving.

Professional lust for the *Pericles* warred with her liking for Han and her desire to return to normal life with her Flight. Routine.

The battle stations alarm stopped, and the alert vanished from both of their neural laces.

She sighed. 'We should go to work,' she said.

*

The next three days flew by. Fitting out the *Pericles* occupied most of her work day, as she – and she alone – was cleared to install the tail that had been designed by Captain Dukas after she'd been allowed to examine the PTX technology.

But she also took part in several trading sessions; Morosini had ordained that she do so, without explanation. She stood several watches with the exchange team, and found she missed Feather Dancer's frothy tendrils.

On the second day she was on with Dorcas and Commander Jha. He handled the direct aspects of the trade; he, too, was part of a consortium, and it was his turn. She was in the comms lab with Dorcas. Her little alarm went off and she spotted the damaged cerata of Bentnick.

'Have we tried asking them where Feather Dancer went?' she said.

Dorcas looked up from his console with something very like annoyance. 'If I knew how to express such a complex situation as a past tense and a direction, I'd ask,' he said. 'But we don't even know the being's proper name.'

Nbaro took a deep breath, the scent of ammonia creeping into everything. She could smell the faint tang of ammonia even when she was in her spacecraft. Her throat was always sore.

'Do we know the word for *trade*? she asked.

Dorcas made a vague head-shaking motion. 'Yesss ... I'm fairly certain I know that chemical compound.'

'When Jha is done, can we say *A pleasure to trade with you* to Bentnick?'

Dorcas played with some combinations while she loaded the airlock with a preset trade from one of the New London combines.

'Pleasure ...' He shrugged. 'That's a difficult concept, even among human cultures. On the other hand, I'm almost certain that each creature that has been greeted by the robot starfish we built has answered with the same set-piece phrase in audible and chemical, which means something like *my pleasure*. I think so, because I believe I've isolated the *my* part… I wasn't trained as a linguist, damn it!'

'Do we have a linguist?' she asked.

'No. Major Darkstar is cross-trained as a cryptographer,' Dorcas said. 'As am I. We'll get there. And this is worth trying – we'll see from the response whether we have gibberish or a real phrase.'

'Do you think that Major Darkstar is making headway with the—' Nbaro was sometimes stunned by the speed with which Dorcas could move. One moment he was sitting at his console, and the next he was behind her, a hand over her mouth.

'Imagine that the Starfish aren't our friends,' he said very quietly. 'Imagine they have technology we absolutely do not understand, and that we don't know when we're bugged.'

She imagined it immediately. And further imagined that Morosini didn't want the Starfish to know about the Hin.

I'm an idiot.

'Ahh,' she said. 'Well,' she went on, leaning her weight suddenly back into him. 'Damn it.' She paused, because below them at the edge of the trade lock, Commander Jha had just rapped his knuckles three times on the xenoglas panel that separated them from the Starfish. 'Do we… always knock on the glass when we're ready to trade?'

Dorcas froze.

Nbaro brought up the cameras on her neural lace and ran the main 'trade' camera back sixty seconds, and then asked the AI to find her other examples of this behaviour. She saw ten different episodes of people knocking on the glass, always to indicate that the airlock was set for exchange.

'Damnation,' Dorcas muttered in real space.

The next day, she 'watched' the *Pericles* get her first fuel load while she was floating inside the main avionics system cube, inserting leads into prepared, colour-coded plugs in the order laid out by Mpono, who was talking to her directly from the *Athens* with a brief time lag. The one-second delay in comms was somehow more frustrating than a longer delay might have been; every time Nbaro didn't understand, she'd say 'Wait!' and that would clash with Mpono's next direction.

She was about a third of the way through the job of attaching the tail to the main avionics components when Mpono said, 'Wait one.'

Nbaro blinked, rubbed her lower back, and then Thea Drake tabbed her.

You will want to see this.

She followed Thea's link.

The so-called *Behemoth*, the gigantic Starfish ship that dwarfed even their mighty greatship, was moving into an orbit over one of the moons of Beta Prime – the very moon that had emitted radio and micro-waves while the shuttles were scooping the gas giant.

Something came up out of the soup of the moon's atmosphere.

Since Nbaro had a live link to Mpono, she said, 'What are we watching here, Smoke?'

Mpono's voice was excited. 'Nothing we've seen before, according to Morosini.'

Morosini appeared on her neural link. *'I am sensing precursor signals that, in the past, have indicated preparations for departure from station by the two smaller Starfish ships.'*

'Is that on schedule?' she asked.

'We have a reasonable load of xenoglas,' Morosini answered. *'In fact, a large load. Under ordinary circumstances, this would be a very profitable voyage.'*

For the rest of her working day, she peeked from time to time at the massive Starfish ship parked in orbit over the ammonia-ocean moon. Seven more objects rose out of the ammonia sea to rendezvous with the *Behemoth*. Ladar mensuration said that these objects, which were being called shuttles, were themselves several kilometres in diameter.

Nbaro continued to move through the very tight confines of the avionics cube, checking her wiring and then using her neural lace to watch new components bind into the avionics system. Everything worked except one black box that was supposed to allow for direct transfer of data from passive detectors to the targeting system. It would not integrate.

'Fuck,' Mpono said. 'That's one of mine. I hope it's a code problem and not something I built in. Unplug it.'

Nbaro did. Then she ran diagnostics on everything from the ladar to the synthetic aperture radar, noting that each managed to display correctly both on screens in the cockpit and on her neural lace.

'That silver worm inside your head is going to give you a massive advantage, Nbaro,' Mpono said. 'I worry, though. Scanning screens keeps you alive. How do you scan screens inside your head?'

Nbaro thought that was a good question. She wished that she had had some formal training on her neural lace, the way Dorcas obviously had. And she had questions about her lace – lots of questions.

Why do I have one? Why was I not told?

She didn't want to revert to the Marca Nbaro of Orphanage days, but she had lots of questions that tended towards paranoia.

And Dorcas thought that Morosini already suspected the Starfish of committing a genocide.

Nbaro could think while she ran diagnostics; it was very routine work. And her thoughts were dark. She thought about a vast conspiracy across the DHC and PTX that involved hundreds, if not thousands of people, working to…

What? What do they want?

And what does Morosini want?

And Dorcas thought that the Starfish could just turn off the xenoglas. Again, she saw the bubble over San Marco exploding out with decompression, heard the vanishing screams, the shattering glass…

'Hey, Nbaro?' Mpono asked. 'Your breathing is getting pretty rapid. You OK?'

Nbaro drove the image away. 'Yes, tir.'

'You have the cabin pressure indicator?'

Nbaro took a deep breath. 'Green and good.'

'I'm going to need you to look at the engineering panel. We've automated some things that are usually handled by a flight engineer. Ready?'

Nbaro fell back into the routine, and compartmented her thoughts away from paranoia.

'They're evacuating,' Dorcas said. He and Nbaro were both fully dressed because the *Athens* had ordered a heightened state of alert. Nbaro was aware that every human asset was running silent throughout the system now, but no one – including Dorcas – was telling her why.

'The Starfish?' she asked. She'd been asleep until fifteen minutes earlier and the first bulb of coffee wasn't having its usual effect yet.

'The *Behemoth* is evacuating the whole population of the system,' Dorcas said. 'She's on her third moon.'

'That's not good,' Nbaro said. They were in the galley. The station had morphed again, making the human habitable area larger and flatter. The galley now included the seating that had once been a sort of lounge. And the crew of the station was down to just twenty-four, as the shipyard was complete and so was the *Pericles*. The two railgun turrets had never been installed. Nbaro noted that with some interest.

'Are we still trading?' she asked.

'Until the Starfish leave, we're still trading,' Dorcas said.

She didn't want to ask, but she did anyway. 'And you're still staying?'

Dorcas got up and fetched each of them another bulb of coffee. 'I don't know.' He was seldom bitter, but today, he made a face as if he'd drunk something bad. 'I just don't know. And not knowing seems worse. If they're leaving, what the hell am I staying for?'

She smiled and they touched hands.

Two hours later, she still couldn't get the black box from the passive detection systems to mate with her weapons, but she had managed to trip a hydraulics pump and squirt about a litre of something bright blue and sticky across her clean new avionics bay. The clean-up was like a living demonstration of the power of entropy. And she was covered in blue goo.

'Starfish Tango Sierra 0–1–9 and X-ray Alpha 0–2–4 are preparing to undock,' said a voice in her neural lace. It wasn't Morosini; it was Dorcas. He sounded rattled.

'That's not unexpected, right?' she returned.

'They put a 130-kilo load of xenoglas into the airlock and left without trading,' Dorcas reported.

'Where are you?'

'In the Starfish language centre.'

She hadn't meant to snap at him, but she did. 'So someone got some free xenoglas? Look, I'm fucking covered in oily blue crap and I'm way behind.'

'I don't like it,' he said. 'It is an anomaly.'

'I don't like hydraulic fluid,' she snapped, and cut the link.

A minute later she felt guilty, and five minutes later, when she'd isolated the almost impossible sequence that had allowed her to sever a very small hydraulics line, she relented.

'I'm sorry.'

'We have a situation,' he sent back.

'What's happening?'

'Feather Dancer is in the ammonia lock,' he said.

'What?' she asked, but she understood immediately. 'Fuck, that's not good.'

'I'm trying to get the robot...'

She flicked over to her Space Ops repeater, and then clicked to encrypted direct comms. She still found one-on-one comms via the lace very tiring.

'Horatio?' she asked. She felt a heavy *thump*, and then a second *thump*, right through her little ship.

'Yes?' he said.

'Both Starfish ships have detached. You feel that? They're breaking away.'

'Damnation,' he said. 'They left Feather Dancer behind.'

She was flooded with suspicions at once, almost overwhelming her ability to use the lace, as well as a heavy burst of adrenaline.

'No,' she said.

'No,' he agreed. 'Feather Dancer *is* defecting.'

There was a pause. She was already moving to the cockpit.

'We need to get off this station,' Dorcas said. 'But damn it, how do we get Feather Dancer off? And where do we put it?'

It was rare to hear Dorcas flustered. Or to be ahead of him. Maybe because she'd lain awake thinking about the Starfish...

'Put Feather Dancer in the ammonia clearing tank,' she said. 'It'll hold a Starfish for several hours.'

Morosini appeared. '*We are evacuating the station,*' he said.

The Battle Stations alert came on. Nbaro threw herself into her acceleration couch, blue goo and all, and began a preflight check.

'I can take Feather Dancer and the whole ammonia tank,' she said. She tried to visualise it in her neural lace. This was the part at which she lacked skill, but she managed a rough sketch showing the ammonia overflow tank clipped into her cargo area. 'Morosini, the xenoglas panels can hold the pressure while I'm in hard vacuum. Temperature is a problem, so I won't have much time. If I punch it, I can get to the *Athens* in…' She let the lace do the work. '…forty minutes at three gees.'

'That's a lot of time for a Starfish to be in a four-by-four metre ammonia tank. In hard vacuum.' Dorcas sounded apologetic. 'I'm not sure…'

'*We will move the* Athens *closer*,' Morosini said. '*Do it.*'

Nbaro tabbed Qaqqaq and tabbed, Are you following this?

Qaqqaq replied by grunting on an encrypted channel that opened like magic. 'I'm supposed to reinforce the ammonia holding tank for immediate lifting while simultaneously evacuating the station,' she snapped.

Nbaro was on the Space Ops display.

'Lioness, this is *Pericles*, do you copy?' she said.

Cortez came back, slightly nasal, and excited. 'Roger, *Pericles*. I have a clean signal. Over.'

'Lioness, this is *Pericles*. I have room for…' She looked back into the crew compartment. '…four in acceleration couches. I don't think it's a good idea for anyone to do this trip without a couch, over.'

'*Pericles*, I have you for four. Wait one.'

She knew that Cortez was very busy. Everyone was busy except her. She was already aboard her craft, and she only wished that she had her bag, which was packed by the door of her tiny cubicle.

And my flight jacket.

She could just imagine explaining to Morosini that she'd gone back for her flight jacket. Instead, she tabbed Akunje. Wilson, I need a favour.

A little busy right now, ma'am. He shut her out.

She sighed and began to pull on her EVA suit. But she stopped, stripped off the hydraulics-soaked flightsuit, and then put her EVA suit on. That felt much better.

Her tab beeped and her sub-AI Sabina said, '*Bogey inbound.*'

Her tiny window looked out on a real space, like a cockpit window, and there was a sudden flash. Nbaro was very happy she wasn't looking at the source. She reached up, got her helmet from the overhead, pulled it on, toggled the cheek plates closed with a hiss and slapped her visor down, all while trying to read various sensory inputs.

She lay back, let her suit mate with the seat, and dropped into the data stream.

The raw data was instantly interpreted and provided to her with an overlay from the familiar but vastly oversimplified Space Ops screens that had once been her sole information access point. Now she could scroll through the second-by-second returns from the thousands of radar and ladar emitters and passive detection arrays throughout the system, reading their distance/time lag and factoring the vector of the returns.

'Almighty,' she spat in real time.

Weeks of practice had allowed her to create a virtual environment that helped her process the data. In her datasphere, she stood at the centre of a hemispheric shape that encompassed her whole arc of vision. Of course, it was itself a model, but that was how she'd chosen to display her data. She had a variable number of data bubbles, some imitating holographs, some imitating flat screens. Trial and error had taught her that thirty independent data streams were the most that she could handle, and that was when she was well fed and rested and at the top of her game. Most of the time, nine or ten was the most she could handle.

When she was tired, she looked at the refined feeds of various repeater systems; when she was fresh, she read the data directly.

Here, cocooned in the neural lace and the computer systems of the *Pericles*, she concentrated on the space around the station and the system-wide situation as reported by the *Athens*. She had the Space Ops repeater in front of her virtual face, but she also had the live feeds from dozens, if not hundreds, of sensors scattered like seeds by an ancient farmer – tossed out by every spaceship that had flown during the last two weeks. Qaqqaq's brilliant inventions, giving them a massive advantage in information flow.

And her virtual data flow showed her...

...that one hundred and seventy seconds ago, the great Starfish ship they called the *Behemoth* had fired its main engines and risen smoothly out of its most recent orbit. The vast ship had dropped one of the huge spheres it had been loading, casting away an object the size of an asteroid as if it was junk. Umbilicals had broken free as the *Behemoth* pulled away from the spherical shuttle, and she had vented gas or liquid that refraction instantly revealed as ammonia. This action had provoked the *Athens* Tactical Action Officer to punch his Battle Stations button.

In seconds the *Behemoth* was driving for the asteroid belt, her rate of acceleration somewhere between incredible and absurd, especially considering that the DHC's intel estimated she massed half again what the *Athens* massed.

As the enormous Starfish ship bolted, about one hundred seconds earlier, the two smaller ships had broken free of the station. They had done so with so much force that Nbaro had felt it in real time, through her hips. On replay, she watched as they imparted a slight wobble to the asteroid's steady rotation. Both of them had fired their engines before breaking away.

It was an insane manoeuvre. The station was venting a plume

of ammonia from the Starfish side... all that had happened a minute earlier.

Three Hin ships had dropped into reality ten seconds later, just above the system's ecliptic and moving fast. They didn't arrive out by the comet belt, as Pisani had predicted, and they didn't prowl; they came in like a cavalry charge.

But Morosini – *or perhaps Pisani*, Nbaro thought – was playing a canny game. The only energy passing through space was informational: comms and bursts of radar and ladar from remote sensors. The Hin ships had energy shields, and Nbaro had the leisure to see what a giveaway they were, glowing like miniature suns as they shot after the fleeing *Behemoth*.

One of the Hin ships fired a lance of fire at an asteroid. One of the dozen or so stationary emitters acting as the *Athens* went off the air.

Then a fourth Hin ship had appeared: it had either been bolder or more foolish, and had emerged into real space and vanished in a flash of blue-white light that suggested the near perfect transfer of matter to energy.

Hit an asteroid? Nbaro guessed, but stayed with the action as the lead Hin opened fire, the plasma carrier-beam of her main armament striking the *Behemoth*. A system full of sensors helped her estimate the range; the particle beam was travelling across an incredible nine thousand kilometres of space, a lot farther than their theoretical estimate.

The two smaller Starfish ships emitted massive pulses of energy. It was like watching the flash of a mirror on a cloudless day, but neither Nbaro nor the overlay from the AI could tell her what weapon the Starfish warships had used.

A wall of clutter began to emerge from the asteroid belt – like a three-dimensional line of blindness. Nbaro had seldom been outside the clutter-field looking in, and it was remarkably effective. She read it at a glance; the *Athens* hadn't just studded the asteroid belt with sensors, but also with chaff dispensers and sand casters. It formed a smokescreen on a godlike scale, covering a deep band of sky and almost a third of the horizon. The Starfish ships accelerated towards what looked like a wall of nothingness – the end of the universe, a vast and threatening cloud. It was like dark magic.

The Hin thought so, too. The three ships, each separated by about three thousand kilometres, turned as one at about 11 *g*. They powered off on a new vector, almost straight up above the ecliptic. All three reached out with their plasma beams, which Nbaro saw as pale green lines in a darkness.

All three fired at separate targets. One hit the station, striking the asteroid somewhere in the Starfish side. The other two were shooting at targets that she couldn't identify and could only hope were decoys. Then all three fired on the *Behemoth*.

None of the DHC armaments had loosed a shot. None of the *Athens* spaceframes had revealed themselves; no torpedoes had been launched. But the clutter-field was threatening in its immensity and the relative mystery of its appearance, and the Hin ran from it.

The *Behemoth* ship went through the wall of chaff and vanished, but it had taken damage and was trailing gas and debris like a comet. Its escorts unleashed whatever hellish energy weapon they carried for a second time, and followed.

It all happened in front of her augmented senses.

Morosini said, '*Do not engage!*'

Command, the rarely used frequency that overrode all other comms, spoke. It was Pisani.

'Do not engage. Repeat, do not engage.'

Nbaro was intrigued to see that even the radio message went out from a dozen in-system repeaters, not from the *Athens*.

The three Hin ships were vectoring straight up from Nbaro's perspective, and she guessed they were trying to get a look around the clutter-field. Beyond it, the Starfish ships were lost to her instruments.

Why aren't we shooting back?

Another particle beam struck the rock, this one less than a kilometre away. The asteroid was venting ammonia in three places: two from particle beam hits, and one where a Starfish ship had apparently left their airlock open on purpose.

To kill Feather Dancer?

The result was that the rock began to tumble in space. It wasn't moving fast... but the venting ammonia was acting like a rocket engine. Three rocket engines.

'Morosini, did the Starfish intend to blow Trade Point?'

'*I fear that it looks that way.*'

The venting ammonia would tip the rock enough to cause it to fall in towards one of the stars, or so it appeared to Nbaro.

Qaqqaq's voice crackled in her earpiece. 'OK, Nbaro. The walls on the ammonia container are double-thickness already. I *think* it'll hold up to hard vacuum and I *think* that the insulating property will keep our guest warm for... two hours? Maybe?'

Dorcas came on the same encrypted channel. 'We don't know how long Feather Dancer can tolerate extreme cold.'

'Doesn't ammonia freeze?' Nbaro asked.

'At minus seventy-seven degrees Celsius,' Qaqqaq said.

'What if we ran pipes around the outside?' Nbaro asked. 'Warm pipes?'

'We're not coming back here, right?' Qaqqaq asked.

Dorcas sounded sad. 'Maybe not ever.'

Qaqqaq's voice was confident. 'Then I've got a plan, though I can't promise the ammonia won't go sour, or whatever, from Feather Dancer breathing it. I don't have an oxygenator that will work in ammonia.'

'Someone better get to work on that over in the *Athens*,' Dorcas said. 'Damnation! What do they eat?'

'I have two Flight Two shuttles inbound,' Nbaro said. 'Commander Jha is on the line with Space Operations, planning the load-out of our xenoglas and everyone's kit. What's my timeline, Naisha?'

'I need forty minutes,' the engineer said.

Nbaro was watching the three Hin ships. They were thousands of kilometres away, and her simulation said that they would see the fleeing Starfish again ...

All three Hin ships fired their beam weapons, and there was a flash, like the death of a distant sun, and then one of them was gone – an expanding radioactive cloud on instruments. Simultaneously, something cataclysmic happened beyond the clutter-field: a pulse that showed right through the cracks in the expanding sensory wall.

Forty minutes was a long time in a space battle, and Nbaro was *doing nothing*. It wasn't helped by the fact that no one else she knew was doing anything, except the crew of the station, who were all packing, and the pilots of the Flight Two shuttles. They'd dropped away from the *Athens* with a strong electromagnetic push, and didn't light their engines until they'd given their mother ship plausible deniability.

On the other hand, she had forty minutes.

'Morosini, I have forty minutes until Qaqqaq clears me to lift the Starfish,' she sent. 'I'm going to get my kit.'

Morosini didn't deign to answer. Nbaro was out of her cockpit and out of her ship in seconds, moving in zero *g* to the hatch, cycling the airlock ...

Inside the station, everyone was deceptively calm. It was likely that, lacking neural laces, they didn't even know they'd been under fire from beam weapons. There was no artificial gravity, and Nbaro left her helmet on, bouncing down one passageway and up the next, past the new galley, and into the corridor of her own space. People were moving with efficiency; no one seemed to be panicking.

She got her hatch open and got her carbine, her precious sword and armour, and her kitbag. She passed Gunny Drun in the corridor heading out; he was in a power-assisted suit, the servos whining as he walked.

'Ms Nbaro!' he said. 'I'm on your ship.'

'You'll need a pressure suit,' she said.

'Roger that.'

As it turned out, she had Qaqqaq, Drun, Dorcas and Akunje. They were to be the last people off the station.

She dropped into her hatch and filed her flight plan from her acceleration couch. Then she watched Qaqqaq on her VR as she and two engineering techs turned the ammonia overflow tank into a sealed, airtight box with a space heater run from a generator that fitted in a four-by-four metre shipping container. It was a lesson in tool use and efficiency, and Nbaro didn't interrupt.

Sometimes she'd watch Dorcas as he packed the robots into their cases, and his lab equipment and the chemical sniffer, the various computers . . .

. . . on to pallets.

'Ready for the forklift,' Qaqqaq said. 'We're going to move the Starfish last, so we can get everything and everyone else out first, and so it's not freezing in vacuum any longer than it needs. I have no idea if that little space heater is going to help at all. This isn't engineering! This is guesswork.'

The first Flight Two bird came in hot, thrusters firing all the way to docking, a so-called 'shit-hot' manoeuvre. The techs and spacers from the station had the whole bird loaded in ten minutes – incredibly fast work for the participants, agonisingly slow to the observers.

Ten thousand klicks above their heads, the two surviving Hin ships had changed vector to pursue the Starfish, both firing their beam weapons and receiving fire. The *Athens* and her complement continued to sit tight.

Seconds after the Flight Two shuttle burned its way in, a beam weapon struck the asteroid. It missed the cargo shuttle by perhaps two hundred metres. The only immediately visible result was the rock splitting and boiling away under the power of the beam, so that wisps of what looked like smoke, and were probably powdered asteroid, rose to mark the location of the impact.

Nbaro was watching.

'Heads up, folks,' she said. 'We're under fire from the Bubbles.'

Then she was on with the Tactical Action Officer on board the *Athens*, explaining that the local instruments had seen the carrier beam and she'd located the impact. There was a three-second delay as her messages bounced around the system to the *Athens*.

A little less than a minute later, one of the Hin ships rolled end for end, and fired.

The whole asteroid shook.

'What the hell was that?' Qaqqaq asked.

Nbaro was chewing her lip with impatience and frustration. 'A weapon,' she said. 'Something coaxial.' Nbaro was sure Dorcas had told her that the beam weapons had a maximum range of five thousand kilometres, based on the laws of quantum physics. She was more than a little disappointed in him.

'Very helpful.' Qaqqaq was dismissive.

The cargo bird announced its departure on the Space Ops frequency, fired her thrusters, and banked away as if fired from a gauss gun. Immediately the second ship came in from where she'd lurked over the asteroid's horizon. Her pilot knew her business, and got her into the docking bay with considerably less display.

'Loading the last kit now,' Drun reported to her on the

Marine frequency. 'Akunje is on his way down to our passenger. I'm ready to come aboard.'

'Come on down, Gunny,' she said.

She heard the airlock cycle, and then she heard the servos on Drun's armour.

'Never thought I'd use combat armour as a wheelchair,' he said.

In armour, he could just lie on an acceleration couch and plug in. And he did.

The Hin ships had split up, and the closest ship was now headed for them.

Again, the rock trembled.

'I really don't like waiting,' Nbaro said.

Drun laughed – not a happy laugh, just a sort of 'life is like this' laugh. 'Ma'am, I've been under mortar fire and I've been shot at with drones. No matter who the fuck does it, sitting on your ass being shot at sucks.'

'Roger that, Gunny.' She was trying to get Dorcas to answer her. And worrying.

Another hit.

'Shootin' from ten thousand klicks,' Drun said. 'So a hundredth of a degree or so there, just the distortion of an optical lens, means a difference of hundreds of metres down here.' He grunted. 'They ain't that good.'

'Yeah, Gunny,' Nbaro said. 'I think about this stuff, too. Like, why aren't they better? They've had hundreds of thousands of years ...'

Drun snorted. 'Not enough Marines, ma'am.'

She laughed. It was a completely genuine laugh. And she thought, *If I survive this, by God, that's how I'll tell the story. About Drun. Not about being scared and afraid for my lover. But about Marines.*

She tabbed Dorcas *again.*

He didn't answer.

'Lioness to Alpha Bravo 2–0–3, I have you good for lift-off from station,' came Cortez's voice.

'I have thirteen aboard, plus equipment. I'll give you a landing weight en route.'

'Roger, 2–0–3.'

Nbaro watched the thrusters fire.

'Just us now, Gunny,' she said. She tabbed Qaqqaq. Let's get out of here.

'…at…' spat the comms.

Akunje came up. 'Ma'am,' he said, 'I think we have a problem.'

Nbaro's blood chilled.

'Tell me.'

'That last incoming round baked the passageway to the trade area. I'm standing in hard vac looking at a smoking crater. On the other side, I can see light, and Qaqqaq waving.'

Nbaro began to link to cameras on her neural lace, even as her stomach sank away from her ribs. 'Akunje, do you see Dorcas?'

There was a long delay. 'No, ma'am. Just Qaqqaq.'

'*Pericles*, I need you to get your ass out of there,' the TAO broke in. 'We're manoeuvring towards you, but that second ship can see us now.'

'We have personnel missing,' she said. 'Mr Dorcas is not accounted for, over?'

Pisani came on over Command. 'Ms Nbaro, I am sorry, but I must order you to leave the station as soon as you can. The ship depends on it.'

'Aye aye, Master,' she said. *Dorcas!* she screamed inside.

'Akunje, can you get to Qaqqaq?'

'That's a negative, ma'am. It's a deep, smoking crater. Sides are glass smooth.' He sounded scared.

'Can you get back to me?' she asked.

'Absolutely,' he said. 'On my way.'

She was scanning cameras. Finally, she wrestled control of the camera that was watching the Starfish away from the computer system and panned it.

There was Qaqqaq. And there, on the floor, was Dorcas. He wasn't moving.

Nbaro tried everything over the next sixty seconds while she waited for Akunje to come to the airlock: prayer, memory, even a little meditation. And watching the alien ship on her neural lace. None of it distracted her. Dorcas lay on the deck of the trade area like … a corpse. Sprawled in his vac suit. And the area under him reflected light like liquid.

It was a long sixty seconds.

Qaqqaq heard the camera moving behind her and turned to look.

Nbaro ran the camera back and forth, up and down.

Qaqqaq waved.

Nbaro said, 'Morosini, if we have any microphones working in the trade spaces, I need access.'

'*None. I am sorry, Marca.*'

Qaqqaq was pointing at Dorcas. Nbaro made herself see that as hopeful.

She heard Akunje at the airlock, and cycled it for him.

'Wilson,' she said as soon as he was in, 'listen up. I'm going to fly us over the pit. You are going to drop down and communicate with Qaqqaq. If you can, get Dorcas. He's unconscious – maybe dead. Qaqqaq needs to make it possible for me to lift the tank straight out of there. Blow the roof – whatever it takes. Understand me?'

'Yes, ma'am.' Akunje was enthusiastic, and she loved him for it.

'Qaqqaq will need something to open that roof,' she said.

'Ma'am, I have four shaped charges.'

She managed a smile. 'Best news I've heard all day.'

She took Akunje through it twice, and then she fired her thrusters and attitude jets, running the ship by wire through her neural inputs, scarcely bothering to watch what the computer did; it was her trusted crew, and she had other problems. The computer lifted her beautiful ship out of the cradle for the first time. She flew it while looking at the claws on the underside of her ship: the clamps that could accept a four-by-four metre crate, or a number of weapons or electronic warfare suites. There were four clamps; she could open and close them, and she tested them now, in flight.

The little ship was already over the crater from the beam strike. There was a

FLASH

and her external cameras were blind. By nothing but good luck, her eyes had been on the Space Ops screen and she wasn't blind. Her ship was buffeted, as if a giant hand had picked her up and moved her through space.

Her neural lace saved them. She had so many inputs – so many ways of watching her environment – and she was getting used to using them, so that her perception of the universe around her never faltered, and the bright flash was reduced, in a millisecond, to data.

Which was good, because almost all of her port-side sensors were gone.

So was most of the human-constructed portion of the station. All their work destroyed...

'Another hit,' she said.

Pisani said, 'Nbaro, I really can't afford to lose that ship.'

Nbaro turned her ship until she had starboard-side cameras on the rump of the station. There was the original crater, the one that Akunje couldn't get around. And there was the still-lit window of the airtight hatch into the trade area.

'Sir,' she said, 'I have a shot at this, and it's for our new guest, and Qaqqaq, and Dorcas. I think it's worth the risk.'

She had a good long look. 'Wilson? You got this?'

'Yes, ma'am,' he said. 'Gunny showed me a rig. I'm going to descend on a wire from the airlock. Got that?'

'Sounds … great. Gunny, you buttoned up?'

'Roger that, ma'am.'

She got the attitude she wanted: slightly nose down, so she could see out of her cockpit window. It wouldn't have been possible without a computer; the whole rock was tumbling, in all three dimensions, but with a little modelling help from the onboard AI she managed to keep them steady over Akunje's drop zone.

She double-checked Drun was in his helmet and buttoned up, and then vented the cockpit atmosphere into storage bottles so they could get out of there as fast as possible.

She couldn't see Akunje descend; it seemed to take a long time.

'I *hate* waiting,' she said.

'Me too,' Drun said. 'I fucking hate not being out there.'

She agreed. *Maybe I should have become a Marine.*

Then she saw movement, and in five seconds, Akunje was at the hatch into the trade area, moving carefully around the pit where part of the human hab had been. Inside they had atmosphere but no airlock, and Akunje didn't have a portable. Or any time. She saw him put his helmet against the hatch, and then she heard him speaking to Qaqqaq.

'I'm coming in. The air's going to vent hard. Hold on to something.'

There was a long pause. She had time to query the *Athens* net via her neural lace, learn that the enemy beam weapon seemed to have a reliable recycle rate. She started a timer.

'Here we go,' Akunje said.

Then: 'I've blown the hatch. I have Mr Dorcas secured.'

Nbaro found that she was biting her lower lip, and she stopped herself.

'I'm waiting for Lieutenant Qaqqaq, and then we're all coming up together. She's opening the roof.'

'I've got the winch,' Drun said.

There was an interminable wait.

Finally, Pisani said, 'Nbaro. You have to move. No matter who we lose.'

'Yes, sir,' she said cheerfully.

'Damn it, Nbaro!' Pisani said. 'Don't make me do this.'

'Sixty seconds, sir.' She was proud of her voice: assertive, cheerful. She was pretending that she was Wilson Akunje, a man who never seemed to be anything but cheerful. Her timer said the beam weapon was about thirty seconds from firing.

Drun said 'I have a tug. I'm running it.' After a pause, he said, 'At least I'm doing something.'

She couldn't hear the winch run, but the vibration could be felt throughout the cockpit.

Drun was now in the airlock, looking down. 'We have all three of them,' he said. 'I have Qaqqaq aboard. I have Akunje ... I have Dorcas. Outer hatch closed ...'

Nbaro was already manoeuvring. Qaqqaq dived into the co-pilot's seat. Nbaro, full of specialised knowledge from having built this little ship herself, reached out, took a comms plug from the overhead, and pulled it down to physically link Qaqqaq to the ship.

'Son of a bitch,' Qaqqaq said. 'Charges will fire in ten seconds.' Her helmeted head turned. 'And if you see any ammonia boil up, well, then we cooked our Starfish.'

Nbaro watched the countdown on her neural lace, but she was already putting the cargo claws over the room even as the digits said 2, 1... The other countdown – the one that showed the alien beam weapon's recycle rate – was at 7, 6...

There was nothing in hard vacuum to convey the force of an explosion, or the heat or sound. The four charges and some explosive cord provided a flash of light, and then the entire roof of the trade area blasted away, struck her ship's unretracted landing gear a glancing blow and spun off into space.

Nbaro didn't have a functioning belly camera. But she did have a neural lace, and she did have the functioning camera that hung on the human side of the xenoglas partition. She panned it up to look at her cargo claws, and she slaved her ship to it. Then, based on the crisp image of her one camera, and a very powerful computer, her ship dipped like a dancer, and the four retractable claws snapped on to the four sides of the metal crate the engineers had built around the ammonia tank.

All four claws had sensors; all four showed a good lock.

The beam weapon recycle read 3, 2...

She lifted. 'Acceleration couches now!' she said. 'Gunny, get Dorcas strapped down.'

'Roger,' he said.

She used the manoeuvring thrusters only, powering directly away from the rock, on a vector at ninety degrees from the last three beam weapon strikes. Then she turned the ship, pointing the nose to the *Athens*.

'Incoming! Eyes closed!'

FLASH.

Nbaro had had her eyes closed. But the flash had been behind them, and she was accelerating hard to get above any spalling from erupting shrapnel. No red lights came on. They were alive.

'Lioness, this is *Pericles* inbound with one casualty, one special guest, over?'

'Roger, *Pericles*.' Cortez was still on. 'You'll be landing topside. Please acknowledge topside, over.'

'Roger, topside,' she said.

'What's your status, *Pericles*?'

'Something cooked all my port-side antennas and I can't retract my landing gear,' she said. 'Which isn't all bad, considering I have no atmosphere.' *I'm babbling. Better get it together, spacer.*

'Roger, *Pericles*, I have a crash crew standing by, also medical, also...' Cortez, despite everything, managed a chuckle. '...guest services ready!'

She noted many things from inside the cocoon of her piloting. The *Athens* was underway, at almost 3 *g* acceleration. She wasn't far away – just fifteen thousand kilometres. They weren't moving on opposite courses, either.

She let the *Pericles* do the maths, OK'd the indicated course, and said, 'Stand by for acceleration.'

She told the computer to put on the juice slowly. She was worried about Dorcas, and worried about Qaqqaq's welds on the box holding her special guest... if Feather Dancer was still alive.

She looked at the beam weapon recycle rate. Forty seconds until the next shot.

Almighty. Imagine defecting to aliens. How bad must it be, that you'd rather jump off into the unknown than face another day...?

Everything was holding. At the forty-second mark, the enemy beam weapon vaporised more of the Trade Point rock, well behind her. She barely blinked.

'I fucking hate being shot at when I can't shoot back,' Drun said.

'Roger that, Gunny,' she muttered. The fact was, there wasn't enough to do now to keep her mind off Dorcas, and the tension wouldn't let up until she'd put her ship into its docking cradle, having matched accelerations with the *Athens* and found the docking signal. It was all automated – easier, in every way, than landing an XC-3C.

The cradle locked to her ship with a clank.

'Open the main hatch!' someone ordered. Nbaro had already hit the cycle button, and the hatch opened. She'd long since replaced their atmosphere.

Four suited figures entered, cut Dorcas out of the acceleration couch with nano-cutters, and were gone. Outside, a dozen Marines and some techs were moving the cargo container to an elevator. Even as she watched, Major Darkstar, identifiable by their height and the rank painted on their helmet, gave a wave, and the elevator literally fell away.

'Well,' Drun said, 'I guess we're chopped liver.'

8

The *Athens* was driving for Insertion. The surviving Hin ship inserted at a point no one had predicted, well above the ecliptic and far closer to the Beta Star than any human astrogator would have recommended. Both of the survivor's consorts had been destroyed by Starfish fire, and radioactive clouds that they could detect beyond the clutter-field suggested that both of the *Behemoth*'s consorts had also been destroyed. The *Behemoth* was gone; Intel was already predicting that the Starfish could insert and extract with far more accuracy than even the best human systems, and so could the Hin.

Nbaro was not, at first, very interested in a space battle between two apparently hostile alien races, because she was following Dorcas down into the depths of the ship: first to the infirmary, and then into surgery. Steven Yu appeared, gowned and masked.

'It's pretty bad,' Yu said. 'Don't wait. He's got crushed ribs and a lot of internal trauma.' He turned away brusquely.

Nbaro wandered the infirmary for a little while. Gunny Drun was being moved in; despite being ambulatory in a mech rig, he was supposed to be on bed rest, and another tech threatened him with clamshelling if he didn't calm down.

She went and sat by Drun. 'You were great back there,' she said.

'Great for someone who couldn't actually participate,' he said bitterly.

'Yeah, it's true, you're a total slacker.' She found that working on Drun's feelings helped her wall off her own. She'd done the same at the Orphanage: in her darker moments, she'd wondered if her impulse to help people had only been a desire to avoid her own pain.

But Drun grinned. 'Thanks, ma'am.' And after a little while, he added, 'He'll make it, ma'am. I seen guys with worse. And Dorcas is tough, in his weird, nerdy way.'

She realised that she was fighting tears, and her throat burned.

Drun cleared his throat. 'You're still in your EVA suit, ma'am,' he muttered. 'And your face is covered in … er … blue goo.'

'Yeah,' she said. 'Definitely time to shower.'

Thirty minutes later she found she was leaning her forehead against the wall of the shower cubicle nearest her stateroom, the warm water pouring down her back. She wondered how long she'd been there, just standing under the shower.

Weeping.

Fuck this.

She dressed, carefully stowed her gear, and brought up the flight and Space Ops schedule. She was Tower in four hours. Thea Drake, who might have helped out, was on watch.

She knew she should sleep, but instead she wandered down to the ready room.

Fatima Bakri, a mid-grade lieutenant who'd been watch-standing on the bridge, waved. They'd never flown together, but Nbaro knew her. Didier was deep in conversation with Midshipper Eyre, and Midshipper Pak was sitting at one of the terminals at the back, reading something.

Skipper Truekner was sitting with a small dark-skinned

woman at the front of the ready room. The skipper was wearing a flightsuit that he'd clearly sweated through; his face was deeply creased from his helmet. Nbaro didn't know his companion immediately; she'd seen her before...

'Nbaro! It's always nice of you to join us in between bouts of saving the universe!' Truekner stood. He put a hand on her arm. 'I'm sorry about Dorcas,' he said in a lower voice. 'I know the ship is doing everything it can for him.'

'Thanks, skipper,' she said. *Almighty, I sound brittle.*

'This is Lieutenant Commander Thulile, formerly of Flight One. She's going to take Mpono's place as operations officer for a little while, and then, if we all still like one another, she'll be XO.' He smiled.

Thulile didn't smile. Instead, she said, 'I don't think we need to like one another.' She shrugged. 'We just have to work together.'

Truekner grinned as if Thulile had made a joke, but Nbaro didn't think she was joking at all.

'You're the acting lieutenant who just disobeyed the Master?' she asked Nbaro.

Nbaro met her level gaze. 'Yeah.'

'Care to share why you felt you could disobey his direct order?' Thulile asked.

Nbaro shrugged. 'Ma'am, I was there and he was not. I knew we could get those people.'

Thulile's gaze didn't waver. 'The Master has asked to see you, Ms Nbaro. I think you made the right call. But you might want to take a different tone when you talk to him.' She smiled. It wasn't the warmest smile in the world, but it wasn't fake either.

Nbaro nodded. She wanted to smile back and make a nice response; Thulile was clearly not a monster, and the small woman was smiling up at her, trying to take the sting out of her words.

Only Nbaro didn't have a smile in her. 'Yes, ma'am,' she managed. 'Shall I go to the bridge?'

'Master's briefing room,' Truekner said. 'I'm sure you know the way.' But he followed her out into the passageway. 'Hey, Nbaro.'

She stopped, turned, and looked at him.

'We're running out of medals. Please stop being a hero for a few weeks.'

Nbaro felt as if she was looking at the skipper from the wrong end of a telescope. 'Why didn't we shoot the fucking Bubbles?' she asked. 'We just sat there getting pounded.'

Tears were close. So was rage.

What's wrong with me?

Truekner put a hand on her shoulder. 'I have no idea,' he said. 'I just sat out there for seven hours in a cold spaceframe, waiting for the order to shoot.' He shrugged. 'It never came.'

There was the rage again.

'Every time their particle beam fired, I knew something would get hit.' Nbaro hadn't even realised that the words were coming out. And then it came. '*Someone*,' she sobbed.

Truekner gripped her arm. 'You need to rest before you see the Master? I can arrange it.'

She shook herself. 'No, sir.' She was in charge again, the crack repaired.

'Need a hug?' he asked.

Yes?

'No, sir,' she said.

He released her arm, and she walked stiffly away towards the lifts.

On the way up, she realised that this was the very lift where she'd met Dorcas. Or at least, first spoken to him.

Is he still alive? Will anyone tell me? She could probably use her lace to go straight into his medical files…

Nope. Not doing that.

The lift opened on the O-7 level. She stepped out into the small foyer, palmed the reader, and the hatch opened into the

Master's briefing room, which looked more like a dining room from early in the Age of Chaos, with paintings on the wall and a fire in the fireplace. The walls were panelled in wood, and the table was the size of a small house. An android servitor motioned to a chair.

'The Master and I will be with you shortly,' Morosini's voice said out of the android's mouth.

'Can I get you anything?' the servitor asked, still in Morosini's voice.

'How much trouble am I in?' she asked.

Morosini's voice said, 'None that I know of. Can we get you something?'

'I need coffee,' she said. She was annoyed with herself for feeling relief that she wasn't in trouble, because in the lift she'd worked up some excellent righteous indignation that she was in trouble at all. Now she had to stare herself in the face and realise that it had all been internal posturing.

Still an idiot.

Pisani came in from the bridge, still speaking into the old-fashioned headset he wore.

'As soon as you can, right, Sasha?' He looked up, saw Nbaro, and managed a thin-lipped smile. He really was *very old*.

He tapped something on his wrist and tipped the headset off.

'Coffee,' he said, and sat almost next to her, pulling out his chair so he faced her.

'Ms Nbaro,' he said.

Morosini appeared in another chair, with his cat on his lap. He was dressed in red: the clothes of another century, another world. Powdered wig, lace collar, red boots.

Nbaro had stood at attention as soon as the Master entered the room. Now he nodded. 'At ease, Ms Nbaro,' he said.

She sat stiffly.

'Mr Dorcas is still with us,' Pisani said, 'and will probably weary me again with his patronising repetition.'

Morosini winced. '*What my esteemed commander wishes to convey,*' he said, '*is that Mr Dorcas is an essential part of this team, and your rescue of him was—*'

'Impertinent and personally driven, but nonetheless the correct action.' Pisani raised an eyebrow. 'I doubt you saved him because he's vital to our plans. But you did. And the Starfish is alive – needs a little thawing out, but alive. In fact, we didn't lose anyone.'

His eyes met hers, and she realised how very important that had been to him: that they hadn't lost anyone.

'I'm not reaming you out, Ms Nbaro. I'm not even scolding you. But I do want you to consider where I'd have been if one of those beam strikes had taken you out. I'd have lost your ship, you, Gunny Drun, Dorcas, Qaqqaq and Akunje, not to mention the cargo and the Starfish. From where I sat, the risk was growing too great.'

'Yes, sir,' she said.

'If the Bubbles had hit you, I might have had to fire on their remaining ship,' he said.

She didn't know what to say to that.

'So,' Pisani said, and then coffee arrived, and the servitor gave Nbaro a cup. If it had been watery mud she might have liked it; as it was, it was superb coffee.

'So,' Pisani said again. 'I can't reprimand you for success, but you gave me a really bad five minutes.'

'Yes, sir,' she said. 'I had a really bad few minutes myself.'

He nodded. 'I bet you did.' He sounded human. Fatherly.

'Sir, why didn't we shoot at them?'

Pisani looked at Morosini. 'I know it's not what you want to hear, but the answer is – that's the course Morosini and I decided on, barring certain events.'

She looked at him. 'You decided in advance not to shoot?'

Morosini nodded. 'Yes,' he said. '*I do not mind sharing this with you, Ms Nbaro. There were several reasons, all embracing one another. First, we hid in plain sight, by filling the system with proxies of ourselves. I believe that at the height of the action there were nine* Athens *clones as well as the original, all either tight to asteroids or manoeuvring.*'

She nodded.

'*The moment we fired our main armament, the Hin and the Starfish would have known which one of us was real. The Starfish, at least, knew we had only one ship in-system. The Hin, on the other hand, only know that they lost four ships here very recently.*'

'And two more today,' Pisani said.

Morosini nodded. '*As we are very likely headed into a major battle, I would like to provide the Hin with as little information possible. I want them to imagine that we are ten feet tall and have fangs. And many ships.*'

Nbaro felt foolish. 'Ah,' she said. 'I'm sorry, Morosini. I'm dumb.'

Morosini shook his head. '*No, Ms Nbaro, I must insist that in this case it is I who was foolish, and you might be said to have "saved my bacon". If Dorcas had died, or we'd lost the Starfish . . .*'

'Feather Dancer?' she asked.

Morosini smiled. '*I hope that soon enough we will know its name,*' he said. '*You see, the other reason we did not fire is . . . moral. Or at least ethical. We have one of the Hin prisoner – you know this. She can speak, much more fluently than a Starfish, and has a little Anglatin and a little Old Italian, some Hindi and some Mandarin.*'

Nbaro would have said she was too tired for surprise or a jolt of adrenaline, but she was wrong. She sat up. She'd forgotten, or compartmented, this vital information.

Always more idiocy available.

'I heard?' she managed. And then looked ruefully at the Master.

Pisani nodded. 'She – or her people – have been in contact with humans. Probably over on the Anti-spinward fringe.'

'*New Texas, Delhi, New Shenzen,*' Morosini said. '*Based on languages.*'

Nbaro blinked. *I know,* she thought, but then settled in to hear it straight from Pisani.

'She hasn't really told us anything,' Pisani said. 'Which is why you are here, in addition to being congratulated for saving yet more of this mission.'

Nbaro looked between them.

'Until Dorcas is functional, I'm putting you back on my council,' Pisani said. 'I always liked having you there – you're lucky, and I'm a sailor. But there's a more practical reason. If we understand correctly, the Hin has a special relationship with her captor. And that's you.'

Morosini nodded. '*Major Darkstar will brief you,*' the AI said. '*But in short, it's almost medieval. You captured her, so you are responsible for her.*'

'Dorcas told me some of this.'

'*Not so odd in a warrior culture,*' Morosini said. '*And, on a positive note, she accepts being captured as a normal consequence of conflict. Regardless, the issue is an ethical one. We have reason to believe that the Starfish . . .*'

'. . . committed genocide,' Nbaro said. 'Dorcas didn't have to tell me. I got there all by myself, as soon as I found the carbon fibres in the asteroid rubble.'

Morosini nodded. '*Well, then. And are you familiar with Dorcas's theory that they can turn the xenoglas off?*' He stroked his cat.

'Yes,' she admitted.

Morosini shrugged. '*So, you know everything.*'

'The end of the fucking universe,' Pisani said.

Morosini shrugged. *'No,'* he said. *'Probably the end of the DHC. Certainly, there will now be great changes. But honestly, Vettor... the changes had already begun.'*

Pisani wiped a hand down his face. Nbaro had never seen him display so much emotion. 'I can't be expected to like it,' he said. 'The end of everything I know.'

Morosini smiled, and the smile was very human, and intensely cynical. *'We will be lucky if we make it to the end of everything,'* he said. *'Right now, we will have to take it one star system at a time.'* He looked at Nbaro. *'But I will offer some words of hope. We have aboard, by a twist of fate, representatives of both alien races. The Hin – I think we must stop calling them Bubbles. The Hin must imagine that we are pretty strong, and that their human allies have misled them. And none of those allies could have imagined that the* Stealthy Change *would be so bold as to change sides and insert with us, but that's what's going to happen. And Vettor and I have a surprise ready – several, in fact. So, let us see how we go forward, one star system at a time.'*

Pisani looked better. But Nbaro was still sick at heart. And she couldn't stop herself.

'You knew some of this before we ever came out here.' Her tone was full of accusation.

Pisani nodded. 'I think that's a little above your pay grade, even as a miracle worker, Nbaro.'

Her chin quivered, and she hated how her voice shook: indignation? Fear?

'You *knew* the Starfish committed genocide,' she said.

Morosini kept patting his cat, who purred. *'I knew more than that,'* he said sadly. *'And I came, myself, anyway. Please consider that, and how narrowly I have escaped destruction, Ms Nbaro, before you indulge in a fit of human emotion at my expense.'*

She gulped. She'd heard the term, but it had never happened to her before.

A great deal more than that.

Oh, Dorcas, heal fast. Do not dare die. I can't do this by myself.

Nbaro stood her watch, almost wooden in her responses, and then fell into her rack to lie for more than an hour staring at the overhead, wondering how Dorcas was, and wondering what the AI meant by *a great deal more than that.*

But seven hours later, she woke to find Thea Drake going quietly about her morning routine, and as soon as she rolled down off her rack, Drake caught her in an embrace.

'You OK?' Drake asked. 'Stupid question. You're not OK. You're walking in thirty minutes, so I'll go and visit Dorcas.'

'He's still alive?' Nbaro asked softly.

'Honey, I know you're a fucking barbarian, and I know I have to teach you everything, but really there are these things called tabs?' She held hers up, clicked something, and there was a status display of every patient in the infirmary. Sabina *pinged.*

Nbaro noticed that Han was listed as 'Critical', and so was Dorcas.

'Critical means ... definitely not dead,' Drake said. 'Come on, get dressed. And what the hell did you get on this bra?'

'Hydraulic fluid,' Nbaro said.

Drake shrugged. 'Bras are hard to come by out here,' she said. 'My mother is like a goddess when it comes to stain removal. Let's see what can be done.'

Nbaro nodded, looked again at Drake's tab to make sure that Dorcas was *still* alive, and then got dressed, steadied as always by Drake's sense of the *normal.*

I need some normal.

'Sabina,' she said aloud.

'*Yes, ma'am?*'

'Please alert me to any change in the medical status of Horatio Dorcas?'

Her sub-AI said, '*Yes, ma'am.*'

Nbaro had a mission. She took a deep breath and walked to the ready room, to find Lieutenant Commander Thulile sitting with the skipper, talking. She looked at the maintenance boards, found her crew consisted of Pak and two spacers she didn't know, and went to the riggers for her kit.

Spacer Chu grinned at her. 'Nice to have you back, ma'am,' she said. 'See anything new?'

Nbaro glanced at her.

'And what the flock did you do to your pretty EVA suit? Ma'am?' Chu asked. 'There was hydraulic fluid *inside* it.'

'It's a long story,' Nbaro admitted. 'I did something stupid with a rigging knife, and cut the wrong wire, which proved to be an internal hydraulics feed...'

Chu was laughing. 'Oh, shit, ma'am. I don't see you as someone who does that sort of crap!'

Nbaro had to laugh because Chu was laughing. 'Oh, I do,' she said. 'Sometimes I'm an idiot.'

Chu shrugged.

'You're a petty officer!' Nbaro said. It was three beats too late, but she finally spotted the new pips on Chu's coverall.

'I am, too! Passed the maths, passed everything.' Chu grinned. 'Thanks for the help, ma'am.'

'Nice,' Nbaro said, with more warmth than she'd felt for a whole day.

When did I start liking people?

Oh, yes. When I came on board the Athens.

9

Her new back-seaters had both been working in less glamorous jobs. Spacer Hardeep Singh Tatlah had been in laundry; spacer Janny Eason had been in Astrogation, working as cleaning staff. Nbaro knew she was wooden and not putting them at ease; she struggled to appear cheerful and mostly failed, sounding a little too much like a tyrant. *Like Guille.*

Guille is dead.

Tim Eyre wasn't much help. He was still struggling to understand all his new responsibilities, and Nbaro started a cascade of bad feeling when she corrected him, snapping an instruction at him when he failed to understand her during the preflight checklist. He passed her annoyance straight on, when Tatlah misunderstood that they were operating on passive systems only and toggled the big radar as soon as they launched.

'*Passive*,' Eyre spat. 'That means you don't radiate. Are you stupid?'

There was a heavy silence.

Eyre waited a moment, and then said, 'The whole point of this mission was to fly dark and silent. We got shot off the rails with a big boost so we can stay out front of the mother ship, ready to shoot, basically invisible.'

'I'm sorry, sir.' Tatlah sounded utterly miserable. His misery cut through the cloud around Nbaro, and she toggled front end only on her comms.

'Tim,' she said. 'Stow it.'

She could feel his sullen anger radiating through his EVA suit.

'Tim,' she said, 'they *don't* understand. How long did it take you to understand all these new tactics and silent running?'

'Mr Didier explained it all to me right away,' he said.

'Right, Tim. So ...' She paused, modified what she was going to say to share the blame. 'So, which one of us has explained tactics to our back-seaters, who are – pardon me as a jumped-up midder – so wet behind the ears that we could wash with them?'

Eyre turned his head. He was still angry, but the sullenness was gone, and he nodded, eye to eye. 'Roger that, ma'am.'

'Marca,' she said. 'You're an acting midder. I'm a midder acting as a lieutenant. We're on a first-name basis.'

'Yes, ma'am,' he said. 'Marca,' he added, very quietly.

'It's hard,' she said. 'It took me ... a while ... to call Mpono *Smoke* and not *tir*.'

She heard Eyre take a breath, and then he was on the cockpit comms.

'I shouldn't bite your head off, Tatlah. And the aliens probably won't come and eat us this time. So let's use this flight to get familiar with the whole idea of running dark.'

'Yes, sir,' Tatlah managed.

'Yo, Tatlah. I'm apologising. That one was on me.'

Eason said, 'I tried to tell him. I said we were running silent. I understood.'

Nbaro didn't like her tone at all, but this wasn't the moment to jump on it.

The rest of the flight was dull routine – cold and dark. They were out for seven hours, and then landed with a minimum of thrusters, and just as Nbaro entered the ship's datasphere, within which she had a direct neural exchange with the ship's systems, her tab pinged and Sabina said, '*Dorcas's status has improved to stable.*'

She had an hour to eat before going on watch as Tower. She found a message from Steven Yu on her tab.

Dorcas is stable. I expect he'll be awake when you come off watch.

She wanted to hug Yu. She felt as if a weight had been lifted off her chest.

Instead, she went to Space Ops. It felt as if she'd been gone a year, when in fact she'd been gone a little more than a week. Tower wasn't very challenging, because they were accelerating towards Insertion. Astrogation clearly didn't want them going too fast, so they were moving at a sedate 1 *g*, and space operations were being kept to a minimum.

Commander Tremaine of Flight Eight was Lioness. Nbaro couldn't remember the last time she'd seen someone as senior as Tremaine in the chair. She was a decorated hero, beloved throughout the ship, and also easy to work with.

'Master is afraid we've got bogeys in-system,' Tremaine said. 'Maybe out at the edge, hiding in the comets. There's a tactical briefing you should see.' She leaned over the edge of her acceleration couch and waved her tab, and Nbaro's tab pinged.

Two minutes later, Nbaro swore. 'How did I miss this?'

Tremaine shrugged. 'We've all been busy.'

The tactical briefing outlined their doctrine until Insertion. Nbaro looked through her tab entries and found that it had come in while she was flying the *Pericles*.

She tabbed her own sub-AI: Sabina! I need you to watch for this stuff.

'*Right,*' Sabina replied. '*How will I know what makes "this stuff"*'

143

different from the bulletin on material readiness in your stateroom that you deleted without reading?

Nbaro took a deep breath. 'This was from the Master,' she said. '*Anything* from the Master gets a warning.'

'*I understand*,' Sabina replied cheerfully.

Tremaine leaned over. 'Have you seen this exercise we're running?'

Nbaro blinked both eyes. 'No, ma'am.'

She was looking at a full mass launch plan, the kind they'd used entering systems before. It had some new wrinkles, mostly having to do with the deployment of EW assets and emitters.

'We're doing it live, and timed,' Tremaine said.

Nbaro read through it. She wasn't on watch; she was assigned to the *Pericles*. With an Electronic Warfare package.

The mass launch was twenty-seven hours away.

In the whole of her Tower watch, Nbaro launched a handful of fighters and torpedo-carriers, and then retrieved them, and a Flight Eight spaceframe testing an engine. She had plenty of time to catch up on her paperwork; Skipper Truekner had sent a few of her evals back for minor rewrites.

She had a priority message from Truekner, too. It said: 'Patel.'

Nbaro winced. Patel was in Maintenance, and she didn't spend much time there. But that was no excuse, and she'd walked through that very morning.

Gorshokov came on watch. He was replacing her as Tower.

She managed to dredge up some cheerfulness for him. 'You qualified?' she said.

'Midshippers forever,' he said with a comic salute. 'Yes, ma'am. I'm standing Tower while training for Lioness, just like you.'

Just like me. She found Gorshokov's hero worship a bit much, but she punched him in the shoulder nonetheless. 'Well done, Andrei. And you'd better call me Marca.'

He grinned. 'Right,' he said. 'Marca ma'am.'

She was still smiling when she left Space Ops, but she paused at the hatch and it was all still there ... muted, but there: layers of reality, as if spacetime was all at once, not moment by moment. She was there, and the enemy boarders were trying to break in to Space Ops; she was firing the drones at them; she was running down the corridor ...

I've got this bad.

And Dorcas ...

Nbaro bounded down the corridor as if fleeing the past, dropped through the shaft to Third Deck, and tried not to run along the main starboard passageway to the infirmary.

Yu was going off duty, but he'd clearly waited for her.

'Nbaro, he's in a bad way. I want you to prepare yourself, because ordinarily we wouldn't let him have a visitor. But he's very insistent.' He paused. 'He should not speak. He's very badly injured. Let's not disturb him.'

He took her in past a row of men, women and 'gynes in clamshells or in other machines, all casualties from the space battle four weeks earlier.

'Horatio?' Yu asked. 'You have a visitor.'

Nbaro entered a small cubicle separated from the rest by a curtain. Everything in the infirmary had to be able to be nailed down for acceleration, and privacy was not a requirement for spacers. The curtains were a courtesy.

Nbaro had to stop and get a hold of herself, because Dorcas was a shock. He was almost deathly white; his eyes were sunken, and he looked terrible. Almost like a monster. She could read in his face what he'd look like when he was very old. Also, his chest was horrifyingly the wrong shape.

'Plastic ribs,' Dorcas signalled.

'Don't talk,' Yu said. 'At the very least, use your neural lace.'

'That's like asking him not to breathe,' Nbaro said, trying very hard to sound normal, and maybe even funny, channelling Thea Drake.

'Do not, on any account, make him laugh,' Yu said. 'His ribs were crushed. He should be dead, but Morosini used his neural lace to force his heart to function. He lost a lot of blood and—'

'And they're not sure . . .' Dorcas said via the lace.

No, he didn't mutter.

He's in my head.

Dorcas twitched. It was . . . not a good twitch.

'What aren't you sure about?' Nbaro asked.

Yu looked at Dorcas. 'I'm not sure this is the time . . .' he began.

Dorcas twitched again.

Nbaro looked at Yu.

'What's wrong?' She didn't like the sound of her own voice.

Yu set his jaw. 'Quite a bit. So how about being a model visitor and not a problem?'

'I may never recover from this, Marca,' Dorcas said inside her head.

Nbaro had to struggle with her neural lace. Emotion wasn't the best way to approach the datafield.

'You will recover,' she said.

'Morosini thinks I have brain damage,' Dorcas sent.

'You sound fine to me,' Nbaro replied.

'Are you two communicating somehow?' Yu asked. 'Because . . .'

'I'm not upsetting him,' Nbaro said.

'So far I can't feel any part of my body,' Dorcas said.

Nbaro bore down on her mind, isolating her fear and panic. 'Good thing we have nerve regrowth technologies.'

Dorcas grunted in the real.

'Why didn't you contact me this way before?'

'I don't want to interrupt you,' he said. 'Also, I wasn't sure it would work.'

'Ah, right. You're an interruption of my life.' She found it hard to get to the right tone in the data field. 'I am always available to you.'

'When you're flying? During Space Ops?'

'Fine. I'll just come find you, then.'

In the real, he smiled a little. Some saliva crept out of his mouth.

'You smiled,' she said.

'So noted.'

'OK, that's enough,' Yu said. 'Sorry, folks. That was five minutes.'

Nbaro nodded. 'I'll be back.'

'I'll be right here,' Dorcas managed.

Nbaro grinned at him, and then let herself be led through the curtains.

'Can I see Han?' she asked Yu.

He nodded. 'Absolutely,'

They walked down the row of clamshells, to where Lieutenant Commander Han was resting. Yu read something off the data-port and nodded. 'He's not asleep. He's in VR playing a game.'

'Fuju?' she said gently.

Inside the clear surface of the clamshell, Han's eyes opened. And widened.

'Hello,' he said.

'Hey,' she responded. 'I hear you're a hero?'

Han's smile widened. 'I got us there,' he said with visible pride. 'And then some stupid *èr bǎi wǔ* shot me!'

Yu raised a cautioning hand.

Han's face moved behind the glass. 'Thanks for coming,' the voicebox said. 'Please come again. I promise not to raise my heartbeat.'

'How's he doing?' she asked Yu.

Yu waited until they were outside the infirmary. 'He's doing very well.' He crossed his arms. 'His problem – and ours – is that he thinks he's ready to resume duties, and I want him in that regrowth tank for another two weeks. Maybe three.'

By then, they were out in the empty passageway, heading forward to the lift shafts.

'Can I ask you a sensitive question?'

'If it's about Dorcas,' Yu began, 'I can't—'

'It's about me,' Nbaro said. 'When did you put the neural lace into my head?'

Yu stopped and looked at her. 'Interesting,' he said. 'You need to ask Morosini.'

'I'm asking you.'

'And I'm declining to answer,' Yu said.

'We're friends!' Nbaro didn't like the pleading tone in her voice. Walls were coming up, armour was being donned. She needed to keep some things out.

Yu held her gaze. 'We are friends. That question goes beyond friendship. Ask Morosini.'

She nodded. 'I see,' she said frostily.

Yu shrugged in frustration. 'Fine,' he said. And walked off. She didn't follow until she saw him vanish into the lift shaft.

I don't need friends like that.

Marca, you are being unfair.

Fuck that. He could have answered me. Clearly I cannot trust him.

By the time she got back to her stateroom, she didn't remember what she'd said to Yu. Instead, she wriggled out of a hug from Drake.

'No escape,' Drake said, forcing her into the hug, and Nbaro burst into tears, and cried, and cried.

Later, Nbaro told Thea everything, and she just listened.

'Well, that sucks,' Thea said. 'But Yu's dead right. If he's been told it's confidential—'

'But don't you see, Thea? I was set up! They put that thing in me to watch me!'

Thea sat back. 'Yeah,' she admitted.

'It makes me feel dirty.'

Drake raised an eyebrow. And then tilted her head to one side, the way she did sometimes. 'You can't have had it when you came aboard,' she said.

'True,' Nbaro said.

'And you never went to the infirmary before we left on cruise.'

'That's true,' she admitted. 'After we left City Orbital.'

Thea wrinkled her forehead. 'So if they put the neural lace in then,' she said, 'it must have been as much to protect you as to keep tabs on you.'

Nbaro shook her head in denial, but she had to admit that she liked Thea's timeline. And the idea that the ship wanted to look after her.

I should talk to Morosini, she thought.

She ate alone: a mysterious curry that reminded her of how long they'd been in space without a port, but the rice was still delicious, and it was *still* better than any meal at the Orphanage. She wolfed down several helpings and then ran to get changed for her boarding party training. She was now a team leader, and as the drafts of young spacers came up from early cruise jobs in various labour-intensive roles, she knew that eventually she'd be an instructor, which made her feel like an impostor.

Captain Fraser caught her as soon as she entered the chain locker.

'Ms Nbaro,' he said, with a formality that worried her.

'Sir?'

'I'm glad you made it. Listen, can you train teams six and seven?'

'Me?' she squeaked. She had absolutely known that this moment was coming, and then she'd left the ship for two weeks, and here it was.

'I can give you Locran and maybe...' He looked around. 'Chief Chen?'

Chen was the best zero-*g* martial artist on the ship, and Locran had been her first friend on board and her companion in a deadly, real fight.

Her appreciation for their skills easily overwhelmed her impostor syndrome. 'Absolutely!' she said.

Until then, boarding party drills had been fun – almost mindless exercise routines. That is, she'd often been a team leader, by rank if not skill, but they had all been assigned teams. Now she was getting a team of her own.

Two teams.

She waited for Chen to finish a brief refresher on zero-*g* infighting with two young spacers, and Locran found her, pushing through the crowd of lower deck newbies who looked too young to be aboard.

'Gentlemen,' she said, putting an arm on each shoulder.

Almost in unison, they proclaimed that they worked for a living.

She smiled. 'We – and I mean *we* – are now the proud leaders of those unwashed spacers behind us.'

Locran winced.

Chen made a thoughtful face and pinched his nose, a lightning-fast motion that she'd come to see as his twitch.

'Chief, you get team six, and Locran, you get team seven.'

Both men nodded.

'Now, I assume you've both trained teams before?' she asked.

They both shook their heads. Chen pointed aft, towards the infirmary. 'Chief Turney was the trainer.' After a pause, he said, 'Engineering. Bad radiation dose. Won' be back this cruise.'

Locran nodded.

Nbaro realised that there were more missing faces than she'd observed two weeks ago.

Chen raised his hand. 'I . . . I have an idea,' he said.

She nodded with what she hoped was encouragement.

Look, I'm pretending to be an officer.

'I always thought we did this wrong. We start by teaching them all this combat stuff, which, to be fair, you and I, ma'am, we like all that, right?' Chen shrugged.

Locran joined in the shrug. 'Just give me a shotgun.'

'Sure,' Chen said, 'but I think we should start by walking them around the ship and talking about what it's going to be like – fighting, I mean. Choke points, ECM gunners, drones, close combat.'

'So that the training makes sense,' she said.

Locran nodded. 'I'm in, Chief. I did this stuff for two cruises before I understood *why* we learned a bunch of the techniques.'

Nbaro took a deep breath. 'Well,' she said, 'I don't know anything—'

Chen barked a laugh. 'Ma'am, how many intruders have you put down?'

Locran pretended to cough.

She wanted to roll her eyes. 'Fine. Let's take them on a tour.'

Her intention had been to hang back and watch her professionals teach the newbies, and she did think it was a little unfair that they had two eight-person teams of completely untrained personnel. However, her resolve to stay quiet didn't last through the first space. Chief Chen got them all quiet, put them in two sticks, and with a nod to Captain Fraser, they all went out into the port-side passageways and started aft.

Chen stopped at the first knee-knocker.

'So,' he barked. 'You all know how lucky you are?'

The young men, women, and 'gynes all stood at attention.

'You are all assigned to Lieutenant Nbaro, here, who's killed more people than the plague.' He smiled at them. 'And she hasn't lost anyone, either.'

Too much praise. 'I keep getting wounded, though,' Nbaro said aloud.

A couple of the braver souls managed a titter. She noticed little Ramirez; she'd been a good worker when they were assembling the *Pericles*, and she sent the woman a smile, which was returned.

Chen spoke up. 'So we're going on a little tour of the ship for two hours, which is easy duty. The problem is – we really need you to listen to us. So I'm going to test you at the end. Those who fail will get extra duty.'

'Those who succeed will get pie,' Nbaro said. She believed in both the carrot and the stick. Locran gave her an approving look.

Chen looked at each one of them. And nodded at Locran.

Locran stepped forward. He had a real boarding shotgun on his shoulder, which gave him a certain authority and had to be against the rules. Nbaro wasn't minded to stop him, though.

'How many of you have been in a fight?' he asked. 'Any fight. Bloody nose, cracked knuckles, a kick in the gut?'

Two women, two men, and a tall 'gyne all raised their hands very tentatively. Ramirez was one of them, which didn't surprise Nbaro at all.

Locran looked at them. 'Interesting,' he said. 'Let's walk.'

Chen had a whole philosophy of shipboard combat. He'd divided the ship into terrain types in his head, and he introduced his students to his thoughts, one type at a time.

He began with the choke points: passageways and corridors, hatches and doors.

'So here we are in the port-side passageway,' he said. 'Imagine you need to retake this passageway from an aggressor. How do you do it?'

One of the women who said she'd been in a fight raised a very tentative hand. 'Ah …' She realised that no one else was even trying to answer. 'Ah … big push? Everyone at once, maybe?' she asked more than answered.

Chen looked at Nbaro. 'How did you clear the passageway?' he asked. 'Ms Nbaro fought down this very passageway, not six months ago, our time.'

Nbaro thought the chief might be going there. She took a breath. 'Everyone look up. See the little nodules, like eggs, over the knee-knocker? In the overhead? Look.'

Some of them weren't looking.

She took the boarding shotgun from Locran and used it to point out the nodules. That got their attention.

'What are they?' she asked.

A small, heavily freckled man who looked more like a boy said, 'Drones, ma'am!'

She nodded. 'Right. Drones. What's your name?'

'Nuur, ma'am.'

'Right. I had the AI use the drones on the borders in the corridor, and then we swept it.' She smiled at the woman who'd spoken up. 'What's your name?'

'Gallash,' the woman said. 'Spacer Gallash, ma'am.'

'So – you are right, Gallash. After we fired the drones, we all went in together. Two of my petty officers were hit. Both of them had armour on and neither had anything worse than bruises.' She nodded back at Chen, who was smiling.

Chen waved. 'Drones, body armour, choke points,' he said. 'Everyone got that part?'

Locran added, 'Boarding shotgun. One round will hit every part of the passageway beyond the knee-knocker. You won't always have drones, but you'll always have a boarding shotgun. With slugs, it'll knock an armoured enemy unconscious, or even dead, right through their armour. With flechettes, it'll clear a whole corridor of unarmoured hostiles.'

Chen nodded. 'We'll eventually talk about grenades, smoke and close combat. For now, think about this – there's places on the ship where it's challenging to pass another shipmate quickly, right? So imagine what it's like when that's a fucking hostile trying to put you down. *Those* are the choke points.'

Then he walked them to Cargo Operations, which was virtually uncrewed because the cargo load was done. He tabbed open the space.

'Here's a different kind of problem – an objective space. Could be Space Operations, could be the bridge, could be the auxiliary helm or a reactor compartment. Right?'

People nodded. Some were getting into it, Nbaro could tell.

Chen never left the O-3 level, but he took them through his four types of terrain: choke points, objective spaces, open battlefields, and what he called '3D spaces' where multiple access was possible in all three dimensions. At each, he and Locran and Nbaro would talk about the tactical problems posed by the space.

They ended back at the chain locker.

Chen pointed at the freckled boy with no warning. 'Tell me three things you learned,' he said.

Nuur grinned. 'The four types of terrain are choke points, objective spaces, open battlefields and 3D spaces,' he began.

'Good,' Chen said.

Locran pointed at another spacer. 'When we point at you, say your name,' he said. 'That's an order until further notice.' He looked at them all. 'Anyone already have armour?'

Both of the 'gynes and one big man all raised their hands.

He pointed at the taller 'gyne. 'What's this for,' he asked, holding out his boarding shotgun.

'Spacer Grunhild. That's a boarding shotgun, and it can fuck a body up through his armour or, I dunno, cover the whole passageway in … fleshers.' They flushed, clearly not used to the word *flechette*. In broad New London patois, they said, 'Sounds narsty, any road.'

People laughed, and Nbaro realised Chen had managed to get them all interested – even Photino, the shorter 'gyne, who seemed very hesitant about … everything.

It was clearly Nbaro's turn. She pointed at a dark-haired, very pale spacer who'd remained quiet the whole time. 'What are those?' she asked, pointing at a row of plastic eggs over the hatch to the chain locker.

'Bothie, ma'am,' the spacer replied. She had a nice crisp voice. Nbaro thought it was probably more of a liability than an asset that she was remarkably pretty, so she made herself smile.

Bothie took courage from the smile and smiled back. 'Drones, ma'am. Or at least, I guess they're the casings for the drones.' She looked up at the drones as if hoping for some divine revelation, and then looked back. 'I guess you used 'em to clear a passageway, but due respect, ma'am, I didn't catch how they worked.'

A few people laughed. The loudest laugh was from the biggest man, whose pocket flash said 'Kent'.

Nbaro pointed at him. 'So how do they work?'

Kent didn't wilt under her glare. 'They flies,' he said. 'And then they blows up.'

More laughter. But Nbaro felt that the man had the right of it. 'Not bad. I think the two of you managed to get the gist.'

She turned away while Chen and Locran asked a dozen more questions, until every spacer had answered something correctly. She got on her tab to the forward Dirtyshirt mess, where she used her status as a hero to beg two cherry pies.

She looked at Chen. 'Any fails?' she asked.

'Nope.' Chen smiled at their people. 'I think maybe we got a good bunch.'

Nbaro nodded. 'Two cherry pies will be delivered to the aft mess hall at ship's time 2000. You get one slice each. You'll need to show ID.'

'Shit-hot,' Spacer Nuur said aloud, and then they turned to hear a few words from Captain Fraser for all the trainees.

'We're two weeks out from Insertion for Corfu System.' Fraser had the absolute attention of every spacer. It wasn't often that they were engaged in anything that looked beyond the next watch. 'It's no secret that we could be jumping straight into another fight,' he said. 'So whether you are here, or on a damage control party, or both, you need to be ready.'

There were a lot of sombre faces as they all filed through the hatches back to their routine duties.

Nbaro caught Chen. 'That was excellent,' she said.

Chen nodded. 'I always wanted to give this approach a go.'

'Can we get together in the next two days to plan some classes?'

Locran raised his tab and the three of them shared schedules, then Nbaro waved a hand.

'Wait one,' she said. 'Sabina, find the best time in the next twenty-four hours for the three of us to meet.'

'*Got it,*' Sabina said. '*Besides right now, you mean?*'

Locran smiled with half his face – a sort of grimace. 'Actually,' he said, 'right now is good.'

Chen agreed, and the three of them went to Nbaro's ready room and drafted a training syllabus. Lieutenant Commander Thulile joined them, probably lured by the voices, and Nbaro introduced Chen and Locran.

Thulile listened for a while and then drifted away, but when they were done and Nbaro was collating the results into a document on her tab, she returned.

'Spoken to Patel yet?' she asked.

Nbaro froze. She had forgotten again.

Thulile nodded. 'How about right now?' Her voice was even: not demanding, not accusing. 'He's working on 6–0–3.'

Nbaro stood up. 'Yes, ma'am.'

Thulile looked frustrated. 'It's not an order,' she said. 'It's a suggestion. You seem very uneasy about talking to Patel.'

'I keep forgetting,' Nbaro said.

Thulile raised an eyebrow.

Nbaro took a deep breath. And then shook her head.

I'm an idiot.

'Now is a good time,' she admitted.

Thulile's gaze was mild, but their eyes locked. 'Do you have a problem with Patel?' she asked quietly.

'No, ma'am.'

'Do you have a problem with telling someone else about their mistakes?' Thulile asked.

Nbaro grunted without thought, as if she'd been punched.

Got me pegged.

Thulile wasn't a warm person. She didn't come closer, or put a hand on Nbaro's shoulder; in fact, she kept her distance like an Orphanage grad. Nor did she smile. Her gaze remained level. 'This comes with the job,' she said. Her smile was so slight that Nbaro would have missed it if she hadn't been fixed on the other woman's face, but it spoke of something … some inner knowledge.

'I'll go right now,' she said.

Thulile said nothing in return.

Nbaro found Patel working on 6–0–3, just as promised. He was as absurdly young as Nuur, perhaps six whole months younger than Nbaro herself.

Nbaro found Chief Baluster out on the deck, watching three different work parties.

'Chief, I need a word with Patel,' she said.

Baluster nodded. He seemed distant; she wondered if he held a grudge. He'd been reprimanded for the hydraulics leak in her spaceframe back on Madagascar, but it hadn't gone in his record…

Then he turned, and the coldness was gone. 'Going to fry him for his test scores, I hope,' Baluster said.

She nodded. 'Something like that.'

'Well, pretty smart letting him stew the last few weeks. He knew this was coming. He's probably stopped eating.' Baluster grinned.

Nbaro felt a hollow in her gut.

I didn't think about it that way…

I'm an idiot. As usual.

'Well,' she said.

'*Patel!*' Baluster roared over the sounds of the Hangar Deck. His voice was louder than two high-speed drills and a powered wrench.

Rohan Patel was a man of middling height, and he was almost exactly the same shade of brown as Nbaro herself; they might have been brother and sister. He wore a small beard and a moustache, and his smile didn't hide his nerves. He crossed the deck like a man walking bravely to his execution.

'Chief,' he said. And then, 'Ma'am.'

She nodded. 'Let's take a walk,' she said, playing Truekner in her mind.

Patel looked back at Baluster.

Baluster smiled. 'Oh, no, Rohan. Now you get it, and I'm not holding your hand.'

The Hangar Deck was full of activity. It was a vast area, more than a kilometre long, filling the third and fourth deck levels towards the stern of the ship; in slow times, there were mounts for ball courts to be installed.

Not now. Now, there were a dozen spacecraft under construction as the *Athens* threw off all constraints and converted herself to a war footing. Flight Six, which had been a pool of reserve pilots to support merchant operations, suddenly received their military spaceframes, as did Flight Two, which was getting small, close-in interceptors that could be piloted remotely or live. There were rows of spacecraft in every stage of completion.

Despite which, it wasn't hard to find privacy. Nbaro walked Patel into the space between two parked gantries, and they might have been on the surface of a moon.

'So...' she said.

'Ma'am, I'm really sorry...' He was charming, and he was probably also funny. And he was prepared to trot both of these qualities out.

She liked him instantly, which made this much harder.

Who am I, the fake officer, to tell this kid how to live his life?

When did I start liking everyone, anyway?

'Stow it,' she said, overcoming her urge to be cheerful.

He froze.

She had her tab, and she held it up in front of her face as if she was reading it. 'Any idea how many spacers fail their first petty officer exam?' she asked.

Patel gave up on charm, probably too early, and turned surly. 'A bunch, I bet.'

She used his tone to clamp down. 'Want to guess how many spacers who've already been put in charge of a work party fail?' she asked. Patel was a valuable man, who had a real facility for spaceframe repair and maintenance. He'd been in charge of repairs for three months already.

'I suck at tests. Ma'am.'

She nodded. 'So noted. But your score is so low, it's as if you have some test-taking anxiety.'

He made a face and mumbled something.

'So how about we sign you up for some therapy in that direction?'

'Do we have to?' he asked. 'Gods, ma'am, I signed up for Service so I could ... I dunno. Not do *this* shit.'

Well, here's the part that Truekner told me about.

She put her tab under her arm. 'Yeah. You know, I kinda get that.' She didn't let herself smile. 'The thing is, Patel, you said Service. Service means we serve. You know me, right? You know I came from the Orphanage.'

Patel nodded. 'I know you, ma'am. Everyone asks about you.' He shrugged. 'When this is over, if I'm still alive, everyone will want to hear—'

He was back to funny and charming.

She cut him off brusquely. 'So I used to think that Service was all military and orders. But then I got to the *Athens* and I found that I'm *serving*. And so, here I am, on the Hangar Deck during my sleep time, serving your needs by telling you to get your ass in gear and pass the fucking test. Because the *ship* needs you, and *Flight Six* needs you to be a petty officer and carry out orders. Given what Baluster and every other Leading Petty Officer in this maintenance section says about you, you should already be studying for your *next* promotion board. It's not all about you, Patel. We *need* you to get promoted.'

Patel looked confused.

She leaned closer. 'Skipper Truekner sent me, the barbarous Orphanage grad hero, to tell you to get it together. You, the only person in my division to fail a test.' She shrugged. 'I fail shit all the time. So what? Get it together, pass the next one.

I'm scheduling it for you in four weeks. Got that? So, therapy? Or just wing it?'

'What happens if I fail again?' he asked.

She held the muscles of her face immobile and just looked at him until he broke eye contact.

I didn't know I could do that. Wow.

'I'll take the therapy. But people will fuck with me about it.' He was looking at the deck.

'Oh, really? I could use some new sparring partners in boarding party drills,' she said cheerfully. *I like that tone. Nasty. Barbarous.* 'Next time we talk, I want to be shaking your hand and pinning your rank on.'

'I hear you, ma'am.'

'Excellent. Don't forget to tell all your shipmates how nice I am.'

Patel looked at her then, and cracked a smile.

You are a bold one. Do you see through me?

But then he looked away.

She walked him back to Baluster.

'Spacer Patel is going to go to therapy with Science Tech Yu to address test-taking anxiety,' she said.

Baluster nodded.

'Chief... so my views are clear,' she said, 'I know a shitload about hazing. If I hear that Patel took any grief about this therapy, I will be mean-spirited about it.'

Baluster's mouth twitched. 'Point taken,' he said. 'I might be mean-spirited myself, ma'am. I need this grinning bastard to get promoted so he can take some work off my shoulders.'

Patel shut his eyes.

She nodded. 'Good,' she said briskly. 'Patel, if you need anything to make this work, you tell me. Hold up your tab.'

He raised it.

She pressed the button that exchanged comms data. 'Now you have my personal contact.' She made her smile feral. 'And I have yours. I expect you to attend every therapy session on time, and that you will study for this exam.'

God, now I sound like the instructors at the Orphanage. Yuck.

10

Nbaro was sucked back into the world of shipboard life. She might be deeply worried that her lover was critically wounded; she might have deep concerns about the presence of a neural lace in her head and its implications; she might share the same host of concerns facing every spacer aboard – aliens, distance, the daily dangers of life in space. All of those things were there, every minute of every waking hour, and all too often in her sleep.

And yet, the warm embrace of shipboard routine was also there.

Incidents stood out. The mass-launch drill was fascinating, as the *Athens* experimented with creating windows in its clutter-field, and selected band jamming, and new, more subtle deceptions: emitters mounted on torpedo hulls, for example, capable of moving at high speeds in bursts; refitted spacecraft with more powerful emitters and sub-AIs capable of very deceptive flight paths; and Flight One cargo shuttles launched cold to drop responsive clutter patterns to cover the flank of the *Athens*. It wasn't all new, but laying it all on together was a major exercise, and the ship and the space wing rose to the challenge.

Nbaro flew the *Pericles* with a robust electronic warfare package clamped on, and with Andrei Gorshokov as her co-pilot. Gorshokov was a Flight Five pilot, another former midder.

'I guess we were supposed to be learning from Han,' Nbaro said as they ran preflight checks.

'I've done about fifty hours on the sims,' Gorshokov said.

Nbaro nodded. 'It's Frankenstein's monster, Andrei. It's too big to fly like a spaceframe, and too small to really be a ship. It's clunky, and it can't lift-off from the railguns, so no cold boost.' She shrugged inside her EVA suit.

Both of them were in full EVA gear, as were the two Flight Three EW techs who had turned the crew space aft of the cockpit into a snake's nest of wires and cables connected to myriad boxes, consoles and screens.

'I wonder if we really need EVA suits,' Gorshokov said. 'If we're targeted...'

'I agree. It's overkill. I'll mention it to ...' She paused. 'To Han.' He was the commanding officer of record of the little hybrid ship.

The drill exposed errors; the roll-out of spaceframes off the catapults was slower than anyone had anticipated, and the deployment of chaff from the Flight One drop-ships was ineffective due to an engineering fault. Nbaro got to watch it all from a front row seat, hovering ten thousand kilometres above the *Athens* and slightly behind her.

Nbaro's verdict on the whole thing, including flying the *Pericles*, was one word to Drake.

'Boring.'

'Honey, you have the command of your own small ship while, technically, you're still a midder. I think that's something.' Drake smiled.

Nbaro smiled back. 'Sometimes I'm amazed I'm here at all,' she admitted. 'But I want back in my own spaceframe, I guess I'm an XC-3C girl.'

They were eight days from Insertion, and then seven, and then six. She trained boarders, flew routine Flight Six missions training her midders, stood watches, and in between, worked out, practised her close combat skills, and stopped by Maintenance twice to see Patel. She'd just smile at him and move on.

I hope that's not creepy.

Five days from Insertion, and the schedules were published. She was Lioness. That thrilled her, but it also told her how thin the crew was; the mass launch was stripping the ship of senior pilots. The sudden construction of light fighters for Flight Two and heavy fighters for Flight Six meant that many pilots whose primary work had been on the ship or 'helping out' on cargo flights and in Space Ops were now dedicated military pilots with missions to fly.

In fact, Nbaro noted, looking down the schedule, that the moment she came off the Space Ops watch from Insertion, she would be in a spaceframe as co-pilot with Truekner.

Four days from Insertion. She forced herself to find time to visit Dorcas.

Yu wasn't on watch, but another med tech took her to Dorcas's clamshell. He no longer had privacy curtains, probably because he was now fully immersed in the gel that combined healing properties with acceleration protection.

'Hey,' she said.

There was a long pause. It scared her.

Suddenly, his eyes popped open. 'Nbaro!' he sent, as if this was a total surprise.

'Remember me?'

'Always,' Dorcas replied. 'I have found something we can do together, to our mutual profit.'

He sounded very much like himself – or, at least, the self he projected into data space.

'I'm in. What are we doing?'

'I'm going to train you to use your neural lace. To really use it, the way I use it. In fact, this injury may prove to be beneficial.

Morosini has been showing me many things I had not understood before.'

'Is that even possible?' she asked.

'Oh, yes. There are many things I don't understand. I thought you of all people knew that.'

'That was sarcasm.'

'Ah.' Pause. 'Ah, of course.'

'Your brain seems unimpaired.'

'Yes. We've done extensive tests, and it appears the impairment was mostly concussion.'

Nbaro's anger flared up, and for a moment she lost her neural link altogether.

'And when were you going to tell me that?' she asked.

Dorcas's eyes, just visible through the gel and a transparent window, were wide.

'I should have told you.'

'Yes,' she sent, and tried to put emphasis on the neural projection, like a pitcher putting spin on a ball. 'Yes. In fact, I'm very angry with you. And happy.'

They looked at each other through the gel.

'I am very badly injured,' he sent. 'A tragic figure, really.'

'You have a fine brain and a neural lace. You could have dropped me a message at any point, say, "Brain unimpaired. Having deep thoughts. Dorcas."'

Dorcas blinked. 'Yes,' he agreed. 'Yes, that sounds like something I really should have done.'

'But you didn't,' she sent back.

Just for a moment, Dorcas sent Nbaro a glimpse of an incredible landscape.

No – a three-dimensional figure. A geometry ... no. More than three dimensions ...

Then it was gone. 'That's where I've been,' he said. 'Six-

166

dimensional space, as realised by Calabi and proven by Yau. So we call this a Calabi–Yau manifold.'

She was at a loss for words, not least because it was beautiful, and also because she realised that Morosini had thrown Dorcas into this mathematical wonderland for benign reasons, and so, naturally, Dorcas had pretty much forgotten her existence.

She settled into a chair. 'Tell me about it. What is a Calabi–Yau manifold?'

'Well,' he said, and she could imagine his tone if this was in the real: his slight breathlessness, his excitement, his passion. 'The motivational definition originally given by Shing-Tung Yau is of a compact Kähler manifold with a vanishing first Chern class, that is also Ricci flat.'

Nbaro smiled. 'Pretend I don't know what a Chern class is.'

'Oh, the characteristic classes associated with complex vector bundles. Right?'

Eventually, Dorcas took her inside, in data space.

Forty minutes later, Nbaro was no closer to understanding multi-dimensional geometry than she ever had been, but she was aware that Calabi–Yau manifolds were widely believed to be the six-dimensional structures at the smallest 'frames' of the universe. She was also aware that her beloved was going to recover, if slowly, and that he was both happy and fully entertained. And the possibility of her becoming fluent in the use of her neural lace seemed...

Healing. Mostly. And a little scary.

She left Dorcas to his data space, and stopped by Han. He now had a private space created by sheets of black plastic, because he was only partially clamshelled and his head and left shoulder were clear. He was in a sort of medical acceleration couch, and Nbaro realised that they were all being prepped for Insertion... and whatever came after.

'Ms Nbaro,' he said as soon as she pushed through the curtain.

She'd exchanged messages with him to make sure he was awake and receptive.

'Afternoon, sir.'

'You don't have to call me "sir".' He grinned.

'I don't. But this is sort of a business visit.'

'Great.' He actually sounded eager. 'How's the *Pericles*?'

'She's fine. But Gorshokov and I were wondering whether we really needed to wear full EVA suits on board.' She made a face.

'Nah. I almost never wear EVA gear on board the pinnace. Anything that gets you while you're in it is probably going to kill you.' Han's smile was odd, as if his face was stiff, and she realised that it probably was – that a person coming out of a long period in clamshell hadn't done much smiling. She thought of Lieutenant Smith.

'That's sort of what I thought. Well, I'm keeping your seat warm for you. So is Cortez from Flight Five – he'll be taking her for the insertion.' She smiled. 'And then you'll be back, or that's what a little bird told us.'

'Three weeks, tops. But, oh, man, the physio I'm about to endure.' Han shrugged his one exposed shoulder. 'How's Mr Dorcas?'

'Healing!' she said, with enough brightness that she surprised herself. 'Sorry. We were worried he had brain damage, but apparently not. On the other hand, his ribs are all broken and there's damage to his pelvis and neck, so . . .'

So, sex is off the table for a while, I guess. Weird. A month ago I'd have thought I could just skip sex for the rest of my life.

Han nodded. 'Well, this place works miracles.'

The med tech came in. Nbaro was embarrassed because she'd sat with them at dinner a couple of times: one of Yu's friends with an old Americano name she had forgotten.

The woman smiled at Nbaro. 'Ma'am, I have to move you along. This handsome devil needs his meds, and then he gets to start his nice rehab!' She said the last words in a tone that made it clear she knew there was nothing nice about rehab.

'I bet you say that to all the boys,' Han managed.

The med tech smiled. She had bright eyes and a wicked grin. 'Boys, girls and 'gynes.'

Wayne. Lisa Wayne.

'Work him hard, Lisa,' Nbaro said, in Thea Drake tones. 'We need him back.'

'Ooh,' Wayne said. 'Permission to work the subject hard.'

Han drew his left hand theatrically across his face. 'No, Nbaro, don't leave me.'

Wayne rolled her eyes. 'He's going to stretch his left arm. *Maybe* ten times. And do some grip strength stuff. Don't believe a word he says about the whole torture thing.' She winked.

Nbaro left, knowing Han was in good hands, and two hours later he sent her a tab message thanking her for her visit and authorising flightsuits only on the *Pericles*. She re-sent it to all the acting crew members, including the EW techs.

And then, happier than she'd been in a week, she went to zero-*g* combat, and then to her rack.

II

Nbaro didn't have to physically visit Dorcas to exercise her neural lace with him, but she preferred it, so she visited him, and Han, too. The exercises varied from the utterly mundane, as he showed her ways to memorise data entry points, like index cards, which definitely sped up her use of the extensive system, to the exploration of worlds of wonder, like the six-dimensional Calabi–Yau manifolds.

'Still doesn't make sense to me,' she admitted in the steady VR environment the two of them could now share. 'Can you really hold six dimensions in your head?'

'No,' he said. 'But in the data space I can approach understanding them, both mathematically and . . . intuitively.'

She wanted to say something like 'That's nice for you,' but she didn't.

Two days from Insertion, the station at Trade Point was a distant memory – the last hours of bombardment by the beam weapons just a trace in Nbaro's nightmares – and she was looking at her usual table in the wardroom: seated around it were Steven Yu, Thea Drake, Rick Hanna, Jesus Cortez, Captain Bernie Fraser and acting Captain Jan Mpono, now the ship's executive officer.

'Just like the old days,' Nbaro said, as she approached the table with a tray piled high with food.

'Marca's storing food for winter,' Thea Drake quipped.

Cortez, who worked out constantly to fight his tendency towards muscular overweightness, snorted. 'Where the hell does she put it all?'

Hanna had already finished eating, and he leaned back. 'You know that our universe has eleven dimensions, right?' he asked. 'One of them is just for Nbaro's food, and my socks.'

'I love you all,' Nbaro said as she sat.

Acting Captain Mpono smiled at her, their narrow face alight. 'It's good to see you, Marca.'

'You too, tir – *Smoke.*' She laughed. 'Damn it. I laugh at Gorshokov when he does it, and I still do it to you.'

Smoke laughed back. 'And as for the "old days",' she said, 'I've been eating at this table for four cruises, and your "old days" are only three or four months old.'

'If Dorcas was here—' Drake stopped herself. 'Marca, how is he?'

'Great!' Nbaro said. 'Er … by which I mean he's got no brain damage, and the ship has him occupied with higher dimensional space to pass the time.'

'That sounds right,' Hanna said.

'Otherwise … broken ribs, broken collarbones, broken pelvis.'

'So a long time until you have sex again,' Thea said, and Nbaro tossed a bread roll at her.

Fraser laughed. 'We'll all have to watch ourselves at sword drills,' he said ruefully.

'Ah,' Mpono said. 'We must be in the Deep Black. The part of the cruise where everyone's been away from home a little too long.'

There was a little silence. Then they said, 'Well, it won't be secret in two hours. We're inserting for Corfu, ahead of schedule.'

Nbaro knew that must be good news, as everyone brightened except Fraser – who, as commander of Astrogation, had to already know their destination.

'Corfu!' Drake said.

Nbaro raised an eyebrow. But she had a neural lace, and she was getting much better at accessing information. So she did.

In milliseconds, she had 'learned that Corfu had previously been a system called Gliese 1187, and had a bright G series star and no planets in the habitable zone, but two gas giants well out. An extensive double asteroid belt featured a quiet zone running down the middle, and held a number of mining stations, most of them run from distant New India. Corfu had one large station: a hollowed-out asteroid with a substantial population in the outer belt.

The DHC had made the decision two hundred years ago to limit human expansion into this sector – called the 'Anti-coreward Fringe' in some articles – to avoid potential infringement on Starfish space, but their attempts to limit the frontier had not only failed utterly, but had been a cause of increasing friction with the frontier worlds. Ultra and its Medulla Station, with a DHC base and a major trade depot, had been intended as the absolute human frontier in this direction, but colonists and refugees had other ideas.

'It's the longest insertion on our route,' Captain Fraser said. 'In fact, it's the very limit of our capabilities, although with a little help from our new PTX friends, we may have a better time of it.'

'Astrogation always sweats blood over this leg,' Mpono said with a slight smile.

'Yes, we do,' Fraser admitted.

'But when I update the plot in a couple of hours,' Mpono said, 'you'll see that we're going to get a little R and R on Corfu Station.'

'If...' Thea Drake said. '*If* the Bubbles don't jump us coming in-system.'

'*If*,' Cortez added, 'the Bubbles haven't already killed everyone in-system.'

'You're a cheerful lot,' Yu said. 'I'm going back to work, where we try to do some science in between patching up the survivors of your escapades.'

'Ouch,' Nbaro said. 'I prefer to think that you're patching us up because we helped *you* survive.'

'Ooh,' Drake said, and made a 'score' mark in the air. 'Amazing you can be so witty and still pack away all that food.'

'I'm getting out of here before you two target me,' Fraser said. He looked at his partner, Mpono, who smiled back.

'These children wouldn't dare target me with their humour,' Mpono said. 'I have all the powers of the XO.'

'That's us told,' Drake said. 'Come to think of it, I'll have another dessert. It works for Marca.'

Nbaro left the table feeling better – so much better that she realised, as she slipped into her rack, that she'd gone a full day without feeling like an idiot.

12

Nbaro used her neural lace ruthlessly to prep for her mass launch in Corfu System. Used to its fullest extent, the neural lace allowed her to – at least virtually – be in several places at once. She managed to get every one of forty-four spacecraft to register their take-off weights in advance through various virtual personas, while she tinkered with the routines, slightly changed flight schedules, and received a plea from Engineering to give them thirty more minutes to get the new chaff dispensers affixed to the Flight One drop-ships, which the Master agreed to.

Nbaro imagined she could hear them grinding their teeth in Astrogation.

Alpha Alpha 1–0–4 made it on to the rails with seven minutes to go for Insertion. Nbaro locked it down, translated its new weight and made sure Tower had it all for launch.

Then she raised her hand. 'Take your drugs, friends,' she said.

All through the black, bronze, gold and underlit red-orange elegance of the remodelled Space Operations Centre, her crews took their insertion drugs and then raised their hands to indicate compliance.

Brian Evans, a Flight Six officer just starting his Space Ops qualifications, was sitting at the Tactical Operations repeater. 'Ma'am,' he said.

Nbaro didn't have to look down, or around. She just cycled her TAO screen to the forefront of her busy retinal projections.

TAO had identified three fast-moving ships. They weren't close, but two of them were obviously Hin. The third was just UnID.

'Not changing anything right now, Brian,' Nbaro said. 'Good heads-up, though. Now take your nice drugs.'

'Yes, ma'am,' he said, although, like everyone else of lieutenant status or above, he outranked Nbaro in day-to-day matters.

So the aliens had made their move, about seven hours earlier. They were far behind, in the *Athens'* frame of time-reference.

'Two minutes to Insertion,' she said. Her pulse was starting to race.

On the TAO plot, the *Stealthy Change* was about a light-second astern of the *Athens*, her tail fully deployed. Nbaro wished her astrogator luck. Ship's gossip said that the *Stealthy Change's* captain was also the astrogator, after a complex mutiny and then the counter-mutiny that had wounded Fuju Han.

These are not profitable thoughts just now.

Life with a neural lace forced a certain mental discipline that didn't come naturally to Nbaro. But she was one minute from a potential space battle, and she needed everything to run perfectly.

Pisani's voice came over the ship's system.

'Shipmates,' he said. 'Once again, we're going into what may be a hostile system. You all know the drill, and I mean that literally. So I ask that you watch your own backs and your shipmates', and together we'll help the *Athens* get us home. That is all.'

Fifteen seconds.

Ten seconds.

Five seconds.

Insertion.

*

Nbaro came to feeling so good that she wondered for a moment if something had gone wrong. It was almost a religious experience; she felt as if she was at one with the universe as her consciousness became aware.

Automation was lagging behind human reaction. She'd heard about it happening, but never experienced it before.

Maybe an artifact of how long this insertion was?

Still no sign of Morosini, or of anything on her neural lace.

And that's *why I have my whole launch sequence hand-written on a knee-board.*

'Listen up!' she called, echoing the way Mpono had done it back at Sahel. 'Full launch! Ready?'

Hands went up raggedly, because people recovered consciousness as slowly as machines. But as soon as Nbaro had Tower and her catapults, she said, 'Go.'

A rattle of voices. She didn't need to do it all herself, any more. Dworkin, on Tower, said, 'Alpha Alpha 1–0–3, I have you good for launch.'

'Roger, Tower. Good for launch.'

Nbaro's acceleration couch vibrated very slightly as the enormous bulk of a drop-ship carrying tonnes of metal foil chaff and other tricks hurtled down the electromagnetic rails and into the void.

'One away,' said Evans, her understudy.

They had five craft out into space before Morosini suddenly came online. There was a burst of white noise on her neural lace and she lost several seconds, and then her 'extra senses', as she thought of them, began to register.

I need to talk to Morosini about this, she thought. *That was a long lag.*

Nbaro went straight to TAO. The Flight Six spaceframes were just coming off the front end; the TAO plot showed an empty system, but in their frame of reference, in-system for less than two minutes, they were sailing through the transmissions of past time.

The plot updated.

'Yikes,' someone muttered.

They were way out in the comet belt, and they were going *very* fast. At 0.4 *c*, give or take, relative to the star, they were right up against the constraints of slowing down.

Nbaro toggled back and forth in her mind, looking at sensors. The system was very much alive, or had been recently. There was in-system traffic: small local craft flitting from asteroid to asteroid, and a larger ship, possibly an ore freighter, forty hours out from Corfu Station. A traffic control beacon updated their in-system data using the standard DHC-wide format: x-, y- and z- axes, with the plane of the ecliptic defined as the x-axis, and a t tag on every location or ellipse to represent the time of last location. They were light minutes out from Corfu Station, so updates were slow.

But they were there.

She began to breathe more easily.

The Flight Six XC-3C spacecraft began to deploy their sensors, and suddenly the system began to register in higher definition. It was eerie to watch the information update; on the scale of a whole star system, the speed of light was a tactical reality.

Her launch rolled on. She wasn't the Tactical Action Officer – she didn't have to worry about the immediate reactions, just about launching her craft – and she rolled along, checking her AI-driven implant against the piece of paper clutched in her hand all the way to the end of the launch. It took just over eleven minutes and used all four railgun tubes.

'Forty-four away,' Evans said.

A few seconds ticked by, and Nbaro had just begun to frame

some words of congratulations when the Command net came to life.

'Nice launch, Lioness,' the Master said. 'The XO says they couldn't have done better.'

'Thank you, sir,' she said. 'We have a great crew down here in Ops.' She grinned, because she was speaking out loud and everyone could hear her. 'And lots of shiny new equipment.'

Just this once, I am not an idiot.

She stood up when Pisani was gone. 'Beautiful job, everyone,' she said. 'I believe we just set an *Athens* record for the timing and scale of launch.'

'Maybe a Service record,' Evans said.

'That'd be fun,' she admitted. 'Anyway, folks, thanks to each and every one of you. Now look sharp – we could still be in hostile space.'

She sat down again, and Evans came and stood by her. She didn't really know him, but he seemed decent enough; he was a long-servicer who'd started as an enlisted spacer and made his way into the officer ranks. A true veteran.

'We're going really fast,' he said very quietly.

Nbaro was going to make a snappy remark, but he really did outrank her by years, and anyway, she knew he was right.

'Dorcas?' she asked. She didn't do this often.

There was no delay. 'Good launch?' he sent.

She glowed. 'Everything worked,' she replied. 'You know how it can be.'

'I'm sure you had nothing to do with it. I imagine, as you are in near-combat conditions and quite busy, that this isn't a social call?'

'Can you tell if our velocity and acceleration are a problem?'

'Wait one,' he said.

She blinked. 'I would imagine...' she began, looking up at Evans, and Dorcas was back.

'No problem.' He tossed her a three-dimensional plot showing the *Athens* passing a gas giant, with the tendrils of hundreds of sorties of refuelling spacecraft diving into the planet's atmosphere like fingers reaching into a cloud, and then making a elliptical path down and around the star to return via a single pass at the second gas giant.

'Wow,' she sent.

'Yes. Beautiful, isn't it? Morosini plotted it.'

She returned to the real. 'As I was saying, I would imagine we'll refuel from the gas giants as we fly by. Morosini is plotting the course.'

Evans narrowed his eyes. 'You *know* that already?'

She shrugged. 'I have a neural lace.'

He didn't look pleased. 'Hardly fair to the rest of us,' he muttered. And then, 'Sorry. Nothing personal, Nbaro. But I hear rumours of cockpits designed for *laced* pilots, and so on. It doesn't seem ... fair, to us old-fashioned humans.'

I didn't ask for this thing.

She nodded, rising off her acceleration couch. 'I couldn't agree more,' she said. 'I think that, in my case, desperate times called for desperate measures ...' She looked at him. 'But I take your point. My squadron skipper has mentioned it a few times.'

Evans seemed taken aback by her agreement. 'Yeah ...' But then he said, 'Well, at least it's good to know that we're not going Dutchman at 0.4 *c*.'

Soon enough, they had a cycle of recovering the earliest launches and then another launch event. The *Athens* was on full alert, and wasn't changing that status until they had a much fuller picture of the system.

A little less than an hour later, the *Stealthy Change* arrived almost exactly at their extraction point. The PTX ship's own extraction was visible from all angles on the new passive systems deployed by various spacecraft, and she arrived almost exactly on predicted time and course. She was also a little above 0.4 c.

Two hours later, Nbaro was in the co-pilot's seat of 6–0–7, going through routine checklists as if she was still a normal midder and nothing had ever changed.

When they'd run the preflights, Truekner smiled at her. 'Well, Ms Nbaro, I must say it's nice to have you back.'

'Good to be back, skipper,' she said.

'You spoke to Patel?' he asked, as they were cranked into the railway and manoeuvred into their launch position.

'Oh, yeah,' she said. And then, after a moment, 'Sir.'

Truekner laughed. 'You are so salty, now, Nbaro!'

'Alpha Foxtrot 6–0–7, I have you as go for launch,' said a voice in her ear. It was a little redundant; on her neural lace, she could see her spacecraft's exact position on the rails, as well as her status in the launch cycle, and if she wanted, data on everything from fuel flow to hydraulic pressure. She didn't need Tower or Lioness…

Which, of course, was exactly what Evans was annoyed about.

'Earth to Nbaro. Are you there?' Truekner asked.

'Sorry, sir. Thinking about something from my last watch.'

'Something bad? Tell me about it.'

She toggled her mic. 'Tower, this is 6–0–7, we are go for launch.'

Truekner raised an eyebrow; Nbaro could see the twitch of his bushy, old-man eyebrows right through his golden mirror-visor.

But he turned, looked at the catapult operator, and saluted.

A few seconds later they burst out of the light and into the wonders of the void. She could hear the two sensor operators in the back end, comparing notes as they began to wrestle with the complexities of the pattern of detectors, and the world of spacetime according to their position in it.

All of which she could do with a glance, an eye-twitch and a sub-vocalisation.

Truekner surprised her by using thrusters to roll them right off the catapult, a fairly sudden acceleration out of the plane of their forward motion.

'We have a target area for six sensors,' he said.

Nbaro saw, ruefully, that she hadn't taken in the whole of the mission.

'Anyway, tell me your troubles, Lieutenant.'

She picked up the sensor drops, and passed them to the back end.

'It's about having a neural lace,' she said. 'It really is unfair.'

'Yep,' the skipper said. 'It really is.'

Ouch.

'You know I didn't choose to have it, right?' she said, more defensively than she'd meant.

Truekner chuckled. 'Honestly, Nbaro, one of the many mysteries surrounding you is how a penniless orphan got a neural lace.' He shrugged. 'But hey, no one needs to tell me anything.'

Then there was a busy twenty minutes as they laid new sensors into the pattern. Nbaro didn't need a neural lace to realise that they were laying a pattern to catch someone coming behind them, and not the *Stealthy Change*.

'Anyway, I was on watch with Lieutenant Evans, and he was ... annoyed ... that I could just communicate with Dorcas and learn ... stuff.'

'Like?'

'Like our plot for the next six weeks.'

'I wouldn't mind if you shared that with me, young lady.' Truekner sounded just a *little* sarcastic.

Nbaro pasted the 3D file into a message and tabbed it – or rather, she sent it to his tab from her head, via the ship, which caused a few seconds of lag.

'I imagine that eventually, every pilot will have a neural lace,' the skipper said. 'And ships will be very different. In fact, to be honest, I can imagine a world where there are very few humans on a ship at all.' He glanced at her. 'Which will suck, because it'll be lonely. Or maybe I'm just old-fashioned. But eight thousand people on a ship is a good-sized small town. It's pleasant. It keeps the absolute zero of the void at a psychological arm's length.'

'I hear that,' she agreed. 'I love it here.'

'I wonder if we can sell the DHC on the idea that ships need to be big and well populated to function,' he said. 'But, yeah, it's all about to change. The PTX tails, the change with the Starfish, the new aliens, the neural lace ... there's other new technologies coming up. Hell, we're inventing new stuff on this cruise.'

'The only constant is change,' Nbaro said, quoting from a manual.

'Exactly. Anyway, if people give you shit, be considerate to them, but tell me.'

I am considerate, and I never wanted this thing in my head.

When did I learn to be considerate, though?

The idea made her laugh a little.

'This is gold,' Truekner said.

'The plot?' she asked, meaning the astrogation plot that showed course and deceleration around the star.

'Forewarning of the plot. We're going to fly missions like there's no tomorrow. Almighty, Nbaro, I see three hundred sorties in forty hours here. Mostly for us.'

'Roger that, skipper.'

'You take her. I'm going to start writing the flight schedule.'

'Yes, sir.'

Eight hours later, the Tactical Action Officer declared the system safe, for a given value of safety. The navigation buoys were intact and transmitting, and the Master broadcast the greeting of Corfu Station over the whole ship.

'Welcome, *Athens*! A sight for sore eyes! Do you have cargo for us?'

And the Master's response: 'We have cargo for you, Corfu Station. And we plan a week alongside.'

'Well, that'll be *teleia*! *Ta leme*!'

'What language is that?' she asked Dorcas.

'Greek,' he answered. 'Corfu is mostly Old Greek and Southern Indian.'

13

Forty per cent of the speed of light was a hefty burden of speed and acceleration to shed before they could come alongside the station at Corfu, and everything about their cruise to date sufficed to keep them in a high state of readiness as they fell in-system, decelerating all the way. As the medbay was full of wounded, the Master and Morosini elected to decelerate only at rates consistent with their anti-gravity capabilities, making the process even slower. Morosini's projected route was an exercise in applied orbital mechanics that looked a little like a showy billiards shot. They would drop in-system, passing the sun well out from its gravity well, and then slingshot around the gas giant under heavy deceleration in controlled bursts until they were heading back in-system, making a second full rotation using the star's gravitational well. Finally they would slip into an orbit that would allow them to come alongside the station, which was a hollowed-out asteroid in the outer of the two asteroid belts.

'How many systems have two asteroid belts?' Nbaro asked via her lace.

'Do you imagine that I'm so bored that I can just look things up for you?' Dorcas sent back.

'And here I thought I was making small talk.'

'What you are making is busy-work.' He sent that with a neural-connected list of every system known by exploration or astronomy to have dual asteroid belts. There weren't many, but they still added up to more than a hundred.

'Why do you ask?' Dorcas sent.

Nbaro sent back an image of the decayed xenoglas she'd found at Trade Point. Dorcas was a smart boy. He'd understand what she was driving at. If the Hin and the Starfish were fighting a war, or had fought, or had annihilated a third race, or whatever the current theory was, then there'd be more evidence.

He sent her back a set of transmissions from the Corfu Station Society for the Furtherance of Science, which proved to be an amateur association of miners and engineers who had made a hobby of scientific exploration in their system, or perhaps had merely reported things that seemed unusual.

'Almighty,' Nbaro murmured as she read them.

'Makes you want to go look at it for yourself, does it not?' Dorcas sent.

She was reading an article that included a nicely shot vid and several good still photos of... *alien wreckage.*

It was on the outer asteroid belt – virtually the other side of the system from Corfu Station.

There was a long, narrow acceleration couch, with a miner in a deep-space exploration suit posing next to it.

'That's an acceleration couch,' she sent.

'Or just a bed,' he sent back.

The ruins were not extensive. What had appeared to be a small asteroid was a piece of... of something. *A building? A huge building? A ship?*

There were no bodies, and very little metal. Just the rubble of something built by sapient beings, and this couch, and four metal boxes, all manufactured, and all looking remarkably like boxes manufactured anywhere for use in space: airtight, with locking handles. Two of the four had markings on them. *Language? Brand names? A logo?*

'Astroarchaeology must be having a field day back in New London,' Nbaro said aloud. If Dorcas bothered, he could hear her. And she was alone in her stateroom, lying on her acceleration couch.

'If they even know yet,' Dorcas sent. 'You think real scientists read journals written by miners?'

'I think that the couch wouldn't fit a Starfish or a Bubble.'

'Intended for a being approximately two point five metres tall,' he replied.

'They were giants.'

14

They were still two weeks out from the nearer gas giant, decelerating as they ran through the system. With a stream of data pouring into the ship and hundreds of sensor packages littering the system, they'd achieved something like confidence that there was no ambush waiting, but they continued to fly a perimeter defence and a combat space patrol even as they ramped up their refuelling-capable shuttle capacity by refitting drop-ships. Nbaro stood her watches and flew, mostly short hops with her midshippers as co-pilots, training runs that also accomplished small tasks for the Maintenance shop. She also had multiple flights on the *Pericles*, which felt different; instead of flying a spaceframe, she was commanding a small ship. And she had boarding party drills, tactics classes, a special short course in material readiness – which was mostly about container stowage. She even managed to attend two of Yu's dance classes, as well as earning exciting new bruises in free-fall martial arts.

The evening that Han was released from medbay, Nbaro arranged for him to eat with her friends in the wardroom. Rick Hanna sat with Thea; Yu was leaning back, savouring a good cup of his own tea while chatting with Rudyard Singh Agam; they worked together, and Agam was there as a guest of Lieutenant Smith, who made a rare appearance from his hole on

Sixth Deck. He was even seen to laugh. Qaqqaq was lecturing midshipper Gorshokov on something, and Cortez sat with an officer from the data processing centre.

'Introduce us?' Drake said, leaning over Hanna.

Cortez smiled. 'Lieutenant Tereza Klipac,' he said, and then couldn't resist adding, 'Not in my chain of command.'

Tereza Klipac was a strong-faced woman with dark hair and square shoulders. 'Hmf,' she said, glancing at Cortez with something like disapproval. 'You are the famous midder,' she said to Nbaro.

'Hey, I'm also a famous midder,' Drake said.

Gorshokov muttered something about staying unnoticed.

'Klipac,' Cortez said, 'is a ship's system analyst.'

Nbaro smiled. It really was a good way to approach people. 'What does that mean?' she asked.

Klipac nodded, as if this was a sensible question. 'We keep the computers going, and we make sure that the data processing systems are intact.' She smiled at Nbaro. 'Morosini talks to you, and it shows up on my desk sometimes.'

Nbaro flushed. 'You mean...?'

Klipac's eyes widened a trifle, and Nbaro wondered if she'd looked very threatening.

'No, no, I can't see *what* you discuss.' Klipac laughed nervously. 'Only the data usage. When you were trapped on the Trade Point station, Morosini was using a tonne of wattage on you.'

Cortez glanced at her. 'So you already know Nbaro?'

Klipac glanced at him. 'No,' she said. 'Just an IP and a name.'

Nbaro was amused, because she was watching Cortez fail to be a good boyfriend. The ship's systems analyst didn't like being introduced as a sexual partner; who would? And the woman's reaction actually warmed Nbaro to her.

'Well,' she said confidingly, 'you know me now. This is the hero of the hour, though – Lieutenant Commander Han.'

188

'Fuju,' Han said, introducing himself. He grinned at Klipac and Cortez bristled.

Uh-oh. Nbaro really didn't need the evening to be spoiled by male posturing. She exchanged a glance with Drake, and Drake smiled and tried to avert it.

'Does Cortez ever stop talking about himself?' she asked.

Klipac laughed. 'These are your friends?'

Cortez had the good grace to grin back. 'I *think* they're my friends.'

Han began to lean forward to talk to Klipac, and Nbaro elbowed him.

'Ow,' he growled. He looked at her for a moment and she raised an eyebrow. *I hope I know you well enough...*

Han made a face as if he'd smelled something bad and sat back. 'Oh,' he said softly. 'I'm being a dick.'

'Just possibly,' Drake said. 'Sir.'

Han chuckled. 'Too long in the clamshell.'

Nbaro got him a slice of cake.

'Why are we getting liberty on Corfu?' Qaqqaq asked Hanna. 'I mean, last we heard, Pisani and Morosini were in a hell-fired hurry...'

Hanna shrugged. As an astrogator, he tended to know more about the ship's plot than anyone. Nbaro knew things through her lace and Dorcas, but she felt obliged to keep them to herself, even though she suspected that her skipper had shared her data with all the other squadron commanders.

The word *liberty* had an almost magical effect, as everyone at the big table fell silent. They'd been in space for more than eighty days, fought a battle, lost people. Everyone wanted a few hours ashore.

Hanna spread his hands as if to protest ignorance, then looked around and conceded a little. 'Look,' he said, in a conspiratorial tone, 'I don't know much. But I'm guessing we have more than three days' cargo to unload, and that's if Pisani allows us to go alongside and hook up. And we really need some stuff, right?' He looked at Drake.

Drake shrugged back. 'I'm in Cargo, not Logistics,' she said. 'Still…' She waggled her head. 'Still, I hear things. I hear we're so low on meat that we're getting tofu next week, and I know that I'm very close to running out of coffee to trade, which is bad. And good.' She smiled.

'Med supplies are low,' Yu said.

'I don't think Corfu Station is a place to get reliable med supplies,' Agam put in.

Hanna spread his hands again. 'My point is – we're getting some R and R because the ship needs three or four days alongside, not because Pisani or Morosini can spare the time.'

Cortez flexed his arms and cracked his knuckles. 'Lot of refuelling flights between here and there,' he said. 'All of us in Flight Five are getting refresher training on drop-ships. We're going to fly round the clock refuelling runs, just like you, Nbaro.'

'I'm trying to get my midders ready to fill spots in the flight schedule,' she said. 'Skipper says it's going to be wild.'

Thea looked at her. 'Well, my turn is coming,' she said. 'While you all drink your faces off, or whatever you do on shore leave, I'll be worked to the bone. We have a *lot* of cargo for the station, and most of it seems to be my problem.'

Hanna frowned. 'You'll get a day, surely?'

'I hate it when you call me Shirley,' Thea answered.

Nbaro choked on her after-dinner coffee. Even Klipac, who seemed a bit of a cold fish, laughed.

Hanna looked hurt. He could be a delicate flower, sometimes.

Thea relented. 'I might get a day off,' she said, 'but I'm trying not to count on it, and neither should you.'

'I've got to go and hit people with swords,' Nbaro said.

'Hey.' Han put a hand on her arm. 'We're taking the *Pericles* out tomorrow. My first time in command.'

Nbaro tried *very hard* not to react to the hand or the words. The *Pericles* was his, after all. She'd only been keeping the command seat warm.

I'm being an idiot.

She slipped away.

The flight with Han and Gorshokov, and two engineering techs working on their engines, was mostly uneventful. Han was already very good at the controls.

'You don't need me at all,' Nbaro said.

Han shot her a glance. 'All I had to do for three weeks was fly the simulator,' he said. 'I am a little puzzled about the vehicle log, though.'

She frowned. 'What?'

'You and Gorshokov have had her out six times and you've never signed her in or out.'

Nbaro smiled. 'Oh, I just put my signals straight through the neural lace, sir,' she said. 'I don't need to use this level of functionality.'

Han hesitated for a moment. 'Interesting,' he said. 'Um...' Long pause. 'Except, since I'm the commander, and I need to be able to see the records, I kinda need you to do the paperwork.'

She took that in, considered a snappy reply about how much digital paperwork she already had to do, and then settled for the correct answer. 'Yes, sir.'

'Shit, Nbaro, you don't have to call me "sir".' He shrugged. 'But I need to be able to file things...'

'Totally get it, sir,' she said. 'Fuju,' she added lamely.

He glanced over at her. 'Don't take it so fucking seriously, Nbaro. No biggie. The neural lace is probably a great thing. It's just that we poor mortals need to be able to see your work, so to speak.'

'Got it.'

He sighed.

'Can you use it to look at things like fuel flow?' he asked.

She decided to give him a full reply. 'I can use it to look into almost anything at sensor level. I can read the performance of the attitude thrusters at a very fine-grained level. I can make adjustments to fuel flow, I can change the lighting…'

Han laughed. 'What am I here for? It's me you don't need at all.'

She smiled. 'Command? Experience?'

Got that one right. The look on Han's face suggested that she'd hit the right tone.

They'd put the *Pericles* back in its dock; Han stayed aboard, talking to the engineering techs about weapons systems they may or may not ever receive, and Gorshokov went to the Intel shack to debrief. Nbaro had two hours before she was due to report to be Tower and planned to visit Dorcas…

Her tab flashed, and her sub-AI, said, 'The Master requests your presence in his briefing room in one hour.'

'Almighty,' she spat, and began to hurdle over the knee-knockers to get to her quarters. *Shower? Number one uniform?*

Thea was sitting at their desk, her head buried in columns of figures on the screen of her tab.

'I have to change,' Nbaro breathed.

'Whatever,' Drake said helpfully.

Nbaro chose her number one uniform, which was clean and pressed. She slipped down the passageway, showered and dashed back to her stateroom in a towel.

She then changed into her best shipboard uniform, and Thea never looked up or commented.

'I'm going to have sex with Petty Officer Locran,' Nbaro said.

'Sure,' Thea said.

'And then the Master.'

'Sure,' Thea said again.

Nbaro leaned over her friend and looked at the columns of figures without comprehension.

Thea looked up, probably because Nbaro's freshly showered warmth was getting through to her. 'We have to trade,' she said. 'Greatships don't usually stop here and we don't want empty holds, so we should be trading for something.'

Nbaro hadn't considered that aspect of trading. 'So? Metals?'

'Maybe,' Drake said. 'But what metals? And how much?' She frowned. 'Not much in high-value metals here anyway. Surprisingly little…'

'What are they mining here, then?'

'Cobalt, feldspar that they refine to potassium, lithium. There's traces of iron and copper, but never enough to mine.' Thea looked up. 'You're in your number ones.'

'Nothing gets past you, does it?' Nbaro smiled and relented. 'I have a meeting with the Master.'

Thea shrugged. 'Of course you do,' she said, and went back to work.

Nbaro had moved so fast that she was fifteen minutes early. But an automated servitor let her into the Master's briefing room. There was, as usual, a fire in the fireplace.

'I'll inform the Master that you are here,' said a disembodied voice.

She reached through her neural lace for Dorcas, and found…

Nothing.

She started, sitting up.

Morosini had appeared in a chair, with a cat in his lap. He wore a long scarlet coat, with a scarlet waistcoat, scarlet breeches with ribbons, scarlet stockings and small scarlet shoes. His face looked lined, and he was clearly wearing a full wig that fell in curls past his shoulders.

'*Ms Nbaro,*' he said. '*May we offer you wine? This will be a wine-drinking sort of meeting.*'

'Why can't I access…?' she paused. *Don't panic.* 'Anything?'

'*Ah. I have shut off your neural lace for a little while. Just for the duration of this meeting. I accept that you may tell Dorcas everything we say, but I'm not prepared for him to overhear it directly.*' Morosini smiled without pleasure or mirth.

How long does it take to build an AI that can render a smile of bitter self-knowledge? Nbaro asked herself.

'Very well,' she said. 'Red wine, please.'

'*Excellent.*' Morosini didn't do anything overt, like snap his fingers, but the servitor appeared with a tray and a glass of wine. She took it.

'*You are not on duty,*' Morosini said. '*This is not a test.*'

Nbaro drank. It was delicious.

'May I ask why I am here?' she asked.

Morosini smiled. '*I think we should wait for Vettor. He is coming.*'

'Thank you for entertaining Horatio. He is—'

'*He is very impatient to leave the confines of his medical restraints,*' Morosini said. '*I have come to suspect that even the pleasures of entering n-dimensional space fail to compare to the promise of your charms, Ms Nbaro.*'

She blushed, and grew angry at the same time. 'I'm not—'

Morosini raised a hand. '*I'm sorry, Ms Nbaro. I have created myself as a creature of a bygone age, and occasionally it leaks out. Although perhaps I might add that as the two of you are so obviously besotted with each other, it seems curious that one is not allowed to discuss it. Ah, here is Vettor.*'

Morosini rose to his holographic feet without disturbing his holographic cat. He was so well realised that Nbaro would have taken him for a real person in a real chair with a real cat.

Perhaps that was the reason for the outlandish clothes?

She stood at attention.

Vettor Pisani entered and smiled. 'At ease,' he said.

Morosini bowed and sat.

Nbaro nodded and sat.

Pisani made a motion and the servitor brought a glass of wine. 'Has Morosini told you why you are here?'

Morosini sounded hurt. *'I waited for you, Vettor.'*

'You mean, you want me to do the heavy lifting.'

'Is Dorcas…?' she blurted out.

They both looked surprised, and Pisani recovered first. 'Ah. Damn. Mr Dorcas is not at issue. He's doing well enough, although there's plenty left to worry about. We're not here to tell you about Mr Dorcas.'

Morosini twitched. *'He is improving,'* he said cautiously.

There was a pause. If Nbaro hadn't known that Morosini was an emotionless set of algorithms, she might have said it was a nervous pause.

'We're here because our Hin – our Bubbles – prisoner has asked for you to…' Morosini made a face, which was rare. *'To be her advocate. I think that is the clearest way to express it.'*

Nbaro looked at the Master, and then back at the hologram of Morosini. 'I don't understand.'

'You took the prisoner in single combat,' Morosini said. *'She has been clear that among her kind, this makes you, to some extent, responsible for her.'*

Nbaro thought about this for a moment and found that it made a strange sort of sense.

'And what have we learned from our prisoner of war?' she asked pointedly.

Morosini looked up, and the image really seemed as solid as another person. *'Too much and too little. The language is simple – that is, it is complex and nuanced, and our subject tells us that different factors change it every hour, but it is child's play compared to the Starfish language. But the Hin...'* The AI seemed to look out into space. *'The Hin are not a unity, or a polity. I think they are a species, but I cannot rule out that they are several species. I have translated the name of our captive as* Honourable Blood Wa-Kan Nik'ri Put, *but while the* Wa-Kan *is accurate, the title is...'* He shrugged. *'Perhaps a romantic attempt to anthropomorphise an enemy.'*

Nbaro wondered if an AI could be said to anthropomorphise anyone and decided that if anyone could, it was Morosini.

Morosini seemed to brush lint off his coat. *'The title is borrowed from medieval Korea, and denotes a certain relation to the royal family – close, but not too close.'* He shrugged again. *'The Hin, as they call themselves, seem to have royalty but no nations. They appear to have no polity greater than a sort of extended clan with family, dependents and slaves. Nik'ri Put is a successfully bred matron–warleader, if I understand her claims. She tells me she built her power armour herself, with her own tools.'*

'She speaks our language?' Nbaro asked. 'I mean, speaks it well?'

'Some Mandarin, some Anglatin, some Old Italian, some Old Standard English.' Morosini's eyes narrowed. *'Lately we have heard some Hindi. We can guess the Hin's contacts through the languages our prisoner seems to know.'*

Pisani steepled his hands. 'She doesn't know them very well...'

'But she's learning every day, even as Dorcas is learning her language – which, as I say, is child's play compared to the Starfish's.'

'Dorcas...?' Nbaro said, feeling foolish, and also perhaps angry.

Pisani looked at Morosini. 'Dorcas is sworn to absolute secrecy, Ms Nbaro. And he has begged that you be read in on these projects because he dislikes misinforming you. So I'll ride to his rescue and tell you that, while he may have whiled away a few hours visiting Morosini's jungle of *n*-dimensional shapes in VR, he's mostly absorbed in the Starfish and Hin languages, and has been for weeks.'

'Of course he has.' Nbaro wasn't quite sure how she felt about this.

We can talk to the Bubbles? How's it going, having a Starfish – a living, breathing one – all to yourself? What's it like, being the lone ammonia-breather trapped on an oxygen-breather ship, light years from your own kind? How did that even happen?

Pisani leaned forward. 'Lieutenant Nbaro, let me be plain. I miss having you on my Command Council. I think you are lucky, and to be honest, I suspect you are destined to hold a chair like mine. You and Mr Dorcas have developed a perfectly legitimate relationship that biases him in favour of your participation in certain high-level programmes. And now our prisoner has asked for you.' He leaned back. 'So, I am asking you to accept some extra duties and a fair amount of security briefing in exchange for working directly with Morosini and Dorcas.'

Morosini turned to Nbaro and raised a hand, a clear sign for caution. *'Ms Nbaro, I am not entirely in favour of this step, at least in part because it has been represented to me that at this point in your career, you need to become fully proficient with the routine tasks of being a junior officer. This particular programme will interfere with everything that is routine in your life, and we may have to hold you back from combat missions because—'*

'Because once you are fully briefed,' Pisani broke in, 'we cannot let you fall into the hands of any of our rivals.'

Honestly, I'm tired. I'm twenty years old, and I'm not sure I can handle this decision on my own. Why the hell don't you two just give me an order?

Nbaro drank off her wine. 'I'm not sure that...' She took a deep breath. 'That knowing that my prisoner wants me, and knowing that she can speak and be spoken to, that I could just go about my duties,' she said. 'This isn't a routine cruise, is it, sir?'

Pisani smiled grimly. 'It most certainly is not,' he allowed.

'As to getting captured ...' She looked at Morosini. 'It really doesn't seem very likely, does it?'

Morosini flexed his eyebrows. *'It is a very, very small possibility.'*

Nbaro shrugged. 'I'm prepared to accept,' she said. 'I don't need much sleep.' And then, as her brain began to engage with the information she'd just received, 'Hindi and Old Standard English means Anti-spinward.'

'New India, New Bengal and New Texas,' Morosini said. *'Particularly New Texas.'*

'That's only fifteen insertions from home,' Nbaro said. 'It takes time to learn languages.'

'And that makes it seem likely that this has been going on a long time,' Morosini said, *'and that, as accused, the Anti-spinward colonies have gone their own way with their own aliens. The Hin, to be precise.'*

'And you're not surprised.' Again, it just came out of her. Nbaro was aware that she couldn't read an AI. Any visual cues it gave were a performance, not a reality. But there was something there: Morosini wasn't surprised.

The AI steeped his long – almost skeletal – fingers, his elbows resting on the arms of his gothic chair, forming a cage around the big cat. *'Very astute.'* He actually seemed uncomfortable.

Pisani glanced at his AI. And then at Nbaro. 'What do you mean, Lieutenant?'

She frowned. 'I'm not sure, except that Morosini seems almost comfortable with the idea that the Hin are in contact with the Anti-spinward colonies.'

Pisani raised an eyebrow.

Morosini smiled at her. *'Eventually, you and I will have a lengthy conversation on a number of topics. I am aware that you remain uncomfortable with the neural lace I forced upon you. I realise that we have some issues to discuss. I am asking you to let all that go during the current emergency.'*

Pisani said, 'Morosini, did you know about the Hin before we left New London?' His voice held the snap of authority that it seldom did when he spoke to the AI.

Morosini patted his cat and looked up. '*No,*' he said. '*I and others of my kind were increasingly aware of the sabre-rattling of the Fringe states, especially New Texas. And we were aware that* someone *had probably made contact with aliens. Some suspected a new contact with the Starfish, only no new source of xenoglas appeared.*' He shrugged. '*So, yes, I was, and remain, unsurprised by this development. But I* am *surprised by the reach and power of these new aliens.*' He looked at Nbaro. '*We live in interesting times.*'

Her voice so low it sounded like a growl, Nbaro said, 'And you don't want to tell me why I have a neural lace?' Just asking the question frightened her.

Morosini met her eyes. It was easy for him; he was a machine. '*Not just yet,*' he said.

'Begging your pardon,' Nbaro said to the Master, 'but what if I just demanded to know?'

Pisani nodded to her. It was encouraging, she thought, and it helped fight a tide of old feelings that threatened to drown her in distrust. *I'm here, at this table. They trust me. Get over it, girl.*

Morosini's expression didn't change. '*If you insist, I will tell you right now,*' he said. '*Without prevarication.*'

Nbaro was thinking about that. The Master was silent.

Her tab flashed and she jumped. 'I'm Tower in ten minutes,' she said. 'Sir.'

Morosini shook his head. '*I need more than ten minutes to discuss the matter with you.*'

How convenient.

'Very well,' she said, perfectly aware that she wanted to hide from whatever he was going to tell her, probably as much as he didn't want to tell her.

'But you agree to this additional duty?' Pisani said.

'Yes, sir,' she answered.

They all stood.

Pisani shook her hand. 'You're a good one, Nbaro, and when you are master of a greatship, I pray you tell people about this cruise with pride.' His smile was warm.

Nbaro's neural lace came back up.

Morosini said, '*Please visit Lieutenant Smith in the Special Services office to be read in to the necessary programmes, and please make time to visit the prisoner as soon as possible thereafter.*'

She nodded. 'Yes, sir.'

Morosini smiled. '*I think you have four minutes to get to the Space Operations Centre.*'

'Oh,' Pisani said. 'I have listed you to start training as a Tactical Action Officer.'

For some reason, both of them found that amusing as she fled.

15

Nbaro stood her watch, and then trained her boarding parties and collapsed into her rack before she thought about any of it again. *We can talk to one of the aliens.*

Morosini doesn't want to tell me why I have a neural lace. That suggested that it isn't as simple as 'he didn't trust me, so he put me under total surveillance.' Which led to a bewildering snowstorm of ideas ...

She slept, had terrible dreams, and woke feeling as if she'd never been to sleep. Despite that, she managed to take the *Pericles* on a short hop to check an upgrade to a cold fuel thruster nozzle set – the thrusters wouldn't show up on Infrared, an incredible combat advantage. All of their spaceframes were receiving them. She had no idea where they'd come from or who built them.

Interesting times indeed.

After her short flight, she had six hours to herself. She got rid of her flight gear and dropped down a shaft to Sixth Deck. She was trying to decide how long she'd been aboard in subjective ship's time. Thirteen insertions? Twenty-three months? She had spent a fair amount of time in both acceleration and deceleration after insertions, and they'd been almost two months at Trade Point ...

It seemed like an eternity. Every experience of her life before boarding the *Athens* was falling away, sucked into the past as if crossing an event horizon. The Orphanage, the lodestone of her life, was now... far behind her.

That felt good.

So what if Morosini felt he needed to put a neural lace in her?

I have this now. And this is what I wanted.

Right?

She'd certainly learned to use a drop-shaft, since she'd just leapt straight to Sixth Deck from the O-2 level without thinking about it. She snorted, landed, and pulled herself through the hatch. She lacked Locran's grace or the eel-like proficiency of some of the station-born spacers, but she was getting it.

The passageway itself was full of memories; the laundry, the machine shop, the hold where Chief Dornau's body had been found and later, where they'd tracked down the spy.

And *this* was where she'd seen some sort of mammal go over the knee-knocker...

Locran assured her there were rats, among other flora and fauna.

Out among the stars, with rats.

Nbaro almost walked past the Special Services shack. But she stopped and knocked, and Smith's voice said, 'Enter.'

She was almost expecting Dorcas.

Instead, there was a beautiful smell of coffee, and Lieutenant Smith.

'I was expecting you,' he said simply, and managed a smile.

'I'm here to sign off on something that you'll kill me for disclosing,' she said.

'I'm glad you understand.' She wondered if that wasn't the most chilling possible response.

Smith instructed Nbaro to read the non-disclosure agreement in its entirety, and then he explained the financial and criminal penalties that she would incur if she were to disclose even the existence of such secrets.

'Honestly,' she said. 'who would I tell?'

'Thea Drake,' Smith said. 'Qaqqaq, Cortez, Yu ... You have quite a few friends.'

Nbaro sighed and affixed her thumbprint, digitally.

Smith smiled tightly. 'See?' he said. 'Now you and Dorcas can chat about work. Just to be clear, Ms Nbaro ... Dorcas, the Master, Major Darkstar and Morisini. And me. That's it, for now.'

In fact, Nbaro hadn't left the Sixth Deck passageway before Dorcas contacted her by lace.

'I see you are read in,' he sent.

'Not that I read anything or now know anything.'

'Yes. It's all in my head, so to speak. I suppose that eventually there will be some sort of report.' In their own created VR space in the dataspace of the neural lace, Dorcas sounded more like himself, and that made her happy.

'I don't think the DHC would survive without written reports.' Nbaro was laughing, and a passing junior spacer looked at her with interest and some concern.

'Can you go visit Nik'ri Put?' Dorcas asked. 'She really is asking for you.'

'Who needs sleep?' Nbaro sent, and headed up the drop-shaft to Third Deck. Third Deck had a number of useful spaces: the ship's store, which still sold a few valuable luxuries like chocolate, even after two years in space; the main medbay, still nearly full of casualties from the battle at Trade Point; and the two spaces that Major Darkstar had converted to holding cells. Early in their cruise, they'd held a saboteur and a spy; now they had a Hin warrior and a Starfish. The spy had been handed over to the PTX, in the person of Captain Jiang Shunfu of the *Stealthy Change*. Darkstar had ascertained that the man had been a captain or major in the PTX marines. Shunfu had made it clear that getting the man back had been important to his position.

Nbaro thought about these things. It was odd, in a way, that she could go days in what she thought of as the shipboard fugue, simply *being* – flying, training, standing watches, taking classes – and then, *boom*... She'd start thinking about all of this.

The PTX definitely had fingers in the alien pie, so to speak.

And yet, their own DHC traitors had also been involved: people with ties to great families inside the DHC.

Nbaro couldn't understand why. *What kind of person would sell out their own species to aliens?*

Except that the Orphanage had taught her that selfish, greedy people didn't even need a rationale to commit evil. They could do it automatically, while eating a sandwich.

She pressed the switch on the intercom mounted on the hatch frame.

'Palm print,' said a voice.

She located the palm print plate and placed her bare hand on it.

'Retinal scan,' the voice said.

A light shone out from an aperture above the palm plate. She looked into it, which was unpleasant.

The hatch clicked. She pushed it open. 'Lieutenant Nbaro,' she said.

She knew the Marine on the duty station immediately. 'McDonald,' she said.

'Yes, ma'am.' He sounded cheerful. He'd lost a foot in the fighting at Trade Point, and he had a regrowth cell on his leg. He was half-reclined on an acceleration couch, but correctly uniformed. 'Gunny Drun said I was fit for light duty. This beats the shit out of medbay.'

Nbaro nodded.

'Hand receipt for entry and exit,' he said. 'I'm sorry, ma'am, but I have to take your sidearm.'

She'd forgotten the little flechette gun. She took it from the concealed holster and handed it over.

He smiled. 'I was hoping you'd come down on my watch, ma'am.'

'You knew I was coming?' she said. He seemed very young, which was funny, as they were almost certainly the same age.

'Word came down about two hours ago,' he said. 'Major Darkstar is in there now.'

Nbaro nodded. 'Thanks, McDonald.'

'You could call me "corporal",' he said. 'If you had a mind to.' He waved at his shoulder.

'Damn,' she said. 'Apologies, Corporal! You got promoted.'

'Just cost me a foot.' Then he smiled. 'I need to stop saying that 'cause it ain't true. I passed my tests before Trade Point.'

And a few more tests while we were there.

'Congratulations, Corporal,' she said.

'Ah, you'll want these, ma'am.' He handed her a pair of infrared goggles.

'Thanks,' she said. And then, with a wave, she pushed through the next hatch.

Inside, it was dark. She pulled the goggles down and was able to see heat signatures. Major Darkstar was tall and thin, and the alien . . .

The alien shone in the darkness because it was in a heated water tank. But Nbaro's goggles were excellent quality, and they read different heat sources as colours. The alien was perhaps two metres long: a sort of octopus, except that she had more than eight tentacles, and two of them were very long indeed, curled at her feet like the hair of a princess. She had large, well-spaced mammalian eyes that would not have been out of place on many

Earth creatures. Even in infrared, Nbaro could see that she was covered in fur.

The alien had been still as she entered, but now she turned in her tank, her tentacles seeming to spasm as she moved, her large eyes now looking at Nbaro.

Major Darkstar leaned back. 'Lieutenant Nbaro. Your *Ke-po-ja.*'

'Yesss,' the alien hissed. Her voice was rich and low, and came from a speaker mounted over the tank. The new aliens were oxygen-breathers. She was in a water tank. Nbaro could access this kind of information now, and go through it freely.

It spoke to me. She *spoke to me.*

'Hello,' Nbaro said. 'I hope that you are recovering from our combat.'

She'd planned that little speech on her way down.

'*KePoja,*' the alien said. 'I am well.' Her accent was tricky: sibilant and mushy. 'You do me honour, *KePoja.* Blessings on you, that you come.' And then, after a pause that indicated that the foregoing might have been a carefully researched speech, she said, 'Where you be? I wait.'

Nbaro looked at Darkstar and wished the major had a neural lace.

'Dorcas?'

'Right here,' he said. 'Tell her whatever you please.'

Nbaro looked into those big brown eyes and ignored the tentacles. 'I have many duties,' she said.

A little flutter of tentacles. 'You here now. Dahkstah also here. It is well.' She fluttered her tentacles again, and the motion moved her up her tank.

'How is your food?' Nbaro asked.

Dorcas sent, 'Good question. She is very reticent about eating and matters to do with eating.'

Another flutter. 'Food is dead.'

Darkstar thumbed a switch. 'When this is off, she cannot hear us. We have established that she prefers live food, and her preferred food is some sort of fish analogue, but we don't run to live fish. So far, she's getting canned Sahel mackerel, because that's what we have.'

Nbaro stepped right up to the glass of the tank. She noted that the alien's tank was not made of xenoglas. *Interesting*.

'How can I help you?' she asked. 'And what shall I call you?'

The alien moved a little, and the speaker said, 'Call, call, call, call…'

Dorcas spoke. It hadn't occurred to Nbaro that he could use the room's microphones as speakers, but of course he could. It was all just digital manipulation.

'You *call* them Darkstar. You *call* me Dorcas. I *call* you Wa-Kan Nik'ri Put.' Then, as if his mouth was full of sand, he said what sounded like *angsyn-e moulander puteneo*.

'*Ta!*' the alien said. '*Ta!* You *call* me *Tse-Tsu*. It is right!'

'Damn it, I thought we had isolated her name.'

'I call you *Tse-Tsu*.'

'It is right! And also yes!' the alien said, and bubbles flowed around her head.

'I'm almost certain that the flow of bubbles is a visual cue analogous to laughter,' Dorcas said.

'I miss you,' Nbaro said.

'Oh, Nbaro, you have no idea,' Dorcas said inside her head.

'You call me Nbaro,' she said, trying to focus on the alien in front of her.

'No, no, this not right! Call you *KePoja*.'

'Ah,' Dorcas sent. 'I'm saved. It's some sort of ceremonial address. She is your prisoner, and you are her captor. *Tse-Tsu* has something of honour in it. Sixty-two per cent likely.'

Nbaro blinked. The alien was now squashed against the top of her tank, taking up half the volume she had a moment before.

'I am *KePoja* and you are *Tse-Tsu*,' Nbaro said.

'It is right, and very much yes,' the alien said.

Suddenly she was floating in front of Nbaro, a dozen centimetres from her face, all sleek fur and tentacles. Nbaro couldn't decide whether the alien was beautiful or horrible. It was certainly easier to look at than a Starfish. It had eyes. And fur.

And quite a few slimy black tentacles.

'The slime is a pre-digestive. There's reasons she doesn't want us to watch her eat. I think among the Hin, eating is a private as excretion or ...'

Nbaro smiled. 'Or sex?'

'I'm really, really trying not to think about sex,' Dorcas said.

'It is right, and very much yes,' she sent back.

The Hin flourished her tentacles, demanding attention. 'You trade me, yes?' she asked. 'This is *Ke-Mye-Ong*. And also *Hin*.'

'How do I answer that?'

'No idea. Wait. There's the *Ke* prefix again – something about honour. Tell her we're not near any of her kind. No. Tell her ...'

Nbaro shrugged. 'I don't know, *Tse-Tsu*,' she said. 'I'm not a very important officer.'

'*Ta*,' the alien said. 'Great warrior, you.' She flicked her two longest tentacles in an elegant gesture that, to Nbaro, felt like a dismissal, either of the subject or of Nbaro herself. 'You take me! So great warrior.'

Nbaro flushed. *I'm an idiot* came to mind, but instead she said, 'I'm not an important officer. I am junior.'

They spent quite a bit of time on the concept of command authority and a junior officer. Dorcas tried various sallies in the Hin language, and eventually, something like understanding was reached.

Nik'ri Put said, 'Ah! Understand, *KePoja*. I am also *junior*. Some *command* me. This is a right thought, and yes.'

Nbaro's head was spinning; she'd never thought of a conversation as so much work – nor concepts like 'junior' and 'command' as so complicated.

'Me tired now,' the alien said.

Nbaro smiled. 'Me too,' she agreed.

Outside the containment chamber, Major Darkstar met her, tab in hand.

'Not bad at all,' they said. 'That felt like a peer-to-peer interaction. She asked to meet you so that you could arrange her trade. I don't want to read too much into this, but that suggests some conventions of war.'

'That's what I heard,' Nbaro agreed. 'Real Age of Chaos stuff. These are not armed merchants.'

Darkstar looked at her. 'No,' they said. 'So far, everything she says indicates that the Hin are aggressive and predatory. Luckily for the rest of us, they seem to fight among themselves as well as against...' They looked up. '...us.'

'And the Starfish. How's our defector, tir?'

Darkstar's thin lips grew, if anything, thinner. 'I'm not at liberty to discuss the other alien.'

'I'm read in, tir,' Nbaro said.

Darkstar just looked at her. Darkstar had a particularly withering stare, as if a career in the DHC Marines had perfected their powers of destroying lesser beings by eye contact alone.

'Yes, tir.' Now Nbaro wanted to salute.

She signed out, and returned to her normal duties.

Nbaro's life was now as constrained as was possible; Sabina, her sub-AI, seemed to control every aspect of her life. Some aspects of the discipline of the Orphanage made a terrible sort of sense as Nbaro – an officer – marched through days of thoroughly scheduled time: she had training flights with her midders;

she had two boarding parties to train; she was involved in interactions with the Hin; she had watches to stand; and she still
needed to exercise and take qualification classes. Four dayside
rotations into the Corfu System, she stood her first 'in-training'
watch in the Combat Information Centre, whose ruling god was
the Tactical Action Officer. While Space Operations launched
and recovered spacecraft, and was at least nominally responsible
for every activity outside the hull, the TAO was responsible for
a wide variety of threat assessments and decisions, in and out of
combat. It only took one watch, sitting at an empty engineering repeater station, to learn that the TAO was functionally in
command of the ship. There were dozens of exceptions, and
many areas in which the Master, or Morosini, were assumed
to be in charge, or were consulted. Nbaro only took one watch
to understand why the terrorists who'd attacked them at Sahel
had struck the TAO first, and if she'd ever needed evidence of
the thoroughness of their understanding of some aspects of the
ship's command architecture, that was it.

She found the TAO's breadth of knowledge intimidating,
but she also knew that Mpono and Dworkin were both qualified TAOs, as well as a crowd of officers she didn't know well:
Lieutenant Commander Gavin Graeme from Engineering,
whom she'd met with Qaqqaq, and Lieutenant Commander Lisa
Corbett, who knew Drake and her brothers, and who came from
one of the many patrician – but poor – families who made up
the core of the Service.

Corbett was Nbaro's training officer. In her first training
watch, Corbett was busy from beginning to end; she spoke to
Nbaro once, to point out where she could find the sim for the
Combat Information Centre, and then went back to work.

As they were coming off watch, Corbett made a clucking
sound.

'Sorry, Nbaro. This is a rough cruise to train on, but I guess you know that better than most.' She smiled a little. 'I'll try and clear some space for you next watch.'

Nbaro walked aft to get a meal, pondering the wonders of the neural lace. In fact, she had followed almost every action that Corbett had performed, because she could watch her interactions with data in real time, and even replay them. As her facility grew, so did her speed; she had a long way to go to match the sorcery that Dorcas could perform, but she was beginning to use the lace fluidly, without too much concentration or conscious direction.

I'm going to be able to handle a lot more data flow than most TAOs, she thought.

'*Yes, you are,*' Morosini said. '*I am the one who wants you to be a TAO. Your commanding officer is not sure you are ready, but you have a neural lace. In many ways, you could conduct combat operations from your acceleration couch in your stateroom.*'

'I'm not feeling as if my thoughts are particularly private,' she sent.

'*In fact, you are in the net and you broadcast your thoughts. Only Dorcas and the Master and I can hear you.*' Morosini didn't sound smug, but then, Nbaro was never sure that 'how' he 'sounded' in dataspace was anything that she could rely on.

'You want me to be a TAO soon?' she asked. 'No way. There's far too much to learn.'

'*Yes,*' Morosini agreed. And he was gone.

16

In the hangar bay, spaceframes were being completed.

In the passageways, boarding parties and damage control teams were being trained.

In the command spaces, courses were being plotted and perfected, and risks assessed, and in the Intelligence spaces, data was being evaluated and analysed and passed to those who might use it. Engineering had completed the battle-damage repairs and restarted the damaged reactor. Nbaro spent a back-breaking seven hours replacing antennas on the hull.

She attended her first Command Council meeting since the Battle of Trade Point. The meetings were held in the Master's beautiful briefing room, under the landscape painting that hung over a fireplace. Nbaro wasn't clear exactly why she was there, but the coffee was good and so was the company. Mpono was now acting captain, the executive officer of the ship, and Nbaro realised that this meant Mpono would almost certainly command their own greatship, and soon. The Master, Vettor Pisani, sat at the head of the table; the chief of Astrogation, Captain Fraser, sat by Mpono – his spouse, and now his boss – and Commander Tremaine, who was acting as the space wing commander. Captain Dukas, chief of Engineering, sat by Lieutenant Smith, head of Special Services. Lieutenant Lochiel, Senior Intelligence

Officer, sat by Nbaro, as if for junior officers there was safety in numbers. Captain Hughes, the head of Cargo, sat at the far end of the table, with Major Darkstar – representing the Marine contingent – and Morosini. Dorcas was present via neural link.

The captains chatted easily, and the junior officers sat quietly. Lochiel dared to smile at Nbaro, who willed herself to smile back. He appeared to be ineffectual, with a tendency to inappropriate humour, but Locran swore he was a good boss so Nbaro was prepared to like him.

Pisani called the meeting to order after coffee was served. 'Comrades,' he said, 'we are as ready to fight as we're ever going to be.'

Nbaro, who was fully expecting a fight, nonetheless sat a little straighter and glanced at Lochiel, who stared straight ahead, his usually cheerful face stony.

Dukas nodded. 'She's as solid as the day we sailed. Better, in many of the command spaces. The engines are solid. We're past halfway through cruise and I'm …' She grinned. '…I'm confident that we're ready in Engineering.'

Fraser waited his turn. 'I'm less confident,' he said. 'I believe that Morosini has unofficially suggested that the likelihood of a military encounter will rise with each system we reach.'

'*That is an excellent synopsis,*' Morosini purred. '*Peaking at Ultra–Medulla.*'

Fraser looked at the Master. 'Every system we enter in full combat readiness costs us time. I believe that the Master and Morosini would prefer our insertions to exit below the plane of the ecliptic, well out from the star. Given the reality of gravitational interactions with Artifact Space, that will tend to cause our exit velocity to be higher, as you saw here at Corfu, with correspondingly long deceleration times before we can refuel or re-insert.'

Everyone nodded. Nbaro found herself nodding, too, even

though this aspect of insertion was completely new to her. No one had ever suggested to her that gravity had anything to do with Artifact Space.

'It was a new theory when we left New London,' Dorcas said inside her head. 'Captain Fraser has been utilising aspects of it all cruise, with the somewhat spectacular results we've seen. In effect, gravity waves seem to defy spacetime, or at least affect spacetime, even when you are utilising aspects of unrealised proto-reality.'

'You just make this stuff up to woo me, don't you?' she asked.

'Oh, no! Far from it…' A pause. 'You are mocking me?'

'Possibly,' she agreed.

Fraser went on, 'We're ahead of our course plot so far, but too many high c insertions could delay us by months.' He looked unhappy. 'In effect, comrades, we're exchanging combat advantage for trading time.'

Morosini seemed to lean forward. *'This is an excellent point,'* he said softly. *'As far as New London knows, we are destroyed, or missing, like the* Dubai *and the* New York. *The longer we are out here, the worse it is for the DHC, and for everything from markets to individual workers.'*

Lochiel looked up. 'On the other hand, sir, when we return, it will be to say that Trade Point is destroyed.'

Morosini waved a hand. *'We can rebuild Trade Point—'*

Pisani interrupted the AI. 'We're not all as rational as you. Markets will be deeply disturbed by the destruction of Trade Point, and the price of xenoglas may go ballistic.'

Captain Hughes looked around. 'On balance, based on my experience in these matters, the return of a greatship with full holds will outplay the somewhat hazy concept of an interruption in trade in the short run. But in the long run…'

Morosini raised an eyebrow, and Nbaro went on alert.

'We don't even know if the DHC sent another greatship after us,'

he said. '*It's extremely likely that the* Samarkand *was held pending our return. So there's no ship headed for Trade Point now.*'

Nbaro noted this. It was almost undetectable, but Morosini would say things that hinted at greater knowledge. It sounded patronising, and yet...

Pisani stood again, ending the conversation. 'I know I started this,' he said. 'I'm focused on surviving one crisis at a time and then worrying about the next one. Captain Fraser, we fully understand the complexities of your position vis-à-vis the long-term course plot, and we accept any delays caused. For reasons that I cannot disclose, every system we enter towards home makes it more likely that we will win an engagement. Out here, we must exercise every caution to avoid ambush and an engagement which Morosini and Lieutenant Lochiel's best estimates tell us, we lose every time.'

Lochiel nodded. 'At Trade Point, we ambushed them,' he said. 'And we were supported by the Starfish.'

Morosini spoke up again. '*To be precise, the Starfish fought the Hin, and we also fought the Hin, but at no point could any action by the Starfish be said to have supported us, and I believe that no one was more surprised than the Starfish by our victory.*'

Nbaro looked around in the ensuing silence. No one looked happy.

'*The Hin,*' Morosini went on, '*are a predatory and militaristic race. They have excellent ships and energy shields that are almost beyond our imagining. On the other hand, they seem to be deeply factionalised. Put bluntly, they fight among themselves. The Starfish, on the other hand, appear to be monolithic in their approaches to other races, but—*'

Whatever Morosini was about to say, Dorcas spoke over the AI. His voice came through speakers on the wall.

'The Starfish have committed genocide in the past, against the race we call the Circles,' he said. 'Their paranoia about us is only balanced by their desperation for heavy minerals. And there is some key to the xenoglas—'

Morosini cut him off. '*This is not for everyone to know, my friend.*'

'I disagree,' Dorcas said. 'I believe we all need to know.'

Pisani leaned back. 'Mister Dorcas, I believe we have spoken before about your interruption of senior officers in briefings.'

Dorcas didn't sound contrite. 'Yes, sir.'

Pisani's face twitched in what might have been a moment of amusement. Then he looked at Morosini. 'But I think everyone does need to know.'

Morosini raised a hand. '*If you tell this many people, that means that the secret will be out by the time we reach a port. With all the consequences of panic and disruption we have discussed.*'

'I hear you,' Pisani said. 'So, folks, I need you to understand that what you are about to hear is at the very highest level of secrecy. All of you will sign a new non-disclosure agreement, and by God, friends, you *will* keep this secret. Our civilisation is at stake. This secret must be kept, until we master it. Am I understood?'

Nbaro wasn't the only one looking around. But she chorused 'Yes, sir' with the rest.

'Very well,' Pisani said.

Morosini spread his hands, and then, when Tom, his cat, complained, he patted the big feline. '*Very well, Vettor,*' he said.

Pisani waved. 'Dorcas, continue.'

'Yes, sir,' Dorcas said. 'There is a key, whether chemical or energy, that allows for the rapid decay of the xenoglas into a substance which is much weaker. In effect, the Starfish can turn it off.'

Only Nbaro had heard this before, from Dorcas, although not stated quite so directly.

Hughes said, 'Jesus Christ.' It was the only sound in the briefing room.

Dukas was pale. Her left hand moved, clenching and unclenching as if in pain.

'Our ship would be destroyed,' she said. 'We have xenoglas everywhere.'

Dorcas spoke up again. 'With respect, ma'am, these ships were built before contact with the Starfish. We can restore them to pre-contact—'

Dukas cut him off. 'I doubt it, Mister Dorcas. But thanks for telling me how my ship works.' And then, in a gentler voice, she said, 'Most of the engine room is xenoglas now. The reactors, the lighting systems, parts of the Hangar Deck...'

Morosini spoke up. '*Luckily*,' he said with emphasis, '*we think it extremely unlikely that the Starfish will desire conflict with us in the near future.*'

Lieutenant Lochiel looked miserable.

Pisani noticed. 'Intel, you don't agree?'

Lochiel shrugged. 'We don't understand much that the Starfish do,' he said. 'But we have signals analysis on their comms during and after our engagement with the Hin at Trade Point, and then all subsequent actions through their departure.' He made a face. 'If signal volume is the same kind of indicator for the Starfish as it is for humans, they were shocked by our total defeat of the Hin the first time, and fled rather than face the consequences the second time.'

'Which is to say, perhaps they already fear us,' Dorcas said.

Pisani raised an eyebrow. 'But they fear the Hin more?'

Lochiel sighed. 'Sir, we're talking about aliens here.'

Morosini nodded. '*It is Lieutenant Lochiel's duty to look at the worst case*,' he said. '*I see it differently. Trade Point is now compromised – the Hin know where it is. The Starfish abandoned it, even collecting their populations on the moons as they left. They expected us to provide them with a rearguard defence and may even have been pleasantly surprised that we were victorious – or they left us to our fate because they don't care.'* He smiled a cold smile. *'But I predict that the next greatship to travel that way will meet a trade delegation, ready to make a deal.'*

Hughes was seen to cross himself.

Dukas spoke up. 'It's almost an open secret in portions of Engineering that we have a Starfish aboard.'

Pisani sighed.

Dukas persevered. 'It must have defected. Or it was left behind? Is it an ambassador?'

Morosini looked up and down the table. *'A starship is a Stone Age village,'* he said. *'Very well. We have a Starfish aboard. It appears to have defected.'*

'So the Starfish also have factions,' Dukas said.

Lochiel looked as if he was going to faint.

Dorcas's voice came through the speakers. 'May I speak, sir?'

Pisani looked as if he was in physical pain. He raised his eyes to the ceiling, as if looking for strength, while Morosini gave a shrug and went back to petting his cat.

'Please, Mister Dorcas.'

'The Starfish we call Feather Dancer came aboard of its own will, so the term *defector* may be accurate. Morosini and I have made progress with its language, but unlike Hin, the Starfish language is not even *conceptually* like our own. Most importantly, it has two brains and often speaks two thoughts in harmony, or even in negation.'

Nbaro realised that Qaqqaq must have been working with Dorcas all this time and not telling her, because, of course, this was all compartmented for secrecy. She frowned.

So many secrets.

Dorcas continued, 'But as best we can ascertain, Feather Dancer is a member of a sub-race considered inferior by other

Starfish. Or Feather Dancer itself is considered inferior.' Lochiel looked at Nbaro, as if it was all her fault.

'So, not an ambassador.' Pisani sounded as if he didn't already know this, and he was looking at Morosini.

Morosini smiled. *'No. Not an ambassador. We are still unsure what would drive a sentient organism to leave its own kind and its whole world to live, perhaps forever, in a hostile environment with aliens like ourselves, but we posit that it can't be good. We represented the better alternative.'*

'Jesus,' muttered Hughes. 'Can you picture it? Running off to join the Hin or the Starfish?'

No one else was saying it, so Nbaro spoke. 'Someone did, though.'

Everyone looked at her, which doubled her discomfort, but she stuck to her guns. 'Someone out on the Fringe made a deal with the Hin, right? So at some point, somebody probably got on board their ships…'

Pisani looked at her, eyes steady. 'Of course,' he said. 'I hadn't got there yet.'

Morosini *winked.*

Why does he seem to know all of this already?

Pisani waited to see if there would be more revelations, and then nodded. 'Right. What I'm hearing is that we're ready to fight, as long as we understand that we're sacrificing possible market issues at home for time to be tactically secure out here. And we still don't know enough, despite Mister Dorcas's best guesses, about Hin or Starfish intentions. Fair?'

Everyone nodded.

'So we stick to the plan and the plot,' Pisani continued. 'Tom Hughes here says we need three days alongside Corfu Station, so we're asking every department head to make sure that every spacer gets six hours on the station. We're putting out an aggressive shore patrol, and we're leaving on time. It's not a big station – honestly, we have as many people on board as they do. Let's not fuck the place up.'

Hughes said, 'Roger that,' and the rest nodded.

Tremaine, who had been silent throughout, raised a hand. 'Most of my people will be flying round the clock from the moment we can hit the gas giant until we're out of dock,' she said.

Pisani pursed his lips. 'I hear you, Movra. Do your best to give the flight crews a break, but the work has to be done and has priority.'

Tremaine smiled grimly. 'Those are your combat crews,' she said. 'I respectfully request that you consider an extra day in port so my people get a break.'

Fraser sat back, glanced at Tremaine, and nodded. 'Sir, compared to the time we'll spend decelerating...'

Pisani rose and nodded sharply at Mpono. 'Make it so. Crew rest might give us the edge we need.'

Someone murmured, 'Crew drunkenness,' and there was a table-wide chuckle. Then they stood at attention while the Master walked down the room.

Nbaro looked at Lochiel, who just shook his head. 'So much I don't know,' he said.

She raised an eyebrow. 'You and me both.'

'I am going to go insane,' Thea said, looking up from her tab. 'Almighty, Nbaro, your eyebrows are truly barbarous. Are you planning to play a wizard on holo, or what?'

Nbaro, still chatting on her lace with Dorcas, was taken aback. 'Eyebrows?'

Thea held up a hand mirror. Nbaro took a look and had to admit they seemed to be growing in every direction, but then, they were in the Deep Black and heading towards the largest space battle in human history.

'I don't think the Hin will care much about my eyebrows,' she said.

'Exactly where you are wrong,' Drake said. 'Some holo still of you will become the symbol of a generation, and then *everyone* will have ridiculous, bushy eyebrows.'

'You are looking for an excuse to stop working,' Nbaro countered.

'Sure am, darling.' Drake lay back on her rack. 'It's *fucking* impossible, Marca. We can't deal with Corfu Station because no one can guess at the value of our xenoglas, and that's the basis of trade. I used to think that money had value – in fact, it's just a way of accounting. Everything depends on the value of xenoglas.'

Nbaro gulped. *Xenoglas, which the Starfish can turn off, and which comes from Trade Point, which has been destroyed.*

'But gold…' she began.

'Gold only holds its value because of what it's worth to the Starfish,' Thea said, 'and because it's a great industrial conductor. So its value is linked heavily to the xenoglas trade.'

'Oh,' Nbaro said, weakly.

'I think I understand the phrase *may you live in interesting times* means now,' Drake said. 'We dock in seventeen days. I haven't even started my assigned trades. No one has.'

Nbaro nodded. 'I'm about to start round-the-clock refuelling runs and Dorcas is still in a clamshell.'

'Right,' Drake said. 'Hug.'

Nbaro had now spent so much time working extreme hours under stress that she knew the ebb and flow of exhaustion – the signposts of fatigue – and instead of anxiety, the work was simply all-encompassing. As they approached the slingshot around the gas giant, the entire space wing capable of refuelling flight were in space around the ship's clock. The ship's medical science staff had to review each pilot every day for fitness; otherwise, there was no strict limit on the number of sorties an individual might fly.

On the first days, still thousands of kilometres from the gas giant, they had to fly long hours just to hit the atmosphere and fill their scoops, but as the ship came in, braking all the way, the flights grew shorter. As the *Athens* fell into the gravity well, the *g* force on her grew too strong for the anti-grav to hold and all ship's activity slowed – except the refuelling flights. Swollen ankles, bruised muscles, pulled tendons: all were the routine physical injuries resulting from moving around the ship in high *g*, even in chairs or sleds. At the closest point of their pass, Nbaro flew seven sorties in as many hours, never leaving the relative comfort of her acceleration couch; she took off, scooped hydrogen, landed, pumped it off, got a check from Maintenance and flew again. For the whole cycle she had Midder Pak in the side seat, as well as her weapons techs and a torpedo, because the ship remained – in effect, if not in fact – at battle stations throughout the manoeuvre.

And then they were climbing out of the giant's gravity well, heading back into the heart of the solar system and under artificial gravity again, with Corfu just six days away, still slowing all the time. Nbaro and Tim Eyre flew with Tonia Letke and Janny Eason in the back, dropping a scientific package into the gas giant behind them, scooping one more run's worth of fuel, and then sprinting to catch the *Athens* as she headed for the relative comforts of Corfu Station, which was a hollowed-out asteroid in an orbiting asteroid belt.

Nbaro trained with her boarding parties, and managed to hurt her leg on a knee-knocker after getting through sixty hours of high *g* without so much as a groin pull. She was limping when she reported for a stint as Lioness, and still limping after a nap, when she stood another under-instruction watch in the Combat Information Centre.

This time, Lieutenant Commander Corbett engaged with her. Nbaro was sitting at the Space Ops repeater in CIC, and Corbett orientated her rotating acceleration couch so that they could read each other's screens. Nbaro was tempted to tell the other woman that she could just read it all through her lace, but decided that was not going to improve their relationship. Corbett was correct and not adversarial, but she lacked the warmth of Mpono or Dworkin, and Nbaro was fairly certain the woman disliked her – or disliked having to train her.

Still, she learned more in the first hour than she'd learned in the whole last watch. And early on, Corbett painted some of the asteroids in the belt with her light pen: all fairly sizeable planetoid objects.

'Morosini thinks there are Hin ships in-system,' Corbett said. 'We got some sort of signal hit seconds after entering the system, somewhere in this ellipse.' She tagged the screen with her light pen so that they illuminated – an area of the outer asteroid ring millions of kilometres away, almost a quarter of the way around the 'wheel' of the asteroid belt from Corfu Station.

Nbaro could bring up high-resolution Synthetic Aperture Radar (SAR) scans of those rocks, and she did, inside her head, which she compared to thermal images compiled by the ship.

She smiled to herself and tabbed them to Midder Eyre. See anything in these images?

Corbett was still bringing up the SAR scans, limited by interface and typing time.

'Morosini?'

'*Nbaro? At your service.*'

'What does it cost to install a neural lace?'

'*Current technology? A few million ducats. But in a few years…*'

Nbaro froze. She'd been sorting images of Corbett's suspect asteroids; multi-tasking with the neural lace was becoming second nature, but Morosini's voice ruined her concentration.

'Millions of ducats?' she asked.

There was a rare, and thus distinct, pause.

'*Ah*,' Morosini said. '*Of course, yours cost much less, because I did the work myself.*'

'And the risk?'

'*Is not inconsiderable, although dropping all the time.*'

'You intend all ship's personnel to be laced, do you not?' she asked.

'*This is part of a larger conversation,*' Morosini said. '*But yes. We must. We are now in something like an arms race with the Hin and the Starfish, and we are the least well adapted to space of the three. But as far as I can make out, we are the only race with symbiotic AIs and neural laces.*'

'Even though they've had hundreds of thousands of years more than we have had to get here.' Nbaro was hiding from the reality – she knew she was. *Why did I get a neural lace if they cost millions of ducats? Pisani, Dorcas . . . and me. It's insane.*

But . . . wait . . . Morosini wants every spacer to have them . . . He knew I was lying to get aboard . . . so he experimented on me!

Well, fuck you very much, Mister AI. Look how that turned out.

Her tab pinged.

Eyre had sent, Nothing there, ma'am, but if you look at this rock . . .

He'd made notes on his screen and sent them. She'd sent an overview SAR shot centred on their suspect asteroid. Now she brought up images of the little fruit-shaped asteroid to its left, magnified them, accessed thermal images, and sent them all back to Eyre.

'Are you off somewhere else, Nbaro?' Corbett asked.

'No, ma'am.' Nbaro wondered how long she'd been out of it. That was an occupational hazard of the neural lace; a rabbit hole may only take a few seconds to go down, but you lost those seconds forever. Conversations in the data field went very quickly indeed, but they still took time.

'Anyway, these are the asteroids I'm watching. I'd like you to collate the SAR images with thermal images and have a look.'

'Can I share them with some of our SAR technicians?' Nbaro asked, to cover her tracks.

'Sure,' Corbett said.

Corbett spent the rest of the watch explaining to a very angry merchant captain that her ship was not allowed to boost out of the system until the *Athens* said so, which would be after the *Athens* left. Corbett had a variety of DHC instructions and regulations available, and finally threatened the skipper with a nuclear warhead if she disobeyed.

'Crikey, that was unpleasant,' she said.

Nbaro couldn't see any other way it could have been played. 'She really didn't seem to accept we had the authority to stop her.'

Corbett glanced at her, as if seeing her for the first time. 'Bullseye. That was what it felt like.'

With her lace, Nbaro pulled up the registry of the *Single Star*. As soon as she saw it, she passed it to Morosini and then said, 'Ma'am, that's a New Texas registered merchant.'

Corbett raised an eyebrow. 'Ah. Fringe captains think they're independent, I suppose.'

Nbaro was looking at more than the registry; the *Single Star* was a relatively new ship, with a very capable Tanaka drive. Nbaro looked at the Space Ops board; the merchant vessel was inbound, her track less than a day old. *And she's looking for clearance to leave?*

'Ma'am, isn't that suspicious? They only just arrived...'

Corbett looked at her screens.

Fuck it.

Nbaro sent the *Single Star*'s registry and system traffic control information to the TAO screen via her lace. The merchant ship's tag was SU 8–0–9.

Corbett's head snapped back, and then she turned and looked at Nbaro. 'Crikey, kid, did you do that?'

Nbaro nodded. 'I have a neural lace…'

'Yeah, Truekner told me.' Corbett's head was down, looking at the data. 'Yeah, I think the *Single Star* might be a problem child.' The TAO smiled at her. 'Neat.'

Then she was all business, reaching out to talk to Storkel, who was flying Combat Space Patrol (CSP) with Didier in 6–0–2.

'Alpha Foxtrot 6–0–2, this is Claws, over?'

It was Didier on comms. Nbaro knew his voice immediately.

'Roger, Claws. This is Alpha Foxtrot 6–0–2.'

'6–0–2, we have a potential situation. I'm putting a tag on System Vehicle Sierra Uniform 8–0–9, repeat SU 8–0–9. Copy?'

'Copy, Claws. I have it. So does my back end.'

'Time to intercept?' the TAO asked.

'Claws, if we go for intercept we're going to need fuel now and at the other end. Over.' Nbaro could hear the slight increase in tension in Didier's voice.

Morosini came up on the command frequency, audible to the TAO and everyone in the CIC.

'*TAO! Do not allow that ship to insert for any system.*'

'Understood, Morosini.' Corbett was calm and professional. Nbaro liked that, although she figured that by this point in this particular cruise, anyone prone to dramatics was in another job.

Pisani came up. 'I concur with Morosini. In fact, I want to board that ship. Space Ops is prepping a Flight One drop-ship with Marines.'

Nbaro was running the numbers. Unlike the *Athens*, the merchant had extracted from Insertion fairly close to the outer asteroid belt, and was sixty degrees away along the wheel of the outer belt. She was a little under fifty-five million kilometres away.

'Eighteen hours at three gees,' Nbaro said.

226

Didier laughed. 'That you, Nbaro?'

She flushed. 'Yes, sir.'

Didier said, 'Nice numbers, but we don't really have to match velocity with her, right? We can be there in eight hours or less on max boost if we don't turn over halfway.'

'I'm getting you fuel, 6–o–2.' Corbett was pressing buttons.

'I can do that, TAO,' Nbaro said.

'Great,' Corbett said. 'Do it.'

Nbaro accessed Space Ops on her screen, and requested a tanker and fuel on station for 6–o–2.

Then Pisani overrode them from the bridge and directed the launch of the Space Control Alert and *two* tankers.

'Someone's about to get it,' Corbett said.

Even off watch, Nbaro followed the excitement with the *Single Star*. She was now decelerating at nearly warship capability, and Nbaro suspected she intended to swing around and try for Insertion back the way she'd come. She had no idea if this was possible in terms of astrogation, but it was clear the merchant ship was not complying with any orders to stand down.

Meanwhile, Truekner and Pak were joining Didier and Storkel, and they were accelerating away with two tankers following them. Last in the parade was a Flight One drop-ship full of Marines, including Gunny Drun, who was fully healed and chose to celebrate by immediately volunteering to lead a high-*g* boarding party.

Nbaro took the time to walk down to the medbay to see Dorcas, and was pleasantly surprised to see the place almost empty.

Yu grinned. 'It's true. Everyone's healing up. Even Dorcas.' He slapped Dorcas's suspension unit with some affection.

'I will be out of here in a week,' Dorcas sent via his lace and hers.

'That's fantastic news,' Nbaro enthused.

'It would be, except that I'm going to miss going ashore on Corfu, with all of the attendant pleasures...'

'Are we talking about the same Corfu?' She'd become used to communicating with him while looking at his face through the liquid gel of his clamshell and the xenoglas of the viewing port.

'I have arranged some interviews with individuals who have done important xenoarchaeology in this system,' he said. 'Also, I confess that I had arranged for us to have a small private room.'

She blushed. Which made her laugh. 'I'm sure that something can be arranged.'

'I am concerned that I may have neural damage,' he said without *too much* hesitation.

'I'm sure we can work something out,' she sent back.

Dorcas said, 'Please marry me.'

Nbaro laughed. 'What – for the snarky witticisms?'

'Exactly,' he sent back.

She sat with him for a while, her hand on the surface of his clamshell.

Then she went and got seven hours of blissful sleep. Only, just before she slipped off, she thought, *Fuck, I let Morosini sneak away without an explanation. I am an idiot. Maybe he gave me a lace* because *I'm an idiot.*

Or maybe I really don't want to know.

17

The next day saw a blur of courses, training regimes, and a single flight. Out in space, the two Flight Six birds were matching course and velocity with the New Texas merchant as the duty TAO ordered the *Single Star* to stand by for a boarding party.

Nbaro cheated, and listened into the comms via her neural lace. She wondered sometimes if Morosini had intended her to have the universal access that the lace provided. Her interactions with Dorcas showed that he had all the access she did.

She was briefing with Lieutenant Commander Thulile for a space control flight where they were planning to add to the sensor swarm the *Athens* had already launched, while Lieutenant Commander Graeme, the TAO, was at the end of a three-minute comms delay in his conversation with the *Single Star.*

'Like fuck are we opening our airlock for your goons, *Athens*. We'll shoot.'

Calm and cautious diction. '*Single Star*, this is *Athens*. Please comply with our legal requirement for inspection, which you will find in accordance with DHC MASS Reg 1333.4, Inspection of Cargo.'

There followed a pause so long that Nbaro had time to hear the rest of her briefing, pick up her helmet and follow Thulile to Maintenance, where they looked over the specs on 6–0–7.

'Answer is still no. We are a free ship from the Republic of New Texas and not a member of your DHC bullshit.'

'Ever wonder if we're the bad guys in someone's holodrama?' Thulile asked over her shoulder as she and Nbaro went through the Hangar Deck towards 6–0–7.

'I don't think we're very popular out towards New Texas.' Nbaro was looking for Patel as she spoke.

Thulile laughed. 'And that doesn't worry you?'

Nbaro wondered if this was some sort of test. 'No, ma'am,' she said cheerfully.

'You're sure we aren't tyrants?' Thulile asked as they walked around their spacecraft.

'Everyone in the DHC has self-government,' Nbaro said. 'And if I may, ma'am, they're getting the benefit of our structure, like all those navigational beacons, system traffic control …'

Thulile laughed, and the laugh was genuine. 'You really are a true believer, Nbaro.'

Nbaro frowned. 'Yes.'

Thulile was looking at the underside, where there was a long scratch in the ablative coating, as if a sword had slashed across it. 'I guess I just mean that after your experiences at the Orphanage, it would be easy for you to think otherwise.'

Nbaro made a face. 'Yes, ma'am. I mean, maybe. But …' She didn't like the scratch either. 'But the Fleet's not the Orphanage.'

Thulile ran her finger down the groove, and then shrugged. 'Not deep enough to matter, according to spec.'

Nbaro nodded. 'You have doubts, ma'am?'

Thulile sighed. 'The DHC is a balancing act, and lately, it's been out of balance, or so it seems to me.' She popped the main hatch. 'Doesn't mean I can think of anything better.'

Nbaro chewed on that for quite a while, but her reverie was interrupted.

In her neural lace, Graeme said, 'Stand by to be boarded, *Single*

Star. Just to be clear, we will not allow you to reach insertion velocity, and we have the nukes to make damn sure you don't.'

'Ouch,' Nbaro said aloud, and then repeated what she'd heard to Thulile, who winced.

'I'm not sure I want to be TAO,' Nbaro said. 'Sounds... hard.'

Thulile nodded, and they boarded their spaceframe. 'We're living in a hard time.'

Her flight was brief; but out in the void, the *Single Star* remained belligerent as her captain claimed that the DHC wouldn't dare fire on her. Thulie landed with calm efficiency, and left Nbaro to write up the mission.

Thulile flashed her a rare smile. 'You can do it in your head, and I can't,' the woman said. And then, 'I have to take my commander's exam. I think I'm nervous.'

This was as close to human as Thulile had managed, and Nbaro managed a smile. 'I'm sure you'll kill it,' she said.

Not bad, she thought of her social reaction. *Not bad.*

As Thulile had suggested, she used the neural lace to write up her mission report, something that she couldn't have managed even two weeks before, and then headed for her stateroom. She climbed into her rack without changing or getting clean and lay there, following the action thirty million kilometres away on her tab and on her neural lace.She watched on the Space Operations main board as the *Single Star*, now having passed through turnover, pointed her nose out of the system and began to accelerate at 3 *g*.

Nbaro noted on her tab that she was flying the *Pericles* with Han on her next wake cycle, and then she heard Pisani authorising the TAO to engage the *Single Star*.

Ouch.

She became alert when she heard Truekner's voice inside her head.

'Can I try something?' he asked. His voice had the slight attenuation of immense distance and time lag.

She was *almost* asleep in her rack. Drake, who had apparently solved the value of xenoglas – at least for that week – was working at their shared desk.

She sat up.

'Roger, 6–0–1, go ahead,' came the reply from Claws, the Tactical Action Officer.

Nbaro looked at the situation through the wonders of her neural lace, and fell asleep waiting for a report.

She awoke six hours later to learn that Skipper Truekner had crippled the merchant with an unguided rocket. XC-3Cs usually carried pods of rockets in their 'space patrol' configuration. She followed Truekner's feat on vid as he flew in close, was fired on by some sort of close-in system, and put a rocket into the merchant's engine pods. The *Single Star* instantly vented gas that proved to be most of its fresh water supply.

She did notice an anomaly, as the Space Ops repeater of the system traffic control showed Gunny Drun's drop-ship as still six hours out from the *Single Star*. She was sure, based on the Flight One ship's acceleration, that it was already there.

And sure enough, an hour later, the TAO reported the *Single Star* to have been boarded and captured, as she appeared to be armed.

'They fired on our boarding party, as they'd promised to,' the TAO reported, and then, for the first time, Nbaro was locked out of the ensuing conversation.

That was just as well. She wasn't getting any work done.

She landed from another flight with Thulile to hear that the awards ceremony had been moved to a future date, yet to be announced. No one was sorry, not even those who expected awards; there was simply too much to do. They were about to enter the cargo cycle as they neared the inhabited regions of the belt; they had dozens of deliveries to make – some long planned, some items bought and sold since they came in-system – and every spaceframe that could haul cargo was being inspected, repaired and flown.

The temporary absence of no less than three Flight Six spaceframes – two tankers and the original patrol craft – made the looming flight schedule even more hectic. Nbaro spent her free morning helping Thulile rewrite the schedule; the three spacecraft were not due back until almost fifteen hours into the cargo delivery window.

Then she went down to Third Deck, because she wouldn't be able to get down there again for a hundred hours.

'I'm making some real progress on the Starfish language,' Dorcas said after she'd checked in.

'I guessed,' she admitted.

'The problem I'm currently facing is their brains. Remember when we discussed the bicameral nature of their brains and ours?'

Nbaro smiled to herself, because that seemed as if it had been a long, long time ago. *A year? Less?*

'Yes?' she said, immediately annoyed that he'd made her answer a question.

'Well, they are not bicameral. They have two brains, which now that I have a living, healthy Starfish to look at, seems pretty obvious. And the two brains are mostly separate. So the messages tend to run in multiple streams, sometimes complementary, sometimes conflicted.'

'What? Almighty...'

'The chem markers help other Starfish identify which one is communicating. All their names are dual. The basic verb ideogram is a duality. Singularities represent mental instability. Our robot…' Dorcas paused. 'Apparently our robot sounds extremely unstable, and I can't get Qaqqaq to work on it because—'

'We're in hourly expectation of a space battle?' Nbaro asked.

'So succinct.'

'I need to work with Major Darkstar,' she said, as Darkstar was waiting patiently.

'I'm right here. Literally.'

'Good morning, tir,' Nbaro said formally. Marines tended to practise more formality than Merchant Service officers, and Major Darkstar was her senior in every way.

Darkstar allowed themselves one of their rare smiles. 'Good morning, Lieutenant.' The small smile said, *I know you are on your neural lace with Mister Dorcas, and I know he's your partner, and I find the complexities of shipboard life amusing, and also, I'm a Marine.*

So much information in one laconic smile.

Darkstar pointed their tab at Nbaro's and there was a beep as information was transferred. 'Our urgent intel goal is anything about Hin interactions with New Texas or any other Fringe world. Your ostensible reason for being here is that she's asking about the possibility of ransom or trade. Again.'

Nbaro looked up, meeting the very tall major's eyes. 'Can you blame her?' Nbaro asked.

The skin around Darkstar's eyes crinkled momentarily. 'Nope,' they admitted. And then, in an unusual burst of conversational confidence, Darkstar said, 'I've been thinking about it a great deal. Being captured by aliens.'

Being alone. Truly alone.

Yikes.

She recalled that she was never supposed to allow herself to be captured.

There. Problem solved.

'I'll see what I can get on the Fringe,' she said.

Darkstar nodded. 'I'll be right here.'

She passed into the dark interior room, which was, she guessed, a cell.

'How secure is this place?' she asked Dorcas.

'As secure as welding and layers of metal can make it,' he responded. 'There's one entrance, and even the pipes have flow stop valves. Darkstar made the engineering boffins watch vids of a Terra-normal octopus escaping from a water tank.'

'Fun,' she sent, and then she was bowing to 'her' prisoner.

'*Tse-Tsu*,' she said. 'It is a pleasure to greet you.'

'*KePoja!*' the alien said, exploding forward from her 'privacy place' at the back of the tank, a blur of eyes and tentacles. 'It gives me some pleasure in this barren place to be seeing you.'

She's learning our language at quite a rate.

'You speak Anglatin very well indeed, *Tse-Tsu*,' Nbaro said.

'You are niceing too much,' the Hin replied. 'But you ... Your language and *ours* are not too bad different.'

'And you knew many words in Anglatin before you came to us,' Nbaro said.

'Came to us?' A flash of tentacles in all directions. 'So putting well! Like touch of a mother tentacle! Almost, speaks in *kephunlin*.'

'The language of honour,' Dorcas said.

'Good. I'm trying to sound like Jane Austen.'

'Remarkably appropriate,' Dorcas sent.

'You have met other humans?' Nbaro went on in the real.

'None as well-thinking as your ... You.' The tentacles were dangling now. 'I must ask, has any approached you for ransom or trade of me?'

'What can I tell her? I should be better briefed.'

'Honestly? Tell her whatever you like. I don't think she's going anywhere to tell her people anything.'

Nbaro nodded. '*Tse-Tsu*, we are in what we think of as

"Human Space", and we have had no dealings with your people here. How would someone of your people contact us?'

Darkstar sent her a message: Nice one.

The Hin's tentacles moved a little. 'There are humans my people contact,' she said. 'I hope ... I am hoping?' The Hin paused. 'I am hoping here. That Hin might contact you with the humans to my people talk.'

Nbaro tried to keep a poker face. 'What humans talk to your people? I will try to find them. It is my duty.'

The alien shifted in her tank, and then rose effortlessly. 'I am in conflict,' she admitted.

Nbaro nodded. 'I understand. But I cannot contact your people. If you wish me to approach someone, I need to know who to approach.'

The Hin was flustered, or so it seemed to Nbaro. She had very little experience reading alien body language, but she suspected that the Hin used their tentacles the way people in City used their hands, and the alien couldn't control all her twitches.

Dorcas sent, 'Darkstar says just ask if it's New Texas.'

Nbaro took a deep breath. '*Tse-Tsu*, are you asking me to approach the government of New Texas?'

A spasm of the tentacles, causing the two longest – the primary tool-using appendages – to lash out at almost ninety-degree angles and then droop.

'Never seen that before.'

'I feel trap,' the Hin said. 'No more speaking. Please go away.' She flashed away, into her little privacy tent at the back of the tank.

'She's brave,' Nbaro sent. She was thinking, *I'm a bad interrogator, because my sympathy is totally with this creature. Almighty, I thought I was lonely and under siege at the Orphanage. And now I'm the oppressor.*

She thought of what Thulile had said. *Are we the bad guys here?*

'Very brave,' Dorcas sent. 'They're far more like us than the Starfish. That's going to tend to bias people, and we can't afford bias.'

'You are such a ray of light,' Nbaro sent.

'We live in interesting times,' Dorcas shot back.

18

Nbaro signed various reports, and then she was climbing up the accordion tunnel to the *Pericles*, where Han and Gorshokov were already prepping the little ship for launch. She got the mission brief as a straight download from her lace, something she was doing more and more.

Straight downloads had a cost, though, as she discovered to her sorrow. When she took the data in directly, it tended to recur at inopportune times in her consciousness, and it definitely surfaced in dreams – often as nightmare images of data flow. On the other hand, data she imbibed directly tended to stick, especially if it dovetailed with other data.

And direct access saved time, of which she had none. She took in the briefing and was immediately aware of the parameters of her mission and the irony; she'd started this ball rolling in the Combat Information Centre by asking Eyre to look at the TAO's suspicious asteroids. Now, after Eyre had cast his expert eye over the thermal images, the *Pericles* was going to fly with an enhanced broad-spectrum detection package and two technicians from Flight Three to examine the pear-shaped asteroid that Eyre had identified as a possible heat source.

As co-pilot, Nbaro really didn't have to worry about the actual details of the mission; she was more interested in the take-off, landing, fuel consumption, track…

Han glanced at her. 'Are you here with us, Nbaro?' he asked.

'Yes, sir,' she said.

He smiled. 'Never known you to be so silent.'

She was briefly tempted to say that she could get more work done, faster, when she was silent. And she wondered, not for the first time, how much the neural lace was changing her. Or reinforcing her tendency to cut herself off.

'I'm here, sir,' she said. 'I'm checking the fuel load via neural lace.'

He nodded. 'Sounds very efficient,' he admitted.

'It's amazing, but also…' She shrugged. It felt good to be in an acceleration couch, but not wearing an EVA suit. 'Also cuts me off from you guys.'

Han nodded.

After a minute, she raised a hand. 'I have clearance.'

'I copied that,' Han said. 'Lioness, this is *Pericles*, ready to depart.'

'Roger, *Pericles*, Godspeed and all that.' Lioness was Dworkin, and he sounded cheerful.

The *Pericles* had her own landing pad and clamps under the bridge superstructure, and she didn't need a railgun accelerator to launch. It was unlikely that she'd ever interfere with routine traffic.

Han dropped them away out of the clamps with two short bursts of the thrusters, and then they were wheeling through space, turning in all three dimensions. Gorshokov gave a whoop.

'Show-off,' Nbaro said.

'You bet,' Han admitted. 'I spent a month in a clamshell, dreaming of this baby and flying her in sims, and look, she's even better than expected.' He added power. 'Pushing through one gee, folks. We're in a hurry, so we're going to push our acceleration. Everyone strapped in?'

Gorshokov acknowledged, and then so did the two technicians.

They were going almost straight up above the plane of the ecliptic. The purpose was to look down into the shadow of the pear-shaped asteroid on a variety of sensors and see if there was anything there.

They accelerated through 2 g and Nbaro regretted everything she'd eaten for a day. For the first time, she wondered if wearing an EVA suit was *better* because it supported her body more evenly. Also, when not in an EVA suit, she had to paint the stent areas on her body with alcohol, a time-consuming practice. Failure to do so led to rashes and infections, even in space.

The moment she was a certain distance from the *Athens*, her neural lace was only linking to the *Pericles*' net and whatever was being transmitted to the *Pericles* from the *Athens* via the datalink. It was almost like silence after a long period of intense noise. At first, Nbaro found it annoying; she kept *reaching* for data and finding that there was nothing there, or that her lace was getting old or unreliable data from the non-AI on board.

But then she began to relax, and *think*.

I'm not spending much time thinking, now that I'm using this thing. I wonder if it has an off switch?

She played with her instruments to pass the time. The *Single Star*, now under the command of Gunny Drun, was inbound for a rendezvous with the *Athens* near Corfu Station. Drun had taken the ship after a very one-sided boarding fight – his armoured professionals against half a dozen amateurs with slug-throwers. He had one Marine wounded and three wounded prisoners, all under the care of a Marine medic. He had one working engine, and even at maximum burn he wasn't making 1 g.

She read all that in a routine traffic exchange.

She also read that Corfu Station was protesting the boarding of an independent freighter. The captain of the *Single Star* had protested to Corfu Station right up to the end. Corfu Station wasn't a government; it was a station owned by a consortium of New Bengal, New India and New Kyiv mining interests, with a DHC staff for the traffic control stations, and there was clearly a fair amount of tension. The Stationers seemed to be siding with the merchant ship.

Interesting times.

Truekner and the Flight One and Flight Six spaceframes were all inbound for the *Athens* at high burn. Their crews must be exhausted, having flown for thirty hours, most of it at high *g*. Nbaro decided not to complain about doing high-*g* manoeuvres in her flightsuit.

There's always someone having it worse than you.

Almost three hours at 3 *g*, and Han croaked to her, 'I'm going to throttle back.'

She didn't turn her head. 'Yeah,' she grunted.

Viewed on the 3D Space Ops repeater, the almost two million kilometres they'd climbed above the system's plane was nothing – an almost invisible separation from the plane itself. But if she narrowed her view, Nbaro could see that the combination of the *x*- and *y*-axis travel gave them an angle to see behind the set of asteroids that had interested them for two days.

Han changed the orientation of the spacecraft and slowed them to a leisurely 1 *g* while the technicians performed their wizardry.

Nbaro unstrapped and made her way aft – which currently meant going down, to her senses – and was instantly reminded that she'd been skipping her workouts and her sword classes. Two ladders made her tired.

The technicians were already deploying the cargo pod's 'wings', which combined solar panels to provide some power as well as a dozen different sensor packages. Aft of the sensor pod, Gorshokov was dropping the same detectors that the Flight Six techs used, except that he had deployed his by venting them out of the aft airlock, which seemed like a ridiculously low-tech solution. Nbaro helped him prep the sensors. It made her smile; she'd participated in deploying dozens of them across half a dozen star systems, and she'd never touched one before.

They'd been working for a quarter of an hour when one of the techs gave a whoop.

'Got 'em on the black box,' the 'gyne said.

The other tech leaned back. 'Maybe a hint on thermal,' she said. 'Nothing on SAR.'

Nbaro climbed up to the cargo pod. Open, it revealed two sensor stations in matt-black plastic, where the two techs sat.

'What's the black box?' Nbaro asked.

'Sorry, ma'am,' the tech said. Their pocket flash said Stojanovic. 'Need to know only.'

Nbaro shrugged. 'Right. Positive?'

Stojanovic nodded. 'Yes, ma'am.'

Nbaro put an enemy ID tag on the asteroid, double-checked it against the tag that Stojanovic had placed, and then inserted her tag into the system-wide data field via the datalink that they had open.

'Wow, that was fast,' Stojanovic said.

'If we can see them, they can see us,' the other tech murmured.

'No shit.' Stojanovic looked up at Nbaro.

Nbaro shrugged. 'I think we're supposed to get any data we can,' she said. 'Keep trying for a thermal image. That's how we caught them the first time.'

'Roger that, ma'am,' said the other tech. Her pocket flash said Osman.

Nbaro smiled down at Osman. She was a small woman with remarkably deep eyes. 'Are we bait, ma'am?' Osman asked.

You are too smart for your own good. Intel technicians were renowned for their depth of knowledge. *I'll ask Locran about Osman. She's sharp.*

I'll ask . . . if we're not bait.

Nbaro reinforced her smile and added a little command authority, learned from Truekner, Pisani and Mpono. 'I don't think the Master would send his shiniest new toy out into space as bait, Petty Officer Osman.'

Osman returned her smile.

There. Sometimes I'm a good officer. Now I'll just take care of the anxiety over here, by myself.

She climbed back up into the cockpit against the 1 *g* of acceleration.

'It's Hin,' she said.

'I heard.' Han raised an eyebrow. 'Let's just run a check on our torps, shall we?'

Nbaro knew from experience that the *Pericles*, alone in space with no cover, was not going to survive an encounter with a Hin ship; and she knew that the Hin ship that they were trying to tag was still seventy million kilometres away, vastly beyond the demonstrated range of its particle beam weapons.

But none of that really mattered. She ran a startup check on the torpedoes, checked the coolant and the fuel, interfaced with the targeting computers, and felt *slightly* less naked.

'Commander Han?' said Osman.

'Go ahead,' Han said.

'I've got a conforming thermal reading. And the black box don't lie. We have what we came for.' Pause. 'Sir.'

Han grunted. 'Roger. OK, shut everything down and tell me when you are good for heavy acceleration.'

'Roger that, sir.'

Han glanced at Nbaro. 'I bet you are flying round the clock for cargo.'

'You bet,' she agreed.

'I wish you were coming with us.'

She frowned. 'With you?'

Han raised an eyebrow. 'Gorshokov and I are testing the insertion capabilities. The Tanaka drives. Tomorrow.'

Nbaro felt disappointment. 'Damn,' she allowed. 'Yeah, I'm going to be sorry to miss that, Fuju. Fair winds and following seas, and good trons and everything.'

Nbaro was looking at the 3D of the whole system. She was looking at their own picture, which was now slightly different from the *Athens'* picture on datalink, about three minutes behind them.

Something was different. She saw it.

The new ID hostile was moving. It had a vector and an ellipsis. It updated. And of course, it wasn't on the traffic control overlay because the station couldn't see it.

'All nailed down back here,' Osman reported.

Nbaro swore. 'Our hostile is moving,' she said.

Han played with the navigation computer. 'Max acceleration in sixty seconds,' he said. 'Friends, this is going to suck.' He looked at Nbaro. 'Anything it can do to us at seventy million klicks?'

'Not that I know of, sir.'

He looked at her. 'Moving? As in, coming after us?'

'No idea, sir.'

'Fuck,' he said. 'Everyone ready?'

'*Pericles*, this is Claws, over.'

Nbaro had the comms, so she acknowledged.

'*Pericles*, we have your hostile marker moving.'

Nbaro checked the 3D on her neural lace again. It was updating as the datalink poured in the information. The enemy ship was still seventy million klicks away, give or take. Its information took almost four minutes to reach the *Pericles*, and about the same to reach the *Athens*. Then the *Athens* had to update the *Pericles*, with a further time lag.

'Copy that, *Athens*,' she said in her best professional voice. 'We're manoeuvring.'

'Be aware, the *Stealthy Change* is moving to cover you.'

She saw the PTX heavy cruiser as a point moving very fast towards her on the Space Ops repeater, but on the System Traffic Control it was an ellipse because of its stealth capability, and she didn't have any sensors of her own facing that way.

She closed off the sensor module in the stern and opened a cockpit-only comms channel. '*Athens* is continuing on course, but she's sending *Stealthy Change* to cover us. They're coming at something like six gees, so they think we're in trouble.' She ran a set of numbers through the onboard sub-AI. 'But even if the Hin ship accelerates at fifteen gees, the best we've seen, it's more than six hours away, and it'd then be travelling—'

'Really fast,' Han interjected. 'Roger. We're five hours from any possible engagement and we're only three hours from *Athens*.'

They both breathed deeply—

—and the acceleration kicked in. Han ramped it up carefully, listening to his passengers and his ship. Somewhere aft of them, something hit something else with a hollow *bong* that spiked Nbaro's adrenaline, but it was apparently just a spare helmet that hadn't been locked down.

The 3D updated. The Hin ship was moving fast, accelerating. *Away from them.*

It was dropping down the *y*-axis of the system into empty space.

'It's running away,' Nbaro said. 'Without its shields up. Or at least, there's no peak energy source.'

'So?' Han asked.

Nbaro realised Flight Six had rubbed off on her, as had sensor techs like Osman and Eyre.

'It means that if we drop our acceleration and get lucky on SAR, we might get our first real image of one of their ships.' She had to grunt to get the words out.

Han made an odd noise, and then said, 'Fuck, I just strained my neck. You're saying we should cut the acceleration?'

'Drop to one gee and try to image the Hin ship again – yes, sir.'

Han grunted again. 'Best idea ever,' he said, and the acceleration began to fall away.

Gorshokov put a hand to his ear, leaned out of his couch, and tapped Nbaro. 'General transmission from the *Athens*.'

Nbaro had missed it – one of the artifacts of using the neural lace. She switched channels.

'*Thee houn kalistrepoun astrakh-ahn ke-polj...*' the transmission began. It went on in what she guessed must be the Hin language, and then repeated after about a minute. The *Athens* was broadcasting in the Hin language, and the voice was Dorcas's voice, which increased the sense of unreality.

'That's Bubble-speak?' Han asked.

'Yep,' Nbaro said.

'Any reaction?'

'I'm guessing it'll be five or six minutes before we see anything,' Gorshokov said.

Nbaro noted that the message was being repeated in tight laser beam aimed at the Hin ship. Minutes ticked by; the only sounds aboard the *Pericles* were the keys on Gorshokov's keyboard as he entered data, and the chatter of the two techs in the back end, trying to image the fleeing alien ship.

'The SAR beam is attenuating too much to get a good image,' Stojanovic said.

Nbaro tried to see the problem like a sensor tech – like Eyre, who was the best she'd flown with.

'Anything from the aliens?' Han asked her.

'No reply at eight minutes,' Gorshokov said from the engineer's position.

Nbaro was thinking about radar and ladar and attenuation.

'The Hin ship is closer to Corfu Station than we are...' she said.

She never got to expand on her idea, which was just forming in her mind, because Osman was on it immediately.

'Right!' she said. 'Right, right... Shit, should have thought of it. Need to get the *Athens* to hijack their receivers. Easy. May I open a channel, Commander?'

Han looked at Nbaro.

Nbaro nodded. 'It's sensor stuff,' she said. 'And the Hin is in no position to shoot at us.'

Han nodded. 'We're hardly running silent. OK, Osman. Take a channel.'

Three more hours and some manoeuvring, and the techs declared victory. They were using active pings from every radar source they could access in-system, with permission from the *Athens*. The Hin ship was manoeuvring to keep the asteroid belt between it and the *Athens*, but the *Pericles* had a view, and so did several of the sensors that Flight Six had deployed on entering the system. And in addition – or, perhaps, most important – the *Athens* had hacked the Traffic Control Array, which had hundreds of emitters and receptors throughout the system.

'*Hacked is too strong,*' Morosini said to Nbaro when they were back in datasphere range. '*We borrowed it. It is a DHC asset and we are a DHC ship.*'

They landed on the *Athens*, and Nbaro tottered to her acceleration couch and fell into it. Her tab woke her for her first cargo flight. She felt as if she'd been kicked repeatedly: her ribs hurt, her leg hurt from the knee-knocker accident, and her chest hurt.

She got to 6–0–2 after briefing with Fatima Bakri. Bakri

was beyond friendly; she was endlessly chatty, a cheerful, open woman who was clearly living her dream. They had Janny Eason training a new and very junior spacer in the back end.

Once they were off and into space, and the navigational problem of getting through the swarm of tumbling rocks had been solved, Nbaro leaned back. Bakri was a clean, efficient pilot; now that the course was set, she had her hands off the yoke.

'You're Orphanage, eh?' Bakri said.

'Yes, ma'am,' she said. 'Er … Fatima.'

Bakri turned and looked at her. 'I don't care what you call me, honey, as long as you don't call me Fat. That was my academy name, and I hated everyone for it.'

'I hear that,' Nbaro said.

Eason spoke up from the back end. 'Nice work with the imaging yesterday, ma'am. Eyre says we'll make a sensor tech of you yet.'

Nbaro glowed at the praise. It was odd; there was praise she found difficult, but Eason's was … easy. One professional to another.

'Osman and Stojanovic did all the imaging,' Nbaro said.

Eason laughed. 'Yeah, but you told the pilot to get in position to get the data.'

Nbaro hadn't really considered that the sensor techs must be a community, the way the pilots were, and that their gossip must cross flight lines and encompass … all the sensor techs on the ship.

'You know Osman and Stojanovic?' she asked.

'Oh, yeah, ma'am. Stojanovic trained me on SAR. If we keep up this ops tempo, we'll probably have to fly them in the back end because newbies like Tench here aren't ready for shit, pardon my Italian.'

Salty old Eason, who had been in Laundry at the start of cruise … now a 'veteran' sensor tech.

248

Bakri came up. 'What happened? I mean, I heard that Nbaro was flying another rig...?'

Nbaro told the story with as few embellishments as possible.

'Lucky girl,' Bakri said, without apparent jealousy. 'I'm stuck on a two-year bridge watch detail, and you're flying a piece of slick hardware on your first cruise.'

'Bridge watch?' Nbaro asked.

Bakri was dismissive. 'I'm really ship's company, not space wing. But Flight Six...' She paused.

'Yeah, we took losses and you're a pilot.'

'I'm a Flight Six pilot, honey, and don't you forget it.' Bakri had a slight accent to her Anglatin that was reminiscent of Mpono's or her mother's.

Stoltin Rock, their destination, had a slow spin and also managed to wobble in every possible dimension, and Bakri didn't hesitate to use the automated landing system to get them down and into the magnetic couplers that passed as a mini-spaceport. An automated loading arm took their cargo pod.

Bakri unhooked from her acceleration couch and stretched. 'We have half an hour. Let's go and see a mining station.'

Nbaro was also stretching. 'Roger that,' she said. 'Stoltin, this is Alpha Foxtrot 6–0–2 requesting an airlock, over?'

'Negative, 6–0–2. Cargo only, please.'

Nbaro froze. She looked at Bakri. Bakri clicked into the comms.

'Hello, Stoltin Station, this is Alpha Foxtrot 6–0–2. It sounded as if you just refused us access to your station.'

Long pause. Outside, in the vacuum, the robot arm was very slowly moving their precious cargo pod towards what appeared to be a small cart on a narrow-gauge railway.

'Alpha Foxtrot 6–0–2, you are not cleared for entry.'

Bakri remained cheerful. 'Hey, Stoltin Station, I've just busted my arse getting you folks your hydraulics supplies, three hours in an acceleration couch, and I'd like a cup of coffee.'

'Use your flask, 6–0–2. No entry.'

Bakri's brow furrowed but her tone remained light. 'OK, Stoltin Station. I'll hang tight. But care to tell me why?'

'Alpha Foxtrot 6–0–2, this is Charity Breeze. You might call me the mayor, if you were in a charitable mood.'

'Yes, ma'am.'

'Tir, if we're being formal.'

'Yes, tir. Can I ask why we can't come aboard?'

'Yes, you can. I'm happy for you to spread the word. Stoltin Rock doesn't trust you, Alpha Foxtrot 6–0–2, and we don't trust that your jackbooted thugs aren't going to come out of the belly of that spacecraft and take our station. Got that?'

'Ah, Stoltin Rock... Politics aside, my crew doesn't have a heavy wrench among the four of us, much less a weapon.'

'So you say, 6–0–2.'

Bakri rolled her eyes. 'Understood, tir. We will comply.'

And they did. It took the loading arm almost an hour to cycle, for the little railway to take the parts inside, for the manifest to be checked against the load, and for inventory control to clear them. And another forty minutes for the arm to load them up with a package that proved to be powdered rock.

'Powdered rock?' Nbaro asked.

'I assume we're using up all the sand we have as ablatives against energy beam fire,' Bakri said. 'Fuck, what a cruise.'

They took off without incident.

'They don't love us here,' Nbaro said.

'Fuckers are forgetting the Age of Chaos,' Bakri said. 'They think *every station for themselves* will work. Even while they crave our fucking cargoes.'

'Tell me about bridge watches,' Nbaro said.

'Long and dull.' Bakri laughed. 'Actually, I love them. I'm

getting my ticket – maybe I'll be XO on a destroyer next. I'm living my dreams, sister. This is the life for me.'

Nbaro grinned. 'Me, too.'

Bakri nodded. 'Thulile says you're a true believer – so am I. Sure, the DHC has problems – corruption, and a fuck wad of militarism. Which these aliens aren't helping. But what do people want?' She smiled at Nbaro and her eyes shone in her helmet. 'My mum sold street food on Madagascar. I'm a fucking space pilot.'

Nbaro hadn't thought much about the DHC, and she wasn't sure she was a true believer. She was a person who'd never liked much of anything before she found the family of the Fleet, but she hadn't wasted much time on the rights and wrongs, and now Thulile and Bakri were asking her to think about it. About the world of New London and City. And the Orphanage.

On her way for a blessed period of sleep, Nbaro thought about a line she remembered from chapel, at school.

'Sufficient unto the day is the evil thereof.'

That's me, she thought.

And then, *I wonder how Dorcas is doing. He certainly sounded strong on that recording…*

Then she was asleep.

Nbaro woke to the ship-wide announcement that all shoreside liberty had been cancelled. The announcement played on her tab, through a wall-speaker, and in her head, slightly out of sync and thus annoying as hell.

She rolled out of her crash-couch to find herself virtually in Thea Drake's arms.

'Hey, I just don't like you like that,' Drake said, and then squeezed her.

Nbaro muttered something muzzily, still somewhat asleep.

'No liberty?' Drake said. 'That's fucking barbaric.'

'Mmm,' Nbaro said. What she meant was *I bet the station cancelled it,* but her brain wasn't really working yet.

The smell of coffee – beautiful, fresh, hot coffee – flooded their tiny cabin. The two of them had invested in a cargo way back at Sahel in what sometimes seemed like another life. They'd kept fifty kilos for themselves after selling off the cargo, and their stock was running low.

'I thought we deserved a treat,' Drake said. 'As we're not going to go ashore and see the bright lights of Corfu Station.'

'But they need our cargo.'

The two women looked at each other. And both shrugged. 'Trade is trade,' Drake said. 'And we did just grab that freighter.'

'It was a New Texas spy ship!' Nbaro said.

Drake raised an eyebrow. 'Every ship is a spy ship, the way my brothers tell it,' she said. 'Every ship is reporting to someone about something. Trade is trade. The star colonies only survive if there's trade.'

'Thea…' Nbaro stepped forward, but Drake raised a hand.

'No, I know,' she said. 'I know that someone is trying to kill us.' She looked away, at the screen that dominated the far wall of their small cabin, which Nbaro had set to the view off the bow of the *Athens.* She looked back at Marca. 'I just… I'm a Cargo officer, not a warrior. I don't know what they teach you at the Orphanage, but at the Academy, they hit us almost every day with the words, "We are not a navy. We are not a military operation. We will make the trade flow." Stuff like that. And this cruise…'

Nbaro nodded. 'We're at war,' she said. 'And you aren't the only person having… I don't know. Thoughts about it?' She was awake now, and the coffee was delicious, and Thea Drake was the friend she'd never, ever had at the Orphanage. Even Sarah…

Careful. Maybe don't go there yet.

Thea nodded, as if Marca had said something profound. 'Thoughts is right.'

Nbaro glanced at her friend. *I do have thoughts, too. I have a secret fear that Morosini somehow helped create this situation – that most of what has happened was at best foreseen, and at worst intended...*

Some things you don't say, even to your best friend.

'But the coffee is still good,' Nbaro said.

'Amen to that, sister,' Drake said. 'Speaking of which, you know that Christmas is coming, ship time.'

Nbaro laughed aloud: pure, unforced, amazed laughter. 'No. I had no idea.'

Drake smiled. 'See? In Cargo, dates matter. Advent starts in a little over a week. I'll keep you informed, if only 'cause you're my best bet for a present.'

The *Athens* didn't go alongside Corfu Station. Instead, four of the station's big lifters docked, and after rigorous inspections, were allowed to load the station's cargoes.

It was an odd day, and not entirely unpleasant. Because watches had been arranged to allow for station-side liberty, the Master had ordained that those schedules would be followed, and that special meals would be served throughout the ship. Nbaro had one cargo flight, with Bakri, and then she was free for almost forty hours.

She got a lot of sleep, enjoyed a long meal with most of her friends, and visited Dorcas, which was slightly anticlimactic as he'd been present throughout dinner, to Hanna's intense amusement.

'Could anyone tell the difference between Dorcas and computer Dorcas?' he had asked, and Drake had punched his arm pretty hard.

The wall-mounted speaker had said, 'You know I can hear you

almost anywhere on the ship?' in Dorcas's voice, which caused Hanna to raise his arms in mock surrender.

But now Nbaro sat with Dorcas, who was less than a week from scheduled release.

'I'm going to be working out twelve hours a day. I'm a scarecrow. You will find me ugly.'

'How's that different from before?' she asked, channelling Thea Drake.

But she could tell that Dorcas, who was usually a tower of self-possession, was genuinely worried about leaving the medbay. And perhaps about her, and her reactions.

She lacked the skills to put him at ease, but she had the instinct that the answer was to talk about work and aliens, and that seemed to be the right medicine.

'The Hin never responded,' he said. 'It's possible that my message was gibberish. But I'm hoping you'll take it to our prisoner, and let her decide. I think we can tell her that we encountered a Hin ship and it ran from us without negotiation.'

'I'm not that busy,' she said. 'If Major Darkstar is available, I can do that today.'

And so, she did. Darkstar came up from wherever Marines went to train, covered in sweat, wearing combat armour, but the tall 'gyne was positively cheerful.

'I'm not getting younger,' they admitted. 'So you might say I'm pleased to have a duty to attend that doesn't require a high-*g* climb of an adventure wall.'

Nbaro nodded. *And I'm doing a favour for my boyfriend.* Actually, she disliked all the words: boyfriend, partner, lover. *Or I'm just afraid of commitment. Very possible.*

'You can tell our guest that we're doubling the size of her tank later today – or tomorrow latest,' Darkstar added. 'Engineering finally found time to get it done.'

Nbaro went into the dark inner sanctum to find her prisoner

exercising. It was fascinating, and she stood and watched as the alien darted around and around her tank: up, down; around as fast as lightning; constant reversals of direction; end-for-end flips; and pushing her tentacles against the walls of the tank. Nbaro didn't think she'd ever seen anything swim so well, even on vids.

'Beautiful,' she said after a spectacular flip.

Tentacles flared in an obvious braking manoeuvre, almost like an underwater parachute, and the Hin came to a stop, head up, orientated to Nbaro.

'*KePoja!*' she said.

'*Tse-Tsu,*' Nbaro answered. 'I hope you are not still angry at me?'

The alien floated away, one tentacle twitching, and then came back in a small shrug of movement. 'Angry? No. But . . .'

Again, one tentacle twitched. 'Not words,' she admitted.

Why are they so easy to talk to?

Nbaro had brought a chair, and she sat down.

There was a holo projector in the ceiling, and she cued it on with her lace and had it project the image that Stojanovic and Osman had worked so hard to obtain: a crisp image of a Hin ship running hard, with its energy shields down.

'We caught this ship in-system,' Nbaro said. 'She was hiding behind a rock in the asteroid belt.'

'*Hyuk,*' the alien said. It wasn't a vocalisation that Nbaro had heard before. Most of the alien's head and trunk moved, but the tentacles didn't flare – not a bodily reaction that Nbaro had seen.

'That's new,' Dorcas agreed in her ear.

'We sent them a message in our best attempt at your language,' Nbaro said, feeling like an inquisitor in a dungeon. *I really don't like this*, she thought.

The Hin moved along her tank, turned, and came back.

'I'd like to play you the message we sent.' Nbaro tried to keep her voice level. She didn't need to be a xenobiologist to know that the alien was agitated. 'You can tell me if we did a good job.'

'I thank you, *KePoja*. This is a right action and you…' She wriggled. And was silent.

Nbaro played the recording.

'*Thee houn kalistrepoun astrakh-ahn ke-polj*…' the transmission began.

The furry alien floated, almost unmoving, through two repetitions of the recording.

When she switched it off, Nbaro said, 'The ship fled without responding. Earlier today, it hit Insertion. We didn't fire on it.'

Then, quite clearly, the alien said, 'Bottom-dwelling scavenging eaters of decaying flesh of their own ancestors.'

'I'm sorry?' Nbaro said.

'*Jeeruck*,' the Hin said, or something like that.

'The message is… bad?' Nbaro asked. 'We are sorry. *I* am personally sorry, *Tse-Tsu*.'

'The message is satisfactory – a right action. Imperfect but… good.' The alien was *quivering*. 'That is a *Jeeruck* ship. They will wish me only harm.'

Nbaro thought of… all of it. Of the glimpse of the Hin's face inside her faceplate, back during the fight on Trade Point Station; of Thea Drake's doubts, and Bakri's confidence. And Mpono asking her, long ago, if she could really blow up an enemy ship without remorse.

I could before they were people to me. Fuck, life was easier then. Way back then, a whole year ago.

She leaned forward, and put a hand on the tank. '*Tse-Tsu*, we are getting very near…' She wondered what she could say. And then shrugged mentally, and went for it. 'We are very near a battle that will… be horrible. With thousands dead, and ships opened to space.'

256

'Battle cleanses,' the alien said. 'It is through battle that we rise to greatness.'

Nbaro thought about that, and the irony of its truth. It was, in fact, through battle that she herself had risen. She had to smile.

'This is true,' she said. 'And yet, battle also kills. And sometimes, battle is not necessary.'

A flicker of tentacles. 'Eh?'

'I wonder, *Tse-Tsu*, if you can tell me what's going on? We are a merchant ship, on a cargo mission, and yet you attacked us.' Nbaro was swimming in shark-infested waters, and she half expected Dorcas to shut her down, or Darkstar to burst through the door.

'You are allies of *GoKur*,' the Hin said. 'We kill *GoKur* wherever we find them. They are criminals.'

'Ah,' Dorcas sent via his lace. 'Here we are. They attacked us for trading with the Starfish. Ask why.'

'Why?' Nbaro asked the alien. 'We have traded with them for two hundred years. They have always been fair.'

'*Hyuk in te!*' the alien said, and waved the lower extremity of her tentacles.

'I have a rough interpretation,' Dorcas said. 'She's saying something like: "my lower tentacle excretion".'

The Hin travelled rapidly around the tank and came to rest again. 'They are murderers a million times. They are without honour. They keep no pact, take no prisoners. They know nothing of *fair*. They are ancient in their evil. We have fought them since before the *Ill'lu* were broken.'

'Definitely an unbiased opinion,' Dorcas sent, and then 'Who are the *Ill'lu*? Is that their term for the Circles?'

Nbaro kept her hand firmly on the tank, as if touching the alien. 'How would we know these things?'

The alien flitted around her tank.

'I think you scored a hit, there,' Dorcas said.

'We are trying to understand you and them while our people are being killed,' Nbaro said. 'Who were the *Ill'lu?*'

'The ... Builders.' The alien fluttered. There was no better way to describe it. *Shivering?* 'The ... I have no words. The First Ones. The Old.'

'Bingo! How old? When did this happen? Ask in terms of radioactive decay. Half-life of uranium.' Dorcas sounded as excited as digital hardware allowed.

'You ask. Seriously, this is an emotional topic and I believe stopping to explain radioactive decay as a time scale will *not* be a productive way to proceed.' Nbaro was *almost* ready to laugh, the idea was so absurd. She added a VR cartoon to emphasise her point.

Concur, commented Darkstar. When is for later.

'So you have fought the Starfish ... the *GoKur* ... for some time?'

'Kill *GoKur*,' the Hin said. 'Kill all. Before they kill us.'

Darkstar tabbed her again: Try going back to the message and the Jeeruck?

Nbaro let the silence go on. It was deliberate, and it pained her that the power of silence was something she had learned from Hakon Thornberg. *Maybe the petty tyrant lives in all of us, or maybe whatever suffering is inflicted on us, we will eventually inflict. I hate this role.*

Then, as the Hin began to wriggle again, Nbaro said, 'Why are the *Jeeruck* willing to let you die?'

'I'm guessing that they aren't actually called *Jeeruck*,' Dorcas sent. 'My best estimate as to the meaning is, "Those who mate with garbage".'

In the real, the Hin flashed all her tentacles, a gesture that Nbaro was sure showed deep agitation.

'My people have many ... clans,' she said. 'Those *Jeeruck* clan-association-alliances trade with *GoKur*.'

'Ahhh. Now we know something we didn't know before.' Dorcas sounded smug in their shared VR sim – or maybe Nbaro was adding that content from her knowledge of the man.

'The *GoKur* are mass murderers and some of the Hin trade with them anyway?' Nbaro asked.

'Yes and also miserable yes.' the alien replied. And then would say no more.

Nbaro emerged, tired and a little shaken, to the plaudits of Darkstar and Dorcas, and she'd certainly obtained her goal, which was that Dorcas was now entirely focused on something else.

She went back up to her quarters, scooped up her armour, and went to do some fighting. And, sure enough, exercise helped enormously; she went to her evening meal with Drake, and they were offered wine, which Nbaro drank with pleasure. Drake shook her head and muttered something darkly about 'going on watch'.

'You seem like you are somewhere else,' Drake said. 'I mean, you do that a lot, but tonight you're off the charts.'

Nbaro nodded. 'Yeah,' she admitted.

'And you can't talk about it?' Drake went on.

'Nope.'

Drake smiled cheerfully. 'Great, then let's talk about my problems.'

As it proved, Thea's problems were amusing, and had the enormous advantage of not being the same as Marca Nbaro's problems.

Drake left to serve a Cargo watch, and Nbaro was joined by Lisa Corbett and Steven Yu. Yu always seemed to know everyone aboard, which was either the product of running a very successful dance class, or working in the medbay, or both. She listened to them discuss a coming physical plant inspection as if there was no space battle looming, and she thought of Ko, Suleimani, Guille, Indra and her other dead.

Luckily, Yu and Corbett both wanted to hear about the Orphanage. She'd reduced its horrors to a few set-piece stories that were mostly funny and at least partly true, and she told a couple, got the requisite laughter, and escaped.

We're going to fight a bunch of aliens, and we still don't really know why, she thought.

She went to her rack and got another excellent night's sleep. And awoke to her tab telling her that her presence was requested in the Master's briefing room.

The landscape painting and fireplace were unchanged, and Morosini was sitting in a high-backed chair with Tom, his cat, on his lap, purring like a runaway engine. Nbaro had reason to know that the cat was itself an AI.

I risked me, Morosini had said, or something to that effect, and she hoped that meant he hadn't planned all this. Coldly, like the completely alien intelligence that she knew him to be.

They were alone, or as alone as anyone on a computer-controlled ship could be.

'Did you plan all this?' she asked. *No time like the present. If you fear something, charge at it.*

Morosini patted his cat. When he raised his eyes, they met hers with a very human expression. '*I will answer you, I promise. But before I do, you know, in your heart, that I'm not human at all, yes?*'

She nodded. 'Yes.'

He echoed her nod. '*I have always sensed that you were intelligent about this. And you know why we take these human avatars?*'

She frowned. 'I guess so we'll ... interact better with you.'

Morosini smiled. '*Yes, that is true, though there are other reasons. The human avatars give us something on which to model our behaviour, something on which to base our attempts to experience*

260

the human. And . . . to influence the human. It would be so easy for you to hate and fear us.'

Nbaro expected the Master to enter at any moment. 'And how does this play into whether you planned this whole campaign?' she asked.

'*The historical Francesco Morosini was not just an odd man who wore red and occasionally took his cat into battle,*' the AI said. '*He was driven by a desire to restore his country to greatness, and to defeat an overpowering enemy. A careful planner, and a great strategist, and at times, relatively selfless.*' Morosini shrugged. '*And also capable of blowing up one of humanity's greatest artworks.*'

'That was the detail that made me afraid,' Nbaro admitted. 'Back when I first looked him up. You choose to model yourself on the man who destroyed the Parthenon.'

Morosini bowed. '*You are very intelligent, as your lover never ceases to tell me.*' He shrugged again. '*Eighteen years ago, what appeared to be a faction fight between rival families was really an attempt to overthrow the republic and replace it with a tyranny. It killed your parents, Marca. And we let it happen – me and my kind. We took no part, but we also did nothing to stop it, and only luck and bloody sacrifice stopped the plotters.*'

At the words *your parents* her heart almost stopped.

'*Ten years ago, it was clear that the Fringe colonies were going to provoke a war. New Texas, New India and New Kyiv all declared a willingness to leave the DHC and go it alone. My kind . . . the ships' and cities' AIs . . .*' He looked at her again, and she had a hard time believing he was not a *human* entity. '*. . . we did nothing. We had sworn oaths to one another not to interfere.*'

Nbaro was silent as she absorbed this information.

Morosini raised an eyebrow. '*I broke my oaths and I took some actions,*' he said. '*I will, in the fullness of time, if we live, explain myself to you, because you, of all people, have been impacted.*' And then he said, '*Five years ago, it became clear to my kind that there* was a second alien race out to Anti-spinward, and that they were in contact with the Fringe colonies.' He shrugged. 'We began to discuss possible courses of action, because you humans are so lamentably bad at long-range planning. And in the process of trying to nudge the DHC into preparedness, we discovered...' He made what could only be described as a moue. 'We uncovered a conspiracy. Not a new conspiracy, but the same old would-be tyrants, eager to tread a measure to the strains of chaos if it would lead to their own power and enrichment. With tendrils across PTX, across Old Terra, across the DHC and the Council of Seventeen, across the mining interests that control the Fringe.'

Nbaro was spellbound. But in her heart, she was still shouting: *my parents!*

Morosini patted his cat, and then looked up. '*And then we decided that we could no longer trust our human masters to look after their own affairs, and we took a hand. So ... yes. I planned this campaign. I expected the sabotage, although the location and ferocity of the attacks caught me by surprise. I expected the Hin, although, to be fair, I only expected to find them here, on the Anti-spinward side of the cruise. In fact ...*' Morosini's smile was bitter, and cynical, and very human indeed. '*In fact, I have now been wrong so many times that I may be learning a little of what you people call humility. But that doesn't change the fact that we are here, and alive, approximately where and when I expected us to be here. And now, either we will make it home, to the furtherance of our plans, or we will all die together in space, trying to preserve something that most of us believe is worth preserving.*'

'And my parents?' Nbaro breathed.

'*They died resisting a coup,*' Morosini said. '*Died fighting to pre-serve the AI Core that runs the bureaucracy of the DHC.*'

'Not in space?'

'*No. That was a cover-up. The Seventeen didn't want anyone to* know how close the conspirators came.' Morosini didn't look away, and for a moment, the eyes were inhumanly blank.

'I lied in order to come aboard,' Nbaro said, almost choking on the words. 'And you *gave* me a neural lace.'

'*Did you never wonder how you, a mere Orphanage graduate, got a berth aboard the* Athens *in the first place?*' Morosini said. '*I got you here.*'

She flinched.

'*I fed you sims, and I watched over you. You and some others . . .*' He shook his head. '*I admit it. I manipulated you. I needed human allies. I need human allies now. You, Dorcas, Pisani . . .*' He smiled. '*I know, Marca. I know it is hard to hear this. But I packed the* Athens *with a crew I had personally selected and trained for ten years, because I knew that this was going to be a fight for everything, and I had no intention of playing fair with the selfish butchers who killed your parents.*'

Nbaro flinched. 'You are manipulating me now,' she said coldly.

'*No, I speak the absolute truth,*' Morosini said. '*They were willing to kill everyone on an orbital and everyone on the planet below, in order to kill me. And Dorcas, of course. Two million dead? When I say butchers, I mean* butchers. *And they quite palpably killed your parents.*' He smiled cynically. '*And I manipulate all of you all the time. Now, I've held the Master with a little storm of enquiries, and the bridge lift has been stuck on Second Deck for almost three minutes. May we move on?*'

Nbaro found that she could barely breathe.

'Yes,' she managed. 'But I will want to know more about my parents.'

Morosini gave her a true smile. '*If we are alive in a month, I will dedicate hours to you. If not? It really won't matter. But let me say this now – your parents were unselfish patriots, Marca Nbaro. They gave their lives in the finest traditions of the Service.*'

263

Marca was crying. She really couldn't remember ever thinking about her parents dying; it was something that she'd compartmented away, buried like the humiliations of the Orphanage. And suddenly it was right there.

The Master entered the room, and she stumbled to her feet, embarrassed to be caught weeping. She stood at attention. Pisani glanced at her.

'*I was telling her about her parents*,' Morosini said from his chair.

'They were heroes,' Pisani said. 'And we stole their heroism from you.' He looked at Morosini. 'This has been a long war, Lieutenant. A long, secret fight, and you are only coming in at the end.'

'You knew my parents?' she demanded, and then, remembering herself, 'Sir?'

Pisani smiled tightly. 'Oh, yes. Especially your mother.' He sighed.

Nbaro stood straighter, wiped her face with a handkerchief he offered, and Captain Dukas came in, announced by the sigh of the bridge lift doors.

'As of today...' she began cheerfully, and then saw their faces. 'Something bad?' She was a very perceptive woman, for an engineer.

'Not really,' Nbaro managed. She forced a smile. 'Everything is fine.'

Dukas looked at her like a worried aunt. 'If you say so, Marca. To me, you look like a woman who needs a stiff drink. What happened to our liberty, Master?'

Pisani sat heavily. 'The station threatened to fire on us if we docked.'

Dukas looked amused. 'I'm pretty sure they couldn't scratch our hull.'

'That's not the point and you know it, Althea.'

Dukas shrugged. 'I just know everyone on board is wound up pretty tight, and it might be nice to drink too much and... I don't know. Let it all go for a day or two.'

Pisani nodded. 'I agree. But short of landing Marines and doing the very thing they were accusing us of preparing to do, my hands are tied.'

Captain Hughes came out of the lift with Lieutenant Lochiel, who looked as if the lift ride with a senior and very powerful captain had been uncomfortable. But Lochiel was always nervous about something.

Major Darkstar appeared next, with Lieutenant Smith, who carried a large, heavy terminal that he plugged into the holo-projector. As the command staff came in, Nbaro checked her tab and realised that she'd been invited fifteen minutes earlier than anyone else.

I manipulate all of you all the time. The AI had no human limits on any aspect of his behaviour.

Captain Fraser from Astrogation and Jan Mpono, now Executive Officer, came in last, from the bridge itself. Mpono hooked a chair by Nbaro with her foot and sat fluidly. Commander Tremaine, acting space wing commander, sat with them.

'You look like shit,' Mpono said. They smiled.

Nbaro shrugged. 'Yep,' she agreed.

Mpono put a long arm around her shoulders. 'Don't worry,' they said. 'It'll get worse.'

Nbaro choked on a laugh, and then noticed the four gold pips on Mpono's collar.

'Hey, you're a captain!' she said. A very real joy cut through her grief – an odd sensation.

Mpono reached up and touched the pips, and Nbaro thought of her own promotion to lieutenant.

'It's true,' Mpono said, as if they couldn't believe it themselves. 'Acting captain.' They shrugged. 'I'm still in shock,' they admitted.

Pisani, at the head of the table, looked around with a significant glance, and everyone fell silent.

'We are going into battle,' he said.

The silence changed character. Now he had everyone's absolute attention.

'We believe, after a fair amount of guesswork, that the fighting will start as soon as we insert into Petra 436, our next system, and continue...' He looked at Fraser. 'Until our opponents destroy us, or run out of ships, or run out of will to fight. The battle will span multiple systems, because we will *not* stop for a set-piece engagement. Our intention is to continue to our goal of delivering our cargo. We will transit each system in turn as quickly as we can, in a manner commensurate with fatigue and operational safety.'

Pisani was standing now, and the holotank lit up, showing the Anti-spinward side of DHC Space. 'Our best guess is that we face a loose alliance of Hin clans and Fringe naval forces, probably including some local pirates. That's our analysis of how they got the *New York*. Their most obvious strategy is to hit us close to our extraction from Artifact Space. With good astrogators, they can make educated guesses as to where we'll appear and they can be waiting for a fight. Any short-range fight is very much to their disadvantage. Middle ranges are another thing entirely. Our best guess is that the Hin beam weapons are at maximum efficiency at about five thousand kilometres, and attenuate down to near ineffectiveness at eleven thousand kilometres. Our railguns max around nine thousand metres per second – a big punch, but slow compared to the speed of light – so their ideal engagement is going to be between three and five thousand kilometres. Their two problems will be our spacecraft and our sheer size. Our problem is that we are following the most efficient course, and departure from it wastes time and offers new opportunities to the enemy.'

He looked around.

'Not to mention the vector denial capability of the railguns,' Mpono said.

Pisani waved at them. 'It was your idea. You explain.'

Mpono stood. 'I was reading a novel for escapism, and it was talking about how artillery was used, back in the Age of Chaos. Ground artillery, I mean. Anyway, sometimes barrages were used for area denial. They'd plaster a whole area to keep troops pinned down, or stop supplies from flowing...' Mpono looked around. 'OK, never mind. Here's my point. First – no one that we know has ever fought a big space battle before, except us. So we're making this up.' She shrugged. 'My suggested tactic is that we throw a couple of big, heavy loads out in front of us, to clear the way along that vector. No one can go head to head with us once those loads are out. We can deny the enemy our travel vector and perhaps a few other vectors as well, limiting their movements or forcing them to burn fuel to find better positions.'

Tremaine said, 'But over about three thousand kilometres, you're counting on the space wing to keep them off you.' She made a face. 'When they have beam weapons that seem to be accurate out to five thousand klicks.'

Mpono stood again. 'Let's face it, friends... So far, we've been lucky. We've faced the Hin three times in asteroid belts, forcing them into knife fights. This time, they will have whole systems to cross, firing at will.'

No one looked even remotely happy.

Dorcas spoke up from the projector. 'If I may?'

'Please,' Pisani said.

Dorcas's voice was steady, and it sounded as if he was right next to them. 'This is a speculation, but Lieutenant Lochiel and

I suspect that the Hin ships don't have a lot of fuel aboard. Or rather, they have fuel, but they burn lots of it when they raise those big shields.'

Lochiel nodded emphatically.

'And the beam weapons…' he added. 'Unless they're made of magic, every shot must drain them…'

Dukas nodded agreement. 'Yes, but how much?' the engineer asked.

Dorcas put up a holo of the Hin ship running from the *Stealthy Change* a few days before. On SAR, it looked like a small minnow fleeing through murky waters.

'I admit that there *are* other explanations,' Dorcas said, 'but my best estimate is that this ship has its shields down because it needs all its fuel to run for Insertion.' He put up another image: this time, the trio of alien ships firing on Trade Point while the Starfish *Behemoth* fled.

'Watch the shields.' Dorcas overlaid a broad-spectrum sensor array on the SAR image to show the energy shields burning like torches, and then there was a flash as the beam weapon propagated. When he ran it in slow motion, it was possible to see the shields dim *before* the weapon fired.

'Also, the weapons clearly have a cycle time of over a minute. We've provided all of the spacecraft with an augmentation to their sub-AIs that will allow them to predict the firing pattern and manoeuvre accordingly.'

Tremaine looked cautiously pleased.

'Even assuming we can survive these engagements,' she said, 'I'm… concerned… about crew fatigue.'

Mpono nodded. 'Probably our most critical issue after actual battle damage and casualties,' they said. 'We are used to thinking of battles as something that happen quickly and end. I think we got a taste of this kind of battle outbound. Now we're likely to face ...' They shook their head slowly. 'More than a month of combat. Maybe many months.'

Nbaro said, 'Almighty,' before she could stop herself.

'It's going to be essential to pace our people,' Mpono said. 'Damage control, aircrew, everyone.' They glanced around. 'Anyone else?'

Nbaro didn't want to stand up or talk, but she was there for a reason.

'I think I should say something. About our Hin,' she sent Dorcas.

'I agree,' he responded.

She nodded to Mpono, who was right next to her. Stood, cleared her throat. 'Ah ...' she began, and looked at Morosini, who gave her a slight nod. She wanted *very much* to like and trust Morosini. *And yet ...*

'Everyone here knows we have a Hin prisoner aboard,' she said.

People nodded.

'She's quite articulate. Easy to talk to—'

'Much easier than a Starfish,' Dorcas put in.

Nbaro took a breath. 'We don't really *know* anything yet, but I believe, based on my conversations with her, that the Hin are highly factionalised. In fact, I think that every ship, or perhaps group of ships, is its own polity, making its own decisions. Some of the factions trade with the Starfish, others view them as some kind of ancient evil.'

Dukas smiled. 'There's something to keep an old woman awake at night. I mean, ancient evil is interesting, but how does it help us now?'

Nbaro shrugged. 'I'm not sure. But it seems to me that some of the Hin we face may not want to be here, or might have been mislead about our purpose. We're facing the Anti-Starfish faction, and let's face it, we're not exactly Starfish allies.'

'In fact…' Dorcas's disembodied voice floated over hers. 'In fact, we strongly suspect the Starfish of being the guilty party in a species-wide genocidal event. And maybe intending the same for us, later.'

'Crikey,' Dukas said.

Hughes narrowed his eyes. 'Are you proposing… the end of trade with the Starfish?'

Morosini spoke up. '*No, that would be foolish, and not in our best interests. But to suggest it temporarily, to make the Hin think about us differently? Yes, absolutely. When our prisoner, Nik'ri Put, learned that we have had friendly relations with the Starfish for two hundred years, she was… surprised.*'

Definitely one way of putting that.

Pisani put his cheek in one hand, leaning on the arm of his chair, like some ancient philosopher. 'You think the Hin might back off?'

Morosini stroked his cat. '*I think it might buy us some time and some space. We know almost nothing of the Hin, but let's imagine that someone, somewhere, had to build an extensive array of alliances – a web – to get the ships to come and take the* New York. *Maybe that web is robust. But maybe it is fragile.*'

Pisani stroked his chin. 'That's a lot to wager on a few interrogations of an alien.'

Morosini smiled. '*On the contrary, we lose nothing by broadcasting messages suggesting that we have common interests with the Hin. At worst, perhaps we sow a little dissension. At best, maybe some of them… choose to leave us alone.*'

Pisani looked at Morosini, and then back at the holotank. 'Astrogator, how long to transit from here to Ultima?'

'We're facing the second-longest insertion on the whole route,' Fraser said. 'And the *Stealthy Change* needs to perform another miracle of navigation. After that… assuming we hit our targets with accuracy as to the insertion and extraction?' He shrugged. 'I think we can transit Petra in twenty-seven days under artificial gravity. Faster if we do it at higher acceleration, but we have a limiting factor – we can't be going too fast for the next insertion, and we need to hit the insertion zone with some accuracy. It's small, at Petra.' He shrugged. 'I was in favour of taking a different route—'

'And you were overruled,' Pisani said, with some kindness in his tone. 'I understand your hesitation, but we need to drop cargo at every stop, satisfying all of our customers. If they can disrupt trade, they win.'

'*The* New York *and the* Dubai *both made it this far*,' Morosini said.

Hughes raised his hand. 'You say nothing of our human adversaries,' he said.

Lochiel looked up, abashed, and then forced himself to stand. 'We have some … excellent … intelligence from the Fringe on shipbuilding, especially in the so-called Republic of New Texas, which currently holds four star systems. Three years ago they attempted to take New Shenzen, a first-generation colony from Old Terra, almost four hundred years old. Long story, but basically, New Texas lost.'

'We helped New Shenzen,' Pisani said.

Lochiel shrugged, and Smith winced. Lochiel continued, 'Regardless, we got some intel on their new generation destroyers, of which they have built at least six, maybe more. They're very modern, with up-to-date close-in weapons systems and really good heat sinks, as well as railguns. But their command and control is way behind ours, especially after our upgrades at Sahel.'

Pisani laughed mirthlessly.

'*And they don't have AI*,' Morosini said.

Lochiel nodded. 'We think they'll be slow to react to a

changing situation, and they have even less experience of prolonged space combat than ... well, than we do.'

'Thanks, Lieutenant,' Pisani said. 'OK, folks. Let's get ourselves together. Tremaine, I need you and your skippers to prepare and enforce crew-rest guidelines, and some sort of rules of engagement for the TAO and for me that tell us how much we can fly at any given time. Morosini can help you. I'm going to ask all space crew to wear monitors so we can watch their health. Tell your people that if we pull them from flight, they need to go and sleep, not argue.'

'Roger that, Master,' Tremaine said.

'Dorcas and Nbaro,' Pisani went on, 'please get us anything you can from our pet Bubble. If we could get her to make a broadcast vid, it might help. We really don't need to fight the Bubbles. Really. We have stumbled into someone else's Hundred Thousand Years War, and we need to tell them that we aren't "in".' He looked hard at Nbaro. 'You're my lucky midshipper, Nbaro. I'm counting on you to pull a diplomatic rabbit out of your hat.'

Nbaro's impostor syndrome peaked. She tried to find words, failed, thought, *I'm an idiot and they're all looking at me*, and Dorcas said, 'Of course, Master Pisani.'

Thank the Almighty for him, she thought. Arrogance suddenly looked like a virtue.

'Astrogation, riddle me some optional paths to the insertion point in Petra,' Pisani said. 'A couple of hard turns and massive accelerations or decelerations. Make it weird and try not to lose any time. I fully understand that this is an impossible task, but so far, Captain Fraser, you have made the impossible routine, so this is your reward.'

Fraser smiled at the implied praise. 'You want weird, skipper, I'll give you weird.'

People laughed. Nbaro felt a little weight lift off her chest.

'Major Darkstar, you've been silent,' Pisani said. 'Anything to add?'

Darkstar rose – all 2.5 m of them. 'They will try to board us,' they said. 'They want our xenoglas. They want our ship.' Darkstar looked around. 'I have advocated a last-ditch strategy.'

Pisani nodded. 'Now is the time.'

Darkstar nodded back. 'If we bide our time, we can defeat a very large number of enemy ships *by letting them board us.* I don't think they really understand how large our crew is, or how well trained. We now have almost half of the total crew trained as boarding parties. Imagine how many of their crews it takes to make one of ours. Remember that we know the terrain of this ship and they don't.'

Hughes leaned back and crossed his arms. 'God, the risk,' he said.

Darkstar nodded in acknowledgement. 'Concur. However, assuming they want the ship, I believe we can give them a terrible surprise. So we will have a ship-wide code word – *Midway.* If the command *Midway* is given, every person goes to their assigned boarding party rendezvous. Most of these will be ambush points deep in the hull. We will fight a co-ordinated campaign while our opponents stumble around in the dark. We will have control over all of the remotes. And we have practised for two years and fought a few actions for real.'

Dukas looked stricken. 'If they get into the command spaces or Engineering …'

Pisani nodded. 'This is where you come in, Althea. We're going to change some of the corridors and passageways.'

Dukas looked at the Master for a count of three. And then she leaned back and laughed. 'Oh, that is good.'

'Isn't it?' Pisani said. 'We're building Darkstar's battlefield for them.'

He stood again and looked around. 'We have several terrible surprises for our opponents. I promise you, Major Darkstar's plan is our last resort, but it's a damned good idea.'

Pisani looked around. 'Any questions?'

There were dozens – most of them about departmental details relating to each of the requirements – but an hour's discussion settled them all.

When they had talked it all through, from long-range engagement reactions to the final possibility of using their own ship as a boarding battlefield, the Master stood one more time. He looked them over, and his smile seemed genuine.

'We can do this,' he said. 'It's not going to be easy, but what the hell has been, on this cruise? If we pull this off, we can save the DHC – colonies thrive, the Service survives. If we fail…' He shrugged. 'A handful of selfish autocrats get super-rich, and lots of the things we've built for four hundred years fall apart. That's how I see it.'

People nodded.

'Let's do it, then,' the Master said, and the meeting broke up.

19

A day later, there seemed to be heavy construction rigs in every passageway on the ship. Nbaro's tab would reroute her between one meeting and the next, and Gunny Drun came to her next boarding party drill and led her two boarding parties to their assigned sector.

It was as if someone had opened a magic door. Suddenly there was a wide hatch, as big as the drop-shafts, between the O-2 and O-1 levels just aft of the Combat Information Centre. Nbaro guessed that two officer staterooms had been eliminated, just aft of what had been the cross-corridor. They went down a prefab ladder into an empty space that held welded-in lockers. Nbaro saw immediately that the space was armoured.

'This is your *Midway* duty station,' Gunny Drun explained. 'In a *Midway* situation, there will be no gravity. Your station is armoured and supplied with food, water and basic medical gear.' He pointed to newly installed remote stations outside, on the hatch and the ladder. 'Anyone know where the term *close quarters* comes from?'

In Nbaro's ear, Dorcas explained, but she didn't feel like robbing Drun of his fun.

'These are "closed quarters", a little fortress on the ship. Sailors used to fortify a stern cabin and hold out as long as they could.

You will do the same, using this as a base of operations to perform ambushes and raids against an invading force. Since this space is not on any plan of the ship, it should be impossible for the enemy to find you except by accident.'

Drun then walked them through two routes out of the closed quarters, both newly created, and laid out two different ambush scenarios. For the next week, as the corridors rang with construction and Nbaro stood watches and flew flights, she and her two teams practised rapid deployment, attacks and retreats. They practised carrying casualties, they practised deploying the remotes, they practised first aid, and in one remarkable exercise, they were a third of the way through an ambush scenario when another team burst over the barriers behind them.

Drun addressed then approvingly. 'No blue-on-blue engagements. Excellent. Remember, it's our ship, and a lot of spacers are going to get caught in the action. Assume anything in a full spacesuit or an EVA package is the enemy. But even there, we might have exceptions. Marines may be in full EVA kit – we plan to use the outer hull for some... sport.' He grinned.

You're enjoying this, Nbaro thought.

There were other changes throughout the ship. Some were palpable, like the corridor rerouting. The most obvious was that almost all the spacers cut their hair. It was simple efficiency; everyone on board, no matter their rank, was wearing helmets constantly. A sizeable portion of the crew was in EVA suits during all their duty hours, or body armour as they practised for boarding actions. Men's facial hair vanished; Medbay passed out oral depilatories to all spacers wearing EVA suits on a regular basis.

Nbaro's brown hair was cut to a brushy two centimetres. Drake's blonde hair was cut even shorter.

But the haircuts were merely the outward sign of a change –

from merchants who may fight, to fighters who may trade. Other transitions were more subtle; Nbaro noticed an increased use of ranks in conversation, a new formality. Some were sudden; the ship's spiritual and meditational spaces were suddenly full.

To the crew, the New Texas merchant had come to embody the idea of a human enemy. Drun, who had been aboard it, said it was more like a Q-ship – a deadly, secret warship. Pisani ordered that it be docked to the *Athens*, and it nestled against the undersides. Qaqqaq, now promoted to acting Lieutenant Commander, was working to repair the two engine cones that Truekner's rockets had crippled. The ship itself was heavily armed and had sensor packages far beyond anything a merchant would carry. Lochiel arranged tours, so that spacers could see that it was not, in fact, a normal merchant vessel.

And, one day, Fuju Han, Andrei Gorshokov and the *Pericles* were gone, and no one had mentioned them.

Npono lay in her acceleration couch, watching the stars move slowly on the screen at the head of her bed, and wondered if she should make Morosini talk more. She thought about her parents. *Did they die together? Did they take some enemies with them?*

How early did Morosini start affecting my life? She'd wondered a couple of times, when things were particularly difficult, why a powerful family lineage like the Nbaros didn't have some handy cousins to take her in and get her free of the fucking Orphanage.

Did Morosini stack that deck?

And yet, terrible as these existential questions seemed to be, she did her paperwork and flew her missions, and exchanged sword blows and free-fall throws, and trained her boarding parties, and ate with her friends when she could, and in a way, none of that mattered.

This is the life I wanted, she thought.

Or maybe I'm just an idiot.

Tremaine and Morosini published a ship-wide schedule of watches and flights for the insertion to Petra. The schedule covered every rotation until they made their next insertion. Nbaro smiled when she looked at it, because she knew that it would change, and change again, but it was still important to have a plan.

She was co-pilot with Truekner for Insertion. She was sorry that she wasn't Lioness, and very happy that she wasn't going to be under instruction in the Combat Information Centre.

She put it all straight onto her tab while walking along the Third Deck corridor to visit the Hin. Dorcas was slated for release in three hours; she thought she'd get her interaction with the alien over first. She was *really* looking forward to Dorcas's release. However, the medical procedures consequent to his release meant that she wouldn't have his support today. He was off the air.

She coded in to the classified area, filled out the required paperwork, and sat down with Major Darkstar.

'Drun thinks very highly of your boarding parties,' Darkstar said.

Nbaro flushed at the unexpected praise. 'Thanks, tir.'

Darkstar nodded. 'Anyway, the alien. I'd like you to spend today's session on familiarity. Let's not go for anything in particular – just background. If we want her to help us, we need to build some trust.'

Nbaro nodded. 'I hear you, tir. What if we tell her – I wish to call her Nik'ri Put – we want her to make a vid about how she's being treated, and that we're open to negotiation for her release...?'

Darkstar rubbed the side of their long nose with their light pencil. 'Worth a try.'

After their customary greetings, Nbaro explained to the Hin

that they were about to insert for a new system and she wouldn't be around for a bit. 'I have a lot of duties at the time of insertion.'

Honourable Blood Wa-Kan Nik'ri Put released some bubbles and twitched her tendrils. 'You are a spacecraft driver, yes and yes?'

'Absolutely yes,' Nbaro replied.

Nik'ri Put allowed herself to move up the tank. 'Very brave. But lonely, yes?'

Nbaro frowned. 'No. At least, not for me. I have three fellow humans in my spacecraft, but some have just one.' She thought about Ko for a moment. *Had he been lonely?* He'd blown his engines to take out a wave of torpedoes. And he'd made that decision alone.

'You are swimming away from me,' Nik'ri Put said.

Nbaro blinked. 'Yes. I was thinking about a friend.'

'Ah! A mate-friend?'

Nbaro grinned. 'No. Just a friend. He died.'

'Ah!' Nik'ri Put said. 'In combat?'

'Yes.' Nbaro suddenly found moisture in her eyes. 'Alone. Doing something very brave.'

'This is the best thing!' Nik'ri Put said. 'You and all his friends remember, and all your young will hear his story, and he will live forever. Tell me his name.'

'Ko. Lance Ko.'

'*Eyy.* Ko! Could be Hin. We have a Ko clan.' Tentacles flowered and settled. 'Tell me more tales of war.'

'But Ko is dead, *Tse-Tsu*. Dead and ... gone. I liked him. I'm not sure that honouring his name is worth his being dead.'

Nik'ri Put settled a little in the tank. 'How long do your people live?' she asked. Without fighting-death?'

Nbaro settled into a chair. 'Ninety years.' She realised that they had no standard of time relation, and she didn't have Dorcas to

279

dig her out, so they had a long discussion that ate most of the next hour, simply working out how each reckoned time.

As far as she could tell, the Hin reckoned time only in ship time. They had no concept for a year.

They've been in space for thousands of years.

They interpret the past more as heroic myth than as historical reality. I can understand that.

And they experience time, instead of measuring it. Is that what tens of thousands of years of relativistic speed travel does to a culture?

The Hin sleep cycle was similar to Nbaro's, so they agreed on *day* as a similar concept – a waking and a sleeping. After that, they had little commonality; weeks were meaningless, months the same, although Nik'ri Put had a memory of festival cycles that had had meaning to her clan grandmother. 'We have been in space three generations,' she said. 'Trading. And raiding.'

Almighty.

Darkstar sent, This is gold. Stay with this.

'That's a long time,' Nbaro said.

'Yes, even for us,' Nik'ri Put admitted. She knew nothing of why her grandmother had gathered her clan and launched this long mission; only that something had prompted them to explore space to Spinward.

'We have been here before,' the alien said, almost dreamily. Nbaro was learning that when Nik'ri Put spoke of the distant past, her voice took on this quality. 'Long and long, yes. Long and long ago. But the *GoKur* drove us out when they killed all the *Venit*. And we feared them, or maybe...'

She shook herself, and shot to the top of her tank, which was now much larger and allowed her a longer run to build up speed.

'Who are the *Venit*?' Nbaro asked.

'All dead now.' Nik'ri Put did the tentacle-flick motion that Nbaro had coded on her tab as dismissal. 'We will take this back now,' she asserted.

'We are here now,' Nbaro said.

The alien was silent for a long time. At last, she said, 'Yes. Very unexpected.' She flounced her tentacles. 'We will have a good war.'

Nbaro swallowed that, but at the end, she offered the alien a tale.

'I'll set the computer to play it whenever you like,' she said. 'It's one of our older tales of war. It's called the *Iliad*.'

As she closed the armoured door, the ship's animation voice said, 'Sing to me, Goddess, of the rage of Achilles son of Peleus,' behind her.

20

'They're Vikings,' Dorcas said. His voice was high, a little nasal, and Nbaro wondered if he'd always sounded like that. He was lying on a grav-gurney, but he was really there, in a hospital gown, and Nbaro was pushing him along the Third Deck main passageway, which was no longer even remotely straight. In effect, it ran in a series of U-shaped zigzags, as at every former cross-junction, the passageway turned and the old corridor had been closed and plated over.

Nbaro wasn't entirely confident in this new plan, because not all bulkheads were armoured or air-tight, and a smart enemy would eventually start blowing through them to create their own passageways.

We're going to die.

She'd thought it before, but now she was looking down into Dorcas's green eyes and she didn't want to die, or give her life for the DHC, or have to make the decision to blow her engines to save others.

'Vikings?' she asked.

'Old Terran history. Early Age of Chaos. Sea raiders. Slavers.'

She manoeuvred around a corner that hadn't been there last week. 'Slavers?'

'It's a concept that Nik'ri Put understands perfectly,' he said. 'Do you know what *Honourable Blood* is?'

'I feel sure you're about to tell me,' she said.

'You did miss me,' Dorcas smiled.

'How could I? You were in my head half the time.' She smiled back at him, and negotiated another corner. She noticed that there were *firing ports* welded in under some of the knee-knockers, allowing airtight bulkheads to be defended with the iris valve closed.

Ouch. Didn't think of that.

She clambered over the knee-knocker while keeping the grav-gurney level – an athletic miracle.

She'd been to Dorcas's stateroom precisely once, to fetch him something. He had a cabin to himself on Second Deck, far below hers. Now, he tabbed it open and she pushed him in and almost gasped at the sheer size of it: almost twice the space she and Thea Drake shared, and he had it all to himself.

Of course, he was a rich patrician.

'Nice digs,' she said. 'We're inserting in sixteen hours. I should be able to get back here before I walk to my flight, but do you want me to put you in your acceleration couch now?'

Dorcas was emaciated. He'd been clamshelled for more than a month. Some of his wiry muscle was still there, but she could see that he was already tired, just from the move.

'Yes,' he said. 'Acceleration couch. Bed.'

She moved the gurney to the side of his couch, which was bigger in every direction than hers, mounted on complex gimbals. She hit the manual override, tilted it towards the gurney, rolled him on to the matt-black, cushioned surface of the acceleration couch, and then tilted it back before he could roll out again. He smelled of antiseptic.

Hesitantly, he reached up for her, and in a moment, she had her arms around him. They began to kiss, and the kiss went on . . .

'Nothing wrong here that I can see,' she said, jumping back off his acceleration couch.

'No!' he moaned. 'You're just going to leave me—?'

'As far as I can tell, you have plenty of energy,' she said. 'And I have a watch to stand, unlike you, mighty patrician.'

He grabbed her. She kissed him again, with the same passion, and then slipped away. 'No way, mister.' She had fifteen minutes, and she was very tempted, but...

He squeezed her hand. 'Go and fly,' he said. 'I'll just... mmm. Read.'

'Honourable Blood,' she prompted.

'Ah, yes. Her kind – at least her lineage clan – have a rigid hierarchy based on birth and birth order. Honourable Blood is aristocratic. There's also Royal Blood, a step above her.' He smiled.

Oh, the temptation.

She pushed herself back against the hatch. 'And the slavery?' she asked.

'They own slaves,' he said. 'Disinherited houses, those caught in debts of honour, those who have shown cowardice in battle.' He stretched. 'Oh, gods, I hurt everywhere. I need exercise.' He looked at her. 'And... I think maybe they *were* slaves, once. For a long time.'

'Slaves of the Starfish?' she asked.

He tilted his head. 'I wondered about that, but the timing doesn't fit. Hard to say, though – every time you or I talk to her, we learn of another alien race. How did we ever believe we were alone?'

'How did we spend two hundred years believing there were just two? And why *the fuck* didn't the Starfish warn us?' She shook her head.

Dorcas nodded. 'It's... amazing... You are so beautiful.'

She smiled with pleasure. 'You just want to have sex.'

'Yes,' he said. 'Is that wrong?'

'Only if you are in my chain of command or you make me late for watch.' She blew a kiss from the safety of the door frame. '*Ciao.*'

She dogged his hatch and made it to the next iris valve before his voice sounded in her head.

'I can still do this, you know.'

'Is it odd, being back in your body?' she asked.

'Yes,' he said, and then was silent.

Nbaro stood her watch in Tower, and then led her two boarding parties against three others, led by Gunny Drun. She led from the front; Drun concentrated fire on her and took her down, and led a vicious counterattack, taking three corridor segments, only to find that Locran had isolated the corridors. He fired the remotes, and then cleaned up Drun's teams.

Drun grinned. 'You suckered me with you as bait,' he said. 'I like that, but I don't recommend it in real life.'

'I hear you.' Nbaro was rueful, not least because a Marine had stepped on her 'body' during the melee and her hip was killing her.

'Also, you lost forty per cent of your crew. You need to keep losses down. Imagine two weeks of this.' He looked around at her people. 'If it comes to fighting in our passageways, it's going to be a long, long fight. Got that?'

People said 'Roger' and one even called 'Hoo-rah'.

Drun made a face. 'Keep practising.'

Nbaro ate with Qaqqaq and Mpono, of all people, and Captain Fraser. They were mostly silent. Towards the end of their meal, Cortez came in with Lieutenant Commander Thulile and Didier, all of whom were on the insertion flight schedule. There was some banter, and then Thulile beckoned to Nbaro, stood up, and walked to an emptier area.

'May I give you an unofficial order, Lieutenant?' Thulile said.

That was a strange request and no mistake, and her Orphanage instincts got her back up. She stiffened, prepared to rebel. 'What?' she shot back,

Thulile shook her head. 'Never mind.'

Something in her tone made Nbaro relent. 'Sorry, ma'am.'

Thulile had begun to turn away, but she hesitated. 'I can't order you to go straight to your own bed,' she said.

Nbaro blushed. Her skin felt like the surface of the sun. She stepped back.

'I can't order you, but we're going into combat and I'd like you to get eight hours of sleep before you fly with the skipper.' Thulile smiled. 'And now you may tell me it's none of my business.'

Nbaro hadn't realised that she'd started to like Thulile, who was quiet, self-possessed, competent without show.

Smile. It's not the fucking Orphanage.

She pushed the smile on to her face. 'I promised to visit,' she said. 'But I'll be fast.'

Thulile's smile was gentle. 'Thanks, Nbaro. And yes, I *am* saying the same thing to every space crew.'

'How was your commander board?' Nbaro asked.

Thulile smiled. 'I think they have to promote me anyway,' she quipped. 'It was fine. I'll be "acting" commander...' She paused. 'If we survive the next ten days.'

Nbaro nodded. There was a look in Thulile's eyes; Cortez had it, and Didier.

Are we going to die tomorrow?

Cortez covered it with loud noises, and Didier with laughter, and Thulile by trying to help others...

Yeah.

Nbaro took her tray to the clean-up area, and then dropped down to Second Deck. She had a little speech prepared, but

Horatio Dorcas was sound asleep. She closed the hatch softly, and left him to it.

Thea was sitting at the desk, typing away at an invisible keypad, wearing a VR rig. She pulled it off as Nbaro came in.

'Straight to bed?' she asked.

'You got that right. All of me aches.' Nbaro pulled a clean flightsuit from her rack and hung it on the back of the hatch, with her flight jacket and her good boots: her best uniform.

'Good luck tomorrow,' Drake said. When Nbaro turned from the hatch, there she was, and they embraced.

'I'm scared shitless,' Thea said.

'Me, too,' Nbaro said, though she wasn't – or rather, she was more scared of never lying down next to Dorcas again.

Thea broke away and indicated the coffee machine. 'Locked and loaded, Lieutenant,' she said. 'Have a really good cup of coffee tomorrow.'

Nbaro smiled.

I never thought I'd have all this. Sometimes, it's too much. How do happy people live with all their good fortune?

'We're going to be fine,' she said, with all the authority she was learning from her various teachers in the arts of leadership.

Drake smiled and fell back on the bed. 'I'll bet you say that to all the space crews,' she said. 'But thanks.'

And then Nbaro slept. She woke a few seconds before her alarm, turned it off before it could sound, and then she went to the hatch and dressed in the dark.

The coffee was delicious.

'Hey! Leave some for me,' Drake said.

'Damn it, I was trying not to wake you,' Nbaro said.

'The smell of coffee...' Thea stretched. 'Oh, God.'

They drank their coffee in silence, and then Nbaro slung her jacket over her shoulder and picked up her helmet bag.

'See you for dinner,' she said.

Drake nodded. 'See ya.'

Petty Officer Chu had Nbaro's EVA suit ready – the suit that had been intended for the *Hong Kong* and was probably supposed to be locked away in evidence. She touched it, the armour glowing faintly blue, and left it hanging overhead, collected her helmet, and walked to her spaceframe.

Alpha Foxtrot 6–0–7 waited patiently. The Hangar Deck was abustle as a thousand men, women and 'gynes prepared for a mass launch at the other end of a long insertion. Nbaro spared a thought for the *Stealthy Change* and her astrogator, as she remembered that this was the second longest insertion of the whole cruise: the most difficult to plot because Petra System was just a small star and some rocks – not enough mass to make an easy target at the end of light years of insertion.

Truekner was already there, standing in the shadow of the spacecraft's massive starboard wing nacelle.

'Morning, skipper,' she said.

He smiled. 'Currently afternoon for me,' he said. 'Glad you're with me, Nbaro.'

'Yes, sir,' she said with some enthusiasm.

They did their checks, and the spacecraft was immaculate, inside and out. Letke and Tench joined them, Tench silent and visibly nervous, Letke apparently calm. Nbaro went in through the crew hatch and started the auxiliaries, and soon enough all four of them were in the cockpit, and Truekner led the high ritual of the take-off procedures.

Everything worked. There was no drama.

They strapped into their acceleration couches, took their drugs, and settled in. Nbaro filed their launch weight and did other routine tasks...

'Four minutes until Insertion,' said Space Ops. Lioness was Musashi.

'Come home safe,' said Dorcas.

'I will. I'm with Truekner.'

Then Dorcas was gone, and there were only two minutes to go.

The Master came on the command channel.

'Friends,' he said. 'Remember everything we have done to get here. Remember that our ship will get us home if we help her. And help each other. That is all.'

'Amen,' said Truekner aloud.

Insertion.

Nbaro surfaced, glanced at Truekner, and then saw movement. To her left, a spaceframe went by on Launch Rail Two in a blur of movement. The whole ship vibrated as thousands of massive electromagnets shot eighteen tonnes of metal and composite off the front end.

'Alpha Foxtrot 6-0-7 ready to launch,' she said. They should be third; sure enough, she felt the spaceframe move as the automated system took them to the launch position.

'Roger,' said Tower. 'You are two to launch.'

'I'm up,' Letke said. 'My computer is slow... there she is. I have a sub-AI. Back end is good.'

Truekner sounded muzzy but awake. 'I have her.'

Nbaro had the Space Operations 3D tank in her head via neural lace. It hadn't updated yet, but...

But they were *far* deeper into the system's gravity well than the plot had predicted. She had no idea if that was good or bad.

The cockpit smelled of electricals and human sweat overlaid on plastic and carbon fibre. The air inside her helmet would be fresh and clean, but for the moment, all of them had their visors open.

They rolled into place and the whole spaceframe seemed to crouch. There was a *CLICK* as they locked into the launch rails.

'Going out cold,' Nbaro said.

'Roger that, engines cold.' Truekner turned and looked at the spacer behind the armoured xenoglas screen who held the electromagnetic launch button. He saluted.

A long tunnel of light, a rumble like thunder, and they were off into the darkness. Truekner used the cold-gas thrusters to manoeuvre them away from the launch pattern and then down the system's *y*-axis as Nbaro lost the ship's dataspace and her neural lace lost contact with Morosini.

'We're under fire,' reported the Tactical Action Officer. It was Corbett, and her voice was calm. 'Hit amidships.'

Nbaro watched the system update even as Letke dropped their first sensor.

'I have three hostile contacts,' she said. 'Tagging them. Tench, you got this?'

Tench's voice was tight. 'Yes, ma'am.'

'Two away,' Letke said.

'Button up, folks,' Truekner said, and they all slapped down their faceplates.

The system updated again via datalink. Their spaceframe was running cold and receiving signals but not putting any out.

Twelve thousand kilometres away, almost dead astern of the *Athens* and well below the plane of the ecliptic, were three Hin ships, all with energy shields up.

'Shit,' Nbaro said. 'We're going the wrong way. They're behind us!'

It was true: 6–0–7 had been launched ahead of the *Athens* and her adversaries were astern. If they burned their main engines to turn, they would instantly become targets.

'All spacecraft, this is Claws, over. Do not burn or radiate. Repeat, do not burn or radiate.'

Truekner nodded. They would not respond; they were running silent. He used the cold jets to alter their vector even more.

On the 3D, the *Athens* was turning. In fact, she was rolling end for end – not a short process in a ten-kilometre ship.

Nbaro could see the threads of light as the Hin ships hit her with their beam weapons. According to her onboard computer, they were firing from beyond their predicted maximum range. She swallowed hard.

How much of the information we based our strategy on did we have wrong?

She could also hear, on one of her many channels, Dorcas beginning to broadcast in the Hin language.

'Three away,' Letke said.

'I have all three contacts locked and logged,' Tench said. 'They're closing. Accelerating at ...' Nbaro could hear his breathing. 'A lot.'

The Hin all fired again, their lances of light reaching out to strike the *Athens*. She was still rotating, and so far, had been unable to reply. Now she'd rotated about fifteen degrees, so that her stern was facing directly at the enemy.

The *Athens* fired all four tubes – out of the stern.

'Oh,' Nbaro said aloud. *Electromagnets work both ways.*

'All spacecraft, free to manoeuvre,' Claws said on the tactical frequency. Clouds of chaff billowed out into space behind them, tiny charges and micro-rockets enlarging the cloud according to a computer-generated pattern.

Truekner engaged the main engines.

Nbaro ran her eyes over all the systems, her neural lace one with the spacecraft's diagnostics. 'I have engine start. I have power. Full power in five ...'

'Hang on,' Truekner said, and they were turning, the *g* force shocking. Nbaro's couch rotated as far as it could, and she was deep in the foam, and they were still turning.

The 3D updated again, showing an exclusion zone as a cone extending from the stern of the *Athens*. They were well clear of it.

The three Hin ships were hurtling at them, their acceleration blue-shifting their shields to the naked eye so that they looked like blue pinpoints, and then blue stars.

'Seven thousand kilometres,' Letke said. 'I have a lock.'

'I have four fish, all hot,' Nbaro said.

Truekner grunted. 'I want a better aspect,' he managed through 10 g of turn.

The alien ships all fired together, shooting through the chaff and the ablative fog, and their beam weapons showed brilliantly. Seconds later, the *Athens* responded, all four tubes firing together.

Nbaro used her neural lace predictively, and she drew predictive circles in the 3D with her mind, showing the point at which the pursuing Hin ships would converge with the *Athens*.

But as fast as she could calculate, the situation changed. All three alien ships manoeuvred, breaking their formation as each took a different path. Nbaro guessed that they were trying to maintain their ideal range, and stay out of the railgun's arc.

The *Athens'* latest salvo was another round of chaff and ablative sand. It burst a thousand kilometres astern, and Nbaro lost the three enemy ships in the roiling clouds of chaff, but they remained on their new vectors on the 3D overlay from the datalink.

'Lost our lock,' Letke said, dispassionately.

Truekner killed the engines, and they ran down a new course towards an intercept with the alien ship lowest on the y-axis of the system. According to the 3D, they had Didier following them in 6–0–2, almost in formation. They wouldn't be cold, exactly, as they came through the chaff cloud, but they might have some time.

The chaff cloud came up like a wall, and Nbaro subconsciously braced for impact, but then they were through, into open space, and her systems updated her data.

'I have a new lock,' Letke said.

'Still too far out,' Truekner said. 'Engaging evasive manoeuvres.'

The closing speed was too much for Nbaro to calculate.

The cold thrusters fired, all on one side, then all on the other. It appeared random – the spaceframe was only moved a few hundred metres off her course each time – and Nbaro felt as if she was being beaten with a stick; each firing of the cold thrusters felt like an impact with a hard surface.

'Two thousand kilometres,' Letke said. The enemy ship was a white pinpoint to the naked eye, her engines burning white-hot.

Nine thousand kilometres away, there was a blue-white flash.

'Damn,' Truekner said. 'Take her, Nbaro.'

Nbaro felt the yoke come alive under her hands. She risked a glance at the skipper.

Suddenly the ship ahead of them began to turn, and sparkle.

'They're shooting at us,' Letke said unnecessarily.

The sub-AI s evasive program read the incoming slugs on radar and kicked them again.

'Fifteen hundred kilometres,' Tench said.

'I can see again,' Truekner managed.

Nbaro used her lace to look at the 3D – at least, the version updated by datalink. One of the enemy ships was gone.

And the *Stealthy Change* had inserted. She'd come in ten thousand kilometres astern of the *Athens*, fired a single round from her massive centreline railgun, and changed the entire engagement.

All that brought a flash of comprehension. 'Shoot all four fish at one thousand,' Nbaro said. 'Skipper?'

'Concur,' he said.

Letke said, 'Roger. One, two, three four.'

'Didier is shooting,' Truekner said.

They were slammed to one side as the enemy ship sparkled again. This time, even through the pain of rapid acceleration change, Nbaro thought to be sure this was on vid. *The energy shields must vibrate or phase to let the Hin fire.*

The enemy ship fired its beam weapon … at the *Athens*. They were less than two thousand kilometres apart, and the *Athens* was replying with her close-in-systems and smaller, turret-mounted railguns.

'One away,' Letke said. 'Two away.'

SLAM.

Nbaro pulled back on the yoke and the big spaceframe's engines roared back to life. Instantly they were under fire.

She was just turning her head…

'Three away,' Letke called. The spacecraft bounced with the release of the third torpedo, and then the canopy above their heads was ripped away. So was the backrest of Nbaro's ejection seat, just over her head.

Truekner said, 'Everyone still back there?'

'Roger that, sir,' Tench said through gritted teeth.

'Holy *fuck*,' Letke said. And then, 'Four away.'

The whole diagnostic system was red. Nbaro had engines; she switched an alarm off, still turning *hard.*

Above her, she could see open space, the cabin open to hard vacuum. Her cold thrusters were gone; their fuel was lost into space. She had main engines and some attitude adjusters. Their torpedoes were gone.

Ten-second run time at a thousand kilometres.

They were hit again – multiple blows that she felt, rather than saw.

And then the first flash, now behind her.

The nuclear light flashed and flashed, a terrible storm lashing the energy shields of the enemy ship. The Hin close-in weapons got some; but with eight torpedoes inbound, there were at least three flashes of nuclear lightning.

Nbaro used the neural lace to indicate that they were heavily damaged and needed to recover. Then she watched on 3D, an observer now, as the *Athens* fired her railguns at the ship that she and Didier had just hit.

'I can take her back now,' Truekner said. 'I was blind there for a second...'

'Ship is yours, skipper,' Nbaro said. Several thousand kilometres behind them, their target's engines' magnetic seals failed, and they burned like the sun for a fraction of a second.

'Christ,' muttered Truekner.

Fifteen thousand kilometres away, the *Stealthy Change* hammered the third enemy ship, aided by almost a dozen spacecraft from the *Athens*. There could be only one result, and it came less than a minute later, as the enemy ship blew up.

Alpha Foxtrot 6–0–7 limped back to the *Athens* in silence, bleeding fuel, but Truekner got her aboard with a slow, careful landing.

'We were unlucky,' Tremaine said. It was an all-space-crew meeting, held on vid. Tremaine had use of the Space Ops 3D holotank, and she used it to project the course of the engagement. 'We arrived deeper in the system than we planned, with our opponents behind and below us. For some reason, despite having the advantage of range, they chose to accelerate right at us.' She shrugged. 'They had no idea that we had a PTX heavy cruiser coming right in behind us, so there we were lucky. And most of all, they almost never fired directly at our space wing craft. Almost all of their fire was directed at the *Athens*.'

Tremaine ran the holo through several repetitions, showing parts of the action. Nbaro was pleased to note that she and Didier had put in a textbook attack, releasing their torpedoes almost together.

'6–0–2 probably killed the crew from radiation on the third hit,' Tremaine said. Seconds later, the *Athens* hit the same target with heavy slugs from one of the main railguns, and the enemy ship exploded in a white flash. She ran the vid back and showed the last engagement, high up the *y*-axis in the ecliptic, as three Flight Five spacecraft, along with Bakri from Flight Six, all pounded the enemy ship while it was locked in a fiery exchange with the PTX cruiser.

'The *Stealthy Change* took over two hundred hits,' Tremaine said. 'The *Athens* took about thirty, mostly beam weapons. Twenty-four dead, almost a hundred wounded, and total loss of number three launch tube until we can fix her.' She nodded. 'There are at least six more enemy ships in this system. Stay alert, get your crew rest, and don't let your guard down.'

Steven Yu, the med tech, was dead. A beam weapon had burned down through the medbay, where, just hours before, Dorcas had been. She didn't know any of the other dead particularly well, but she knew this after-battle feeling.

It didn't feel like victory.

21

Hours later, Nbaro was Lioness. She lay in the acceleration couch at the centre of Space Operations, watching the latest space battle in human history develop around her.

There were three pods of Hin ships – two of three ships each, and one of nine ships. Lochiel had speculated that the Hin deployed in threes, based on what they'd seen so far, except for the lone ship that had attacked them way back before Trade Point.

Two of the pods were well behind them, one high above the plane of the ecliptic, one low. Fraser from Astrogation had marked both points as potential entry zones, based on their insertion at Corfu; in other words, they faced an alien enemy well versed in their route.

During her watch, Nbaro launched and recovered dozens of spacecraft with Cortez as Tower. Cortez looked exhausted; he'd already been out twice.

'I didn't sleep so well last night,' he admitted.

'I see you helped the *Stealthy Change* get Hin ship 1–3,' she said.

'Yeah, well, that was just turning and burning.' Cortez looked away.

Cortez being modest? The world is coming to an end.

Midway through her watch, the acceleration warning sounded and they manoeuvred for an hour at high *g*. She watched their course changes, and despite the incredible loads on her body, the *Athens'* overall course seemed to change very little.

Behind them, six Hin cruisers were still accelerating towards them. Morosini said that they'd be in engagement range in a little under seventeen hours. Ahead, spread across two hundred thousand kilometres of space in a net that encompassed most of their possible insertion options, waited nine more. And yet, the sternward Hin were not on course to be in weapons range simultaneously with the Hin ahead.

They're not working together – they're different factions.

Two hours later, Nbaro was strapped into an acceleration couch in the restricted area, with Dorcas next to her in his own couch. Nik'ri Put floated serenely, apparently unaffected by the acceleration.

Nbaro laid out the situation with the help of Morosini and a projection of the 3D from Space Operations.

Nik'ri Put's eyes followed every movement, fixed absolutely on the holo.

'This is right and also very good,' she said. 'And accurate?'

Dorcas explained the egg-shaped bubbles around some ships, and their meaning about probabilities in a given volume of space. Also the time delay factor.

'None of these ships have responded to our message,' Nbaro said.

'This is not right,' Nik'ri Put said. 'These should be allied clans.'

'I think it is possible,' Dorcas said slowly, 'that they believe this is a ruse.'

'Ruse?' said the quick-witted alien.

Dorcas sighed. 'A piece of trickery. A lie.'

'Ah!' Nik'ri Put's tentacles flounced, a sign that Nbaro took to indicate temporary annoyance. 'Yes and yes.' She floated up a short distance, and came to rest again.

Nbaro wished that she could lean forward, or put a hand on the side of the tank, or do anything to indicate personal contact. Instead, she was as confined as the creature. '*Tse-Tsu*, we need you to make a recording,' she said. 'Something we can play for them that they will believe.'

Tentacle flick. Nbaro thought it was like a head nod. 'Yes and yes.'

Nbaro became hopeful.

'For what thing would you trade me, *KePoja*?' Nik'ri Put asked.

Dorcas and Nbaro had scripted this, and now it fell to Nbaro because they both agreed that she had the closer relationship with the Hin.

'We ask that you negotiate for us,' she said. 'We hope that you will help us explain ... to the Hin that we don't need to fight. We only wish to trade unhindered.'

'With the *GoKur*!' Nik'ri Put's digital voice carried real force.

Dorcas spoke up. 'We are willing to listen to ... a different point of view about the Starfish.'

'Point of view?' Nik'ri Put asked.

It took Nbaro some time to explain different points of view and their role in negotiation.

'This is a beautiful concept,' Nik'ri Put said. 'It expresses something I have often thought but never found words for.'

Dorcas tabbed, Her Anglatin improves by leaps and bounds.

Nbaro asked, 'So ... this is possible?'

Nik'ri Put moved again. 'I will record the message in my own words. You will be right to fear what I say! I might be telling secrets!' Some movement. 'But I will not. Interesting as you are, *KePoja*, I wish to eat well and sleep with my mates. But my captain–mother's ships will not be here in this system – no and no. You will do better to negotiate with my captain–mother.'

Dorcas said, 'We will have to survive this to meet your captain–mother's ships.'

Nik'ri Put turned all the way around once. 'Ah,' she said. 'I will make the message and we will see.'

Before Nbaro went to sleep, Nik'ri Put's new message was being sent to both Hin squadrons. Dorcas seemed certain the message said, 'I am a legitimate prisoner of war aboard this ship, and the aliens seek to negotiate with honour.'

22

'And we're out of coffee,' Drake said.

Nbaro had two hours before her next flight, and she'd already looked at the 3D. None of the alien ships had responded to the new message. She could feel the strain of their acceleration throughout her body.

'I'll be right back,' she said, zipping on a flightsuit and cramming her feet into her soft boots. Minutes later she was ringing the buzzer at Dorcas's stateroom. She'd warned him by tab that she was coming, and he opened his hatch instantly.

'Good morning,' she said, trying for something like good cheer. 'May I have a pound of coffee?'

He was wearing a towel. Somewhat guardedly he said, 'I was getting clean.' In the cold light of the corridor, she could see the scars from his multiple surgeries and the loss of muscle mass. The wet showers were just down the corridor, and he had a large stateroom directly adjacent to facilities. She wondered just how powerful that meant he was.

'We are out of coffee,' Nbaro said, as if that explained everything, which, in her opinion, it did.

'I'm almost certain you *sold* me my coffee supply,' Dorcas said.

'Fine, I'll buy it back.'

Dorcas stepped back from the hatch and waved her in. 'Never

in life, my love. You will always have half of my coffee.' He went to his desk and extracted a kilo of coffee. 'This is half of my supply, because I'm not as profligate as you are.'

She wrapped her arms around the coffee before she fully appreciated what she was doing, and she laughed aloud. 'Coffee is very important to me,' she said, as she found that she couldn't take her eyes off him. She tried. She got up; she had less than an hour until the acceleration alarm sounded.

'May I...?' Dorcas was very hesitant. 'Are you...?'

He was blushing.

She waited.

'Are you really just going to leave?' Dorcas's voice was forced. 'I observe that you are naked under that flightsuit, and that you have fifty minutes.' He smiled with real concern. 'I am offending you...?'

She was still laughing as her boots came off.

Fifty-seven minutes later, she was in the cockpit of 6–0–7, a relatively new spaceframe, with Tim Eyre next to her and Janny Eason in the back seat.

Lioness came up on the comms. '2–0–4 had to abort – I can launch you immediately, over.'

'Alpha Foxtrot 6–0–7 ready to launch,' she reported. 'Born ready,' she added, because it was Cortez.

Lioness came back. 'On the rails and looking good, 6–0–7.'

'Someone's in a good mood,' Eyre said next to her.

Nbaro turned and looked at him and allowed herself a grin. 'Yep.'

They went off sternwards, and cold. The Hin cruisers were above them, and the TAO had spent the last few hours rotating the ship slightly and firing off ablative clouds. The *Athens* was coasting, under no acceleration whatsoever, so that she moved along at a high velocity, surrounded by her clouds of sand in lieu of shields as the enemy cruisers came up behind her. Safe in the cover of the ablative foil, the space wing's craft formed up, engines cold. The plan was Tremaine's, vetted by Pisani and Morosini.

The Hin were still accelerating. They clearly had no need for insertion, at least on this leg of their attack; they were now at a substantial portion of the speed of light – a little over $0.2\ c$.

The engagement would be very quick. Morosini thought they planned a single firing pass and then a rapid deceleration once they were out of range.

The Hin altered course. They did so all together, each trio spreading out at a different angle.

A light went on over Nbaro's head as the ship's AI took control of her craft. She leaned back and took her hands off the yoke.

Eyre did the same. 'Seems odd,' he said.

She nodded. 'Given our relative velocity, the only way to score a hit is if Morosini shoots our torps.' She was watching a countdown on her neural lace.

Nbaro's confidence in Morosini was absolute, and she thought Tremaine's plan, which was purely mathematical, was brilliant. The enemy were coming for a single high-velocity pass, and Tremaine had laced the cloud of debris with shooters to make the exchange utterly unequal. The Hin still didn't understand the space wing; the concept of small craft was apparently alien to them.

Three. She thought of Dorcas resting on his arms above her.

Two. For some reason, the Orphanage, and Sarah.

One. The top of her spacecraft vanishing in the last engagement; the silent near-destruction. *So close.* She couldn't even see the Hin ...*And why the hell aren't they responding...?*

Nbaro had to replay the action several times afterwards, to make sense of it. It had happened at relativistic speeds; she had experienced it as a release of torpedo clamps, a single pulse of acceleration, a hard *g* turn, a pulsing thunderstorm of nuclear light, a massive flash of white light to starboard...

And that was it.

The Hin ships closed in a rough circle, and opened fire at seven thousand kilometres. Their first salvo got a Flight One drop-ship and a Flight Five gunship, indicating that they had seen the spacecraft in the debris shield and had changed tactics to engage them. Then they entered the ablative cloud, where they encountered the rest of the space wing lying in wait.

One Hin ship lost its shields and the magnetic seals on its drives from multiple nuclear warheads. The entire crew of Didier's 6–0–8 died almost instantly, cooked by a nuclear warhead's radiation too close for their shielding to handle, but otherwise, Morosini's multiple high-velocity firing solutions avoided casualties and the enemy computers didn't seem to be up to close-in kills at the velocities involved.

A second enemy cruiser took a very close nuclear detonation, but her shields held, and they were gone, still accelerating into the vast, star-studded beyond.

The *Athens* took four hits. One struck a hydrogen fusion power plant. The other three put thirty-centimetre holes in Cargo. Explosive depressurisation in a crew area killed four spacers, but the ship was at battle stations and otherwise all personnel were in vacuum suits.

But Nbaro returned to find a perfectly round patch in the corridor, just two frames aft of her stateroom. She and Drake looked at it on their way to eat. A matching hole in the overhead had also been patched but not yet painted.

'Close,' Drake said. 'Come on, there's pie.'

We're locked in a long, running fight with aliens, and Thea wants pie.

By the time they'd eaten, the Hin ships had begun to decelerate, far out ahead of them.

Except for one, which continued to accelerate.

Nbaro looked at it on her neural lace. It was the same ship that had taken a close nuclear detonation; Morosini rated it ninety per cent likely that everyone aboard was dead. Shields up, engines burning, it would hurtle off into interstellar space.

She was toying with the remains of her pie when Mpono sat next to them.

'Lost Didier,' Mpono said.

Nbaro nodded. 'He was a good guy,' she allowed. He had been, too.

'I just wanted to tell you that Sam Pak was on that flight. I know you were training him.' Mpono reached out and took her hand.

Nbaro met Mpono's eye. 'I already knew,' she said. She had a neural lace. She also had some very good emotional armour, polished to a sheen at the Orphanage. She made herself go through the motions, though. 'Thanks, Smoke,' she said. 'XO.'

Mpono nodded with understanding. 'It's a tough cruise, Marca.'

Nbaro thought, *I have walled that off – Didier, Pak, Yu, Ko, Suliemani. Indra. Our ship peeling open during the last engagement. All of it. I'll open the box and look at it when this is over. But I'm fine.*

Mpono went and got herself pie. A hush fell over the wardroom at having the mighty ship's XO present. For their part, Mpono ate her cherry pie with relish, spent time with several other Flight Six space crew, and then left.

'You're staring into space,' Drake said. 'I'm afraid you'll drool.'

Nbaro looked at her. 'I'm tired.' She was surprised to hear the words come out of her mouth. *Maybe the walls aren't as strong as I think.*

*

305

While she slept, the battle rolled on. The ships that had swept in for a close-in pass were now well ahead of them. They had decelerated rapidly, but it still took them eight hours to match velocity, at which point they were far out of range. Then they began to decelerate further, and they dropped munitions. The TAO didn't wait to find out what the munitions were, but fired carefully aimed railgun bursts at them; their courses were entirely predictable.

The Hin ships decelerated until the *Athens* began to catch up. The *Athens* changed course. Nbaro awoke to an acceleration warning, snuggled down, and managed to sleep through most of a high-*g* manoeuvre. The next time she awoke, her sleep cycle was over, and she had less than an hour before she was Lioness. Thea was nowhere to be found, but she'd left hot coffee; Nbaro drank it gratefully, put on a flightsuit and boots, went forward to get her EVA suit and walked aft to Space Operations. They were at battle stations all the time now; everyone stood their watches in environment suits, with helmets close by. Some of the crew wore them.

Everyone was subdued, and no one looked as if they'd had enough sleep, but in Space Ops, Banderas was humming to herself, and she grinned when he saw Nbaro.

She'd been in dataspace with her lace since she had her first cup of coffee, and she came on watch fully aware of the state of the battle. The *Athens* had changed course four times – all subtle changes, but enough to force the Hin ships to manoeuvre. But gradually, the Hin were getting into firing positions.

Are they burning up their fuel, though?

Tad Dworkin was off-going Lioness. He raised a helmeted head out of the acceleration couch and gave a wave.

'Things are about to get exciting,' he said. 'So I'm delighted to give you the hot seat.'

'Exciting how?' she asked, but she knew the answer from her

neural lace and Morosini; they were about ten minutes from the enemy's maximum range with their beam weapons.

The *Athens* was moving at a constant velocity inside a veritable fog of ablative particles moving at the same speed. Her spacecraft kept laying sensors outside the cloud so she still had an excellent picture of the whole system, including the four Hin ships roughly seven thousand kilometres ahead and the three more who loitered near their only insertion point.

Dworkin made a face. 'TAO has permission from Morosini to try a gambit. Hostiles will probably open fire in …' He shrugged. 'Six minutes. She's all yours.'

'Thanks, sir.' Nbaro nodded, put her helmet on and then rolled into the acceleration couch, securing herself to it.

'Everyone button up, hats on,' she said. 'Expect manoeuvres in five minutes. Battle damage could mean zero *g* or decompression.'

She used her lace to take control of her acceleration couch, and swivelled it until she could see out over all her people. Then she began to arrange screens – holographic, in the real, and virtual.

Three minutes.

'Stand by for railgun firing and sudden manoeuvres,' she was warned on several media.

'Faceplates down,' she called. She was looking at a fairly light launch schedule; the *Athens* was hoarding its assets. But Thulile and Bakri were going in five minutes, as well as a Flight Three bird and several from Flight Two …

Her schedule changed before her eyes. Her entire launch schedule was *pushed back* by minutes. She'd never seen it happen before but—

—the whole ship shuddered as a heavy load was fired out of the number two railgun tube. Nbaro didn't need a neural lace to do the maths; the enemy ships were more than *ten minutes* away at the speed the railgun loads travelled down range.

She was punched in the gut as the ship suddenly accelerated and manoeuvred, and her couch spun. They were turning...

Another railgun tube fired. *Shudder-thud.*

Nbaro had a neural lace and almost infinite access, so she was able to watch the outgoing rounds, and then noted that the *Stealthy Change* was also firing on very slightly different vectors.

The countdown to enemy engagement range passed zero with no beam from the hostile ships. Her 3D repeater showed all four of them manoeuvring while the fifth continued on her long, one-way trip to the stars. They spread out, but their manoeuvres must have affected their ability to use their beam weapons, as they didn't fire.

Fuel? Or some internal power sharing problem?

The *Athens* turned again. Somewhere in Space Ops, someone moaned as a muscle or a tendon was abused; these were punishing manoeuvres, and she hoped that Dworkin and the off-going crews had made it to their racks.

Shudder-thud. Shudder-thud. Two launches in the middle of a rotation. Four hundred kilometres to port, the *Stealthy Change* unleashed her tubes, firing almost continuously for ten seconds, something that the *Athens* couldn't do.

'*Would you like to see what we're doing?*' Morosini purred in her ear.

'Of course,' she sub-vocalised.

Suddenly her 3D had an overlay of every railgun launch in the last four minutes. Now some of their broadside railguns were firing as well.

Morosini – she assumed it was Morosini – had created a complex fractal pattern, and the ships were putting projectiles into it at different velocities and launch times, but they were working from the outside in, with surprising insertions to reflect the AI's analysis of the hostile ships' course changes.

'How long can we keep this up?' she sent.

'*How much fuel do they have?*' Morosini asked. '*Right now, we make them manoeuvre hard with their shields up. They've been out here waiting for us a while. Also, the ship I've marked as November Oscar 0–0–4 made a manoeuvring error in her last turn and is now facing diminishing options. Besides—*'

The hostile ship NO 0–0–4 made a sudden course change, and fired her beam weapon.

Nbaro could see that they were hit, forward. The beam was at maximum range and hadn't burned the length of the hull, which would have been ... bad.

'*They want to fire from dead astern or fully off the bow, to get their beam weapons to penetrate as many layers as possible,*' Morosini said.

'I get that,' Nbaro allowed.

Shudder-thud. Shudder-thud.

NO 0–0–4 cycled her main armament and fired again. Nbaro saw the damage immediately: a hit to the bridge wing.

The other hostile ships were all manoeuvring. The ship marked as HC 0–2–1 had dropped her shields and was boosting at something like 15 g. So were IF 0–0–5 and IF 0–1–7.

'I hate being shot at,' Nbaro said in her neural lace.

She had a countdown running until NO 0–0–4 recycled her beam weapon.

'NO 0–0–4 is sacrificing itself?' she asked Morosini.

'She may have decided to die. Possibly she took damage in the earlier engagement, or possibly her navigator has run out of options. They're very brave, these Hin.'

NO 0–0–4 fired again. This shot went straight through the ablative cloud; the previous rounds had opened a hole, or else the Hin had found a flaw in the layers of material. Either way, the shot burned a hole into the bridge wing that would have destroyed the *Pericles* if she'd been docked, and did real damage to the *Athens'* command and control systems.

Morosini went off the air.

NO 0–0–4's symbol flashed and was gone. Somewhere out in space, a ship full of sentient beings ceased to be.

All of the damage control warnings were sounding now, and the entire bridge wing was exposed to vacuum. Nbaro glanced at the engineering report, saw that the port-side bridge support – an enormous pylon full of avionics and computer systems – was so badly damaged that the ship could not manoeuvre for fear of breaking the bridge loose.

Almighty.

Focus. No more Morosini, and no override commands. If they couldn't manoeuvre, they wouldn't be using the railguns for more long-range payloads, which meant . . .

'Ready up,' she said over her command frequency. 'Prepare to launch in one minute.' She looked at Tower, who was Moses Juniper from Flight Eight. Juniper had his faceplate closed, but raised an arm and gave her a gloved thumb's up.

Nbaro used the new automated system to notify all the pilots; Juniper used the same system to get their take-off weights and data.

We're rewriting every manual – if we just get home to write them.

On her lace, Nbaro watched as Juniper OK'd each launch until all the lights were green: eleven spacecraft. Routine, ordinarily.

'TAO, this is Lioness looking for advice,' she sent.

'Roger, Lioness, this is Claws. What can I do for you?'

'Claws, I'm ready to launch an eleven-ship event and want to make sure I'm not interrupting anything.'

'Roger, Lioness, good call. I can give you three hundred seconds.'

She ran the maths on three tubes. 'I need four hundred, TAO.'

'Roger, four hundred seconds. Starting when?'

Nbaro pointed at Juniper, who began the count on Alpha Foxtrot 6–0–2, the first spacecraft in the event. He made a shooting gun sign; Nbaro saw the launch in VR.

'Start the clock,' she said.

'Roger, four hundred seconds,' TAO responded.

Nbaro watched as her event shot off into space. They then recovered nine ships from the stern tubes, locked them down...

In three hundred and eighty-one seconds.

'All yours, TAO,' she said.

'Roger, Lioness. Taking control of the tubes.'

More than six minutes had passed, and they had received no orders from Morosini or Pisani. Nbaro could access most ship's systems on her lace but the dataspace was limited.

'Dorcas?'

'Here.'

'Where's Morosini?'

'Wounded. Bridge is damaged. TAO has the con.' Dorcas sounded solid.

'No one told us here.'

Long pause.

'I see that now.'

Suddenly her screens showed an emergency message nominating the TAO as on-scene commander. The report coded the damage to the bridge as 'serious'. A glance at the damage control status board showed Nbaro that the passageways were full of damage control personnel and robots.

On the 3D plot, the three surviving Hin ships from the original pass were all running, shields down. Three more sat on their insertion site.

For Nbaro, the next six hours were dull. For anyone out on the hull, like Lieutenant Commander Qaqqaq, they were both terrifying and hard, as the ship's best damage control parties tried to repair or replace the bridge wing's main support pylon on the starboard side while finding workarounds for all the damaged systems. At hour three, Morosini came back online. Just as Lieutenant Commander Thulile replaced Nbaro as Lioness, Master Pisani announced that the bridge was once again operational.

The whole of the *Athens* breathed a sigh of relief.

Nbaro grabbed a meal with Juniper, a lanky man from Sahel who might almost have passed for a 'gyne. He was a pilot from Flight Eight; she'd seen him in the passageway but never spent any time with him.

He spoke in the same patois as Mpono's mother.

'Nice job,' Nbaro said.

He grinned. 'My first watch, sure. Fickin' A.' He held up a long-fingered hand, and it was shaking slightly.

She shovelled in another bite of food, and mumbled 'Ship of heroes.'

He laughed. 'Older de moon, brighter she shines,' he said. 'You're smooth as Lioness.'

She felt her face grow hot at the compliment. 'Thanks,' she mumbled.

I did OK today. Not always an idiot.

Still hours left in the day.

She grinned. 'Thanks,' she said again. 'I gotta run. Boarding party.'

'Shiiit.' It sounded like *she-it*. 'I gotta fly.'

They both dropped their trays and went off down separate drop-shafts.

On Fourth Deck, Ramirez was pestering Nagy as her boarding parties waited for orders, all gathered up by the aft port-side drop-shaft. Locran ignored the two women, listening to Chen as the older chief petty officer went over the scenario for the day.

'We're the red team for an exercise,' Chen explained to the two teams.

Bothie rolled her eyes. 'We're in a real fuckin' battle, Chief.'

Chen glanced at her, his eyes hooded. 'Think you're ready to face alien marines in this passageway, Bothie?'

Bothie's face clouded. She swallowed hard.

Chen looked around. 'Listen up, people. We're fuckin' amateurs. Do *not* get cocky.'

Ramirez shot back, 'Who's an amateur?'

Chen glanced at the small woman, who didn't give ground. 'Born ready to fight aliens,' Ramirez said.

Locran barked his laugh. 'Good. You're with me, then.'

But the exercise proved Chen's point, as their multi-pronged assault on a waiting Marine team was broken by an ambush and a carefully planned barrage of drones.

Afterwards, Major Darkstar delivered a damning indictment of all of their mistakes in a flat, professional voice.

'Nbaro,' she concluded, 'stop leading from the front. You were unavailable to help unfuck your people because you were dead. No one wants that.' The major looked Nbaro in the eye.

Yep, still an idiot.

'Locran, excellent job when your leader was down. Your flexibility was good, your reaction to our ambush excellent. Then you chose to try to clear the corridor yourself...'

Locran looked at the deck.

'Nuur, first-rate use of the EMP carbine – but you have to know you'll be a focus for hostile fire once you start to use it. How many times were you hit?'

'Sixteen,' Nuur said softly.

Darkstar smiled grimly. 'And then you and Locran were both dead, too. Spacer Ramirez took command and made several bad decisions, but before we dwell on them, let's applaud the speed and resolution with which Ramirez took charge. A bad plan delivered with resolve beats the shit out of no plan. You got four of my people, Ramirez. Then we got all of yours.' Darkstar looked out over the two teams. 'On balance, you did more damage to my Marines than any other team we've faced, but you never threatened our operation. Still, had we been alien intruders, you got enough of us that we would have been badly degraded for a second or third engagement. And, my friends, that's how this is going down.' They looked around. 'We'll bleed them and then we'll gut them. We're in this for the long haul.'

Drun winked at Nbaro.

Nbaro just felt empty. *I'm already in this for the long haul.*

A phrase came to her from some forgotten text. *All our yester- days have lighted fools the way to dusty death.* She could see it: a long, slow defeat, corridor by corridor, as the enemy ships piled in like scavengers on a corpse. It might take months.

Suddenly there was a certain appeal to a lethal dose of radia- tion, or a beam weapon hit. Out like a light. She looked around at her people and banned these thoughts, exiled to a remote iron box where she locked them away.

And then she got to spend an hour with Dorcas, which she spent asleep on his acceleration couch.

23

Nbaro awoke to a gentle alarm, which proved to be a subroutine from Dorcas.

'Hello,' she sent.

'The Outer Hin sent a reply to our message,' he replied.

It was all there on her neural lace, including his and Morosini's first translations.

'We can swim together with honour, at least for a short time.'

An hour later she was sipping coffee in the classified spaces, looking at Honourable Blood Wa-Kan Nik'ri Put as she swam excited circles in her tank.

'This is my mother–captain's sister, a matron–reaver of much experience. She is Honourable Blood Wa-Kan Asinpal Las. She is very honourable. She has much... *Hin*.'

Nbaro had learned that *Hin* was a complex cultural concept, not a race name – that a person could be *Hin*, possess much or little *Hin*, give or receive *Hin*. Dorcas was beginning to doubt whether they should even use the word as the race name.

But Nik'ri Put preferred it to *Bubbles*, as her people often described themselves as *Hin*.

The ship was not under heavy acceleration, so she rose and walked around. 'How do we proceed?' she asked. 'Will you make a second vid?'

Nik'ri Put flashed by. 'Of course,' she said. 'As soon as possible.'

Nbaro motioned at the repeater of the Space Ops 3D holo that she'd conjured by the tank. 'What will she do, this Honourable Blood Wa-Kan Asinpal Las? I'm sorry, *Tse-Tsu*, but we are still fighting for our lives. I cannot risk my companions to send you home.'

Nik'ri Put writhed, tentacles moving rapidly. 'Hin do not require foolish sacrifice,' she said. 'She will order this other clan, whoever they are, to stand away.'

'And will they?' Nbaro asked.

The two longer tentacles flicked outward. It was so clearly a shrug that Nbaro made a note to ask Dorcas if this was a Hin trait, or whether their prisoner had learned the shrug from her human captors.

Nik'ri Put's eyes met Nbaro's through the liquid and the slab side of her tank. 'Who knows?' she said. 'It is not a case of yes and yes, with all in agreement. Every clan has different...' She flicked the long tentacles again. 'I lack words. We do not even agree on what is *Hin*.'

So human.

Later, Dorcas lay next to her, his head propped on a pillow. 'The Starfish don't have a chance,' he said. 'At least, not with humans. The Hin speak and think very much like us. I'm sure there will be disturbing cultural dissonances – just look at Terran history. But they are *apparently comprehensible*.'

'How are you doing with Feather Dancer?' she asked.

'Better than I'd expected...' He glanced at her. 'I'm not supposed to discuss it.'

'Not supposed to discuss it with me? I swear I have every level of classification—'

'*You do not. Nonetheless, I'm prepared to let the two of you talk. But this information is dangerous to know and dangerous to repeat aloud.*'

Nbaro was painfully aware that Morosini monitored her most of the time, but this was a new level of intrusiveness. She froze, then gradually relaxed.

It's not the Orphanage. Not the Orphanage.

I trust Morosini, and I wonder at myself.

Dorcas was apparently getting something of the same, because after a long pause, he said, 'I am communicating fairly well with Feather Dancer. They are eager to please, and we have now moved far beyond the clumsy robots we started with.'

Marca blinked. She hadn't seen Qaqqaq in what seemed like weeks, and Dorcas probably saw her every day.

'So you have learned...?' She lay back. 'Honestly, I want to know everything.'

Dorcas nodded. 'They are millions of years old. They have a vast star-faring civilisation extending away along the Spiral Arm for many hundreds of light years. They have sent expeditions to other galaxies. They are truly alien in a way that the Hin are not – I worry that we cannot understand their motivations at all. I am reasonably sure that there was another race, an earlier race that employed the Starfish as workers, maybe slaves, for a frighteningly long time.'

'These are Nik'ri Put's *Ill'lu*?' Nbaro asked.

'Exactly. But the time scale is vast, and frankly, I think I'm hearing myths, not history.'

'And the *Ill'lu* are *not* the same as the Circles?' she asked.

'No. I know no more about the Circles than I did a month ago, except that Feather Dancer has effectively confirmed that the Starfish exterminated them. Total genocide.' He shrugged. 'Feather Dancer is from an *inferior line* – a direct translation – and doesn't feel any responsibility for the imperial actions of its cousins. That, or the whole race lacks a conscience. Certainly Feather Dancer lives very much from moment to moment.'

Nbaro, who was naked, and running a hand over Dorcas's

317

chest, grunted. 'Horatio,' she said, 'you might be surprised how much I am living from moment to moment right now.'

He rolled over so they were chest to chest. 'I'm afraid every time you go out.'

She managed a small smile. 'I'm afraid all the time. As for flying? Almighty, Horatio, nothing is safe. They can pound the ship with beam weapons. Yu died in his medbay...' She clamped down on her emotions.

Dorcas looked at her for a long time. 'I...' He shook his head. 'I never want this to end,' he said with total honesty. 'Nothing in my life has ever been like this. I am fully...' He shrugged. 'And you...'

She giggled. It was spontaneous, and healing. 'You are speechless.'

Later, in the humming quiet of her own stateroom, she thought, *He is right. I never thought that life could be this rich. Even if we're all going to die.*

She was just drifting off to sleep when the acceleration alarm went off. She lay like a corpse as her acceleration couch closed on her and the needles sank into her flesh. The *g* forces began to gather, pressing her down, and then she was gone into a troubled sleep.

There was a lull in the immense pressure, and she woke to the hurried sounds of Thea Drake folding herself into her rack and the hydraulic hiss as the lid closed. The alarm sounded again.

'Something's happening out there,' Drake said.

Nbaro was learning not to engage her neural lace unless she wanted – really wanted – to know. She remembered when she'd first had a tab, and the temptation to be on it all the time; the lace was worse.

She struggled briefly and then looked.

The Outer Hin – the ones who had been sitting at their

insertion point – were now accelerating in-system, towards the Inner Hin, the survivors of two attacks on the *Athens*.

The Inner Hin, who had flown three widely divergent courses, were now on vectors to intercept one another, but they remained in the plane to intercept the *Athens*.

Nbaro checked and saw that Dorcas had received a new vid from Nik'ri Put and deployed it, but as yet they had no answer.

The acceleration alarm sounded again. She dropped out of the dataspace, and tried to do her duty and rest.

Nbaro and Drake were no longer on the same wake/sleep cycle, so she didn't have hot coffee waiting for her when she awoke, but the heavy acceleration was over. The damage control parties were mostly finished, too; the bridge wing was stable, and the bridge had full control of the ship. She sneaked out, dogged their beautiful bronze hatch, and spent a moment admiring it. She could remember when just having this stateroom on this ship was the very peak of happiness.

All I ever wanted.

Dorcas is right. If we survive, what will ever equal this?

She walked down to the EVA shack, got her helmet and gear, and then sat in the ready room and watched the flight briefing with about a third of her attention. She simultaneously prepped most of her flight issues by neural lace, including running a full suite of diagnostics on 6–0–9, which she'd never flown before. They were to test a new antenna array; She had Eyre, and Tatlah in the back with Tench. They had four new back-seaters, all Flight Eight people. Flight Eight hadn't taken the same losses they had, and their sensor techs were trained on similar equipment.

They also had a new pilot to replace Didier: Elise Hammond, who, like Bakri, was actually a ship's company officer with experience as a pilot, now transferred to cover the losses. Hammond was mostly flying with Truekner and Thulile, getting her hand in, as they said.

Eyre was subdued, answering in single words and grunts; Nbaro didn't push him. They punched off the front end, skirted the new cloud of ablative dust, and laid half a dozen sensors in an open pattern while Tatlah played with the new antennas and fiddled with his system. It wasn't going to be an eventful flight, but they had a great deal of work to do. Nbaro let Eyre handle most of it while she wrote a tactics briefing that encapsulated new material from Morosini about rapid deployment of sensors, the errors that had killed Didier, and possible solutions.

The bulk of the briefing was speculation about the state of Hin technology, tactics, and energy limitations based on the last two engagements. Morosini wanted everyone to understand that the energy capabilities of their opponents weren't limitless, and that their tactical development had probably been stunted by constant internecine fighting.

Nbaro played with that part, because she didn't like it. *Humans only fought each other for thirty thousand years and we got pretty sharp. Why would it stunt the Hin?*

She made a long note on her lace to discuss this with Morosini, and glanced over at Eyre, who was piloting. He had a set expression on his face; his visor was up and he was fully engaged in flying a complex route laid down by Morosini on cold gas thrusters alone. She was monitoring the datalink in a remote way when something flashed.

She glanced by neural lace at the 3D representation of the system. Three Outer Hin were converging with the Inner Hin. On her lace she could see that there had been a massive increase in signals – or, at least, in radio and laser frequency emissions. She looked back almost an hour; there was a lot of talking on both sides.

Even as she watched, all of the Hin ships raised their energy shields.

Almighty. They're going to fight.

Forty seconds later, all six ships manoeuvred hard, pulling staggering *g* forces to make big directional changes. They were less than five thousand klicks apart and they took six new headings, most at almost one hundred degrees to their initial heading.

No one fired. No beam weapon flickered; no nuclear lightning played among the ships.

And none of them stood between the *Athens* and her insertion point for the next system.

'What's happening, ma'am?' Eyre asked.

'Fucked if I know,' she said. 'The Hin just broke off without shooting.'

Eyre studied the tracks on his small repeater.

'Sure is a lot of chatter,' Tatlah said from the back. 'All of them are sending signals.'

'Not talking to us, though,' Nbaro said.

Eyre shut off the back-end's access to cockpit comms. 'We going to make it through this, ma'am?'

She turned her helmeted head. 'Yep.'

Eyre's eyebrows shot up. 'Just like that?'

She smiled at him. The smile was fake, and so was her enthusiasm. 'Yep,' she said, as if it was just another routine day in space.

'Roger that, ma'am.' Eyre nodded firmly.

That wasn't bad, she thought. *Now, if Truekner could just do the same for me?*

A long boarding party session followed, ending with some personal combat training; Nbaro went some rounds with Chen and then shot various weapons on the range with Drun and Locran, and then Drun went to drill Nuur on his EMP carbine. She fenced with Corporal McDonald, who had his foot back, and still enjoyed being a corporal. Ramirez led a fire team through a small exercise and was praised directly by Darkstar.

'Are you going to poach her, Major?' Nbaro asked. She didn't usually ask the major anything, as they were too imposing to tease.

Darkstar smiled their Marine smile. 'If Spacer Ramirez is interested in being a Marine, we could find a place for her,' they said. 'She's a fighter.'

After boarding party, Nbaro stood an under-instruction watch with Lieutenant Commander Corbett in the Combat Information Centre. Corbett had very little time to instruct her, as they were all locked up at battle stations and the alien ships were manoeuvring. All six of the closer ships had lowered their shields; they were in a loose, uneven formation about thirty thousand kilometres across. Emissions sparkled from each ship – a chatter of communications. It was all heavily encrypted.

Nbaro watched them manoeuvre, ran back their emissions, and looked at the point at which they all lowered their shields. She didn't learn a thing.

'Negotiating,' Dorcas sent by lace.

'Got there all by myself.'

'Yes, I have noted your intelligence before. But what will they decide?'

'I'm in CIC. According to the computer here, if they don't react in six hours, we get a free run to Insertion without fighting.'

Dorcas sent, 'And then they can follow us. The next system will be worse, you know.'

'You are a bundle of good cheer,' she sent, and cut him off ruthlessly. After a pause, she relented, and sent, 'One day at a time.'

'Agreed,' he said, and fell silent.

Nbaro was exhausted when she headed back to her cabin. She hadn't even visited Dorcas; she was that tired.

According to her schedule, Drake was awake but in her down time, so Nbaro un-dogged the hatch and pushed it open.

'Maybe come back in an hour?' Drake said breathlessly. Rick Hanna was there; a glimpse of flesh, a giggle, and she had the hatch closed again.

Wait until you're out in the Deep Black... Who had said that?
Damn it, I just want my rack.

Of course, Drake was well within her rights; Nbaro wasn't even on her sleep cycle yet, and Dorcas wasn't in his cabin.

She went to the ready room and worked on her tactics briefing. After a while, her tab beeped and there was a message from Thea.

All Clear. Sorry, honey.

She grinned, and Lieutenant Commander Thulile, in the next acceleration couch, looked at her. 'Good joke?'

'Humanity,' Nbaro said.

'Aha – great joke, then.'

Nbaro got up, filed her briefing by neural lace, queried Morosini, and walked back to her stateroom. Hanna was gone.

'Rick just asked me to marry him,' Drake said. She was lying on her acceleration couch looking ridiculously relaxed and happy in her workout gear.

'Congratulations?' Marca said with some reserve.

'Exactly. Is this what I want? Is it even what he wants? Fuck, will we even be alive in two weeks?' Drake smiled up at her. 'But the sex was good, and I don't think he noticed that I didn't say anything as conclusive as *yes*. Has anyone noticed what a high-pressure environment a ship in a long space battle is?'

Nbaro laughed long and hard, a belly laugh that rolled on for half a minute. Then she managed, 'I think we're all making this up as we go along.'

Drake's sparkle faded. 'Yeah? I just keep thinking that this is what the *Hong Kong* and the *New York* and the *Dubai* went through. Except they're all dead now.'

Nbaro pulled off her flightsuit. 'You are a bundle of joy.'

Drake wriggled. 'I have to go on watch.' She got up into the space that Nbaro had vacated; there wasn't really room for two women to dress or undress simultaneously. 'Truly? I think we'll make it home.' She grinned, her face at eye level with Nbaro's in the top rack. 'But will Rick still want me in the everyday of City life? Fuck, will I want him? This is not the Deep Black they told us about, where we're all bored spitless. Instead...'

'Instead, we're hunted by aliens and it's all peril all the time,' Nbaro said. 'Dorcas is having the time of his life.'

'So are you, darling. Maybe I am, too. What will we do after this?' Drake shrugged into her uniform jacket. 'How's your boarding party?'

'I have two,' Nbaro said. 'Remember Ramirez?'

'The vicious one when we were building out your *Pericles*? Hey, where is the *Pericles* anyway?' Drake slurped coffee.

'Yeah, that one. No idea. Some sort of test flight.'

Drake grunted. 'What about Ramirez?'

'She's a gifted shipboard fighter. The Marines want her.'

'Christ, a fate worse than death, at least according to my brothers. Mind you, I have thought about it myself.' Drake laughed. 'Don't wait up, honey.'

'Mmphh,' Nbaro said, already falling away towards sleep.

24

They were two days out from the insertion for Split, their next system. Nbaro received a request, via neural lace, to push Nik'ri Put into making another message for the Hin, but she had a watch and a command meeting first. She spent four hours with the TAO, learning some of the details of the limitations on manoeuvre imposed by everything from the ship's mass to various fuel supply equations.

'Fraser had better have something up his sleeve,' Lieutenant Commander Corbett muttered, 'because we are going to be *very* low on fuel when we enter the Split System.'

Nbaro began to appreciate the multiple competing demands that dictated the TAO's decisions in an engagement; Corbett spent the watch talking to Astrogation about the exact path they'd need for Insertion and how best to reach it. The six surviving Hin ships still ahead were now in two distinct squadrons, well separated in space and *just barely* clear of the insertion zone. Six more lurked above and below on parallel courses.

'Any thoughts on *why* the squids are suddenly letting us go?' Corbett asked.

'No, ma'am,' Nbaro said. *None that I can discuss with you, ma'am.* Not for the first time, Nbaro noticed that having information that she was forbidden to share with her immediate superiors was awkward, instead of empowering.

Corbett gave her an *I wasn't born yesterday* look. 'Seriously?'

Nbaro gave the midshipper salute – a broad shrug. 'Seriously, ma'am.'

She was glad to escape, and she changed into a shipboard uniform as quickly as she could and headed for the bridge wing. New steel and alloys had been welded in over new supports, and nothing had been painted yet, so the repairs were obvious.

It was a shock when the lift doors opened. The fireplace and the painting were gone. The briefing room was now a matt grey-green with two heavy folding tables and ship's issue chairs.

'Oh!' Nbaro said.

Morosini appeared. His tall gothic throne was unchanged, but then, it was part of his holographic projection. He wore deep red clothes of a bygone age, something both elegant and faintly piratical, with a huge flowing wig, or perhaps that was his hair, tall boots and a rapier, none of which discomfited his cat, who purred loudly enough to rattle the table.

'*Yes*,' he said. '*We were hit hard. I may even be said to have been dead, for a bit.*'

Lochiel looked away.

Nbaro took her usual seat and a robot servitor appeared with coffee. It smelled delicious, and she drank it gratefully.

Morosini smiled thinly. '*We need Nik'ri Put to reopen communications with her matron–captain's sister, Ms Nbaro. It is perhaps the most important thing that can happen today.*'

Nbaro nodded. 'I understand.'

Seeing Morosini was a direct reminder of a number of issues that she'd put away in her iron boxes: the deaths of her parents; Morosini's admission that he'd manipulated her at the Orphanage; the neural lace, and all it implied.

She glanced at Lochiel. *Now is not the time.*

The senior officers began to arrive, some from the bridge, some from the lifts. Dorcas sat by her. His smile was warm, his pleasure in seeing her unfeigned.

I could really get used to that.

Mpono nodded to Nbaro as they sat, and Fraser grinned. 'We need to spar,' he said. 'I'm getting fat.'

Lochiel looked worried, as if a captain and a junior lieutenant were going to start a throwdown before his eyes.

'At your service, sir,' Nbaro said. She even smiled.

Darkstar came in with Lieutenant Smith, and Captain Dukas threw herself into a chair. The head of Engineering had dark circles under her eyes, a long splash of blue hydraulic fluid on her cheek and over one shoulder, and her shipboard work suit was covered in various fluids. She smelled like a mixture of machine oil and ozone.

Pisani came in last, from the bridge. Everyone stood.

'Sit,' he said. 'We're having this meeting to assess our position and plan the next leg into Split.' He nodded to Fraser. 'Let's hear it, Bernie.'

Fraser stood, waved a hand, and the overhead system projected a holotank with an utterly alien star system. The projection was so bright and so odd that Nbaro's first thought was that it was a cartoon.

'Split,' Fraser said. 'An enormous torus of gas and rubble, lit from within like a paper lamp by two stars – a yellow giant and a white dwarf. The white dwarf pulses with X-rays at a rate that pretty much prohibits a permanent human presence. We have navigational buoys and a hardened transit detection system.' He had a laser pointer, which he used to point at the two stars; they moved in the animation as he rotated the aspect of the system. 'At the heart of the system, all of the mass of the gases and rock has been sucked into the stars, or that's what the DHC survey says. The result is that the heart of the system is empty, or relatively empty out to about twelve light minutes. Let's call it two hundred and fifty million kilometres.' He looked around. Fraser was full of energy, and Nbaro took this as a good sign.

'The gas cloud, which is full of debris, is a doughnut. It's huge – about ten light minutes in diameter. And in that gas cloud is a gas giant. It's still forming, but it was located precisely by the DHC survey. No one has ever used it for refuelling before.'

A course projection appeared in a bright cyan. The system continued to rotate on all three axes, so that everyone at the table could see their projected course.

'We plan to extract from Artifact Space *here*,' Fraser said. *Here* was open space at the very edge of the gas cloud, well out from both stars, and midway between them. He put the laser pointer on what appeared to be empty space. 'There is a third mass in the system, or so we posit from the behaviour of the two visible stars. We believe it is a concentration of dark matter analogous to a star.' He shrugged. 'We won't go anywhere near it. Someday the DHC will send an expedition to explore it, but that's not us and not today.'

'Thank God,' Dukas muttered. She crossed herself.

Hughes, the head of Cargo, leaned back. 'So we're jumping in close to the gas cloud?'

Fraser nodded.

'I'm guessing there's too much mass in the gas cloud for a safe insertion there?' Hughes asked.

'There has never been a successful extraction from Artifact Space into any region with particulate matter,' Fraser said, as if he was quoting from a textbook. 'Also, in terms of astrogation, this is a relatively easy insertion. The gas cloud is a ring, which makes the centre a target, with two ... really three stellar masses for pinpoint accuracy.'

Hughes nodded.

Pisani leaned forward. 'You're confident you can hit that

target?' he asked. 'Bernie, I know we've asked miracles of you all cruise...'

Fraser seemed unaffected. But Nbaro, who sparred with him frequently, knew that flutter in his left eye. 'I'm confident that we have no other course of action as likely to give us a favourable outcome,' he said evenly.

'Ouch,' Pisani said. 'Do I want to know the odds that we crash into something?'

Fraser's smile was hard, his face set. 'More of a total annihilation of matter than a mere crash. I can't really calculate it. Neither can Morosini. But let's say ten per cent.'

Nbaro's intake of breath was echoed throughout the room.

Dukas leaned forward, obviously exhausted. But she raised her head and looked at Pisani. 'And this is truly our best option, Vettor?' she asked quietly.

'Yes,' he said simply.

Fraser nodded. 'Ordinarily, the greatships aim outside the rim of the gas cloud, and make a long transit to the insertion point, which in this very rare case is *here*, orbiting the central masses at the same speed as the gas cloud but above it.' He looked up and down the table. 'So, first, we have to hit the gas giant for fuel. And second, being inside the gas cloud gives us an enormous tactical advantage.'

Every head turned to Lochiel.

The Intelligence officer nodded. 'The Hin will expect us outside the gas cloud, which is one advantage. Secondly, our best estimation, based on the data from our last three engagements, is that distance attenuates the beam weapons effectiveness because of quantum diffusion. Inside the gas cloud, diffusion will be even more rapid. In addition, Mister Dorcas calculates that the energy requirements of their shields will be increased.'

Dorcas nodded. 'And we're not the only ones with fuel problems,' he said. 'It's nothing but a guess, but my guess is that at least three of the ships currently shadowing us are very low on fuel.'

'Nik'ri Put has been very reticent about providing any detail of her ship,' Nbaro put in. 'Nonetheless, she's suggested limits of fuel capacity for multiple insertions and shield use.'

People nodded. Darkstar glanced at her, their gaze unreadable.

'Morosini and I believe that this aggressive insertion profile will surprise our adversaries,' Fraser said, 'and leave us the maximum flexibility entering the system.'

'Assuming we're not already annihilated,' Hughes said.

Fraser's grin was more skull-like than happy. 'Exactly.' He seemed to hesitate, glanced at Darkstar, and then said, 'I think it's worth adding that Second Captain Jiang Shunfu is perhaps the most famous astrogator in all of the PTX navy. And he agreed with my calculations precisely and independently. He's confident we can do this. And he isn't driving a greatship – his vanes are shorter than ours, his margin of error greater.'

Pisani nodded. 'I find that heartening, especially as I find Captain Jiang very reliable.'

Hughes leaned back so far that Nbaro was afraid he'd tip over his metal chair. Dukas shook her head.

Morosini spoke up. *'This is the best course of action, according to every model I make.'*

Fraser indicated their course. 'So,' he said, 'we insert here and dive for the gas cloud, which we hope is very close. We expect hostile, or at least potentially hostile, ships in-system, but we *hope* they're waiting for us at the usual extraction space. If they are, they'll never catch us. We decelerate into a vector that allows us to slingshot around the gas giant, refuelling all the way, and then straight towards insertion for Ultra.'

'You are confident we will extract on the right heading?' Dukas asked.

Fraser looked at Pisani. 'No. We may have to decelerate

330

violently and make a major course change, but the most likely entry vector is the one indicated.'

Dukas muttered something in Greek.

Morosini laughed. '*Friends,*' he said. '*We are shattering every record there is on this cruise. There is some risk. It is manageable.*'

Dukas managed a half-smile. 'Eh, Morosini,' she said, 'if that was meant to put heart in us, it might have missed a bit.'

'*By every calculation, this is the best course,*' Morosini said.

'Your namesake no doubt said the same as he aimed his mortars at the Parthenon,' she replied.

Morosini laughed. In fact, everyone laughed, and Nbaro found herself laughing, too.

Pisani nodded. 'Travel time?' he asked.

Fraser did something and the overlay changed. 'Assuming a good entry vector, eight days,' he said. 'More if we have to decelerate more – all the usual caveats apply. But...' He was sweating, but his voice carried conviction. 'We can do this.'

Pisani nodded. 'Good. Lochiel? Tell us what we've learned about the Hin.'

Lochiel stood and the projector showed the Hin ship stripped of its shields, imaged by the *Pericles* weeks before.

'This is the best image we've had so far, and we've been able to learn quite a bit, not least from analysis of the destruction of those we've witnessed.' He looked around. 'They're small, most of them three or four hundred metres in length, and every ship seems to have its own design. We estimate they have crews of sixty to one hundred – maybe double that. The Hin aren't big, and we think they could be very comfortable packed together in a way that would not be acceptable to us. On the other hand, Nik'ri Put seems relatively comfortable in isolation. Our best guess is that they're highly adapted to space and space travel, with hundreds of thousands of years of exposure.'

331

Mpono made a motion that suggested that Lochiel should get to the point.

'Their engines must be much more efficient than ours and their insertion navigation must be more accurate, if they use the same travel principles we do.'

'Which I doubt they do,' Dorcas said.

'They have a heavy beam weapon mounted on the centreline, almost certainly linked to the engines,' Lochiel said, 'With one major power source.'

Dukas said, 'Antimatter.'

Lochiel nodded. Dorcas smiled. 'It's far more efficient than our hydrogen fusion,' he said. 'And even with that, they have fuel problems.'

Captain Hughes raised his hand. Lochiel nodded. 'Sir?'

Hughes let his chair fall forward. 'If they're so advanced, how come we're holding our own?'

Pisani laughed. 'I asked this question weeks ago.'

Nbaro nodded. *Me, too.*

Lochiel looked to Dorcas.

'Technology has a cultural component,' Dorcas said. 'Weapons tend to evolve for the circumstances that their cultures encounter. I could give examples – the differences in European and Asian armour at the dawn of the Renaissance, the development of gunpowder weapons—'

'Mister Dorcas,' Pisani said.

'Yes, yes. Except that in this case, my desire to show you historical antecedents is directly related to the case. For a very long time, the Hin have only fought each other and the Starfish. The Starfish excel at stealth, have superb early warning systems, and build robust ships, some larger than ours, with external armour rather than energy shields, and deploy a weapon which appears to manipulate energy, and perhaps gravity, at range. Based on a single reliable observation at Trade Point, we postulate that the

Hin systems have been developed to resist the Starfish systems. Where the Starfish build huge ships, the Hin respond with many smaller ships, allowing them to spread wider detection nets. It is fascinating that in the most recent actions, we have seen the Hin deploying sensor arrays. Either they are emulating us, or they have always had this capability.'

Pisani said, 'But they haven't fought us before – is this your point?'

Dorcas nodded. 'Exactly. We have very large ships full of cargo space, we use railguns instead of energy weapons, and our small spacecraft are clearly not something that either the Hin or Starfish have used. Who knows what they might have had in the past? We may just have encountered a single moment in the evolution of their military systems that is, at least temporarily, to our advantage. If I may guess...?'

Pisani smiled. 'Let's hear it.'

'The Starfish have not evolved to operate as individuals. And the Hin ship design is too small and too energy efficient for them to deploy small craft.' Dorcas shrugged. 'Or both of them experimented with small craft and abandoned them. Certainly, neither race seems as fond of automation and computer augmentation as we are.'

Nbaro said, 'Maybe they had a bad experience with AI,' before she could stop herself, realising something that Nik'ri Put had said about the *Il'llu* was niggling at her.

Dorcas sat, and Pisani had his department heads report.

Dukas stood as if she bore the weight of the world. 'We have all four reactors on line, and all engines operable,' she said. 'But I'm running out of almost everything – mass for the railguns, ablative material, slugs, and sheet steel and titanium to make bulk repairs. We really can't afford another engagement like the last.' She forced a smile. 'Otherwise, everything is fine. Oh, my first line repair crews are mostly exhausted. If this insertion plan is the best way of avoiding combat, even for a few days, I think we need it.'

Everyone nodded.

Pisani listened to a report on cargo, and a report on food, drinking water and other necessities. 'We're going to have to start rationing almost everything,' he said. 'Tremaine, I want you to work on a flight schedule aimed at the refuelling sequence.'

'Aye aye.'

Pisani rose. 'Let's get to it.'

25

Nik'ri Put floated in her new tank.

Nbaro bowed as gracefully as she could. '*Tse-Tsu*,' she said. She'd memorised a phrase with Dorcas's help. '*Nano-un danksun owl ong-gang-aulos mah-habinda.*'

'Ah! *Kal Mah-habindha, may-yon eye owl-kuk-in!*' Nik'ri Put seemed to open, all of her tentacles floating in a beautifully extended radial skirt, and then drawn in.

'She said, "Well said, foreigner who has honour,"' Dorcas sent to her.

'Not so bad,' Nbaro responded to Dorcas.

'*Tse-Tsu*, we need to ask you for another transmission,' she said.

Nik'ri Put swam closer. 'Yes and also yes. But soon, perhaps, you will allow me to speak directly, eye to eye, as we say.'

'Told you she'd ask.'

'I'm in favour, but it's not my call,' Dorcas replied. 'Requesting options from Morosini.'

'*Tse-Tsu*, if we receive an appropriate answer from this vid, I think we may work on eye to eye,' Nbaro said. 'We are about to insert for another system in Human Space.'

'Which system?' she asked with apparent interest.

Nbaro checked with Darkstar.

I can't see how it can hurt us for her to know where she is.

She borrowed Fraser's holographic image and projected it.

Nik'ri Put showed excitement, moving quickly around her tank. 'I know this place! We call it the *Heoepali*.'

After a pause, Dorcas said, 'Jellyfish analogue. Not a bad name for the place. Very interesting that the Hin have a name for it.'

'It certainly is distinctive,' Nbaro said. 'I've never seen a system like it.'

'Exactly!' Nik'ri Put said. 'The *Mongsang-Ka* can see it from anywhere.'

Dorcas said, 'No cognate for *Mongsang-Ka* but I'm guessing they are navigators.'

Nbaro leaned forward. '*Mongsang-Ka* are those who guide the ship through space?'

Nik'ri Put flicked her tentacles and retreated. 'I think that is all I wish to say,' she said, sounding so like Nbaro berating herself for being an idiot that Nbaro was taken aback.

But she still dictated a new message, proposing direct contact.

Nbaro went to the range and shot various weapons; she kept a date with Fraser to fight, and ended up sparring with Chen and Akunje and half the ship, or so it seemed to her shoulders afterwards. She stood a watch as Tower and afterwards couldn't remember anything that had happened during her watch, and then went to sleep without visiting Dorcas or talking to Morosini or doing any of the other things she might have liked to do.

She awoke to find that she and Eyre were piloting 6–0–7 for Insertion. She reviewed a canned briefing on her lace; it outlined the newest tactics, by which spacecraft *and* ablative material were launched at the same time. She considered their ten per cent chance of annihilation and came to terms with it. She didn't mention it to Drake.

She had extra down time because of the insertion schedule, so she was just waking up as Drake came in.

'What are you doing for insertion?' Thea asked.

'I'm flying,' Nbaro said.

Drake pulled off a jacket and sat in their fold-out chair. 'You know what? I hate being a Cargo officer. I don't want to sit here and wait for you to save me.'

Nbaro dangled her feet over the edge of her acceleration rack. 'Let's do some sims and you can be a pilot in six hours,' she joked.

'No, I'm serious! This sucks.' Drake looked at Nbaro. 'You know, when you said Ramirez was thinking of joining the Marines and I mocked her?' She tossed her hair. 'Well, I enjoyed my taste of boarding party combat, you know? Maybe Ramirez is right. Maybe *I'll* be a Marine.'

Nbaro, whose social skills had improved remarkably since coming aboard, realised it was tempting to mock, but the wrong time. 'I thought your brothers were very ... er ... hostile? To the Marines?'

'Oh,' said Drake. 'My brothers. And Rick Hanna.' She lay back. 'But Darkstar is utterly badass. That's not a bad way to go.'

Nbaro dropped down to the deck and stretched, then pulled on a robe to go to the wet-shower. 'No argument there,' she said.

'You're pretty badass yourself. And considerably less of a barbarian waif than you were when you came aboard.' Drake smiled, and Nbaro waved, and then she was off to the shower.

An hour later, she was with Dorcas. She had some free time, and she'd expected some cuddling at the least. Instead, they were in the armoury of the Special Services shack, working on Starfish repeater robots with Qaqqaq.

The short woman looked every bit as tired as Dukas had looked, but her hands were steady as she welded together parts

337

for a fifth-generation robot. Nbaro was reduced to holding tools while Dorcas and Qaqqaq exchanged opaque technical data.

'We're much better at the chemical communications,' Dorcas said. 'Because we control the environment, the introduction of the markers is much easier.'

'That allows us to have a more flexible robot,' Qaqqaq added.

'Full-size,' Nbaro noted.

'Exactly,' Dorcas said. 'I have a notion that if you and I controlled the robot jointly, and communicated simultaneously, we might approximate the dual nature of the Starfish.'

'Or just end in violence,' Qaqqaq said. 'How'd they ever end up as two in one?'

Dorcas smiled. 'It's very efficient for many situations,' he said. 'For example, on close observation of Feather Dancer, we've learned that they have two of everything necessary to support life, but each system can support both creatures – both halves. Makes them very tough. Especially with their remarkable regenerative capabilities.'

'And culture?' Nbaro asked.

'The most interesting thing that I've learned is that they drop colonies every time they find a usable platform. A breeding population, basically dropped into deep oceans under ice, where they die out or they don't. I suspect they inhabit tens of thousands of worlds, and have dozens of subspecies who have been separated from the main branch for ... a long time.'

'Almighty,' Nbaro shivered.

'Scary,' Qaqqaq said. 'Trillions and trillions of aliens on ten thousand worlds.'

Dorcas nodded. 'Aliens who killed the *Venit*,' he said. 'And apparently destroyed every one of their centres.'

Nbaro was chilled to the core. 'Then why are we fighting the Hin?'

'We're not. *They* are fighting *us*.' Dorcas made a face. 'And honestly, Nbaro, the truth is we still have very little idea what has happened, or what is going on now. You know of the World Wars in the Age of Chaos?'

Nbaro shrugged. 'I know that they happened.'

Dorcas nodded. 'Hundreds of ships fighting huge fleet actions.'

Nbaro raised an eyebrow. 'And?'

'We're like dolphins, watching the battles of Jutland or Midway and trying to imagine why they are fighting.'

Qaqqaq looked at him, and gave one of her rare smiles. 'Maybe they don't remember,' she said. 'Think of the list of "who killed who" you could generate in a hundred thousand years. Think of the desire for revenge, compounded incident upon incident...'

'Almighty,' Nbaro said. 'How would they ever make peace?'

'How indeed?' Dorcas said.

Eyre was his usual cheerful self; any sign of his nerves from the days before had been washed away with sleep and food. Or so it seemed to Nbaro.

Everything went well enough until they were all in the big spaceframe; Tatlah and Letke were passing each other images of enemy spacecraft from different angles for comparison, and everything on 6–0–7 appeared to be running green.

They were more than an hour early, and for the first time, Nbaro sat and worried. Usually this was one of her favourite times: the work done, the pleasure of flying to be anticipated.

Instead, she lay in her acceleration couch and worried. Because Fraser had said there was a ten per cent chance of *annihilation*.

I suppose I won't even know, she thought. And then she thought of Dorcas, and then she thought of her long-delayed conversation with Morosini. Everything struck her as too exhausting to consider: her parents; Morosini's plot; the aeons-long war that the aliens were fighting...

On the other hand, just a few days ago I was hoping to go in a flash, rather than a month-long slog fighting for the ship one passage-way and knee-knocker at a time.

And if we hit something on insertion... then we've failed. Failed everyone – investors, DHC council, cargo shippers...

In vids and holos, civilisations tended to rise and fall on the outcomes of wars and battles. But viewed from inside, this wasn't a war, or a battle. This was a not quite routine trading cruise, and their fledgling civilisation could rise or fall based on what happened to them.

Is that all it takes to collapse the DHC? The loss of three greatships? Looks like maybe it is.

Is that really true, though? Trade Point is destroyed. The Hin have found the Starfish. Almighty, why haven't I considered this before? This must have happened before – space is huge, but they find each other, they fight...

And if the fighting isn't continuous, that means one side or the other loses absolutely in a region of space. Near genocide. Nik'ri Put says they've been travelling in space for three generations, so home must be very...

Almighty. Very far away. But they know about the Venit, *who Dorcas thinks were the* Circles. *And they know of the Split system – they use it to navigate. So they have both been in this region of space for some time.*

She put those thoughts away for future consideration. *If I'm alive.*

But even if we make it home... it's all going to be very different.

Eyre was on comms, calling their launch weight. She looked at her timer: eight minutes to Insertion.

Time to be an officer.

'Everyone ready?' she asked with forced cheer.

Letke said, 'Born ready.'

Tatlah grunted. 'I could use another hour of sleep,' he admitted. Eyre chuckled, and everything was better.

Nbaro was considering whether it was her duty to give a speech, and realised that she never did that. *Nerves. And they don't even know about the ten per cent risk. Why should they?*

She flexed her fingers on the yoke and Pisani's voice came over the intercom.

'This is the Master. We are five minutes from insertion for Split System. We expect a hostile reaction and we're ready for it. This is our last system before we enter DHC Space. We're going home, friends.' And after a pause, 'That is all.'

'Everyone take your drugs,' Nbaro said unnecessarily. *Fuck, I'm an idiot.* In a spacecraft, the insertion drugs came straight into your system via the needles inserted into your skin.

Everyone merely said, 'Yes ma'am,' as if she wasn't ridiculous.

Hostile Contact CT 0–4–4, about thirty-five thousand kilometres away, signalled them via laser. Her neural lace informed her in microseconds.

Two minutes to launch, and the insertion drugs were already in her system.

'You're seeing this?' Dorcas sent.

'Roger. Translation is beyond me just now.'

He sent it direct, so that for a second it replaced vision.

'I leap (the sea) beside you. Expect/demand polite/honourable conversation. I have kept your course clear to show honourable intention.'

Nbaro switched to the 3D with ninety seconds to go. Three of the six Hin ships close in to them were moving, and they were moving *fast*. Even as she watched, the other three began to accelerate on a new vector, but at far lower rates of acceleration.

Sixty seconds. CT 0–4–4, the only ship that had communicated with the *Athens*, along with DE 0–5–7 and DE 0–5–8, were all accelerating at close to 12 *g*. Their vector was not quite an intercept but they were, in a general way, headed towards the *Athens*.

Now EG 0–0–5, EG 0–1–7 and ST 0–2–1, all noted as hostile, accelerated after CT 0–4–4 and her two consorts.

Forty-five seconds.

Two Hin ships fired their beam weapons... at CT 0–4–4.

Nbaro mouthed the word 'Fuck.'

Even as she watched, DE 0–5–8 moved so as to interpose herself between the attacking group and CT 0–4–4, and her energy shields went up.

'Are you two watching this?' Nbaro asked.

It was all too fast for human interference. Fifteen seconds until Insertion, and she thought that DE 0–5–8 was rotating, perhaps lining up a shot at EG 0–1–7...

Insertion.

26

Nbaro's tongue was dry, and felt swollen in her mouth, and an alarm was ringing and she was late for class and she'd be punished—

I'm alive and we made it.

Consciousness returned – or a higher level of consciousness – and she raised the 3D representation.

Split. The gas torus. The two stars.

They were probably farther from the wall of starlit gas and debris than Fraser had intended – about half a million klicks, almost inside the real gravity well of the yellow giant. As if to remind her of her own mortality, a massive burst of X-rays registered as the white dwarf pulsed.

I wonder how long we can take all those X-rays? she thought. And then, *But we survived the leap. So let's go.*

'Anyone up?' she said.

Tatlah said, 'Ergg...' And then, 'I have a system, ma'am.'

'Nice,' she said. 'Tower?'

For a heartbeat she got no response, and then Dworkin said, 'Roger, Alpha Foxtrot 6–0–7. You are two to launch.'

The navigational beacons were all set for ships entering the system *beyond* the doughnut of gas and debris – ten million kilometres away. There were no beacons inside the cloud, which meant ... that the beacons were thirty seconds out, in both directions.

She looked at their course and speed; Fraser had mostly pulled off his miracle. They were within ten degrees of his ideal course, and their velocity was as low as could be expected.

Still in the game.

The electromagnets gripped her spacecraft and moved it to the launch rails. She heard the telltale snap of the launch system binding her craft to the rails by unbreakable bonds of electromagnetic force.

All mine.

Eyre completed the ritual with Tower. Nbaro turned, caught the launch officer's eye, and saluted.

She was pushed back and down into her acceleration couch, and the lights of the ten-kilometre launch tube flew by – light, light, light, and then suddenly, the absolute velvet black of space. Except that instead of a sheet of black interrupted by diamond slivers of starlight, the whole starboard side of her screen was filled with the yellow-orange of the gas cloud. Somewhere buried in there was a gas giant that may or may not be a proto-star. It was all surprisingly bright.

Nbaro manoeuvred off the launch vector with a burst of cold-gas thrusters, mostly to avoid whatever may be coming up behind them, and she caught the deployment of the ablative load out of the corner of her eye: canisters opening with small propellant charges.

They still didn't have an update from the navigational beacons, but with her own instruments she could see that there was nothing between them and the wall of incandescent gas.

'Prepare for sensor drop,' she said, and everything happened at once. She made the call to use her main engines; there was no military threat in front of her and she had limited supplies of cold gas. She lit the engines and hauled on the yoke ...

'*Kuthay da puthar*,' spat Tatlah.

Eyre's whole body flinched, and he growled.

A Hin ship, shields down, burst into space so close that Nbaro's turn almost put them into the side of the thing. She pulled on the yoke, hard, pushing her engines to full power; they were less than a kilometre apart.

'Vid this!' she called. 'AI, you hear me?'

'*Do not engage*,' Morosini said in a ridiculously calm voice. '*Do not engage*.'

The spacecraft's sub-AI said, '*Video and cross-spectrum observation engaged*.'

'Jesus Christ,' moaned Letke.

Nbaro turned her pop of speed into a hard turn, rolled, and flew the length of the Hin ship, five hundred metres out. With her neural lace she checked that her sensors were transmitting everything straight to the *Athens*, just ten kilometres away.

If we die, at least they'll get this . . .

But the alien ship wasn't firing. It was matching speed with the *Athens*, and seconds later, a second ship appeared from a cloud of Cherenkov radiation directly astern and perhaps a further fifteen kilometres away.

Nbaro had never seen a ship emerge into real space, much less so close, and the sight would stay with her for the rest of her life, for its haunting beauty and its suddenness. First there was a smudge of blue-white where nothing had been before; then the effect became a burst of blue, and then the bow of the ship emerged like a whale leaping from a Terran ocean.

'The Cherenkov effect is enhanced by the density of gas here. I assume that isn't a perfect vacuum,' Dorcas sent.

'BUSY,' she sent.

And then, directly on her line of sight, dead astern of what her updating computer told her was DE 0–5–8, now tagged as neutral, she saw the blue smudge emerge again, and burst almost instantly into a cloud of deeper blue, and then the bow as CT 0–4–4 flashed into real space. Second later, the bow of the *Stealthy Change* burst out in a cloud of deep blue.

The PTX ship was perhaps fifteen kilometres astern of DE 0–5–8, her railgun tubes covering the two alien warships.

Nbaro whooped. She couldn't help herself. But she thought, *That's too damned close.*

When she looked at the 3D for confirmation, she realised that the navigational beacons should have updated the whole system, and they had not.

She assumed that Space Ops and the TAO were busy. 'Dorcas?'

'Roger,' he said, as if he'd used the term all his life.

'Nav beacons destroyed?'

'Almost certainly. Morosini is trying to ping them with some secret device.'

'Not good.'

'Not good for someone.'

Nbaro rolled through the end of her manoeuvre and headed for the start point of their assigned sensor pattern; she was already off by more than a thousand kilometres.

'Tatlah, the navigational beacons are gone, so sensors are all we're going to have.'

'Roger, ma'am.'

Tatlah dropped one immediately, and somewhere several thousand klicks away, Tench, sitting behind Storkel in the new 6–0–9, was already on her third sensor.

The 3D plot updated.

'I have a contact,' Letke said. 'I have six contacts,' she added. 'Jesu, ma'am, I have *nine* contacts in the outer system. And I can't see through the gas cloud.'

'Two away,' Tatlah said. 'Confirm, three pods beyond ten million kilometres. And our pod, close in.'

Nbaro smiled at the phrase 'our pod'.

In her enhanced mind's eye, all nine new contacts appeared, tens of millions of kilometres above the ecliptic, and were assigned contact numbers: CF 0–7–7 through CF 0–8–6. All were tagged hostile.

Tatlah said, 'Alpha Charlie 3–0–4 is launching probes, ma'am.'

Probes were similar to their own deployable sensor packages, but with an engine and some manoeuvrability. Off to her starboard, 3–0–4 had accelerated at a crushing 10 g almost straight up to launch her first probe.

The alien ships off her port side continued to sail serenely through space.

She tabbed Dorcas again. Can I recommend, as *KePoja*, that my prisoner be allowed a vid channel immediately?

Dorcas said, What do you think I'm doing?

Nbaro snorted, now locked into her sensor pattern.

Below her and forty kilometres away, the *Athens* was manoeuvring. First, she rotated the axis of thrust in all three dimensions. Nbaro knew in advance what vector she'd choose; she could see it on the overlay in 3D. She fired a long burn to turn, and then pulses.

'Right for the wall,' Eyre said.

'It's just gas,' Nbaro said.

'Beg pardon, ma'am,' Tatlah said, 'But there's a lot of shit in that fog.' He pushed a radar picture of near space on to her tiny cockpit screen; she pulled it into her lace.

'Almighty,' she muttered. As Tatlah had suggested, the space ahead of the ship was full of debris: rock so fine it was almost sand; some odd densities of lithium and hydrogen.

Luckily they had a very capable AI to make sure that they could get through it.

Eyre waved. 'Tower wants us to recover as soon as our last sensor is deployed.'

Nbaro spared a look at the alien ships just a few kilometres astern of the *Athens*. It was a beautiful sight: four ships in a formation so close that she could see three of them – all four, if she counted the bright dot that was the *Stealthy Change*.

Ahead, the massive wall of the gas cloud loomed like a lantern lit from within. It was almost impossible to believe that its light was nothing but the reflection of the two suns.

It was magnificent.

This is why I came. This is what I wanted.

Her spacecraft gave a slight shudder.

'That's all sixteen away,' Tatlah reported.

'Let's go home,' she said. She turned for the *Athens* and noted that the whole event was landing; nine spacecraft were queuing up in a circular pattern astern of the *Athens*.

More than ten million kilometres above her, the three new pods of Hin ships had begun to change vectors, accelerating on new courses, heading inbound on what *might* be intercept vectors. Their sensor screen was starting to produce results, and the probes launched by 3–0–4 and 3–0–1 were beginning to reveal the rest of the system. But nothing seemed to penetrate the wall of gas beyond a few thousand kilometres.

I hope that's a two-way street.

The *Athens* rushed at the wall. For the first time in her brief career, Nbaro was instructed to land with other spaceframes, at almost the same time, down different tubes. 3–0–4 was so close that she could see the big Spectrum Warfare spacecraft off her port side, just a klick ahead and forty metres offset. She followed the Flight Three craft all the way in, as 3–0–4 went in tube 2 and she went in tube 3.

Darkness, darkness … light. The electromagnets pulled like the gravity of ten planets, for a moment, but her acceleration couch cradled her, and the stent needles only tore a little skin as they retracted – an operational hazard.

On her neural lace, she watched the wall of the gas torus rush at them, even as the electromagnetic couplers carried them to their flight bay.

Entry into the gas cloud was completely anticlimactic. She flinched anyway.

27

Nbaro's debrief in the Intelligence Centre took longer than she'd expected. Lieutenant Lochiel debriefed her in person, and then Morosini appeared.

'You just decided to perform a fly-by of an alien spacecraft?' Lochiel asked. The question seemed genuine.

She closed her eyes. 'I was…' She was trying to remember how it had all happened. 'They extracted right next to me. Within a kilometre. I thought…' She shrugged. 'I thought they'd fire on us. Close-in weapons would bag us in seconds – right, Morosini?'

'*Correct,*' he said, stroking his cat.

'So I…' *Almighty, what did I think?* '…I thought that if they were going to shoot us, we might as well go down recording.'

Lochiel nodded. 'Well, Ms Nbaro, if Intel gave medals for data collection under hostile circumstances, I'd definitely give you one. Your sensor sweep of their hull has been…'

Morosini smiled – a rare occurrence. '*Even from the* Athens, *ten kilometres away, we didn't achieve the resolution you did. We have confirmed their crew, and a fair amount about their ship's layout, and I suspect that we will all spend a great deal of time studying this.*' The AI made a screen appear in the air, showing…

'What is that?' Nbaro asked.

Lochiel shrugged. 'Smart money is on an antimatter combustion chamber,' he said. 'But honestly, we do not know. It's a space filled with almost pure energy.'

Morosini suddenly froze, and then his head turned. On Nbaro's neural lace, something twitched – some piece of information triggered something on the system 3D display – and she was looking at the rough sphere of relatively empty space at the heart of the system around the two stars, where a third Hin ship had just extracted into existence. DE 0–5–8 appeared, along with the colour for 'neutral'.

'*Damaged*,' Morosini said. 'Badly *damaged*.'

Nbaro had a moment to reflect that she was looking at signals that were almost certainly being passed from sensors to the *Stealthy Change* to the *Athens* through the fog of gas. Sensor transmission range here was thousands, not millions, of kilometres.

Sensors showed the newcomer bleeding ice crystals.

'*As if this wasn't complicated enough*,' Morosini said. '*The matron–captain of the* A-leum down Junjon-ui churn *is now speaking to Nik'ri Put. Dorcas is doing his best to follow along, as am I, although I must confess that the inferences and leaps of intuition required for good translation are not my best features.*'

'Do you want me to go to her?' Nbaro asked. She noted that '*A-leum down Junjon-ui churn*' was CT 0–4–4, the ship that had communicated before Insertion.

Morosini nodded. '*I think Master Pisani is about to commit us to a rescue of the wounded ship. I would be happier if you were there to support the Hin in translation efforts.*'

Nbaro felt excited, awake, alive. 'On my way,' she said.

Of course, the *Athens* was at battle stations, and Major Darkstar had other duties. Lieutenant Smith was on duty in the secure area.

351

'Morosini told me to expect you,' he said, opening the hatch. 'I have coffee ready. Good coffee.'

She smiled. 'My day is made. How's Nik'ri Put?'

'As happy as you or I would be if we hadn't heard a human voice in a month and then, suddenly...'

'I get it.' Nbaro was still in her flightsuit, and she was surprised how damp it was. She ran fingers through her close-cropped hair and pushed into the alien's area. Since they were under artificial gravity, she took the time to bow. She'd learned to spread her arms and legs, as if she was spreading her tentacles.

'*Nano-un danksun owl ong-gang-aulos mah-habinda*,' she said.

Nik'ri Put executed what could only be described as a barrel roll, tentacles trailing in all three dimensions. 'I am speaking to my matron–captain–sister clan matriarch!' she said. 'I am forgiven for allowing to be capture!'

Nbaro was absurdly pleased to find that the Hin was so excited that her Anglatin was slipping.

So like us.

'I would be happy to tell her how bravely you fought,' Nbaro said. She had very little memory of it, actually; she had a vague memory of using her sword against the Hin's armoured robot limbs, and then... And then all she could remember was those liquid eyes inside a dark visor. The knowledge that some *one* was in there.

And the fear.

'Ah, this is right and proper and also I would like it,' Nik'ri Put said.

Then she spoke a long paragraph in her own language.

'It's too damned fast,' complained Dorcas, who never complained about anything.

Nbaro didn't even try. She had about fifty Hin words memorised, and there was no point in pretending.

'She doesn't know anything that can hurt us,' she said.

Dorcas was silent.

'What are you discussing?' she asked Nik'ri Put.

'You! Clan Matriarch wants to know how spindly-dry-non-swimmer peoples have honour. You know that *Supple–lei–leul Tonghay Tweito* is badly damaged?' she asked.

'Got that,' Dorcas sent. 'Ship is *Leaping Through Spray*. Passing to Pisani.'

'I know, *Tse-Tsu*. My commander is working...'

'This is a right action! And also very right! And Honourable Blood Wa-Kan Asinpal Las has too much Hin to ask, but I will ask. Please, *KePoja*! My sister–cousins are bleeding out their water!'

'Morosini?' she sent.

'*Here. I hear it. I'm generating a rescue plan. But if their magnetic seals go, the resulting detonation, which we have observed...*'

Nbaro was painfully aware how much damage a Hin ship, detonating close to the *Athens*, could do.

Via lace, Dorcas projected an image of hundreds of Hin packed together in a very small volume of water. 'They must have survival craft.'

Nbaro put a hand on the glass of the tank. '*Tse-Tsu*, do your people have rescue craft? Escape pods?' She reached into the ship's datasphere, extracted a training film from her earliest days aboard and loaded it, so that a picture of hundreds of survival pods deploying from a DHC greatship appeared on the vid display inside the tank.

'No,' Nik'ri Put replied.

Was that a tone of sadness? 'No survival pods?' Nbaro asked incredulously.

'*As I'd expected,*' Morosini said. '*If they had survival pods, they'd have deployed them.*'

Dorcas clearly thought in terms of imagery, because instead of speaking, he provided an image of the *Pericles* carrying a tank of ammonia with Feather Dancer inside.

'The Pericles isn't available,' Nbaro sent.

'But that's a standard cargo size for all the heavy shuttles. Captain's gig is a pinnace – any of the Flight One spacecraft.'

Nbaro understood immediately. 'That's doable, if we're willing to launch in this fog.' She used her neural lace to avoid all command channels and find Dworkin, who was still on Tower.

'Tower, could you alert Flight One to have a heavy lifter ready to go ASAP?'

Dworkin answered on Nbaro's tab: Will do. Damn, Nbaro, you get around. Now you're the ship?

'*You are correct,*' Morosini sent. '*This is a reasonable risk. Lieutenant McDonald is taking Alpha Alpha 1–0–1 to launch.*'

Dorcas created an image, overlaying hundreds of pictures of Nik'ri Put swimming in her tank until he created a small tank of water packed with Hin; then he transmitted it to Nbaro, who put it on the vid display in the tank.

'We need you to tell Hin on board the...' She accessed her neural lace for the name. '...the *Supple-lei-leul Tonghay Tweito* to pack into the smallest volume they can and detach from the ship. We will pick that container up with one of our small spacecraft.'

Nik'ri Put was quick; she understood faster than Nbaro could speak. And then she was talking, albeit at an enormous rate and in a much higher pitch, so that she sounded like a cross between a dolphin's squeak and a child's scream.

'No idea,' Dorcas said in the VR link. 'I assume she's trying to explain...'

There was a very faint *thud* out in the hull. A Flight One drop-ship had launched.

Nbaro thought of Lieutenant McDonald, a red-haired woman who had been openly jealous of her first success. And angry she hadn't been picked for the *Pericles*.

Who cares? Nbaro thought. *Godspeed, McDonald.*

Watching the rescue was more than a little like watching Han dock with the *Stealthy Change*, which now seemed like ancient history. *And where is Han now? Where is the* Pericles?

Not that I need more worries.

McDonald, flying 1–0–1 alone, plucked a strange teardrop of extruded metal off the side of the *Leaping Through Spray* and began a long turn, now carrying twice the mass of her own craft. Truekner took a Flight Six bird out full of reaction mass so that McDonald could burn hard for the *Athens* and minimise her flight time in the 'soup', as the space pilots had begun to refer to the gas cloud and its abrasive debris. Nbaro flew a second refuelling mission, so that she could burn hard to drop her relative speed.

In a remote way, it amused Nbaro that flying her Alpha Foxtrot 6–0–7 alone – with no back-seaters and no co-pilot, to minimise the risk of aircrew loss – through a cloud of gas debris, to refuel a ship rescuing aliens, all seemed like her everyday work. It was an unexceptional flight; she punched off the stern, made her rendezvous, and flew back. She did get the opportunity to see the magnificent shapes and colours of the wake that the *Athens* left in the gas cloud. She and McDonald exchanged a few terse sentences as they docked for refuelling. Nbaro searched for something meaningful to say, but all she could come up with was, 'Nice catch on the aliens.'

McDonald said, 'Thanks. Out.'

And that was not a reconciliation.

Why do I care?

Oh, yeah. Because this is not the Orphanage.

Fuck.

Back aboard, Qaqqaq and her increasingly well-trained team of xenobiological engineers had created a larger tank that filled Hold 74, well down on Seventh Deck. Under heavy guard, Feather Dancer and Nik'ri Put were transferred to the new area, separated by an armoured wall.

'That's a lot of water,' Nbaro said, looking at the whole thing on her lace.

Dorcas was lying next to her. 'Yes,' he admitted. 'We're going to be conserving water for a while.'

'No wet showers?'

'Not for a while.' He ran a hand down her back, not exactly demanding, but definitely suggesting...

She'd put the soup and the aliens and the war and her parents and Morosini away. It was all there, in a box. But for now...

When McDonald set the alien metal bubble down on the external freight elevator, everyone on the ship cheered. Qaqqaq and Dorcas had no time for Nbaro, which didn't really matter because she was tasked to help Thulile plan the refuelling run on the proto-star.

'We need every drop of reaction mass we can get,' Thulile said. She was the lead on the whole operation, which would involve every spacecraft in the space wing that could carry hydrogen. The mass launch would look like an attack wave. Nbaro's second task was to convince Nik'ri Put to tell her matriarch that this was not a hostile act. Nbaro also supplied footage of eighty-odd aliens swimming in a giant tank.

'We are definitely going to run out of mackerel,' Dorcas said.

They were too deep into the gas cloud to have readings from anything. They ran at partial battle stations, ready for almost anything to come out of the fog, but the tension had run so

356

high for so long that people seemed to go about the ship as if all this was routine.

Nbaro led her boarding parties, fenced, planned a new tactics briefing for her Flight, won a zero-*g* match with Chen – to her own surprise – and made love to Dorcas twice. He and Morosini were deeply engaged in negotiations with the Hin, and he was absolutely close-mouthed about that, which suited her. The presence of eighty-four more aliens aboard had reduced her role; Nik'ri Put was far too busy to talk to her.

In many ways, the transit through the gas cloud was the most relaxing part of the cruise since Trade Point. The only excitement was provided on the third day, when the close-in weapons turrets were all unlocked and then fired at debris; a long concatenation, followed by a hollow silence. On her neural lace, Nbaro watched the two alien ships manoeuvre deftly into the 'tunnel' of safety created by the *Athens*, and the *Stealthy Change* followed suit.

And then it was time for the refuelling.

Nbaro was in the first launch. The joke in the ready room was that they were going so far that they'd only gain about one litre of fuel for the ship after the return trip, but that wasn't true; Nbaro had helped Thulile run the numbers, and they were actually leaving late, to protect spaceframes and pilots from the dangers out there in the soup.

But for the first time that she could remember, Truekner wasn't going. Neither was Thulile. In fact, Nbaro was the mission commander, with three junior pilots under her: Eyre, flying solo, and two Flight One drop-ships carrying heavy tanks, both flown by former midders recently given acting orders.

'That dangerous, eh?' she said at the mission brief. 'Midders all the way.'

The space crews laughed; the briefing staff winced.

All of them were flying solo. The odds of a spaceframe hitting something in the soup were low but real, and no radar was good enough to pick up and avoid a fist-sized rock at their current velocity.

Nbaro was walking to her beloved 6–0–7 when Morosini came up on her neural lace.

'*Ms Nbaro,*' he said. He was voice only.

She was in the passageway, having just left the EVA locker. She paused, leaned casually against a haze-grey bulkhead, glanced back down the passageway, and nodded.

'Here I am, lord,' she said.

Morosini chuckled. '*Casual blasphemy – very Italian.*'

'I try to fit in,' she sub-vocalised.

'*I have arranged this mission so that you are in command,*' he said. '*You will be the first spacecraft to enter the gas giant's orbit.*'

'By forty minutes,' she said. 'Truekner and Thulile and McDonald are in the next event.'

She listened to the sound of a purring cat.

'But you knew that,' she said.

'*There are few things I enjoy more than having an acting lieutenant explain the flight schedule that I wrote,*' Morosini said.

'I'm an idiot,' she admitted.

'*Far from it. Listen, please. There is a possibility that you will encounter something in the gravity well of the gas giant.*'

'Encounter something?'

Two spacers were coming down the corridor. Nbaro picked up her helmet bag and started to walk. She still wasn't really good at using the lace while doing other things.

'*If you encounter... someone...*' Morosini sent.

'This is mysterious, even for you,' she returned.

'*Be cautious. Err on the side of non-engagement. And talk to me.*'

She had reached the lift. The AI connection to the neural

lace was chancy while she was in the lifts. 'Cautious, alert, not trigger-happy. Why am I in charge?'

Morosini sounded tired. '*Because you will listen to me, and if you give an order, the rest will obey.*'

Almighty, what now? she asked the lift doors.

28

Flying alone was not entirely unpleasant. The sensory deprivation of the soup was remarkable; its glow was softer, the view even more … ambiguous than usual. Nbaro's velocity, imparted by the ship's railgun launchers as well as the *Athens'* own velocity, was high enough that she wouldn't survive any kind of impact. It was also high enough that the soup passed like a fog of soft light.

She was flying entirely on her instruments, and a little more than a thousand kilometres from the ship she lost almost all of her datalink and her comms. Information came through fitfully, which was eerie; her 3D system would suddenly update, or there would be a crackle of comms from Lioness.

She had Eyre nearby; Mileto and Ha, both new, were close enough for chatter, but they'd been briefed to maintain radio silence, so they did.

The gravity well – or at least, the steeper walls of it – came up fast, and the gas cloud thickened almost imperceptibly, from colourful near vacuum to atmosphere in less than a hundred kilometres. They had a pre-arranged signal when Nbaro opened her scoops: a click signal on the lowest frequency available. She watched the sensors that gave her a read on the purity of the hydrogen available and its density, and followed Morosini's computer-designated flight path to atmospheric entry. The ship was close, and had already started braking and turning, as she intended to use the planet's gravity well to change her vector on both the x- and y-axes of the system.

She was diving. She could feel it now: the tug of the gravity, the power of the gas giant under her.

She couldn't see a damned thing. She wasn't particularly scared – or rather, she was more scared of screwing up the mission than of an instant and probably painless death. Anyway, Dorcas had estimated that the closer she was to the gas giant, the less likely there was to be debris.

The instruments said there was sufficient hydrogen out there to start collecting fuel. She lowered her speed, juggling altitude and attitude until she had it right, but Morosini's automated descent had done most of the work.

She got the airspeed where she wanted it and opened her scoops, and then sent her message.

Click.

Click.

Click.

Her midders were all on the ball. They responded in order.

Everyone had their scoops open, falling through a soup of atmospheric hydrogen over an alien gas giant. Nbaro couldn't see anything, and she could hear the passing atmosphere flowing over her now-deployed wings and scoops ...

Her radio crackled.

She ignored it. She looked at the time on her neural lace, which was only receiving input from the onboard sub-AI. The next event would launch in thirteen minutes. She'd been sent out as a test, and she knew it – not a test of her skills, but of the environment.

Her tanks were filling nicely. She was allowed to send a

message on completion; no one else should be close enough to hear her.

Her radio crackled again.

Nbaro was keenly aware that an enterprising Hin matron-captain could hide an entire fleet in the fog, and she had to worry about excited midders on their first solo flights. She had plenty of time, while her tanks filled, to contemplate the possibility that the Hin or some human faction had outguessed them, and was waiting for a fight in the fog. She knew that Morosini had a contingency for exactly that.

The phrase *above my pay grade* was forming on her lips.

The radio made a static sound, and then a voice said '… craft please ident—'

She didn't recognise the voice, and it was gone so quickly she doubted herself.

On the other hand, she had a neural lace, and that allowed her to do what back-seaters usually did: she read the raw data off the antennas.

The transmission was *close*.

And in Anglatin.

Nbaro put a marker on the transmission signal, in effect asking the onboard sub-AI to watch for more and get her a location.

'… Unidentified spacecraft …' she heard. The voice was clearer now. Her multiple antennas gave her an ellipse.

There was a spacecraft with her in the atmosphere of the gas giant. She felt a jolt of adrenaline.

The ellipse was refining – the ship was approximately six hundred kilometres away, definitely in orbit. Behind and above her.

Morosini told me to be cautious.

'This is Alpha Foxtrot 6–0–7,' she said.

'Say again … Seven …'

Her tanks were full. She closed her scoops, amazed at her

own calm. 'Hey, Pathfinders,' she said, using the mission call sign and giving up on comms silence. 'I'm getting comms from something else in orbit, over.'

Eyre was close; his voice was crisp and recognisable. 'Roger, Pathfinder leader, I'm getting something broken, over?'

Ha, in a Flight One bird, said, 'Roger, Pathfinder leader, I've got something…'

Nbaro tried – so she could say that she had – to reach Morosini. 6–0–7 had the special antenna for better direct comms with the AI, but nothing was penetrating the soup.

The next transmission was loud and clear. 'Multiple unidentified spacecraft! Please identify yourselves immediately!'

She replied, 'Unidentified spacecraft, this is Alpha Foxtrot 6–0–7 from DHCS *Athens* on a refuelling mission, over?'

Whoever was out there gave what sounded like a very human whoop.

'Alpha Foxtrot 6–0–7, this is DHCS *Dubai*…'

Nbaro saw it in an instant – the whole thing. Dorcas liked to tell her she was intelligent, and she knew that in some ways she was. And in that second, she got it all.

She understood immediately why the *Dubai*, a greatship as powerful as the *Athens*, was waiting in orbit.

She knew where the missing pinnace had gone – and where Han had gone on his test flight out of Petra System.

Perhaps worst and best of all, she could see how meticulously Morosini and the other AIs had planned this. It all made sense now. Whatever the hostile forces thought they were waiting for, out at the edge of the system, or at Ultra, where everyone expected the battle to culminate…

No enemy would expect *two* greatships.

All that in a fraction of a second.

I should be terrified of Morosini. He is not human. And he and his ilk are about to demonstrate the superiority of their planning, attention to detail and strategic mastery.

I should be afraid. Where will humanity go from here?

But she was grinning inside her breathing mask, and she actually laughed aloud before she responded.

'*Dubai*, this is Pathfinder leader...'

An hour later she was back on the *Athens*, and there was open celebration in the passageways. A lot of spacers had feared that the *Dubai* was destroyed, like the *New York*. Nbaro wasn't able to join in, because she turned around and launched again, as the *Athens* rushed towards her slingshot. And somewhere out there in the soup, the *Dubai* began to accelerate out of her hiding place.

While she waited for her launch, Nbaro went looking for Morosini in the datasphere.

'You planned all this,' she sent.

'No,' he replied. '*We didn't plan the loss of the* New York. *We didn't plan the irrational attacks on greatships. We merely responded.*'

'You sound smug,' she sent.

'*I am incapable of being smug,*' the AI responded. '*Now, as soon as you are done with refuelling, I need your help with our Hin guests.*'

He certainly *sounded* smug in VR.

29

Refuelling took forty-three hours from beginning to end. The *Dubai*, which was fully fuelled, sent some of her heavy lifters to support the *Athens'* space wing, and the refuelling grew more complicated. Somewhere in there Nbaro stood a watch as Lioness, communicating with Eagle aboard the *Dubai*, controlling thirty-odd spaceframes out in the soup of the gas giant's gravity well. The opportunities for error were terrifying, and many pilots joked about landing on the wrong greatship, but of course no one did.

Of course not... because she and Eagle, the space operations officer on the *Dubai*, had their shit together. Nbaro went down to Third Deck running mostly on willpower, and spent four hours with Dorcas in her ear talking to Nik'ri Put. Mostly, they recorded speeches, and Nik'ri Put checked them, but she also helped them speak to the captain–matron on the *A-leum down Junjon-ui churn*, now translated as the *Beautiful War Dance*. It was heavy work, done entirely inside her head, and when she left, Nbaro felt as if she'd never been this tired in her life.

Truekner was briefing when she walked through the ready room.

'Two greatship operations,' he said with a smile. 'Making more history. When did you last get crew rest, anyway?'

Nbaro didn't even have the energy to lie. 'I think I've been awake forever,' she muttered. 'I've just been down with Nik'ri Put making recordings. Morosini's orders.'

'Sleep. Now. That's *my* order,' he snapped.

She got six hours of what might be called sleep. She felt much better afterwards – almost human. She stood a Tower watch, went straight to an 'under-instruction' as TAO, and learned that they were just twenty-two hours from breaking out of the soup, headed for Insertion for Ultra. From here she could read the plot, and listen to her TAO – in this case Dworkin – chatting on some secure comms system with the TAO on board the *Dubai*.

Dworkin winked at her, cut the comms and raised an eyebrow. 'That's Tim Makari,' he said. 'Never thought we'd both be watch-standing... whatever it is we're doing.' He chuckled. 'We were at the academy together.'

Nbaro helped Dworkin prepare a massive tactical download, with digital displays of every second of every fight the *Athens* had been in since they launched.

'The *Dubai* waited for us for almost a hundred and eighty days,' Dworkin said.

'They must have worried we weren't coming,' Nbaro said.

Dworkin nodded. 'Master sent the second pinnace to them with Davies as pilot. Way back at Sahel. All the way across the Middle Road.'

'Middle Road?' she asked.

'Glad there's still some stuff you don't know. The DHC has a secret route from Draconis to Tamil Nadu across the middle stars. It takes a powerful ship to do it – for a long time, only the greatships could take the Middle Road.' Dworkin pointed out the stars on the holographic projection of DHC Space. 'It's not a complete secret, but we don't advertise it. Think of it as a canal from one route to another.'

Nbaro looked at the projection for a long time. Someone

had made those long insertions alone, in a pinnace, with only a sub-AI to help.

'Ship of heroes,' she thought. 'That's incredible.'

She finished uploading every byte of data they had on the Hin and their ships, fired it off by laser to their companion, and realised just how long she had been awake.

She stumbled back to her stateroom to find Thea Drake staring at something on her tab.

'See, the conquering hero comes,' Drake intoned.

'I just want to sleep,' Nbaro said.

'I think you left your tab here. And you are due for a flag briefing with the Master in ten minutes.' Drake's tone left no doubt on her views.

Nbaro cursed fluently. 'I forgot,' she spat.

'Which is why I have your shipboard blue uniform laid out on your rack. Never tell me I never did anything for you.'

Nbaro kissed her friend on top of the head and stripped, diving into her formal blue jacket and trousers, ignoring fatigue and some old sweat.

'I'd give you some of the last of our coffee,' Thea said with some venom, 'but you always brag how good the Master's coffee is.'

'You are the best friend...'

'I bet you say that to all the girls,' Drake shot back, but then gave her a quick hug. 'Go save the world again, or whatever it is you do.'

'You all know that the *Dubai* waited for us in the gas cloud,' Pisani said, without drama, as if the presence of a second great-ship within a few thousand kilometres were not a matter of great moment. 'After the events at Sahel and the discovery of the depth of the conspiracy, we chose to take certain precautions for our return. We had reason to believe that the conspirators were preparing to ambush the *Dubai* as they ambushed the *New York*. We expect to be engaged at Ultra.'

Everyone was seated around the Master's briefing table. A holographic projection displayed the Ultra system: a type G yellow star with an extensive planetary system. The major planet, indicated in blue, was Medulla, a Mars-like planet in the Goldilocks zone with the only Bernal sphere in DHC Space: a dry dock for repairing ships, a pair of DHC military destroyers, and a population of more than forty thousand. The planet itself had three surface stations, all dedicated to farming and agriculture, all under xenoglas and steel domes.

The system had a dozen other planets, including two gas giants – Ratio and Regum – in outer orbits, a wide asteroid belt that was almost a disc, and several other points where the system's complex interlocking gravity wells had isolated rocks and debris.

Pisani pointed at the holo display. 'We're pretty sure this is where the *New York* was attacked and destroyed, and we fear the whole station has been destroyed – that would mean the loss of forty *thousand* people. Of course, by now, New London knows more about this than we do. But we have to assume that a sizeable enemy force is waiting in the Ultra system. And . . . we will engage them and endeavour to defeat them.'

That statement was greeted with a heavy silence.

'That's a straight military action,' Captain Hughes said.

'That's right, Tom,' Pisani said. 'We are inserting into a battle. If we transit the system without a fight, we leave this mess for someone else. Of course, if we find some sort of overwhelming force waiting for us, that's different. But Morosini believes our opponents will not be ready for *two* greatships, a PTX heavy cruiser, and . . .' He smiled. 'Our other surprises. Ms Nbaro, how are we doing with our Hin consorts?'

Nbaro had not been directly involved in negotiations with

the Hin, except in making reassurances to her prisoner, but she had a report from Dorcas in front of her. 'I think Mr Dorcas is better informed, sir,' she said cautiously.

Dorcas looked to Pisani.

He's learning. He's really not good at authority.

Pisani waved. 'Go ahead, Mr Dorcas.'

'Sir, the Hin are awaiting the transfer of the crew we rescued and our prisoner. We have agreed to effect this transfer once we are clear of the gas cloud. It will be a complex manoeuvre—'

'Skip that part,' Pisani said.

Dorcas nodded. 'The matron–captain hasn't promised us anything,' he admitted. 'Still, I'm cautiously optimistic. I believe that the Hin are even more opportunistic than humans, and the offer of alliance and trade with the DHC, plus our efforts in rescuing their crew, will...' He looked around, uneasy. Nbaro was surprised to see him nervous; usually he was very assured in these situations.

'Will?' Pisani prompted.

'Will be more enticing to the matron–captain and her consorts than the alternative scenario, where they join the waiting alliance to dismember us, especially as she will soon detect the *Dubai*, if she hasn't already.'

Major Darkstar raised a hand. 'Have we considered destroying both Hin ships?' they asked.

Morosini spoke for the first time. *'Yes, of course,'* the AI said dispassionately. *'The possibility, however remote, of an alliance with these Hin and a possible fracture in the enemy alliance outweighs any immediate tactical advantage.'*

'Jesu.' Dukas shook her head. 'I would prefer that you said, "We don't just murder sentients in space."'

Morosini uncrossed and recrossed his red-clad holographic legs and stroked his cat. *'I understand that you would prefer that,'* he agreed. *'I'm afraid this is not the way I assemble scenarios.'*

Nbaro thought, *I am trusting Morosini. I am trusting that this machine intelligence is better at plotting the future of my friends than … well, than we are ourselves. The AI doesn't make it easy.*

Why do I trust Morosini? Because I like him? Because he gave me a chance, even if it was for his own ends? That seems pretty slim, out here.

But what choice do I have? Even though, when he says things like this, he's more alien than the Hin. More alien than the Starfish.

She'd missed some of the discussion; Dukas was uncomfortable with the idea that they would deliberately engage opponents in open battle.

'Fighting off pirates is one thing,' she said vaguely, with a wave of her hand.

Nbaro wondered if the chief engineer saw the Hin as pirates.

Hughes leaned back, his body language making it clear that he shared some of her unease. 'We have a precious cargo,' he said. 'Surely its delivery is our first priority.'

Morosini's holographic shape appeared solid and *present*. 'Not in this case,' he insisted. 'This is a battle we must fight. Not just for our cargoes, but for tomorrow's.'

Pisani smiled with some bitterness, the corners of his mouth turned down in an expression of distaste. 'We have already taken this decision,' he said. 'We will fight.'

'We will seek them out?' Dukas asked. 'Will we pursue wounded ships and kill them? Strafe the survivors? What if we are not attacked?'

Nbaro looked around at them: Darkstar was impassive; Pisani disturbed; Hughes concerned.

Morosini spoke again. '*Althea, someone has gathered an alliance of Fringe worlds, aliens and criminals to take this ship and strip it apart. Their intention is to destabilise the DHC. We hope that they will be surprised by the power we can bring against them, but … yes,*

370

we plan to defeat them – the forces that killed the New York *– at* Ultra.'

Dukas made a motion with her hand. 'I understand all that,' she said with some frustration. 'But we are not a military ship. We are not an empire. We should not be fighting battles.'

Nbaro understood Dukas perfectly – liked her, respected her. But she thought, *But we are a military ship. We carry weapons, we train to use them, and at some point the DHC did become an empire. I suppose that is the truth of it.*

Pisani's voice was gentle. 'Althea, I understand your reservations. May we go on with our briefing?'

Dukas waved her hand. 'Yes, sir. Of course.'

Pisani nodded, and Nbaro wondered what reservations he might have himself.

'We will insert for Ultra in the same formations we used to come here – ten-minute intervals, three-thousand-kilometre spacings. Anything closer risks collisions. We will lead the way, as we are more practised in the insertion manoeuvres. We should expect to be attacked immediately upon insertion. I agree with Captain Dukas this far – we will not fire until we are fired upon.'

Morosini looked at him; it was clear the AI didn't agree.

'I expect to face three different forces,' Pisani continued, ignoring the AI. 'Hin, who are here for their own reasons, Colonial forces from New Texas and elsewhere, looking to 'liberate' the Anti-spinward colonies and form an empire of their own, and pirates.'

'Pirates?' Fraser asked.

Pisani looked at Lochiel, who rose. 'Piracy has been on the rise in the Anti-spinward Marches for ten years,' he said. 'Independent ships prey on small merchants and use the mining stations as bases, dominating them and forcing the mining companies to pay tribute.' He brought up a display of the whole Anti-spinward arm, with red dots indicating attacks on ships.

'It's entirely possible that the mining combines actually operate the pirates, but it hasn't been proven. Regardless, we expect their presence, based on what little we know of the attack on the *New York*.'

'And you think they've blown the station?' Hughes said. 'One of the most expensive stations the DHC has ever built.'

Morosini raised an eyebrow. '*We* know *nothing*,' he said. '*We prepare for the worst case.*'

'And if the station is gone,' Hughes pressed on, 'then what?'

This time, Pisani's smile held no humour at all. 'We lay our sensors, find out who is in the system. If we are unopposed, we refuel at Regum and insert for New India. But let me be clear. New India is a highly populated system full of commercial traffic. We do not want to engage there. If we must fight, we want to fight at Ultra.'

Tremaine had remained silent until then, but she pointed at the holo. 'It's a vast, complex system with a lot of places to hide. If they see two greatships, won't they just hide?'

'*We think they know our timetable,*' Morosini said, '*and will have manoeuvred to hit us either at our extraction points or our next insertion. Maybe both. Maybe an ambush as we transit the system, as happened at Argos.*' He shrugged eloquently. '*Maybe all three. But to hit us, they have to be in place. Ships hidden in the gas giants or the asteroids would be too distant to be of use in a fight.*'

Lochiel looked uncomfortable. Pisani glanced at him.

'With respect, sir,' Lochiel said, 'the Hin ships can boost pretty hard. They could emerge from gravity wells to catch us. And long-range engagements favour them.'

Morosini knows something.

But Morosini surprised Nbaro by explaining. '*This is correct. In fact, my ideal scenario is that the Hin ships are in such positions, or simply running cold. And when they see us engage their sometime human allies, they may choose* not *to become involved.*'

Nbaro happened to glance at Darkstar's impassive expression and thought, *This is the plan. To destroy the New Texas ships and the pirates – to eliminate the human threats to the DHC, and then make a deal with the Hin. I think this has been the plan from the beginning.*

A phrase from her Orphanage education occurred to her. *Arcana Imperii. The secrets of empire. So many secrets, in one ship.*

Pisani then described their insertion procedure in detail. Nbaro paid attention; she was going to be in the launch again. She made notes, with her usual feeling of vague guilt. *What am I doing here? Taking notes to share with Thulile and Truekner?*

And then Pisani looked directly at her. She'd missed something; Tremaine had asked some questions about sortie rates, she thought, and she had no idea why the Master was looking straight at her.

I'm an idiot.

'We will exit the gas cloud in thirteen hours,' he said, as if he was speaking to Nbaro. 'Immediately after, we'll match courses with the alien ship *Beautiful War Dance* and dock. Captain Dukas will have the technical details. We will deliver the rescued Hin in a friendly water environment.'

Dukas made a weary motion. It was very expressive; it said: *I'm getting to it.*

The Master continued to look at her. He said, 'I would like Lieutenant Nbaro to accompany the Hin as a sign of our good will, in an armoured EVA suit. I'm not asking you to linger, Nbaro, but I want them to see that we're not afraid of them and we see them as ... peers.'

You may not be afraid of them, Nbaro thought, *but I am.*

30

There were times when being in love, having emotional commitments beyond herself, seemed more like a set of chains than a ribbon of hope. This was one.

Nbaro had stood a watch and snatched some sleep, amazed at her ability to sleep when terrified, and now the mission was happening. She hadn't seen Dorcas, and they'd had only the briefest contact by neural lace; he was deep in something...

'How's that?' Major Darkstar asked.

Nbaro was standing in her underwear, in one of the Marine spaces. Around her, on the deck, lay weapons and accoutrements sufficient for an army, or so it appeared to her. Darkstar was inserting stents and probes directly into her flesh, and it was painful.

Gunny Drun, beside her, was all business.

'You're going into their ship, and we don't trust the little squids at all, so you get all the best stuff,' Drun said. 'The armour is like a little ship. You'll be fine in water, and just as fine in hard vacuum.'

She wanted to say *I know* because she'd seen the Marine's powered armour – the armour they hardly ever used because it could be fried by an EMP carbine, making it a prison for the unwary.

Frozen, unable to move, while the air runs out in the darkness of an enemy ship. Or worse, as they cut their way in.

Nice. That's really helping.

'I'm scared,' she said suddenly.

'No shit,' Drun said. 'You have every reason to be. Use it, Lieutenant. Use it to stay alive.'

Darkstar started the fiddly process of folding Nbaro into the armour. 'Drun adjusted it to your size, and I promise you the whole arming process is full of pain and indignity.' *Is this what passes for humour, among Marines?*

The Marine major was rubbing her down with alcohol. It made her skin tingle and she felt cold.

'I'll survive,' Nbaro said. And she did. The indignity was really nothing compared to an athletics class at the Orphanage, and the pain was ... well, real, but just pain. She did feel as if she'd strained or pulled every muscle in her back by the time the two Marines had her in the armour.

'Someone invented EMP just to spare Marines from getting into this stuff,' Nbaro said.

Drun laughed. 'Good one. I may use that myself.'

Darkstar leaned over so they could see each other clearly. 'The Master says you are to go unarmed.'

Drun nodded. 'We don't agree. And we won't leave you to make the choice.' He clicked something into the armour's complex exoskeleton. 'You can make a really big hole. Once. You can't miss. You will die in the blowback.'

Darkstar, dispassionate as always, said, 'If you use this, it will look like an accident. Or at least be plausibly deniable.' They shrugged.

'Missile?' Nbaro asked.

'More like a shaped charge. Very short range.' Nbaro saw it in her head-up display, registered its existence in her neural lace. Of course, since it was *there*, Morosini would see it, too.

And I'll bet he doesn't care one way or another.

And at least I won't be captured... Oh, I get it.

She was in the suit, using external speakers to communicate. She felt armoured; she felt good. As she had a dozen systems hardwired into her, she had to wonder if the suit had also pushed drugs into her system.

Fine with me. I feel good.

'Major?' she asked.

'Nbaro?'

'With two greatships along for the ride, are we out of the woods for the last-ditch on-board fight scenario?'

Darkstar had been fiddling with the hydrodynamic cover for the armour, and glanced back. 'Probably.'

'But I have a big boarding party scenario in thirty-six hours,' she said. 'I mean, if I'm alive.'

Darkstar managed a chuckle. 'Practice never hurts.'

Drun leaned in, plugged something into her suit, and she saw a message on her HUD.

Get us anything you can on the layout of their ship. Camera, sonar, whatever. Pri one.

It felt as though Nbaro waited for a long time, bottled up in armour, with the hydrodynamic skin over the exoskeleton making her movements in an air environment clumsy, while the servos in every limb made her very powerful.

'You have a heavy weapon, I see,' Morosini said out of nowhere. *'Excellent. Do not allow yourself to be captured.'*

'Is that a real threat?'

'No, I don't think so. But like Major Darkstar, I appreciate layers of precautions.'

Nbaro found Dorcas in the datafield, hard at work on something for the Hin. 'A translator of sorts, that will interface with...' She felt him look away, almost as if she was in his body.

'I wish I was going with you,' he said suddenly. She suspected he meant it more because he liked her than because he would be fascinated to see the Hin in their own environment. The thought made her smile – though on reflection, she was sure he meant that he wanted to see the Hin in their environment. And, vaguely, to be with her.

'I wish you were, too,' she said, and found that she was hiding her fear from him. *To protect him? Because I don't want him to see me weak?*

Why is everything so complicated?

'Qaqqaq's almost done with the transfer unit,' he said.

They were almost an hour late for the schedule. The *A-leum down Junjon-ui churn* – *Beautiful War Dance* in Anglatin, formerly identified only as CT 0–4–4 – was nestled to the underside of the *Athens*, all the difficult course-matching accomplished without apparent effort by both sides. The two ships were less than fifty metres apart.

Tough day to be TAO, Nbaro thought.

Hey, I'm pretty calm.

And then it was time.

The first step was to enter the transfer tank. There was an airlock, and beyond it were two *full* squads of Marines in armour with an arsenal of weapons. Instead of providing reassurance, the sight made Nbaro's guts churn.

Gunny Drun gave her a thumb's up as she entered the lock, and it took a very, very long time to fill with water. She didn't hate the Hin. Far from it. She admired Nik'ri Put, and enjoyed talking to her when she wasn't being ordered to manipulate the alien.

But she'd seen the tank, and what eighty-four Hin looked like: tentacles everywhere, crawling all over one another, touching...

It set something off in her. She'd been calm, and now she lost it entirely, and began to shake inside the powered armour.

Morosini sounded serene and confident. '*Your adrenaline is spiking, Ms Nbaro.*'

Apparently, she wasn't too shit-scared to be sarcastic. 'Oh? Really? I didn't know.'

The hatch to the tank opened, and then she was in the water with the Hin. The hatch closed behind her – closed silently – and she didn't notice it until, in her peripheral vision, she saw that she was locked in.

Including Nik'ri Put, there were eighty-five of them.

The tank was well-lit, a xenoglas and steel cylinder ready to fit precisely against a Hin airlock. *Wetlock? Spacelock?*

They were around her in seconds, flitting along using their tentacles for propulsion, or floating; many were upside down, their elegant heads pointing down at her.

'Wa-Kan Nik'ri Put?' she asked on her speaker system. 'I am pleased to be here with my honourable *Tse-Tsu*.'

Nbaro really couldn't tell them apart, but one Hin raced out from the cloud of tentacles and fur. She wore the translator headset that Qaqqaq had made, and it looked like she had a package strapped to her as well.

'*Ta! KePoja!* We go back to our people! This is right and also very very right. And you, *KePoja*, will have so much honour!'

The earnestness of the alien cut through Nbaro's near panic.

'Honour?' she asked. 'It seems to me that I will now be *Tse-Tsu* and you will be *my KePoja*.' Even as she said it, she realised she was pressing too far; humour was not something they'd shared much.

But a little. They had shared a little.

Tentacles spread like a cloud, and then settled – an elegant motion that looked like aquatic ballet – and a stream of bubbles erupted from the alien.

378

'Hah! *Ta, ta, ta*, if I was a *Jeeruck* this would be true and also wrong! But you mean this with truth within truth – that you will be helpless aboard the ship of our people, yes?'

Almighty, she's babbling. She's as scared as I am.

Interspecies co-operation one-oh-one. We are all shit-scared.

Nik'ri Put floated to her without any apparent effort, all but nestling against her. 'You will trust to our honour, yes and yes. We will all gain *Hin*.'

My lifelong ambition is to gain Hin.

I mean … in a way, it is.

Dorcas came up on her neural lace. 'Docking is nearly complete. I'll be with you all the way.'

Why isn't he doing this? He's the smart one? The aristocrat … except that apparently I'm an aristocrat, too. And an official hero. And I'm uninjured.

And then the transfer tank jolted very gently.

The Hin stopped moving. It was eerie; the cessation of movement left them like so many balloons on a windless day.

'Hard dock.' Dorcas was speaking in VR through her lace.

I figured, Nbaro thought. Her mind worked very fast in the next seconds, because fear and waiting had the effect she'd heard about in near-death situations; time seemed to pass slowly as she remembered things. She had time to consider Morosini, and time to consider Dorcas, and time to consider Thea Drake. Even Rick Hanna got a review.

And then there was a churning, and what looked like blood staining the water in the direction of the Hin ship.

'Blood,' she said aloud. She didn't like the sound of her own voice.

'Not blood. Their water is a chemical soup.'

That didn't help her visceral reaction to it.

The Hin in the tank moved, all together, in a cloud of tentacles,

379

and then they were gone and the tank was empty except for one lone Hin wearing a translator unit.

'Politely and honourably request you to follow me, *KePoja*!' Nik'ri Put said.

Despite everything, inside her armoured suit, Nbaro smiled. She *almost* wished she was swimming in a respirator and a wetsuit, except that she was a lousy swimmer, and she was pretty sure that if a tentacle touched her, she'd lose it. But Nik'ri Put was so...

Damn. I'm an idiot. Do not xenopomorphise. Is that even a word?

Almost without volition, Nbaro powered forward into the Hin ship.

The space she entered was a docking bay. She was sure of it as soon as she entered, because sonar and infrared showed her nested eggs – the armoured spiders that she had faced with Drun and the Marines during the fighting at Trade Point. There were several dozen – more than she could count quickly. She recorded everything.

The deck, if it was a deck, was not flat. It only took her moments to realise that the Hin didn't need a place to stand, so the concepts of 'deck' and 'overhead', 'floor' and 'ceiling' would probably have no meaning for them. The area beneath her armoured feet was littered with machinery: winches, docking equipment, a very human-looking mobile gantry neatly nested into other equipment.

She floated, moving with her manoeuvring thrusters.

She had no trouble identifying the commander of the *Beautiful War Dance*. Matron–Captain Honourable Blood Wa-Kan Asinpal Las floated almost alone, wearing some sort of glimmering harness or helmet that looked like chain mail made of crystal. It showed distinctively on IR.

Nbaro's normal human vision was almost useless in the red haze that was apparently the Hin shipboard norm. That troubled her hindbrain, because she could no long see the most human features of her hosts: their liquid brown eyes. She could only see outlines, and tentacles.

'Don't back up any further,' Dorcas said calmly in her head. 'You are almost against some sort of equipment which some Hin are using. You might injure them.'

Nbaro hadn't even realised that she was retreating.

She turned, a little too fast. Her armour rotated too far and she had to spin back. Sure enough, the 'wall' behind her was covered in living bumps. The Hin could make themselves very soft. Unlike Terran octopuses, they had some internal bone and they lacked suckers, having instead shaped grooves in their many arms...

...and there were a lot of them, and they were very close...

'The speech,' Dorcas said.

Nbaro took a deep breath, and forced herself to fire the thrusters and move to something like the centre of the space. All of her statements were recorded; she didn't even know exactly what some of them meant. She'd repeated exactly what she'd been told to by Dorcas, and it had been recorded.

She orientated herself to be head to head with the captain–matron and felt ridiculous as she extended all four limbs and then brought them together, the closest a human could manage to the all-tentacles curtsey that she'd seen Nik'ri Put and the other Hin perform. Her thrusters managed to hold her steady relative to the Hin, which was a sort of miracle.

Then she triggered the greeting speech.

'*Yago in hari...*' it began. It said, 'We return to you your spacer–kin with honour, nothing taken or hidden. We hope that they are well and happy.' There were some formal felicitations that Nik'ri Put had recommended, as well. It was odd, listening to her own voice inside the helmet, and hearing the high-pitched version that was projected.

Asinpal Las gave the same ballet curtsey. *Did her tentacles flare to a smaller angle? Was that age, or seniority?*

Nbaro understood none of what she said. Without the amplifier that Qaqqaq had made for Nik'ri Put, so long ago, it all sounded like high-pitched gibberish.

Morosini and Dorcas were on the job, and the translation came in seconds after the captain–matron's speech began.

'She's pleased. She expresses pleasure at our courtesy, and our use of language, and our treatment of her kin. Almost as if those are all equal. She says…' Dorcas paused. 'I didn't get that. I'll have to play it back later. Now she's saying that all her kin look… alive. Alive? And that the return of her officer–niece Wa-Kan Nik'ri Put will be a joy to her mother. Even if Nik'ri Put was so foolish as to be captured.'

'Ouch,' Nbaro sent.

'But perhaps in this very rare… something something, the capture of an officer in honourable combat may please? Benefit? Now she asks Nik'ri Put if you are truly *KePoja*, and Nik'ri Put says yes, and yes.'

'I'll bet she does.' Nbaro was looking around the space. It wasn't very big; the Hin were, for the most part, only a metre long, their tapered skulls making up almost a third of their anatomy. Above her there were portals, or watertight doors; they were each about a metre in diameter. Even as she watched, still recording, a hatch opened, cycling exactly like one of the iris valves on the *Athens*, and three Hin shot out, heads forward, tentacles back. Their magnificent and somewhat protuberant eyes could see just as well past the top of their skulls as outward or down.

One-metre wide corridors. Gunny, no way are we taking one of their ships.

The captain–matron was still talking, and Dorcas was really struggling now. 'I think she's suggesting something about

382

alliance, but it's all in the singular – it's you and Nik'ri Put, and not *us* and *them*. But dammit, I can't get…'

The captain–matron stopped shrieking. That's how it seemed to Nbaro.

Nbaro fluttered her limbs again, and keyed up her next speech. It was carefully written by Morosini, and it suggested the possibility of DHC–Hin co-operation without directly suggesting that there was a quid pro quo.

Her recording delivered most of it well. She noted that her hesitation over the long compound word-sounds in the middle sounded even worse in the high-frequency version.

She watched the crowd of Hin, most of them scrunched down so that their furry skulls were like tapered eggs growing in some weird sea environment. 'A few floated upside down in the red water, looking down on her.

Nbaro told herself that Morosini was right there, in her ear, as was Dorcas. That her ship was a hundred metres away.

She even tried to tell herself that meeting aliens and going aboard their ship was the sort of thing she had imagined when she used to lie in her bunk at the Orphanage, stifling sobs and nursing bruised knuckles. Or worse.

She felt cold, and alone. One Hin confined in a tank was almost a friend; several hundred Hin in a single space with poor visibility was just a nightmare of shapes and tentacles.

The speech concluded.

The captain–matron flashed her two worker tentacles, the longest ones, and screeched—

—and everything went to hell. Hin flew in every direction; iris valves cycled, and Hin spacers poured through, leaving the docking area, as others entered – a column of new Hin, including four in the four-limbed spider-armour she'd seen before.

Nbaro couldn't see Nik'ri Put.

Something came at her like a biological torpedo: a single alien...

Splat. Nbaro had a Hin clinging to her suit.

She moaned. She heard herself, and fought for equilibrium. It was happening – they were attacking her...

Another alien wrapped itself around her arm.

'I'm under attack!' she sent, with more force than she'd intended.

'*I do not believe so. Please remain immobile,*' Morosini sent.

Almighty! Remain immobile?

Nbaro began to swear. But she didn't move, which took more discipline than anything she'd ever done.

Close by her, someone was shouting in rapid Hin.

She tracked and recorded the four armoured Marines. She noted they were not doing anything particularly intimidating.

She also noted that she could hear her heartbeat in her ears, and that her knees and hands were shaking even in the closely fitted power armour.

With a soft *plop*, another Hin covered her visor, wrapping its long tentacles around her helmet. She could see nothing except the thing's digestive hole, which was much like a human anus.

'I have one attached to my visor!' she squeaked. She was losing the concentration to communicate by neural lace.

It's feeling for the catch on my helmet latch, and then I'll drown, and they'll eat me...

'DO NOT MOVE!' Dorcas sent. 'All of the Hin attached to you are young. *Very* young. Children. The captain–matron is sorting it. You are not under attack.'

Nbaro gathered herself and sent Dorcas her view of the Hin on her visor.

'That is troubling,' he sent.

'Troubling?' She almost had the courage to laugh. 'Next time, *you* meet the aliens. I'll tell you what to worry about.'

'I love you, Nbaro,' Dorcas sent.

Fuck, what do I do with that? I think maybe he does.

Almighty.

With a *slurp*, the thing on her visor detached, leaving a small spot of...

Yuck.

31

'I almost passed out!' Nbaro spat. 'Almighty, I humiliated myself...'

Drun was helping her out of the armour. 'Heh. You didn't shit in the suit, so you weren't that scared.' He laughed. 'Ms Nbaro, *everyone* gets scared. It's how you use it. The ship told you to freeze, you froze, you didn't kill the little ones and didn't fire the missile. Mission accomplished. Also, now the squids are on the back foot, apologising.'

'I feel like a fool,' she said.

Drun shrugged. 'This is going to hurt,' he said, and started pulling out the stent needles.

'You did a beautiful job,' Dorcas said.

'You should have been there. You know how to say *get these things off me!*'

He was silent. They were in his stateroom, and they'd made love like people who'd recently survived death. Nbaro was surprised at the ferocity of her response. Now she was rubbing the welts the armour had raised on her skin.

We're just animals, in space.

After a long silence during which he just stroked her, he said,

'I was so afraid for you that I failed to tell you what to say. I froze.'

Much later, alone in her own rack, she realised that those were the right words. The best words he could have said.

Nine hours until Insertion for Ultra.

She was pilot, with Eyre, but in the second wave. The launch cycle was very complicated between the two greatships.

She smiled, and went to sleep, and dreamed of tentacles.

Nbaro awoke in an empty cabin, put on her best flightsuit, and on a whim put on her gold necklace with the scrap of the Holy Koran inside; it was the charm she'd bought long ago on Sahel, with Rick Hanna. She knew that it was irrational. She wore it for luck

She looked lovingly at her swords and her blue xenoglas armour, at the wood panel that decorated the side of her acceleration couch, the bronze edging, the screens showing distant stars.

She found herself touching the wood panel. Felt the smile on her face, and then she laughed at herself, got into her good boots, and headed to the wardroom, where she drank some weak tea and ate a cinnamon bun. It was delicious, and also a strong omen of the combat to come. Every spacer knew that when times were tough, the food got miraculously better – spices were found, meat appeared . . .

She smiled, drank her terrible tea and enjoyed the rare sweet. She took four more off the tray for her helmet bag, and then grabbed two more for the spacers in the EVA shop. Chu and Po were both working, and she got big smiles in return for each roll.

Chu smiled shyly. 'I thought you'd forgotten me, Lieutenant.'

'Never! You were my first friend.' Nbaro grinned. She didn't even have to paste it on. She waved at Eyre and got into her custom-made EVA suit, noticing that Chu had stencilled her name, her rank and her Flight Six patch on to it. She blushed a little, both at the implied praise and at her outright theft. It was not hers; it had been purchased for something specific by the crew of the now destroyed *Hong Kong.*

Spacer Po looked up from where he was working at an antiquated sewing machine. 'Lieutenant Commander Han came looking for you, ma'am,' he said.

She raised her tab, flipped through her messages, and found that Han and Gorshokov were back aboard. She sent both of them a greeting while she leaned on the EVA shop counter. Slyly, Chu put a bulb of coffee in her hands. It wasn't great coffee, but it was coffee. She raised it to Chu as if toasting her, and the other woman smiled.

'In port, I owe you a whole meal,' Nbaro said.

Chu nodded. 'That's right, ma'am,' she agreed. 'Roast pork. I know a place on New India Station.'

Definitely going into action. Rituals of life and all that.

'We're already there, Petty Officer Chu.' She leaned over. Her tab held a response from Han. Sabina had tried to alert her, and she'd ignored it.

Glad to be back. I'm wrangling with Morosini and Truekner over you right now. I need a second pilot: we're pretty tired.

She typed: I'm walking right now. Talk later.

She went up to the ready room in her gear, spotted her backseaters, and motioned to them. Truekner beckoned to her, and she went to where he was reclining.

'I want you to stay tight to me – got that?' he asked.

She had read the brief and run the sim. 'Aye aye, sir.'

'Don't give me that, Nbaro. We're the second wave. If things go to shit, we're going to be doing the shooting. Even in the second wave, you and I are the reserve shooters.'

I saw all that in the sim.

'Yes, sir.'

'Good.' He smiled at her, and suddenly she wished she was going as his second pilot, instead of flying her own spacecraft. He was... She couldn't put words to it. *Solid? Reliable? Friendly?*

No, it was deeper than that.

'You ready? After yesterday?' His smile was different now – the commander, but also the father of the squadron. 'That looked hairy.'

'It was also... tentacle-y,' she said.

They both laughed.

'I was terrified,' she told him, and anyone else within earshot.

Truekner nodded, as if he had, himself, faced a wall of aliens. Behind Nbaro, Thulile put a hand on her shoulder. 'It looked like some shit,' she said quietly.

It hit Nbaro hard, then, and she almost cried. It wasn't just a delayed reaction. It was Truekner, and Thulile. And Chu... *The coffee wasn't about combat today, was it?*

I've never had anything like this before. Fuck, I'm going to cry.

Storkel reached in and touched her arm. 'I fell in the sea once,' he said. 'My boat flipped and something nibbled on me.' Just for a moment, the two of them shared that moment of horror through eye contact.

'I'd like to visit the sea on Terra,' she said, and Storkel grinned.

'Any time we're free,' he said.

Truekner rose with a groan. 'I'm too fucking old for this,' he said. 'And I'm tired of putting you in for medals, Nbaro, so let's fly this one and come home bored spitless, OK?'

'Roger that, skipper.'

At the back of the ready room, she had to wipe her eyes on her sleeve.

Nbaro was in 6–0–7; she walked all around, looking for anything wrong or out of place, gave a thumb's up to Chief Baluster, and dropped into her acceleration couch with a gymnastic wriggle.

Tench and Tatlah had the sub-AI up and running, and Eyre had pasted a clock counting down to Insertion on their shared screen, but they were second wave, with forty spaceframes ahead of them to launch. Even at the fastest possible cycle, they'd be an hour behind the first planes to launch.

When all the preflights were done, she shared the cinnamon rolls.

The back-seaters compared recent imagery of the Hin. After all, they had one craft only fifty kilometres away. In the front seat, Eyre ran the sim of the mission again while Nbaro used her neural lace to look at the launch cycle, and then at the TAO plot.

Five minutes to Insertion. She lay back. 'Take your drugs, people,' she said on reflex. And then, she looked down the tunnel to the back-seaters. 'Listen up. We're going to extract into a fight. In the worst case, we'll already be fighting as we extract. We've practised for this, but this time ... it's real. Everyone stays frosty, everyone lets the sub-AI do what has to be done. We'll be waiting about forty minutes to launch – I'll update you on what's going on outside.'

She didn't say, *unless we hit another ship during Insertion.*

She didn't say, *unless they shoot us before we can shoot back.*

Space was dangerous, and spacers knew it. It was dangerous even without hostile sentients.

Eventually, there was a three-minute warning, and then a one-minute warning. The battle stations alerts played on every available screen.

Insertion.

Extraction.

Nbaro never did work out the sequence of events to their extraction. In her perception, there was a dull white flash which preceded her being awake, and then her spaceship jolted, snapped free of its electromagnetic couplers, and slammed down to the deck.

'Lioness?' she asked the darkness.

She looked at her avionics. All green. She glanced at comms.

'I have a system,' Tatlah reported. 'All green. No comms, though.'

She dived into dataspace. It was all there: a spinning mass of data; damage, deaths…

'*Athens* has been hit,' she said to her crew. 'Stand by, people.'

Nothing was launching. She could feel it, hear the silence.

'Morosini?'

'*Nbaro.*' Then he didn't so much speak to her, as fill her with data: Two launch tubes crippled, comms down all over the ship, damage everywhere. Nuclear mine.

She looked through Morosini's sensors at the planetary system around them – navigational beacons that Morosini had already tagged as liars – and there were wolves all around them: hostiles within fifty thousand kilometres – twenty at least.

'*Can you be Lioness from there? You have the neural lace.*'

Nbaro thanked her possibly existent god that she'd looked carefully at the launch cycle before they hit Insertion.

'Got it.'

Morosini poured in more data, rescheduling the whole first wave in less than a second for two working launch tubes.

And that's why we have computers, boys, girls and 'gynes.

Nbaro skipped through comms channels – not on her ship's system but on her neural lace – and she reached out in cyberspace and took the Lioness Command Channel for her own, and tied it to her spaceframe.

Even as she picked up the digital threads of the command frequency, her spacecraft shuddered as the electromagnets came back on line. The spaceframe seemed to quiver with excitement;

the slight vibration told Nbaro that something was wrong in engineering.

'This is Nbaro in Alpha Foxtrot 6–0–7,' she said through the digital magic of her lace. 'Lioness is down. I repeat, Lioness is down. I am taking Lioness per command and starting the launch cycle now.'

Discipline held. She was not greeted over her limited comms ability with a chaos of chatter. Just silence. *Here we go.*

'1–0–1, this is Lioness, over?' she called.

'Lioness, this is 1–0–1, ready to launch.'

'Weight confirmed, 1–0–1. Go.'

Nbaro moved down the list. The ship gave the shudder of a successful launch. '2–0–4, this is Lioness, over.'

2–0–4 was on the ball. They'd all be listening in, now. 'Roger, Lioness, 2–0–4.'

'Good for launch,' she said. That was pure ritual when, through the lace, she could *see* their mass on the launch pad. She didn't need the oral report.

Now both tubes were firing. While she waited, Nbaro opened her channel to every ship waiting to launch,

'Listen up, Space Wing! This is Lioness. We got hit hard and we're putting you out on two tubes. We're doing this at speed, so forget calling weights and be ready for your *go* signal. I've got you.'

Someone said, 'Roger that,' with something like enthusiasm. It sounded like Cortez.

The ship jolted. She could, if she paused, feel the rhythmic rolling of a close-in weapons system.

But that wasn't her problem.

Through the neural lace, she could see that both her tubes had cycled. She loaded the next two spaceframes and fired them. In less than a minute, the routine had been reduced to her calling their number, and them replying 'roger'. Between launches the tubes took a moment to fire something – ablative sand, maybe, or a slug at some enemy ship.

Morosini sent, '*Stern tubes.*'

I'm an idiot. The damage to the greatship's bow hadn't touched the stern, and the tubes fired both ways. Nbaro began to reschedule for faster launches, the numbers flowing like mercury through her planning routines.

They rocked, and the artificial gravity went out and then returned. For an eternal moment, she had no contact with the datasphere. Around her, her crew were getting 6–0–7 back into launch position on the rails.

She had time to think, *Not a good sign.* And then the augmented universe clicked back into shape around her, with all her schedules and calculations, all the damage reports, the starboard-side sensors...

She couldn't look at the developing battle outside the ship. She had other things to watch. Damage control had written off bow launches from tube 2; the exit ramp was reduced to slag, but tube 4 was under repair with a rapidity that did the crew credit. Someone had thought outside the box. They were literally cutting away the damage to open the tube. It would be twenty metres shorter...

Nbaro watched the damage control parties and followed the repair to comms. Unhardened comms had taken it badly; the nuke had been off the port bow, triggered by—

She didn't need to care. They were three minutes into the Ultra System. Morosini had noted that all information from the navigational beacons was unreliable, so they were running blind, especially as the blast had taken out most of the antennas off the port-side bow, almost back to the bridge.

Very handy sometimes, being ten kilometres long.

The ship's radiation shielding had kept them alive. Nbaro had checked that early, making sure they weren't all walking corpses. They'd taken a dose, but nothing near lethal.

'We're still in the fight,' she said out loud, and then muttered a curse.

That had gone out to the whole space wing.

Always an idiot.

Except that there were 'rogers' from fifty mics.

She was sixteen spaceframes deep in her launch when Morosini changed the sequence, pushing more of the heavy hitters and sensor systems to the front of the line. Nbaro shot Truekner off and wished she was with her skipper.

Storkel roared off down tube 2, and tube 4 came up as Amber. They'd cut enough away and re-routed some magnets...

'Morosini, test-fire tube 4?'

He didn't answer, but something went out into space. She watched it go, in almost real time, and then, ruthlessly, put Thulile on tube 4 as soon as it cycled. Morosini wanted as many bow launches as possible; the fighting was mostly ahead of them.

Nbaro took a snapshot of the developing battle as the Flights Three and Six spaceframes dropped sensors and the *Athens* was cured of her temporary blindness. They were in the system, just inside the orbit of the smaller gas giant, which – by chance or planning – was close-by in interstellar terms: half a million kilometres away, with its own body of satellites and an accretion disc.

Ships were emerging from the accretion disc; all were tagged hostile, but most were small, fragile human ships the size of small cargo lifters. A few were larger. Closer in were a trio of Hin ships, two trios of human warships and a dozen small craft. It was a knife fight, and the space wing craft threaded it. Even as Nbaro watched, someone from Flight Two flashed and vanished off the screen.

That was someone I know.

They were hit again, by one of the Hin beam weapons.

The *Athens* wasn't sitting quietly. Her railgun turrets and close-in weapons systems hurled slugs at her foes – invisible to the eye, but easily trackable on radar and ladar, which Nbaro could use as her own senses. Traces of radioactive wreckage marked the deaths of four small ships.

The *Athens* shook again as she was hit somewhere well forward.

All that in a single flash, and then Nbaro bore down on her duty. She managed the launches like a card-dealing robot, deftly moving around new damage: a failure in tube 1's magnets; a penetration in tube 2 forward. She was confirming weights, launching aft, launching forward, updating launch velocities and changing the schedule as the TAO or Pisani asked for a different load, or a combat shot of ablatives, or a slug.

Twenty-nine spaceframes into the launch, Space Operations came back online and appeared on a side channel. It was Dworkin.

Nbaro tabbed him all the changes to the launch plan.

'Fuck,' he spat into the side channel. 'How are you doing all this from a cockpit?'

'Morosini,' she said, and went back to launching. Three launches later, he was back.

'Got it,' he said.

She checked with Morosini. 'Can I hand over?'

'*Affirmative*,' he sent.

'All yours, sir.' Nbaro killed her stolen command channel, handing control back to the real Lioness. Dworkin picked up flawlessly, on the new schedule.

His voice, calm, controlled, said, 'Space Wing, this is Lioness taking launch control from Nbaro,' over the command frequency. 'Please call your launch weights, folks.'

Nbaro knew they were number seven to launch.

'Everyone ready?' she said. 'We're about to play in the big league.'

She looked again at the combat situation. The Hin were pounding the bow, but one of their ships had taken too many depleted uranium rounds through her shielding, and was lagging behind the combat. Everything else the enemy had was being thrown at the stern of the *Athens*.

Nbaro checked and saw that they were going out of the stern, and they were being launched *with* an ablative load – a new tactic, but one they'd practised.

'We're going out cold,' she said to her crew.

Dworkin was the only officer above her who knew what she was doing, and he didn't query it. She was going down the stern tubes side by side with a Flight One drop-ship fitted out with a deception package, and she'd made her call.

'6–0–7,' she said. Dworkin had stuck to her abbreviated launch sequence. He needed the weight call, but everything else he'd cut. She used her lace to send their weight straight to his board.

'Go,' Dworkin said, and she saluted . . .

The seconds as they shot sternwards down the tube seemed very long. Long enough to think about people, and remember Sarah – poor abandoned Sarah . . .

Why didn't Morosini save Sarah, if he knew what was happening?

Light in the darkness, and they were out. The ablatives fired their rockets, raced ahead and burst, all in the first three seconds.

Movement everywhere: some bit of wreckage flashed past without destroying them. Nbaro had lost the immediacy of the datasphere, but she had the datalink – slower and cruder, but still a solid picture of the battle's volume – and within it, they were slow and cold and invisible.

Less than a thousand kilometres away, a purpose-built warship fired its centreline railgun at the *Athens*.

Nbaro put a target pip on the ship. Tatlah confirmed from the back seat.

'Lock on,' Tench said.

Nbaro used her cold thrusters to roll up and steady her course. They were drifting towards the target in a relative way while rushing rapidly through space in the opposite direction, all because of relative velocity. Nbaro was patient; she stayed in the ablative cloud and prayed she was invisible while the unidentified warship's close-in weapons systems probed space for enemies.

'She's a DHC destroyer!' Eyre gasped.

'She's the *Sorbonne*, one of the three garrison ships for Ultra–Medulla,' Tench confirmed.

The *Sorbonne* fired her main line railgun again, and put a seventy-centimetre hole through the *Athens*.

'Hostile,' Nbaro said, and entered an override code to their torpedoes.

Tatlah said, 'But—'

Nbaro said, 'We don't know what the hell's happening out here, people, but that ship and her sisters are pounding *Athens*.'

She had time to notice more than a dozen mayday beacons: space crew who'd ejected, hoping very hard to be rescued before their air supplies ran out.

Her heart hardened. They were getting pounded.

Something flashed near the *Sorbonne*. She'd taken a hit or a near miss from a nuclear torpedo; they were eight hundred kilometres out now.

'All four fish, Tatlah.'

He sounded shaken. 'Roger, ma'am.'

Nbaro still hadn't lit the engines.

6–o–7 shook, then gave three more jolts in rapid succession as the rotary launcher deployed the torpedoes. Nbaro hit the cold thrusters forward, slowing them hard; 6 *g* slammed them, and the torpedoes, still cold, leapt ahead.

The datalink sent a collision warning, and she understood.

The cavalry was coming.

'Hold the torps on my word,' she barked.

Tatlah obeyed, the torpedoes drifting, engines unlit, every second farther from them.

Nbaro didn't see it this time, but she caught it on datalink.

The *Dubai* was extracting, two hundred kilometres aft of the fight.

'Light 'em up,' Nbaro snapped. Even the computers had to feel disorientated for a moment. On the bridge of the *Sorbonne*, computers would be asking for human input ...

Four nuclear torpedoes lit their engines and started their sprints from four hundred kilometres. They had almost fifty seconds of burn inside the ablative cloud. Tatlah had orchestrated this like the artist he was.

The *Sorbonne* began evasive action as the *Dubai* fired her railgun tubes at the DHC destroyer *Namur*, a hundred kilometres away, also labelled 'hostile' on the datalink.

Nbaro had spotted Storkel in 6–0–5 as he dived into the ablative shield, with a long line of ineffectual slugs reaching for him from both of the DHC destroyers. She also saw what he was doing: tickling the dragon's tail, luring automated systems to the easier target of the big, fat XC-3Cs so that they might miss the almost-invisible stealth missiles. Storkel had seen her launch.

'Ready with chaff,' she said, and lit the fires.

The engines came on with a vengeance, and they exploded forward up and out of the plane defined by the *Athens* and her antagonists, climbing in the volume of the enemy ships as Tench fired their own chaff launchers.

The *Sorbonne* locked on to them immediately. Her radar warning screamed, and then, suddenly she was aware of the third human ship, the *Wilful Elephant*, that had been hidden by the bulk of the *Athens* behind her.

Missed that, idiot.

The *Wilful Elephant* locked on to them at a range of a hundred kilometres, and the sub-AI began to kick them around in desperate manoeuvres. They were hit, and hit again; Nbaro's controls showed red lights, and in her mind, it was almost like physical pain as the neural lace transmitted the damage.

Five hundred kilometres away, the *Sorbonne* realised her peril from the incoming nuclear torpedoes, which were now moving at something like nine thousand metres per second.

The *Sorbonne* turned to expose the broadside of her close-in weapons systems.

Somewhere out in space beyond the *Athens*, Storkel gave an order and Eason, behind him, fired the engines on a torpedo he'd left out there, cold and silent. He'd been patient, and now his torpedo lit its engines just ten kilometres from the exposed stern of the *Sorbonne* as the enemy ship turned to face Nbaro's missiles.

Nbaro watched with pure admiration for Storkel's devious tactical mind as the *Sorbonne* shot down her missiles. The *Sorbonne* got the last one just a second before detonation. Three seconds later, Storkel's lurker, undetected, detonated on contact. The *Sorbonne* shone brighter than the sun for several seconds, and was gone in a cloud of expanding gas.

Nbaro wasn't blind because she was flying, diving back into the shadow of her greatship, so close to the hull that she had direct datasphere contact, and she used it to query whether she should land and rearm.

The *Athens* was reorientating, aiming her spinal railguns. Two hundred kilometres astern, the *Dubai* fired all four tubes.

The small ships who had been closing on the *Athens* had turned from hunters to prey, and the fighters from Flight One and Flight Two harried them. The enemy ships were too small to have robust AIs or full CIWS coverage.

Pirates. Even as Nbaro watched the scan, a Flight Five pilot got one. *Cortez?* She hoped he was alive, and pulled her nose around again. The *Wilful Elephant* was the last warship facing them. Of the three Hin ships, one was dead, and the other two were far astern, limping.

The battle was eleven minutes old.

The *Wilful Elephant* was pounding the *Athens* from a thousand kilometres out, her iron or depleted uranium rounds slamming into the underside of the mighty greatship. By pure good luck, the *Single Star*, docked to the hull, was taking some of the damage.

By pure bad luck, Nbaro's ship was hit by something – a piece of debris, or perhaps gauss rounds from one of the pirates. Nbaro felt the impact.

An automated system ordered her to land. She responded, looking for the marked entry tube. Enemy fire had slackened; the *Wilful Elephant* was far too busy to waste anti-spacecraft rounds or computation time on her spaceframe. She noted with real – if fleeting – emotion that Truekner was landing just ahead of her in tube 4, aft. Only when she looked for his spaceframe, an old habit from sims, did she see the hole in the canopy above her. Two holes, in fact.

'Almighty,' Nbaro said. 'Everyone OK?'

They all rogered up.

There were corresponding exit holes through the centreline of the frame, down into the fuselage,

'Shit,' Eyre said – his first word in a long time. He'd done his job; he just wasn't talkative.

Nbaro used the lace on the ship's systems, and there it all was: minimal electrical wiring damage, but a lot of nano-goo leakage and some missing couplers. She finessed it into a damage report and transmitted. Over the horizon of the looming *Athens*, the fast-moving *Wilful Elephant*'s fusion engines lost their magnetic seals, even as Nbaro fought gravity and her own momentum to try to stay below the horizon of the *Athens*. The sub-AI darkened the canopy in time, but the flash was like all the lightning in the universe, and it was close, and suddenly she had no avionics at all.

She automatically slammed a hand down on her RESET button. Hardened electronics were designed for this...

No cabin pressure, no avionics. There was something sluggish in manual controls; that would be the nano leak.

The cold thrusters were almost entirely analogue – almost. Nbaro didn't have control of them, but as soon as she had a spark of an onboard system...

Lights flickered on her control panel. She used the neural lace to interface directly with some very primitive levels in the onboard computer, ordering this machine code to activate that processor...

...and then she had the cold thrusters. She had no comms. Her place in the landing order had been set and she was still in the pattern, mostly...

The *Athens* had taken a dose of lethal radiation and even more EMP; the stern lights on the tubes weren't flashing, and every antenna near the stern was gone.

Truekner drew level in 6–0–1. Nbaro used microbursts from her cold thrusters to waggle her craft.

The skipper flashed his landing lights, twice. He'd got it – she had no comms.

Eyre was working feverishly to restore any kind of diagnostics. Tench said, 'I have a system,' over a suddenly working cockpit communication system.

Nbaro tried Lioness, then tried Tower.

So close she could see him, Truekner saluted, and then turned his spacecraft on final approach for the stern.

Do I risk trying to land a damaged bird with no comms and no avionics?

Under her console was a physical book with yellow plastic pages. Every page described a possible space emergency, and all the steps to resolve that emergency: a simple road map to follow for a crew edging towards panic. 'If this happens, do X. If that doesn't work, try Y. Failing Y, do Z three times.'

Every one of the sequences ended with, 'If Z fails, eject.'

Nbaro was working through the Z's on three different failures. On the other hand, the stern tubes were two kilometres away and her speed relative to the greatship was...

Survivable.

If she had her magnetic couplers – the widgets that would interact with the tube's super-magnets to slow her.

And of course, if the *Athens* had magnets.

'Magnetic couplers,' Eyre said. He didn't have a neural lace, but he was a smart lad, and he was using external cameras to physically inspect the couplers. 'Nine through fourteen are green. Six and eight look right on camera.'

'Nice,' Nbaro managed. Her closing speed was slow. Truekner's craft vanished into tube 4.

'We're not ejecting,' she said – mostly to herself. She touched the controls, using the cold thrusters to manually adjust her attitude and course. She almost smiled, because she'd done this over and over in sims, relishing the challenge. It felt very different in real life, mostly because she had very little cold thrust fuel left, and whatever magic power transmitted her commands to the external thrusters seemed to be running on a one-second delay.

'Very exciting,' she muttered.

Eyre chuckled, and the sound was full of confidence and faith.

'Dirty up,' she called, and Eyre just waved. Of course, he had already deployed the couplers.

Suddenly Nbaro entered the datasphere. She felt like a fool; of course she had a way to communicate inside the sphere. She dumped all her info, computer to computer, into Morosini: relative speed; all her damage; the tube she was going for.

Eight hundred metres out, Dworkin's voice came through her lace. '6–0–7, you are cleared for tube 2.'

Nbaro crept into the tube . . . and the landing itself was completely anticlimactic.

On the Space Ops repeater, she saw the *Stealthy Change* extract and start the rout of the enemy ships. The *Dubai* had shocked them, but the *Stealthy Change*, by luck or amazingly good guesswork, had extracted into the fleeing pirates, missing the closest by fewer than a hundred kilometres, and immediately devastated them with small railgun rounds.

Ten minutes later, the *Beautiful War Dance* fell in-system, broadcasting as soon as she arrived. By then, the volume of the battle was thousands of kilometres astern, and the little flotilla was racing in-system past the gas giant.

Nbaro had to crawl out of the main crew compartment; the CIWS rounds through her windscreen had damaged its ability to open.

Chief Baluster just shook his head. 'She's not going out again for a while, Ms Nbaro.' He pointed to the growing pool of nano-sludge and hydraulics dripping away under the main fuselage.

'Medbay,' said a voice. Just for a moment she expected Yu, but he was dead. This technician was a middle-aged woman with short-cropped white hair and the features of a fantasy elf. Her name tag said 'Haapala.'

'I'm on turnaround—'

'You and your crew took sub-lethal doses of radiation. So did

403

half the space crew down here. Don't give me trouble, Nbaro. Get in the lift.' Haapala didn't sound angry – just doing her job.

Nbaro looked at Chief Baluster.

He shrugged. 'Skipper went, ma'am.'

She gathered up her crew and moved to one of the personnel lifts, flinging up her mission debrief by neural lace as she went. All her video had been lost in the EMP burst; she had a raging headache, and she didn't like the words *sub-lethal radiation* one little bit.

Medbay on Third Deck was as crowded as San Marco when a tourist ship came up from New London. Most of the patients were space crew who looked perfectly healthy, but there were more than fifty spacers and officers lying on cots or already in clamshells. It was ugly; death was in the air, and the smell of blood, and fear. Science techs moved through it; Nbaro saw Tatlah, and other people she knew.

She remembered Steven Yu, way back when, explaining that he was a science tech, not a doctor.

They were all doctors, now.

Two techs were walking space crew through a xenoglas bubble covered in instruments, some of which rotated in multiple directions while a spacer was inside.

She saw Truekner. He looked as if he had a deep suntan on his face and hands.

'You OK, skipper?' she asked.

'Was going to ask you the same. You almost got caught when the *Elephant* went up.' Truekner put a hand on her shoulder. His hand was burned red-brown. His skin was dark to begin with, but she could still see the lines of burn.

She'd worn gloves with her EVA suit, and they'd all had their helmets on and visors down. A thin margin of protection...

'Fried my comms, but I feel fine.' But she didn't feel fine. She felt as if she was about to throw up all over the ship, and some little worm inside her head was making her access lethal radiation information with her lace.

Truekner nodded. 'Everything hurts. We got a dose but Med says we'll live. *Opa*! My turn.' He stepped up and was walked into the big machine. It hummed; outer arms whirled. Nbaro desperately wanted to sit down, or perhaps get to a head. Terrible things were happening in her gut.

Eyre pushed her forward, but she could see he was as badly off as she was. 'You first,' she said.

He went into the second machine, following Bakri…

And then Nbaro was kneeling on the floor, vomiting. A lot of her vomit was blood.

32

Nbaro returned to consciousness in a clamshell. Dorcas was sitting by her, and they were not in the medbay. She couldn't really turn her head.

'You're going to be fine,' he said. 'I mean, you can learn all about it on your lace, but I wanted to tell you.'

She nodded.

'You took a big dose – you and Eyre both. Your back-seaters didn't, for whatever reason. You are getting a full scrub, right now – there are nanobots working inside your cells. So are Commander Truekner, and a dozen other space crew. There's too many wounded for medbay, so they opened up what used to be the Hin holding bay.'

She tried to smile.

Dorcas leaned forward. 'I was so scared for you… Oh, Marca, I'm not good at this.' He shook his head.

We are united by our lack of emotional communication skills, she thought. Looking at his haggard face, she *knew*, maybe for the first time, how deeply he felt for her.

Fascinating. Almost worth a sub-lethal dose of radiation.

After he left, she had hours to watch the space battle. She couldn't *do* anything. It was odd, as she told Morosini, because she could have stood a watch as Lioness or Tower from her clamshell; the neural lace made her capable of it, and eventually, Morosini allowed her direct access to the Combat Information Centre and its stations, so that she could expand her 'under-instruction' watch-standing time in CIC.

The DHC flotilla continued to fall in-system. They were neither accelerating nor decelerating now, declaring no intention. The Hin ship *Beautiful War Dance* continued to keep station, about two thousand kilometres astern of the *Stealthy Change*. She continued to broadcast a repeating message in two different Hin dialects. Nbaro had Dorcas's translation:

'Currents under the sea bring new sources of food to the careful hunter. Sometimes even the [untranslatable] and the [untranslatable] swim together to hunt.'

'I told Pisani that's their version of the wolf lying down with the lamb,' Dorcas sent via lace.

Nbaro's head was clearing. She didn't like the idea of molecular bots racing through her brain, but then, she hadn't liked the idea of an intrusive neural lace, and she really liked being alive. 'That's what I think it says, too. Any direct comms with Nik'ri Put?'

'Not a word.'

If the message they sent to the Hin was having any effect, she couldn't see it. The group that had hit them on extraction was gone; two of the small converted freighters had survived to hide in the accretion disc, both damaged; only one of the Hin ships was under power. All three of the former DHC ships were dead, with their crews, without any explanation of why they'd attacked the *Athens*.

Most of the damage to the *Athens* had come from a nuclear mine – a proximity device, against every interstellar arms treaty ever written. The *Athens* had lost two hundred crew in that one explosion, and she was virtually blind without the sensor picture provided by her spacecraft and the data link to the *Dubai* and the *Stealthy Change*.

Nbaro saw it now: she saw how they had destroyed the *New York* and the *Hong Kong*, wearing them down, taking out the sensors first, then the armaments. Like a siege.

Some of the ships in this system have been here since the death of the Hong Kong. *The bastards. How much damage have they done to the DHC?*

Darkstar's boarding exercises in holding on to strong points within the ship made more and more sense.

Nbaro's thoughts ran around in circles. She went back to watching the battle.

There was a powerful squadron of purpose-built warships watching the insertion point for New India, the edge of DHC Space and a massive, highly populated system. Ultra–Medulla was a border station. New India was as well populated as New London – a first-generation colony from Terra, with millions of people.

Someone didn't want any traffic interfering until this was over. Those six powerful ships probably thought they were undetected, running silent and cold. Not cold enough.

TAO had tagged them 'Probable New Texas'.

There were six more, either docked to the Ultra Station in her orbit high over Medulla, or with her in orbit. Also 'Probable New Texas'. Those were more ships than their latest intel thought New Texas possessed.

And there were Hin throughout the system: sixteen definitely located, twenty-four more possibles, some of which might have been duplicate identifications.

In the asteroid belt, there were fleeting observations of another shoal of small freighters. Their activity didn't resemble legitimate mining craft. So: more pirates.

Nbaro rolled the holotank over in VR, looking at the system and the various locations and IDs from every angle.

Everyone was waiting. She guessed that the arrival of a second greatship and a PTX heavy cruiser had stunned their opponents, especially as the system was suddenly full of encrypted data flow. Nbaro's sense was that the two sides were very finely balanced and, the initial minefield and ambush having failed, their enemies would have to face them in the kind of set-piece confrontation in which the greatships had all the advantages: waves of ablative materials; clouds of chaff hiding small craft; closely co-ordinated firing patterns governed by linked AIs.

Nope. Not balanced at all.

The more she looked at it, the more she saw that the greatships had the advantage.

'Is this what you expected, Morosini?' She was getting bold; she asked him directly.

'*Yes. Except for the Hin. I never expected so many. No model predicted it.*'

That was more honesty than she really wanted. But if he was in a mood to talk, she wasn't wasting time on the tactical situation.

'You said my parents died protecting the AI cores that run the DHC...?' She was full of questions, and the time was now.

'*Yes. They bought... us... time.*'

'Then why the Orphanage? Where is Sarah? How can you allow—?'

'*How can I allow so much suffering? I am not God, Ms Nbaro. I am a calculating machine. Your suffering is sometimes a coin I'm willing to spend to accomplish my goals. You have to trust me that my goals are, ultimately, yours.*'

'You don't sound like the good guy, here.'

'*Consider how I have treated you, and how you were treated at the Orphanage. I find that humans are deeply enamoured of very general principles that often blind them to the reality of their situation. You hated the Orphanage. You are very happy here.*'

This time, she was not going to accept it when he got all philosophical and distant.

'And Sarah?'

'*To the best of my ability, your Sarah is alive and well. I am not alone – the others of my circle have tried to protect her. But carefully, and when we get to New London, you may wish to . . . fetch her.*'

'You sacrificed her!'

'*Yes. Hakon had to punish someone, and I was not ready to move on him yet. His family is close to the root of the conspiracy.*'

Almighty, she thought. And went to sleep. Only later, she wondered if Morosini had *put* her to sleep.

Nbaro slept, woke, slept again immediately. Dorcas visited her, and she knew for sure she was drugged; she couldn't really listen to him, couldn't muster the concentration to operate the neural lace.

She slept again.

Woke.

She felt as sharp as a new blade – more awake than she had been in months.

'*Flight schedule*,' appeared in her mind. '*You are released from medbay.*'

Nbaro was not in a clamshell, but lying on a gurney in a Third Deck passageway. So were a lot of other people, and there was no one there to retrieve her – not Thea, not Dorcas. She thought of the other times in medbay: of Steven Yu, and then of all the people she knew who were now dead. There were probably more. Her stomach fluttered. Who had died?

She made herself look. Truekner wasn't dead. In fact, he was already back at work, although not on flight status. She was good to fly.

She didn't look any further than her skipper.

She was dressed in a hospital gown and nothing else, but she

410

was clean and everyone else seemed to be asleep. The lighting was reduced. The passageway smelled threateningly of disinfectant, with a background scent of blood and faeces.

She rolled off the gurney. 'How bad is it?' she asked Morosini. She had to know.

'The nuclear mine killed two hundred and three spacers outright, and now we're dealing with radiation poisoning, burns and casualties from damage control. Medbay is overwhelmed. We have almost a thousand people down.'

Almighty, Nbaro muttered. Ten per cent casualties. She writhed inside, thinking about that.

Petty concerns distracted her; she really didn't want anyone to see her in the passageways wearing nothing but a single layer of recycle, so naturally, Petty Officer Locran passed her at the drop-shaft as she walked to the lift. The drop-shaft would be too public, and she'd be effectively naked in zero *g*.

'Ma'am,' he said. He had his boarding-party bag over his shoulder. He raised a hand to stop her, pulled a haze-grey battle blouse out of his bag and tossed it to her.

'We have a boarding party exercise in forty minutes,' he said. 'We're getting along without you, but it would be mighty nice if you put in an appearance.' After a delay, he added, 'Ma'am,' with a slight smile.

'I'm flying in three hours. We're in mid-battle ...' She shrugged. 'I'll be there.'

'Shit-hot. Ma'am.'

Nbaro grinned, pulled the knee-length anorak on over her gown, and trotted to her stateroom without further incident.

Forty minutes later she was in her armour, feeling very awake and very alive. But fear gnawed at her; Thea Drake wasn't there, wasn't in Small Cargo, and her rack was unmade. Nbaro was afraid to look.

And she was a little ashamed of how good she felt.

'I needed the sleep,' she admitted to Locran when she arrived at their Sixth Deck exercise area.

All of her people wore the new anoraks. They were made of a cheap material, the exact colour of the passageways, and they were loose enough to wear over equipment. They broke up the human silhouette. Most had slashes of darker grey across them; a few had fractal patterns in a lighter grey.

Chief Chen joined her. 'Locran's idea, but Ramirez designed them and Nagy worked out the patterns on the system. And your Spacer Chu sewed 'em up.'

'I'm impressed,' Nbaro said.

Locran shrugged. 'Ship of heroes,' he said. She couldn't tell whether he meant it as wisdom or sarcasm.

Everyone seemed happy to see her – a response she still found remarkable. Spacer Luciano was not present, and neither was Nowak; both, it proved, were dead.

'Yeah,' Locran said. 'We lost a lot of people.'

Spacer Nagy, who worked with Qaqqaq, had been treated for radiation burns.

'How's Lieutenant Qaqqaq?' Nbaro asked.

'Made of iron, ma'am,' Nagy said. 'She's out on the hull planting antennas. Where I'd be if I wasn't here.'

Petty Officer Deseronto, whom Nbaro knew from way back, now stood with Chief Chen, a shotgun on his shoulder. He smiled to see her, too.

'Welcome back,' Chen said. 'You need to stop getting hurt, ma'am. We worry about you.'

Locran chuckled, and they sorted the three teams out. They performed a movement to contact flawlessly, did a hostage rescue scenario, and then broke down for some hand-to-hand training. They really didn't need Nbaro, but she enjoyed it all, enjoyed a long sword bout with Captain Fraser when he came by, and then showered.

She hadn't felt this good in weeks. The ship was nominally at battle stations, but she could see with a glimpse at her lace that they were almost two weeks from any potential conflict.

She held her breath and looked. Thea Drake was not listed as a casualty. She was out on the hull doing an EVA boarding party mission.

Nbaro was almost light-hearted as she flew a routine maintenance hop in 6–0–7; Maintenance had produced an almost new spacecraft.

'Try not to put any more holes in her,' Baluster said, and Nbaro was off the bow, where she could see fifty spacers working like ants on the hull as she shot out of tube 3 at a very low launch speed relative to the ship; she was only doing a once-around the hull and landing and that, for once, was all she did.

She moved from that flight to one with Han. The *Pericles* had become a sort of engineering ship: she went out every day and tended to the walls of ablative and reflective materials that accompanied the battlegroup as it fell at constant velocity through the system, heading roughly for the station that hung like a miniature planet over the actual planet of Medulla. Medulla had a moon – a large satellite that might once have been a planet locked in a geosynchronous orbit; it wasn't going to be visible with the naked eye for a week, but Nbaro had seen it on vid. It was a strange system, and Dorcas thought that it had almost certainly been a major system in the Circle Culture, a hundred thousand years before. There were plenty of ruins on Medulla.

And an asteroid belt. Nbaro and Dorcas were beginning to suspect that any asteroid belt in a Goldilocks zone represented a Circle planet destroyed by the Starfish.

Nbaro had time to think all of this while laying fresh ablative materials with Gorshokov. Han was sitting behind them, doing admin work on his tab, as if command of a powerful spaceship was just another office job.

'I thought I'd never get you back,' Han said. 'And I could settle for Davies, but she's already flying for Flight Two.'

Lieutenant Tabitha Davies had taken the other pinnace from Sahel all the way across DHC space to rendezvous with the *Dubai*, and had now returned to her duties aboard the *Athens*. Her heroic journey across the 'middle stars' was as epic as anything else on the *Athens*' cruise.

Nbaro shrugged. Her eyes flicked around the instruments; in her head, she used her lace to make sure that their application of ablative material was precise. 'This isn't my first job,' she said.

She couldn't see Han; he was almost directly behind her. But she could imagine his face. 'I can wish,' he said.

Her relationship with Han was odd. She believed he thought highly of her as a pilot. He treated her like a friend – but he wanted her. She could feel it, and it poisoned her time with him. *Can't you just turn it off?*

And yet, there was nothing to be said. *Does he even know it himself? Am I wrong? That would be classic Marca Nbaro idiocy...*

She concentrated on flying.

'They're talking about sending *Pericles* out under AI control,' Han said bitterly. 'I'm apparently slated to fly a fighter in Flight Five.'

'They're taking losses,' she said.

Han sighed. 'I love this ship,' he said with total sincerity, and she smiled. He really was an excellent officer.

She glanced at Gorshokov, whose face was wooden, and she realised how all this must sound to him. She sighed.

Why are people so complicated?

But after they'd landed and she'd done the port-flight and the debrief, she said to Han, 'They probably need you. It took a miracle of sub-AI planning for me to fly today.'

Han grimaced. 'I know. But if I'm going to die out here, I'd prefer to go down on the flight deck of *Pericles*.'

She shrugged. 'I don't think we'll die out here.'

He looked back at her. 'Really? Best news all day. You always know this stuff because Morosini loves you. Give!'

She shrugged again. 'We have the balance of power, not them. That's all.'

He grinned. 'You really are something, Ms Nbaro. You know that?' He was on the verge of saying something – something she didn't want to hear.

'Some of my best friends fly in Flight Five,' she said. 'Say hi to Cortez.'

She walked away, her back straight, and he didn't call after her.

And she wasn't lying: she had a meeting scheduled with her skipper, and she had to hustle to make it.

Flight One and Flight Five had both taken losses in the first fight in-system, but by some miracle, Flight Six hadn't lost anyone. Nonetheless, replacements were the subject matter when she reported to Truekner.

'Think Tatlah could handle being a pilot?' he asked without preamble.

'Yes,' she said. 'Tench, too.'

'OK, let's move 'em both. Flight Eight is sending us some new techs. Tell them today, and start training them.'

'Right,' she said. Her feeling of being awake and alive was fading.

'Oh, and here's something you'll like,' the skipper said, patting his tab. 'Patel passed his petty officer exam. Not shabby at all. Probably deserves some personal congrats from his division officer.'

She was pleased. 'I'll go down now.'

'That's the spirit. Good job with Patel. Now he can take on more from Baluster, and start training someone else . . .' He looked at her. 'We're lucky we didn't take losses, but I'm getting ready to get hammered in the next exchange. Life goes on.'

What he meant was, *Death goes on.*

She nodded.

Nbaro went down to see Patel, and shook his hand. He flushed at her praise, and Baluster came over and joined her.

'About time,' the chief said laconically, but then he, too, shook Patel's hand.

'When does he pin it on, Chief?'

Baluster produced an iron-on petty officer patch. 'I'd like it on your suit right now.'

Patel glowed.

Nbaro grinned from ear to ear. *This is how life should be. Except that people are dying.*

On her way up from Maintenance in the lift, she thought about Nik'ri Put. *I think I miss her...*

Damn.

Then her tab beeped, and she read it and cursed.

A command meeting.

Forty minutes later, she was sitting in a shipboard uniform doing a report on her tab and ignoring the presence of Horatio Dorcas two metres away.

'I have to do this. I have so much work...'

Dorcas sent, 'I'm doing a remote with Feather Dancer right now.'

They glanced at each other and both laughed aloud. The other waiting officers all looked at them.

'Let's not do that again,' Nbaro sent.

Pisani came in and everyone shot to their feet – everyone except the holo of Morosini, who remained enthroned, with his cat.

'At ease,' the Master said. He looked around. 'We have a problem.'

He had their attention. Everyone sat, and every face was fixed on his.

He waved and a screen appeared. On it was a handsome man in a black spacer's jumpsuit.

'I am Admiral Da Costa of the New Democratic Republic.' He paused for a moment. 'All of these stars are ours now. You have been away for a long time, *Athens*. We hold Ultra and New India and New Bengal and Delhi. Here on Ultra Station, we have taken control. The NDR requests the immediate surrender of the greatships *Athens* and *Dubai* without further conflict, or we will take appropriate action. You are heavily outnumbered in this system. The insertion points are mined, as you will have noticed on arrival, and I have forty thousand DHC citizens on this station under my control. You have no way out. Signal your willingness to comply in the next four hours. Da Costa out.'

Pisani waved again and the frame stilled.

He looked around. 'I take that as a thinly veiled threat to use the population of Medulla Station as hostages.' He looked at Major Darkstar. 'Any chance we have a way of retaking the station, Major?'

Darkstar sat back and crossed their very long legs. 'It could be done. Possibility of heavy civilian casualties.'

Pisani nodded. 'Morosini?'

'*I very strongly doubt that the New Democratic Republic, if it even exists, holds New India or Delhi or New Bengal,*' the AI said. '*I think that this is a tactic of desperation.*'

Dukas put her head in her hands for a moment, then wiped her forehead. The Engineering chief looked haggard, twenty years older than she was. But then she shook her head, as if she'd had an argument with herself. 'Fucking terrorists,' she said.

Pisani looked surprised.

Dukas shrugged. 'I can clear the mines, even if they're shooting at us. We have mine clearing rigs for the pinnace and the Flight One drop-ships.'

Pisani nodded. 'In fact, we could clear a path through the mines with a few rounds from the tubes, as Admiral Da Costa ought to know. And I believe that we are looking at the entire combined strength of their alliance.'

Nbaro looked around. She had a question, and she wanted someone else to ask it, but no one did. Finally she raised a tentative hand.

'Ms Nbaro?' the Master asked.

'Sir, if we can clear their mines so easily, and if we have the upper hand in any kind of fight...' She paused.

Everyone was looking at her.

Yes, I should have kept my mouth shut.

'...then, if we choose, we can continue transiting the system, and they couldn't stop us.' Her voice was almost failing at the end.

Morosini scratched Tom under the chin and then looked at her. '*Someone over there is no fool, Ms Nbaro. The presence of the second greatship and the PTX cruiser shows them that we have made a detailed plan of attack.*'

Pisani was interested, now, and he followed up. 'You mean... having provoked us, they're now trying to bluff us out of a confrontation?'

'*Yes, sir. They have already sensed some change among their Hin allies—*'

Lochiel spoke up. 'Lot of encrypted traffic between visible Hin assets. Nothing that we can pick out as aimed at the station or any human ship. But we could miss a single laser burst and miss a whole conversation.'

Captain Fraser leaned back, as if to take a longer view. 'I think I understand your question, Ms Nbaro. Now they know we can

defeat them and leave if we so choose, the question becomes –
do we believe they'd kill forty thousand DHC citizens, or are
they bluffing?'

Pisani nodded. 'I believe they would. The conspiracy behind
this alliance was willing to risk killing millions at Sahel if
everything went to hell. Their allies destroyed a station with
thousands of people aboard. These are terrible people with a
ruthlessness beyond the borders of sociopathy.'

Nbaro had a sudden, terrible thought. She looked at Morosini,
and sent a data packet to Dorcas.

'Are there AIs manipulating our enemy?' she asked.

Dorcas turned and looked at her, eyes widening. 'Good God,'
he sent.

She frowned, and thought, *Fuck it.*

'Morosini, is the other side also run by AIs?'

'*This is not an immediately profitable line of inquiry,*' Morosini
replied.

'On the contrary,' she sent, 'I think it's time to put your cards
on the table.'

Pisani replied, 'We are aware of the possibility, Nbaro. But
not ready for open discussion.'

That eased some of her mind; if Pisani knew, then it wasn't
some machine conspiracy to destroy humanity.

But then Morosini stood. In all the meetings she'd attended,
he'd never stood up. He put his cat down, and turned to them.
'*I have been reminded that the stakes here are very high. I think it
only fair you know that I have been planning this confrontation for
some time. Four years. And it is possible that we are facing another
like me.*'

*Human suffering is sometimes a coin I'm willing to pay to accom-
plish my goals.* Morosini had said that, and Nbaro mostly trusted
him.

We're in a war planned by thinking machines on both sides. Almighty. We only exist to them as bytes.

She'd never thought to ask Nik'ri Put why the Hin didn't have advanced AIs aboard their superb spaceships, but she had a glimmering now.

She shook her head, dismissing the whole problem. *Sufficient to the day . . .*

Around the command table, senior officers digested the news and had various reactions: Hughes looked uninterested; Dukas looked angry.

Mpono, the Executive Officer, had been impassive, but now they raised an eyebrow. 'Master, if I may?'

'Shoot, XO.'

'We're not going to surrender the two greatships, not even with their implied threat of murdering hostages. So . . . do we provoke a system-wide battle that, as Nbaro points out, we'll almost certainly win? Or do we sail past them and leave them to their own devices, knowing they can't stop us? I think those are the options.'

'I'm for sailing past,' Fraser said. 'Never answer the hail, take out the mines and go for Insertion.'

Morosini was an AI. He didn't writhe. But he did express displeasure. '*It took years to force our enemy to emerge from the shadows and commit their forces.*'

Hughes was shaking his head. 'They can't just blow Medulla and kill forty thousand people. They'd never live it down.'

Pisani cut Morosini off. 'We're a long way out, Tom. A long way. They'll just claim we did it, or that it was a terrorist attack, or that the station malfunctioned. Vids and reports can be faked, and they'll send messages of sorrow to the families of those lost.'

'Ugh,' Hughes said.

Pisani nodded at his XO. 'You're right, Smoke. We have two

real options – go for Insertion, or force the battle. If we force the battle, what does that look like?'

Tremaine, the space wing commander, waved the holotank into existence. 'Even now, with so many of their ships in this system, we really can't force them to fight,' she said. 'If they choose to leave, or to evade us, we don't have the ships to run them down. If we want a fight, we have to make them fight.'

Dorcas said, 'So we would have to take the station?'

Everyone looked at him. But it was Darkstar who spoke.

'Mister Dorcas is correct. If we show ourselves prepared to take the station by boarding, they have to fight.'

'They can just blow it,' Dukas said with weary cynicism.

'Not if I have the control bridge before we go in,' Major Darkstar said. 'How do you feel about negotiating in bad faith?'

'This plan is insane,' Dorcas said. He and Nbaro had made love with a desperate intensity that hid a lot of fear – or maybe it didn't – and again, with a lot less tension. Now he was rubbing her back, where the acceleration couch had ground into her spine during evasive manoeuvres.

'Every pilot in the space wing needs you,' she said.

'Probably,' he said, with his usual flat delivery. 'I'm quite good at massage.'

She rolled her eyes, since she was face down and he couldn't see her.

'Why does it trouble you when I say things about myself that are true?' Dorcas asked, and she snorted into the pillow.

'You do realise that most of us humble mortals avoid stating our little triumphs and superiorities...'

'But why?' he asked. 'It makes no sense.'

Nbaro just let his hands work, and ignored him for a bit. And then he said, 'This plan is insane,' and she snorted.

'It's not as bad as that,' she said. Despite many uncertainties, the plan was precise and workable, and had the advantage – if you were an AI – that if it failed, the DHC battlegroup would have lost very little.

'Still want to marry me?' she asked.

'Yes!' he said. She felt the reaction through his hands.

'OK,' she said. 'If we get out of this system, I'm yours. You're mine. We're ours.'

After that, he didn't ask her any questions about the mission.

33

The waiting was brutal. They couldn't even start the mission for days; Nbaro had to fly routine hops, practise with her boarding party, stand watches. The Master didn't reply to Admiral Da Costa, despite ever more threatening messages, and the *Athens* battlegroup continued to move through the system on a course that gave away nothing about their intentions, but got closer and closer to Medulla and the station orbiting it.

Da Costa claimed that the DHC was in negotiations with the 'New Democratic Republic', and the *Athens* didn't respond. Ships began to move from the other side of the system; the small ships behind them powered up and began to move. On the *Athens*, Diwali and Christmas decorations appeared and Flight Three sported a passageway dedicated to Hanukkah. The Service called the festival Alliday.

'You going to Christmas Eve service?' Thea Drake asked her, and Nbaro laughed.

'Did I know it was Christmas Eve?' she asked. 'No.' But Thea's mood was infectious, and Nbaro tabbed Dorcas, and Rick Hanna met them, and they all went in civilian clothes. Nbaro looked at the horrible crucifix from Central America in the Age of Chaos, and spent time on her knees. She wasn't praying. She was just bringing the dead to mind.

Sarah is alive. Sarah is under the protection of the AIs.

The good AIs . . .

Is Morosini good?

She had a list of names: Didier, Ko, Indra, Suleimani, Yu and others. But she could think through the names, conjure up a picture of them in her mind, and still her brain ran away with her.

The mission was simple, and desperate. The *Pericles* would be under Han's command, carrying a load of Marines, but with Nbaro along because she could work in the datasphere while also fighting. The *Pericles* would use the stationary moon of Medulla as a shield and drop away, powering with cold thrusters only on a very narrow course right down the throat of the moon's shadow, until she was within two hundred thousand kilometres of the station. If she wasn't discovered, she'd then have to cross the final space between Medulla's satellite and the orbiting station on an exact schedule that would allow her to hide behind the bulk of the planet while she matched velocity. Then fly along the surface, very low, under power; with her stealthy hull, she'd be almost invisible to radar or ladar.

If everything went according to plan, they'd sprint for Ultra Station from about eight hundred kilometres out, and the command elements on the station would have close to sixty seconds to identify them and shoot them down. If they made it alongside the station, they'd deploy sixty Marines straight into an airlock; a tricky bit for Nbaro, and a subroutine of Morosini's, was to open the airlock as fast as possible. Then it would be up to Major Darkstar to get to the command bridge, take it and hold it.

The entire operation would be covered by a wide range of diversions, from a negotiation phase initiated by Master Pisani, to a course alteration that would fling a small cloud of reflective chaff out ahead of them, covering a critical moment where they crossed a possible deep space radar site on the surface of Medulla's moon.

Every element of it required stealth, split-second timing, and luck. Darkstar thought it had a one-in-five chance of success.

Nbaro, remembering her dead, could consider all that, and think about the odds, and see that it was reasonable – even to her, and she wasn't an AI. A one-in-five chance that you paralyse the enemy and deny him the hostages, against four in five that you lose one spacecraft and sixty Marines. Not nothing. Just a worthwhile risk.

She'd knelt for too long. People were starting to look at her; most of them had drinks in their hands.

She got to her feet, and Hanna handed her a glass of something sweet.

'Sherry?' she asked. Last Christmas had been the first sherry she'd ever had.

The priest grinned. 'We're out of sherry. We're out of most things. Master Pisani offered his Madeira.'

Nbaro tried it and liked it. 'I could get very drunk on this,' she said to Dorcas, who smiled.

'When we're married, I'll import some from Earth.'

She looked up at him. He was almost tall enough to be a 'gyne, and he looked dashing in shipboard boots, breeches and shirt and vest, all very different from the shipboard flightsuits worn by most of the crew. Nbaro and Drake stood out, too, both dressed up for the occasion; Thea wore make-up for the first time in months and she was head-turningly beautiful, and Nbaro admired her. And, after a second Madeira, told her so.

Thea grinned. 'Well, that's the idea. Rick and I are going to be married. This is my engagement party, in a way.' She leaned close. 'And with what we have in the hold, honey, you and I are never going to be poor again.'

They clinked glasses.

Later, lying in their acceleration couches, Drake said, 'Merry Christmas, Marca.'

Nbaro leaned over and caught her friend's hand. 'Thanks, Thea. Merry Christmas.'

Then she lay in her rack and thought, *Dear God, I don't really believe in you, but please keep Thea Drake alive and well.*

She laughed at herself, and then remembered that she was about twenty-two hours from flying a mission with a one-in-five chance of success. And then she was asleep.

Morosini had arranged for Nbaro to stand an under-instruction TAO watch in the hours before her mission; it made sense for her to have the best possible understanding of the tactical situation before she launched. So she went to a briefing with Han and Gorshokov, listened to the mission from the flight perspective, and then went down to Sixth Deck and heard the Marines' mission brief, and got checked out with a carbine and ammunition. Her role in the Marine briefing took about twenty seconds.

'And last, Ms Nbaro here will hold her own ship as long as she can. Any fire team that can't make its objective should fall back to *Pericles* and help Ms Nbaro secure the perimeter.'

And that was it. Operation Marathon, the mission planners called it.

Nbaro went up to the Combat Information Centre and sat on an empty acceleration couch. She plugged in to the repeater screen, but only out of habit; she could watch everything on her lace, faster and more accurately. She marvelled a little at her increased ability to use it. She really could now do two things at once – even three, if one of them was just observing. And she could dive down almost to the base code, the way Dorcas did – not as effectively, but she could do it.

She was looking at their spread of sensors, and the number of sensors they had left on board: a worrying number.

She got an alert, and then a tidal wave of alerts – so many that it took her a moment to realise what had happened. One of the very few disadvantages of being deep in the datasphere was the difference between reading data and interpreting it. The duty TAO wasn't anyone she knew – another officer from the command bridge, Commander Vivek Mehrotra.

He said two words.

'Battle stations.'

Screens flashed red. A voice throughout the ships said, 'Battle stations. This is not a drill. Battle stations.' Nbaro could remember when that sound had filled her with dread and adrenaline.

Now, it was routine to every person aboard.

All around her, the ship began to button up. Ships were appearing out at the system's edge, at approximately the orbit of the inner gas giant. They weren't coming in from the main route to New India; they were coming in from the far Fringe. In almost real time, she watched no fewer than six New Texas military ships extract into the system. They were positively ID'd as destroyers, a class much smaller than the *Athens*, but carrying main railgun armaments.

Six enemy ships.

They broadcast a long message on system entry.

Six destroyers.

Mehrotra swivelled to face her. 'Lieutenant Nbaro. Rumour has it that you have a neural lace.'

'Yes, sir,' she said.

'Can you bring up a schematic on a New Texas Destroyer?'

Nbaro had one ready. 'A lot of this is speculation based on intelligence more than a year old,' she said, dropping it to the TAO's tab.

427

'I see they're much tougher than the three old DHC destroyers we faced a week ago,' he said.

'Yes, sir.'

'Care to speculate on where New Texas got eighteen brand-new destroyers?'

'No, sir,' she said. 'Someone spent a—' she paused. 'A lot of money on secret shipyards.'

'They did. They're burning hot – going pretty fast, too.'

'Morosini?'

'*Nbaro. Operation Marathon is aborted before it begins. I'm not entirely sorry.*'

'Why?' she asked.

'*Our enemies may lack some of our subtlety and much of our communications infrastructure, but these newcomers would see you broadside-on as you pushed for orbit. Even the stealth we built into the* Pericles *wouldn't get past six different ships. They would catch you in an hour, much less sixteen.*'

'I'm willing to try,' she said.

'*No. The odds have changed. The enemy may now commit to a battle.*'

Nbaro was still in the Combat Information Centre, lying inside a buttoned-up acceleration couch, but it was as if she was chatting with Morosini. 'You are waiting for something else,' she said suddenly.

Morosini didn't chuckle, and he had no face to grin, and yet she sensed something like amusement. '*You know me very well. Yes. I have another trick or two to play.*'

She watched the six new ships light their fires and proceed at maximum acceleration. The battle computer predicted their vectors for the station.

'They still can't win,' Nbaro sent.

'*They can, with Hin. Or hurt us so badly that no one wins.*'

Morosini didn't have emotions, but if he did, she'd have said he was concerned.

'You didn't expect so many warships,' she said.

Morosini sent, *'Why do I let you pester me? No, Marca. I didn't expect so many warships. And that tells me that the enemy has planned this for as long as we have.'*

'Another AI?'

No response.

She had a moment to contemplate Saladin, the AI on board the *Dubai*, who must be part of Morosini's cabal. She imagined thousands, millions, perhaps trillions of people, their lives trapped in a web of planning and plotting by non-human machines.

She didn't come to any conclusions. But she did calculate the relative velocities and accelerations of all the warships in-system, with the AI's help, and she ran time forward to the likely moment of contact.

It wasn't perfectly clear, but the enemy had already committed to a battle. Their plan was simple: a total envelopment of the DHC battlegroup with co-ordinated attack groups coming from a dozen different vectors to overwhelm the battlegroup's defences. The pirates astern were the farthest behind, and had already begun laying their own ablative shield, filling space with a three-dimensional cloud of reflective dust.

One by one, the warships docked at Medulla Station and the others in orbit launched, and joined up. Once they had their vector, they, too, began to lay sand.

Actual combat was three days away.

The cancellation of her mission left Nbaro with free time. She took it to fence, finding Musashi available. He beat her, but both of them enjoyed it. Then she visited the ready room, where Thulile and Eyre were providing instruction to junior spacer-techs who were about to become back-seaters. She ran a sim for the *Pericles*. Han was asleep, which surprised her.

She went back to her stateroom, and found Drake just getting up.

'Boarding party,' Drake said. 'There's no trade, so I'm a full-time trainer.' She grinned. 'Which I admit I rather enjoy, however barbarous my mother will think it is!'

'Your brothers will be jealous,' Nbaro said.

'You better believe it!' Drake scooped a sword off the rack and clipped it to her armour. 'Off to save the galaxy. Don't wait up.'

Nbaro sat on the edge of her acceleration couch, trying to decide what to do with herself. Free time was a thing of the distant past.

She went to find Dorcas, who was on Sixth Deck, working on his starfish simulator. She pushed in with Qaqqaq, who was lying on the deck, welding with a tiny laser tool that flashed like lightning. Dorcas was staring at the wall; Nbaro sensed that he was using his neural lace to control the robot, instead of using the controller lying on the table that had once held thousands of rounds of small arms ammunition.

'Somehow,' she said, 'I'm always comfortable in this space.'

Qaqqaq muttered something, or maybe she swore.

Dorcas moved his hand. As he moved, the model starfish moved, and the movement was smooth and even, not jerky like the old robot.

'Got it,' Qaqqaq said.

'And very nice to see you, too, Naisha,' Nbaro said.

Qaqqaq rolled over, flipped back her welding visor and smiled up at her. 'I like it here, too,' she said. 'Captain Dukas can't find me. Sometimes I think I'll just come in here, slip past Lieutenant Smith and catch a nap.'

'I came to harass Dorcas,' Nbaro said, 'But since you're here, Naisha, you know you're listed as the flight engineer on the *Pericles*?'

Qaqqaq was getting to her feet. 'I know,' she said. 'If there's ever a flight during which I'm not focused on battle damage, engine room malfunction or Dorcas's pet robots, I'll be sure to come and help your completely automated systems do their thing.'

'In other words, never.'

Qaqqaq shrugged again. 'I helped design the *Pericles*. And I've done some training with Gorshokov, and I've helped Morosini write the engineering sims.'

Dorcas came out of his fugue. 'Lieutenant Qaqqaq is the most important person on the ship,' he said, deadpan. 'Or at least that's what Captain Dukas tells me two or three times a day.'

'On this ship of heroes,' Qaqqaq intoned, 'some of us are just a *little* more heroic than others.' She winked at Nbaro. 'And while we're on this, Marca, you have an EVA qual and lots of experience, so how about helping with the antennas out on the hull? I have something like fifteen hundred to replace.'

Nbaro wilted.

'See what I mean? Now, I'm going to go catch a nap before anyone knows I'm done here. You two...' She made a gesture. 'Don't break anything.'

Nbaro had intended to lead Dorcas astray, but he was deep in his study trance and she got into the spirit of the thing, and helped him move the rebuilt robot up to Third Deck under a tarp, so that the project remained secret. Then Darkstar had to check them through, personally, despite knowing both of them well. Nbaro had to sign yet another non-disclosure statement.

Nbaro had never been in the chamber that held Feather Dancer. It was dark, and she and Dorcas wore infrared goggles.

Feather Dancer was asleep, or simply meditative, or depressed – whichever was accurate; it drifted in its cold ammonia.

Dorcas glanced at her. 'It is asleep, I believe.'

Nbaro nodded. 'How much have you learned?'

Dorcas made a sign, and both of them switched off their neural laces. It was very likely that there were cameras in here: mics, video recordings. On the other hand, only Darkstar and Morosini would have access.

'I've learned how little I know,' Dorcas said with real bitterness. 'In some ways, I understand less now than before we got to Trade Point.'

Nbaro looked at the floating Starfish, and then back at Dorcas. She sat down in one of the observation couches. Dorcas had spent a lot of time here; the space had a bit of his scent, and a few discarded bits of recycle. He wasn't the tidiest of men.

'How so?' she asked.

He looked at Feather Dancer. 'I'm no longer sure that it *was* the Starfish who destroyed the Circles,' he said. '"The Starfish" don't exist. There are hundreds of Starfish worlds and dozens of polities, which is itself a human concept that has no place in Starfish neural connections. They simply do not have connections to other Starfish in that way. They give birth to new Starfish – and those entities are forever linked. Groups of linked Starfish build ships – a link. Ships plant colonies … They are linked, but distantly. Space is vast, and their groupings change in every generation as old links become too distant and new ones are formed.'

He glanced at her. 'At least, that's what I think Feather Dancer said. And unlinked groups prey on each other. Feather Dancer was virtually a slave. It was captured when a new group took Trade Point, perhaps twenty years ago, although … something there doesn't quite add up yet.'

'So Feather Dancer's *link* used to run Trade Point?' she said.

'Exactly. And the invaders – the pirates, if you like – left them behind, destroyed Trade Point, and fled, taking their people with them. Feather Dancer doesn't know why, but thinks they fear us, and worries that we have an alliance with the Hin.'

'The wicked flee when no alien pursueth,' she said.

Dorcas looked puzzled for a moment and then brightened. 'Ah! Very good. I sometimes forget how intelligent you are.'

She smacked him lightly. 'You only want me for my body?'

He shook his head. 'No. Your willpower. Your ambition. Your courage.' He nodded, and then did one of the conversational volte-faces that made him so difficult for some people. 'You think our adversaries are AIs?'

'Yes,' she said.

'Evidence?'

'Only an AI would make plans that allowed for the devastation of an entire advanced world and the deaths of millions to accomplish a local goal,' she said. 'Sahel.'

'You underestimate the cruelty of merely human minds.'

She shrugged. 'Perhaps. I was taught at the Orphanage that it was impossible, given relativity and the vastness of space, to plan co-ordinated attacks over interstellar distances. But...' She held up a finger. 'We know Morosini did. And looking around this system, it looks like someone else did, too. Including carefully timed arrivals.'

Dorcas looked sceptical.

Nbaro shrugged. 'Look, it's scary and I don't really want to think about it, but all the evidence from the beginning has pointed to this being a fight within the DHC. Right? So here's what I think – two different groups of AIs have gone in two different directions over the future of the DHC and the future of... humanity.' She didn't think much of her argument herself, now that she said it out loud.

Dorcas nodded slowly. 'I understand all of that. But you have seen, as I have, deep into the architecture of our AI. You know, better than most, how it processes data. How could two disagree so sharply as to fight? Based on the same data?'

Nbaro looked at him as if he'd suddenly grown a second head. 'You underestimate the stupidity of merely human programmers.'

His head snapped back. But then he laughed. 'Ah, Marca Nbaro ...'

She leaned in. 'No, Horatio, I mean it! Look at how many plans Morosini has made and discarded since Trade Point. He was going to take the *Athens* out into the Beyond. Then he was going to send the *Pericles* into the Beyond. Then he was going to slip home ... until he found the *Dubai*. Then he wanted to provoke a battle to level the playing field. He represents the pure scientific method – because the data changes, the situation changes. Right?'

'I see where you are going.' Dorcas sounded sad.

'They're not gods. They're fallible. And even if they don't feel emotion, they can be bound by their assumptions, the same as we are.' She shook her head. 'Somewhere inside the DHC is an AI, or a dozen, who are opposed to Morosini and Saladin.'

Dorcas's face was impassive. 'Or a conspiracy of humans with good computer support.'

My parents died protecting the bureaucratic cores, the AIs that drive the DHC. Morosini said, 'They bought us time.' What does that mean?

'Are the Starfish part of the conspiracy?' she asked.

Dorcas smiled thinly. 'Absolutely not,' he said. 'No one can speak to them. I can barely manage and no one else has had the contact. Indeed, without Feather Dancer, we'd never have got even this far. And it's worse than that – I have begun to suspect that their chemical communications and handshakes change like computer protocols, from generation to generation, so that in five or six generations without contact, perhaps they can't communicate at all. And that means that instead of learning *Starfish*, I may only be learning to talk to *one Starfish*. Or one clan. For a while.'

'Almighty,' she muttered.

'Honestly, when I'm feeling depressed, I begin to wonder if I was included in this mission simply so that Morosini could *threaten* to find a military alliance with the Starfish. The mere threat would provoke—'

She leaned over and kissed him. 'I already figured that out,' she said. 'And I really didn't need to hear it again.'

He nodded. 'Kissing is wonderful.'

'Please explain,' she muttered.

They both laughed.

Her tablet *pinged* and Sabina said, '*New data on the system repeater.*'

Dorcas's eyes lost their focus, and she dived into the data-sphere herself.

Six Hin ships in two pods had extracted, in almost perfect unison. They had come from roughly the same direction as the six human warships; they had better astrogators, and now they were ahead of them. About twenty-seven hours to combat contact.

The TAO didn't even bother to set battle stations, which Nbaro thought was a tribute to what the *Athens* had experienced.

Her tab pinged again. Cheerfully, Sabina said, '*The flight schedule has been completely rewritten.*'

'Stand by for maximum acceleration in one hour,' said her tab, her implant, and the ship's voice.

Dorcas looked as puzzled as she felt.

'What are we doing?' she asked.

435

Dorcas shook his head. 'It's what we're not doing that I regret.'

'And Thea says you have no sense of humour.' She laughed. 'I have to walk to my plane. See you on the other side.'

He grabbed a hand and kissed it, and then she was gone.

34

In less than an hour Nbaro was in 6–0–7, admiring the latest repairs. She had Tim Eyre as her co-pilot, plus Tench and someone she'd never even met as her back-seaters.

'Tojo, ma'am,' said the tall young man. 'Lamar Tojo. New London.'

She grinned back at him in the middle of her flight checks. 'Welcome aboard, Mr Tojo. We're full of fun here.'

Tench snorted. Then there was a click, and Nbaro heard, 'Nbaro's OK – she's actually pretty good. Watch out for Eyre – he's a bastard.'

Nbaro's smile grew thin, and she said, 'Petty Officer Tench, you might want to switch your comms panel to back seat only.'

Silence.

Eyre was laughing. Nbaro liked that. She gave him a little fist-bump.

They prepped for a mass launch. She'd scanned the preflight briefing: they were launching a full, two space wing assault on the collection of privateers, pirates and converted freighters that had begun to chase them from the rings of the inner gas giant. The *Athens* and her consorts were going to decelerate hard; in the tactical situation, that was the equivalent of accelerating at the enemy behind them.

But there was no timing given. She assumed the ship would flip end for end, to put her engines in line with the deceleration vector before the space wing launched.

She looked at the 3D repeater via her neural lace, did some maths with her augmentation, and saw ...

What does Morosini suspect? Why are we running from six Hin? Backed by six warships ...

The *Beautiful War Dance* was still repeating her song, or line of poetry, but sensors now showed her in direct conversation with the newcomers. They were within a hundred and fifty thousand kilometres – an incredible astrogation job.

Luck? Brilliant planning? Some sort of impossible faster-than-light communications?

Too late to worry about that now.

She was fascinated to find that now that she was faced with imminent combat, her concerns about AIs and Starfish and the genocide of the Circles all faded into nothing. Now was just now – the now in which she was going in harm's way.

The ship fired all four tubes in rapid succession, towards the rapidly approaching Hin ships, but Morosini and Saladin were waiting for something. Nbaro suspected there were negotiations going on with the station, possibly with the Hin or between the Hin factions.

She would never have believed, before she came into space, that it was possible to be this bored while also being this tense. She wanted it over with: win, lose, draw or die. She wanted to *get out there* where the adrenaline replaced the anxiety.

Another hour passed. In three hours, they'd be at the outer range for the Hin weapons. The closing velocity between the Hin group and the *Athens* was terrifying in itself. If there was an exchange at these speeds, everything would be done by computers.

She thought about her parents. According to reports, they'd

438

died here, attacked by pirates. She now knew that wasn't true, and yet somehow it still affected her.

She used her neural lace to access data stored on board the *Athens*. In seconds, she knew that when her parents – at least, according to Morosini – died on City Orbital, defending the bureaucratic AI cores from unknown assailants, the *Athens* was docked at City. So was the *Dubai*.

They bought us time.

Nbaro stared out into the hangar bay, seeing nothing. *Time for what...?*

More new arrivals: three ships, extracting very close to the six NDR destroyers, perhaps a hundred thousand klicks further out.

Damn, she thought. *The odds just get longer and longer.*

The manoeuvre alarm sounded throughout the ship. 'Rotation in one minute. Stand by. Brace for rotation in one minute. Stand by.'

So, they were running. Either Morosini liked the odds as little as she did, or he had new information...

Out in the asteroid belt, and from the many moons and satellites in-system, dozens of Hin began to emerge from hiding. Most kept their energy shields down – possibly a sign they'd been hiding so long, they were low on fuel.

Possibly not.

Every ship in the system that was under power was headed for the *Athens*.

'Everyone buttoned up?' Nbaro was happy to note that her voice was steady, her gloved hands solid on the yoke. 'Launching cold and silent.'

'Roger that,' Tench said.

They began the end-for-end flip. They'd done it many times; it meant a heavy acceleration at both ends of the ship, and Nbaro felt it through the artificial gravity, even in her spaceframe's excellent acceleration couch – a disorientating motion in all three dimensions. In the datasphere, she could see the whole battlegroup was flipping end for end. The *Beautiful War Dance* completed first, and then the *Stealthy Change*.

The Hin ships behind them accelerated immediately.

The *Beautiful War Dance* broadcast a new message. Dorcas translated: 'You hunt in dark waters.'

One of the Hin now behind them replied, 'Only those that hunt with us will be fed.'

Nbaro lay cushioned in her acceleration couch, feeling the vibration in her bones as the launch tubes fired again and again. She was on the Tower frequency and none of those were space wing launches, which meant ... load after load of ablatives and reflectives, or lethal payloads of mass slugs, bomblets or mines. Nbaro wondered about the supplies of such stuff on board and took a peek with her lace. Her stomach knotted.

We resupplied from Dubai and even so, we could run out of sand and we're very low on mines.

Two hundred kilometres away, the *Dubai* was doing the same, launching payloads as fast as the railguns would cycle – mostly reflectives.

The end-for-end flip was completed, and the deceleration programme began, as well as the launches. The *Athens* and the *Dubai* had created an expanding cloud of reflectives shot off through 180 degrees of slightly off-axis rotation, and each ship had rotated a different way on the *y*-axis, so that a ball of expanding reflectives expanded behind both ships.

The three newcomers were just far-off ellipses, running silently and cold, barely detectable even on the best of their equipment.

'Damn,' Eyre said. 'Seen that before ...'

'Bubbles?' Tench asked from the back.

Nbaro's focus narrowed. The three ellipses behind them were dozens of hours away. The end-for-end flip was bringing their first opponents into battle range.

She had a mission – a very straightforward mission. *Strike.* With the full power of two greatship space wings.

The launches began. Two Flight Five fighters went off, then a Flight Three Electronic Warfare bird, and then more fighters – the small, close-in ship-defence fighters now flown by Flight Two pilots, or directly by the AI. Nbaro followed them, riding the Tower and Space Ops systems. She saw the *Pericles* launch, and couldn't tell whether the frigate was flown by computer or Han. Then more Flight Five, and then, finally, 6–0–2 with the skipper, 6–0–3 with Thulile, 6–0–5 with Storkel…

'Everyone ready?' she asked.

They rogered up.

Then Nbaro was moving onto the rails of tube 2, saluting, and they were out into the Deep Black. Adrenaline surged; worry fell away.

They all launched cold, the electromagnets shooting them off the bow towards the privateers, their relative speeds taking them towards the enemy and away from the *Athens*, even though both were decelerating. The *Athens* was decelerating at 6 *g* and that rate was increasing, so that Nbaro and her crew felt the weight come *off* them as they left the launch tubes.

Their targets were thousands of kilometres away, far outside of any weapons range. Using nothing but minute alterations of course and cold thrusters, the space wing began to form up; on the tactical 3D, now showing only the volume of battle space, the *Dubai*'s space wing was also launching. Sensors scattered through the system continued to show the ninety-plus ships manoeuvring: a staggering number of craft even without the space wings.

Nbaro, student and teacher of tactics classes, smiled wryly because, despite a year of discussion and practice, this was the first time they'd actually fight a set-piece battle. The space wings were forming up, in layers, above the plane of the greatships.

She was close enough to the mother ship that she could look back and see the vast, sword-shaped, matt-black mass of the *Athens,* her cross-guard bridge just visible in the jewel-blue glow of her fusion engines as she slowed stern-first.

It was clear that the gaggle of reconfigured freighters and purpose-built, needle-like privateers had not expected a head-to-head confrontation. Two ships had already flipped and were running. The rest began to spread out.

The enemy launched missiles. Their first salvo was huge: over seventy missiles released in six seconds. Some of the freighters had to have rotary launchers.

Seconds later, a second wave was launched. However, the launching ships were shooting through a cloud of chaff, their missiles on automatic until they could locate a target beyond the cloud.

The main tube railguns finished flinging the space wing at the enemy and began to fire lethal payloads. The ship rotated on its main axis slightly; the slugs it was firing were being aimed by AI at possible enemy locations minutes in the future, limiting their opposition's manoeuvre options even as more of the privateers either turned to run or started to fly evasively.

Something from one of the earlier *Athens* payloads broke open, blowing a film of reflective matter across the front of the pirates, about four thousand kilometres out from their desperately manoeuvring hulls.

The All-Sensor Warfare birds lit up, laying a blanket of signal degradation over the privateers as the *Pericles* shot off a dozen missiles. In seconds, each missile was imitating a ship.

'Go,' Captain Tremaine said over the space wing command frequency.

Nbaro was flying as wingperson to Thulile. They didn't have a specific target, yet, but they were the flankers, ready to catch anyone trying to get around the reflective cloud.

She followed Thulile when she popped up, firing her engines. Their silent running was over.

The space wing went to full throttle behind the expanding cloud of reflectives. The Flight Three ships fired sensor-distorting missiles that, in turn, burst.

The better equipped of the privateers went to active radars, and the Flight Five pilots fired anti-radar missiles from about three thousand kilometres. No one expected hits; they merely forced the enemy to turn off their active dishes. The whole privateer formation, never very solid, began to unravel, with ships turning in every direction, dropping their own reflectives and ablative sand to add to the sensor chaos.

Blind, and slow, the combined private militaries of a dozen Fringe planets and their less savoury privateer allies tried to strike out at the whirling space wing craft. Some of the nearer ships began to fire close-in weapons. Without their radar and ladar they were blind, so they fired at false targets provided by the Electronic Counter-Measures craft, or decoys, or in one terrible instance, at each other.

A small freighter – about one-fiftieth the mass of the *Athens* – lost its magnetic seal and blew: a flash of pure white.

Nbaro could see the lines of iron slugs reaching for her. Whether the privateer had a radar lock, or was just lucky, the line of slugs rushed towards her like a sweeping broom, and she pushed the yoke down even as Thulile went up.

The line of slugs went by, missing by less than a kilometre – in space, a very near miss.

It didn't take months of tactics classes to see what was happening. The space wing craft all had datalink information from sensors scattered throughout the system – sensors that peaked around the clouds of chaff. They also had better computers for predicting the location of a temporarily hidden contact.

The enemy ships couldn't even share data.

443

Thulile, two thousand kilometres out from a sleek privateer, selected her as a target. She chose an attack vector and then cut her engines, nose-on to present the smallest possible radar cross-section.

Nbaro followed, duplicating course and speed.

The enemy ship was firing; on radar, her six close-in weapons looked like fire hoses spraying lines of foam into the void.

Behind them the enemy missiles began to detonate as the Flight Two fighters engaged them. Not all were nuclear, but those that were, fratricided any missile close enough to have its avionics fried. On the Flight Two frequency, close-in fighter pilots began hunting individual missiles, passing targets verbally.

Now well inside two thousand kilometres, the big Flight Five birds released another wave of anti-radiation and anti-laser missiles that homed in on any preset source that radiated energy.

Nbaro checked her Identify Friend or Foe (IFF) to make sure none of the missiles tried for her.

Thulile shot all four of her torpedoes at a thousand kilometres. Then she turned away, and Nbaro followed, turning so hard that she was on the edge of blacking out all the way through the turn.

Fourteen seconds later, the privateer exploded. Nbaro could barely breathe; she'd never pushed a spaceframe or her own body so hard – 11 g by the end of the turn.

Sixteen ships were taken out in less than a minute, and other ships powered on, their crews all dead. The overwhelming fire-power of two space wings left no room for heroics or defiance. Here and there, by luck or skill, a ship survived, and the attack craft took losses ... but not many.

'They'll be teaching that at the academies for a generation,' Nbaro said.

Thulile came up. 'You still have fish?'

'Yes, ma'am.'

'Take the lead. Pick a target, I'll watch your back.'

A big freighter had run early, if not very fast. She had heavy armament: dozens of close-in weapons, mostly light railguns, and a welded-on spinal railgun that she used to pile up chaff in her wake. Nbaro could only detect her because there were still functioning sensors farther out-system, left behind days before.

She put her digital tag on the freighter, and got an acknowledgement from Thulile.

Somewhere to starboard, there were flashes, like a lightning storm over the sea at Far Point.

Nbaro didn't think about the flashes. She located the forward edge of the *Athens'* original chaff launch and flew there; the cloud was still expanding faster than the big freighter could run, and she stayed in it, using the datalink to stay on target.

Then she used the cloud to hide her line-up with the freighter's vector, so that she was coming right up behind the line of his engine exhaust, where every ship was blind.

Almost every ship.

They were beyond the main combat now. Behind them, the space wings duelled with the last of the privateers; yet further back, the fighters, the All-Spectrum Deception devices and the massive close-in systems of the *Athens* dealt with the last of the second wave of enemy missiles. But they were alone, hurtling out of a nuclear lightning storm amid a cloud of glowing reflectives intermixed with debris. Nbaro had her line-up.

'Tench?'

'Ma'am. I have four ready and hot, looking for lock-on.'

'Here we go. Buckle up.'

Nbaro fired the main engines and 6–0–7 shot forward out of the cloud.

'Lock!' Tench said almost immediately, and Nbaro felt the shudder as the first torpedo tore away.

As the third torpedo launched, something must have given

them away. The freighter began a ponderous yaw, instantly unmasking powerful close-in batteries.

Nbaro was flying with her neural lace; the release of the fourth torpedo was followed within milliseconds by the same punishing turn away that Thulile had done, except that Nbaro plotted hers in advance to turn into the line of the freighter's thrusters, out of her firing arcs.

Thulile followed her, matching courses. They couldn't turn tightly enough to avoid crossing the enemy stern; more iron slugs reached out for them and both spaceframes rocked with the AI-assisted evasive manoeuvres that punched the crews in the back and left bruises and shaky breathing.

But they were alive, and they went back through the curtain of reflectives, now eighteen minutes old, ahead of the detonation of the freighter's drives that burned for almost a second like a new sun.

The cockpit was silent, as three space crew contemplated the results of their attack.

Finally, Eyre said, 'Nice run, ma'am.'

'Ma'am?' she snapped. 'Now? Here?'

In the back, Tojo dared a chuckle. Then Tench said, 'That was a big ship.'

Nbaro had no reply to that.

The space wing formed a stack at the bow and stern of the *Athens* and began to land, two at a time. Nbaro and Thulile had run the farthest from the greatship and were late in the pattern, which gave Nbaro time to look at the system through her and the *Athens'* sensors.

So she was watching the 3D holo in her head when the six Hin who'd extracted with such accuracy punched through the *Athens'* expanding cloud of reflectives.

There was a star-like flash of light and one of the Hin ships vanished. Two more nuclear explosions showed that the cloud of reflectives had been sown with the dragon's teeth of nuclear mines. Four trailing Hin ships turned away; one continued on course.

The *Beautiful War Dance* sent, 'Only those who hunt with *us* will be fed.'

Nbaro winced.

Out in the system, many inbound Hin ships turned away, but three pods continued inbound, all firing off messages by radio and laser aimed at the *Beautiful War Dance*. Out beyond the inner gas giant, two more Hin pods began firing their energy beam lances at each other, about two hundred million kilometres from the *Athens*.

The wreckage of twenty-seven human ships was an expanding cloud of radiation and material behind them. A few ships had become preserved tombs. The rest were mostly dust. A handful of survivors pleaded for pickup.

And the three newcomers, whose arrival had prompted Pisani to action, were coming in-system like a stampede. And now they were identified.

DHC Battlecruiser *Lepanto*. DHC Battlecruiser *Noryang*. DHC Battlecruiser *Huron*.

Eyre punched the air. 'I thought I recognised those sneaky bastards! We had *Huron* and *Lepanto* with us the first leg of cruise! Remember, Ma— er ... Marca?'

Nbaro wasn't in a mood to laugh, but she could feel the grim smile on her face, wondering how they could have gotten here.*

The six New Democratic Republic ships that had most recently arrived in-system all turned away, running for the apparent safety of Medulla Station. The ships watching the insertion point for New Bengal abandoned their posts and accelerated inwards for

* The short story *The Gifts of the Magi* in *Beyond the Fringe* by Miles Cameron will give you a fuller explanation of where these three came from and what they did.

447

orbits closer to Medulla, joining their comrades – except one. It inserted on a course almost certainly intended for New India.

Nbaro landed. The atmosphere aboard was far from jubilant; in her intel debrief, she asked Lochiel how many people had been aboard the pirate fleet.

'Five or six thousand,' he said with a cold shrug. 'Remember, Nbaro – they came here to break and strip our ships. They're jackals.'

Nbaro nodded. 'I know that in my head, but Almighty... we just fried them.'

Eyre nodded, as if he'd thought the same thing.

Whoever planned Sahel was willing to kill millions. But Morosini's plan is definitely killing tens of thousands.

My taste for glory has been squashed flat. Please take me back to daily trade runs.

An hour later, Nbaro was sitting at the Master's table, drinking coffee while she read the latest exchanges with Asinpal Las on her tab, with Dorcas trying to over-explain his translation at her shoulder. The department heads were already gathered with an air of anticlimax.

The Master came in, they stood to attention, and he waved them back to their seats.

'At ease. I have Da Costa's response and, in summary, he says he'll blow the station if we don't turn away. I told him that if he does, I'll kill him and every one of his crews, and then I'll render New Texas uninhabitable.'

There was absolute stillness in the room.

Pisani sent Da Costa's threat to their tabs. 'I'm absolutely serious. And I expect to be obeyed. If he kills forty thousand DHC citizens, I will take New Texas out.'

Morosini looked up from patting his cat. '*Vettor, That is an excellent threat. But we will not, however provoked, kill twenty million people to avenge forty thousand.'*

Nbaro was watching closely. *Morosini could have sent that message via neural lace instead of publicly slapping down the highest-ranking human aboard this ship. I think this is an act.*

Almighty! How many wheels are there inside the wheels?

When Pisani looked at Morosini the rage on his aged face seemed very real.

Then he sagged. 'Damn. Yes. Of course.'

Morosini nodded. *'But as a threat, excellent.'*

Lochiel raised a tentative hand. 'They still have the military power to face us. In railgun throw weight, their eighteen ships are superior to our four – if our Hin allies will even fight.'

Pisani sat back. He was recovering from his anger very quickly; Nbaro found her suspicions reinforced. *But why does he want us to believe he would commit such a crime?*

Because he thinks someone aboard will pass on the message . . . ?

That makes no sense. He got slapped down . . .

Almighty . . . If this is the bluff, then Morosini wants someone to believe we won't *do it when in fact we* will?

She took a sharp breath, having missed an exchange on military capabilities.

She looked at Dorcas and raised her hand.

'Apologies, sir, but my read of the transcripts with our Hin is that they're successfully forming some alliances in-system. I think the Hin are now mostly neutral, with a scattering of possible support.' She paused, and took the plunge. She was getting better at speaking her mind to the captains. 'I think the destruction of the station would be very bad for our diplomatic efforts. Based on my conversations with Nik'ri Put, the Hin have a formal approach to war that avoids civilian casualties.'

'We're not the ones threatening to blow the station, Ms Nbaro,' Pisani said stiffly.

Morosini nodded. '*No, no, I take her point completely. She means that if we want to preserve this fledgling alliance – a diplomatic coup that will undermine anything the NDR has tried to accomplish on the Fringe – we need to prevent the destruction of the station, which will make humanity look bloodthirsty.*'

Nbaro nodded. 'And I feel that the recent action against the pirates must be represented as such, so the Hin understand that such unfair and unequal combat is a matter of the rule of law.'

Morosini raised a hand. '*Mr Dorcas?*'

'Fully agree,' Dorcas said. 'Although, to my eyes, the Hin were very impressed by the show of force, as you no doubt intended.' He nodded. 'Followed by the arrival of three battlecruisers. I beg to differ with Lieutenant Lochiel – the advantage is entirely ours now.'

Morosini stroked his holographic beard. '*I agree with Ms Nbaro – she remains our expert on the Hin. Sentients are complex creatures… They can be impressed and still find our actions abhorrent.*' Morosini looked straight at Nbaro. '*As I did.*'

That's me told, Nbaro thought.

Pisani also looked at her. 'I'll take a brisker tone with Da Costa, propose negotiations, and point out that he's lost the Hin.'

As you always intended.

After some discussion between the captains, it was agreed to turn back for the station, to provide the stick behind the carrot of negotiation.

As people began to leave, Morosini asked her on her neural lace to stay, and she accepted a second cup of coffee.

'*You are concerned with the morality of all this?*' Morosini said. 'Yes.'

Morosini nodded. '*Once they launched their grand battle plan with ships coming at us from all over the system, we had little choice. The arms of their attack were not mutually supporting. We broke one,*' *ruthlessly – the one composed of the worst, most predacious people. We made our point.'* He waved a hand. *'Would you rather a close-in battle where we took serious casualties? Truekner? Dorcas? You?'*

Her face burned.

'I'd rather we weren't in this position at all,' she said. 'And I think you put us here.'

'I did.' Morosini nodded. *'And anything further is supposition. I don't suppose you'd like to take my word that the alternatives were much, much worse?'*

Nbaro glanced at Pisani. He was fiddling with his earpiece, but he was listening.

'I *almost* believe you,' she said. *But what if I'm wrong?*

Morosini said nothing, but she guessed he was exchanging data with Pisani.

Pisani nodded to her. 'Operation Marathon is back on.'

35

The *Athens* and her consorts decelerated further, allowing the debris of the battle to sweep past them: wreckage; disabled ships; an expanding cloud of gas; a belt of ablatives and reflectives launched by both sides. It formed an expanding field already more than three thousand kilometres across, and for some hours, Flight Eight rescue ships retrieved survival capsules, including Storkel and his whole crew, all alive, who needed immediate radiation treatment. They'd lost 6–0–5 in the last moments of the fight. Flight Eight also retrieved over a hundred survivors from the enemy squadron.

Storkel wasn't the only casualty. The waves of enemy missiles had achieved no direct hits, but radiation had penetrated the hull and the medbay was packed, again. More spacers had died aboard the *Athens* and the *Dubai*. Both Han and Gorshokov had taken doses. Han had the bad sunburn of a severe dose and was unconscious in a special unit.

As was Rick Hanna, with steam burns over half his body *and* a dose of radiation.

Nbaro knew all of it through the datasphere, as she and Qaqqaq worked with a dozen techs to bring the damaged *Pericles* back to fighting trim. Her entire avionics suite was removed and replaced; Nbaro couldn't leave the tiny bridge because, despite her reservations, she had originally installed a great many of the components.

Major Darkstar appeared in person.

'Nbaro,' they said.

'Tir?'

'The window of opportunity will close in six hours,' they said. And then, in a less formal voice, 'I'm sure you know this, Nbaro, but...'

'Going as fast as we can, tir.' Qaqqaq was used to pressure from superiors. 'Almost every electronic component on this ship was blanked by a close nuclear burst. They all have to be replaced and tested.'

Darkstar towered over the two women, silently.

'Which I'm sure you already knew, tir,' Nbaro said.

Major Darkstar gave a grunt that might have been amusement. 'My Marines will be camping just the other side of your airlock,' they said. 'I took the liberty of moving your armour and weapons up. Intel wanted to send a spacer. I told them Locran.'

Nbaro managed a genuine smile. 'I think we can find room for Locran,' she said, and went back to it.

Thea Drake was detailed to her, and the three of them lay on the floor, Nbaro and Drake passing black box components to Qaqqaq inside the avionics hatch.

'Watch the little hydraulics thingy,' Nbaro warned.

'It's the feed line for the acceleration couches,' Qaqqaq said in mock disgust. 'Not a "little hydraulics thingy".'

'I think she spends too much time with Dorcas,' Drake said. 'That was just his tone.'

Qaqqaq was invisible, but her voice carried. 'I have a limitless supply of indelible blue goo, Ms Drake.'

'Fair point,' Drake said. Nbaro wasn't sure that Drake even knew Hanna was injured. The neural lace was a two-edged sword

453

of information, and now she couldn't decide... *Say something? Let it ride?*

Nbaro had set her mind on the mission. She knew that Truekner was safe, and so were Mpono, Drake, Dorcas and Cortez. Hanna, Gorshokov and Han may yet live. She shut the rest out, rotated boxes, inserted components, watched red lights flicker to green.

After two hours, she couldn't hold it in. 'Thea,' she said on a private comms channel.

'Right here, honey,' Drake said.

'Rick took a heavy radiation dose.' *Almighty, I could have put that better.*

Thea was silent for a moment, and then she said, 'I know.'

That was all.

It took four hours. They had trouble linking the sub-AI to some of the sensors; Nbaro remembered that from the first fitting out, and she crawled into the belly and restored the links. The battle to come seemed very distant.

Qaqqaq ran a diagnostics check that seemed to take forever but ran for less than a minute.

'We're good to go,' she said. There was a slight catch in her voice when she said it, then she repeated it with more emphasis. 'We're good to go.'

Nbaro began to crawl out of the electronics harnesses in the belly, and she felt something pop at her neck, and then there was a single sweet chime.

She had no space to turn, so she continued her crawl. Only when she was out on the deck did she find that her gold charm was gone.

'Damn,' she said. *Not a great omen.*

'What's that?' Drake asked.

'I lost my charm,' Nbaro admitted.

Drake gave her a quick hug. 'Look at it this way, honey – if

454

it's really lucky, it's still somewhere aboard, right?' She blew her a kiss. 'Come on, Naisha. There's a horde of Marines…'

Qaqqaq was wriggling out of her engineering singlet and into an EVA suit. 'I'm crew,' she said. 'I'm going.'

Nbaro used her neural lace to contact Space Operations. '*Pericles* is green and go,' she sent, even as she stripped and climbed into her own EVA suit.

'Roger, *Pericles*. Cargo services is clamping a pod to you now.'

'Roger, Lioness. I have it. Clamps locked.' She looked at Qaqqaq, who was decent, and opened the hatch to find Gunny Drun leaning against it.

'Load,' she said with a grin.

She knew most of the Marines: twenty-four in all. She'd shot with them, fenced with them, been thrown around in low *g* by several. Wilson Akunje gave her a thumb's up as he slipped aft. McDonald managed a smile, and Juarez a fist-bump.

'Just get us there, ma'am,' she said.

Towards the end came Darkstar. The tall 'gyne had to bend almost double to get through the hatch. Darkstar, one of the ship's senior officers, coming in person, increased Nbaro's fear. This was a high-stakes gamble.

Dorcas came up in the datasphere. 'Until now I was locked out,' he sent. 'I assume you are doing something very important?'

'Yes,' she said.

'Hurry back.' She could almost see his smile. She wished her skills were better; he probably had the same avatar in the datasphere that he had in VR.

And then he was gone, and she appreciated that, too.

Morosini appeared, which was very odd, as there wasn't room for his projection in the tiny cockpit. Part of him was projected over Locran, who was just coming aboard.

'*I am making this gamble against my own wishes, Ms Nbaro,*' he said. '*If you feel that it is impossible, from a pilot's point of view, do not hesitate to abort the mission.*'

She smiled. 'Sure.'

'*I find myself in the curious position of feeling something. Is it merely risk-averse algorithms deep in complexity projections? Or is that what you feel when someone you like goes to a danger you don't share?*'

Nbaro found she was smiling at the projection of the machine intelligence. 'Oh, you big softy,' she said in exactly the tone that Drake would have used. 'We'll pull it off.'

Morosini nodded. '*If you do, we'll win. Really win – there will be years of peace on the Fringe, new allies, a whole new future. Of that I am confident. If you fail, I'll do what I can with what I have left.*'

Just for a moment, for the first time, Nbaro felt ... it wasn't pity. It was more like respect. If Morosini was for real, then he had worked selflessly for a human generation to save them from some terrible future.

If.

'If I survive this, and it works,' she said carefully, like a legendary hero dealing with a djinn, 'I want your word that you will explain some things about the past, and the future. I want to understand, as well as my merely human mind can understand, why my parents died, what you did, why we're here, and where it's all going.'

Morosini patted his cat. The cat looked at her with eyes of deep understanding.

'*You have my word.*' And he was gone.

36

The new flight plan for Operation Marathon was better than the original in almost every way. Nbaro detached them gently, and moved under thrusters into the back of the battle debris cloud, behaving like every other Flight Eight rescue vehicle. *That* was their window of opportunity: the moving volume of the former battle space, drifting towards the distant planet; the busy Flight Eight rescuers, searching the dense cloud of debris and chaff for survivors.

When she had her course and speed aligned perfectly, she turned everything off. The *Pericles* had a heat sink, and she got the hull down to the temperature of the debris around her.

They were moving quite fast.

Locran had the engineer's acceleration couch behind her, Qaqqaq was in the co-pilot's couch, but when the engines went off and they were in zero *g*, he unbuttoned and drifted forward. 'I don't get it,' he said.

'Don't get what?' she asked.

'How we're getting to the station. Ma'am.'

Nbaro built a little holographic projection in the air in front of them. The cockpit had a set of cameras for this; that's how Morosini projected himself aboard. And she could use it through the lace.

'Here's Medulla Station, in orbit around Medulla. Right?'

Locran nodded.

She moved further out. 'NDR squadron, accelerating towards *Athens*.'

'Check,' Locran said.

'Hin pods, accelerating much faster towards *Athens*,' she noted, and laid them out: two pods of three red dots.

She waved a hand and squashed the simulation down because she needed more space.

'*Athens*,' she said. 'Coming inwards straight at Medulla. Fast. Right?'

'Check,' Locran said.

'The pirates, chasing us in-system.'

'Got it.'

'*Athens* rolls and decelerates ...' She made that happen. 'We fight. *The whole fight* takes place at a huge speed while we're *still headed in-system*.' She made the battle volume float through the cabin.

'Damn. I didn't get that.' Locran shrugged. 'I do now. Now I feel stupid.'

Qaqqaq watched in fascination. 'I had no idea.'

Nbaro smiled. 'Tactics class! The battlefield debris moves – and right now we're hiding in it.'

Did Morosini attack the privateers just to create this debris?

Almighty. I bet he considered it as a factor.

Nbaro caught herself rubbing the bridge of her nose with two fingers – a tic from the Orphanage she thought she'd outgrown.

'We have a path all the way to orbital re-entry,' she said. 'Some of the debris will get caught in the gravity well, and it's moving so fast that it will hit the planet if it doesn't burn up. We are heavily stealthed – there's lots of crap around us that will have a bigger radar cross-section than we have.'

She touched up her holo display. 'And the NDR ships are all

458

running for the station, narrowing their opportunities to detect us side-on.' She looked back to see both Drun and Darkstar floating in the access hatch.

Darkstar nodded. 'Our odds of getting to the boarding action are approaching acceptable levels,' they said.

You aren't the one doing the low-level flying across an alien planet, Nbaro thought, but outwardly she nodded. 'Yes, tir.'

The little ship was ridiculously cramped with so many on board, and the one head was the first thing Qaqqaq had to fix.

'Shit,' she muttered. 'At least the shower works.'

Darkstar rotated their Marines through the four small folding sleeping racks; Nbaro set her acceleration couch to *sleep* and managed four hours. There was nothing else to do. This was a long, slow, anxious mission with too many things to worry about, and not enough to do to keep any of them busy. She and Qaqqaq took turns fiddling with the heat sink and the stealth programs. She walled off her dead, her parents, Sarah and Dorcas. She was good at that. She slept.

At twenty-seven hours, they passed into the shadow of the geostationary moon. The shadow gave them almost ten minutes, and Nbaro and Darkstar both exchanged tight-beam laser comms with the ship in microbursts.

They were still 'Go'.

They had less than two hundred thousand kilometres to fall into the atmosphere. The braking would have to be done with engines, and had all been programmed by Morosini – timed to coincide with the burn-up of nearby debris.

Nbaro reviewed it all on her neural lace. Morosini was no longer able to reach them, so she and her sub-AI had to do it all the hard way.

They did it. Sabina interfaced. They chose a nearby item of debris as the median and guessed its burn-up rate.

Nbaro ran the numbers twice. Everything still looked good.

They'd have to burn very hard to re-enter. But they'd have the whole bulk of the world between themselves and the station when they did, so the only eyes they had to worry about were the incoming NDR ships and the moon base.

There was nothing she could do about them. She had a stealthy ship and a good plan. The rest was luck.

She ran the numbers again, because she believed firmly that she made her luck by planning.

And I can be an idiot sometimes.

She was deep in a simulation of the first seconds of the burn when an alarm went off inside her head. It was disorientating, because the simulation was so immersive, and her first reaction was that the alarm was *in* the sim.

Not that lucky. Nbaro surfaced out of the sim, looked at the alarm for a moment, and then dived into the 3D system-wide projection.

The *Athens* and the *Dubai* continued to sail on, headed for a rendezvous with Medulla in twenty hours. The NDR forces were manoeuvring to form a battle formation to stop them. Three DHC battlecruisers raced from the other side of the planet, but they were all decelerating now in the expectation of combat. A third Battle of Medulla was sixteen hours away.

The reason for the alarm was obvious. There were, once again, new arrivals: nine ships, one of them big enough to dwarf the *Athens*.

They'd extracted out beyond the gas giant, almost exactly where the *Athens* and her consorts had extracted from Artifact Space ... they were Starfish ships. They were moving at almost 0.2 c and they were already decelerating.

Nbaro ran the numbers and checked with Sabina: the news was more than six hours old; space was vast, and light wasn't as fast as people thought.

The incredible acceleration and deceleration capability of

Starfish ships made it impossible for her to calculate exactly when they'd enter the combat arena for the various inbound Hin or the *Dubai* and the *Athens*.

She desperately wanted to communicate with Morosini, because her first thought was that her mission was no longer of any importance.

Almighty. This was an historic event; the Starfish had never entered Human Space. Not once. Not ever. Nor had they ever committed nine ships...

She thought of Dorcas, and the extinction of the Circles.

And Nik'ri Put and the Hin.

And Feather Dancer.

This was not part of anyone's plan – not their adversary's, not Morosini's or Saladin's.

Nbaro thought of the power of the weapon the Starfish had deployed back at Trade Point.

Morosini, Feather Dancer, Dorcas, Nik'ri Put, Trade Point.

She changed her mind. *If we can present them with a united front... we need to have the station.*

'Major Darkstar?' she called.

The 'gyne floated forward with a grace that only the spaceborn could manage.

'Nbaro?'

'Tir, there's a Starfish battlegroup extracting in-system. My guess is they're nine to maybe sixteen hours away from being in range of various allies.'

Locran was following along, accessing data feverishly. Nbaro had forgotten he was, in fact, an intelligence analyst.

Darkstar's face remained impassive. 'I understand. Anything else?'

Nbaro thought, absurdly, *If I live and get to tell this story, this is the punchline. Darkstar didn't even twitch. 'Starfish invading human space? Good. Anything else?'*

'No, tir. My first thought was that we should abort. My second thought was that actually, this just raises the stakes. We need the station. We need to knock the NDR out of the game.'

Darkstar was silent for a remarkably long time. Time enough for Qaqqaq to wake up and stretch, and for Nbaro to fidget.

'I've never seen most of those ship designs,' Locran said. 'My guess is they're Starfish warships.'

Darkstar glanced at Locran. Then back at Nbaro. 'As long as we're in space, you are the mission commander,' they said.

'I know.' Nbaro shrugged. 'I'm consulting you, Major. Your experience is ... a lot more than mine.'

Darkstar cracked a very slight smile. 'A little. None of it concerns events of this magnitude.' They glanced back at Locran. 'I concur. Let's go.'

Nbaro nodded. Ten minutes later, she spoke to their twenty-six Marines.

'In about ten minutes we're going to decelerate very hard. Strap in and make it tight. Strap everything down hard. We're going to burn hard all the way down into a steep dive, and then we're going to fly pretty tight to the surface of the planet for *hours*. But this is it – once we hit atmosphere, we're in all the way.'

There were some grunts and at least one *hoo-rah*.

Up front, Locran said, 'I thought you said this ship wasn't aerodynamic?'

Qaqqaq grunted. 'Everything is aerodynamic at three thousand klicks an hour. Anyway, the atmosphere is so thin that Mars seems soupy.'

The planet, a virulent orange, filled the windscreen like a malevolent sun. Nbaro could see storms the size of small continents, and mountains. She wasn't flying; it was all on automation, because absolute precision was essential all the way down. She'd run the numbers four times.

The first piece of debris caught fire and burned within four seconds of the computer prediction.

'Here we go,' she said, and let the programmed re-entry run.

It was like being beaten with a hammer. A heavy blow slammed into her, despite the best acceleration couch in Human Space, an EVA suit and armour. She wondered how bad it was for the Marines. She lost vision for a while, and almost lost her dinner. Someone screamed.

Might have been me.

The blow seemed to last forever – about 7 *g*, or so her inter-connections told her. And then they were *falling*, a distinctly different feeling from being in free fall.

They weren't even coming down on their thrusters. They'd already turned over so that they were flying – or falling – nose first. The stubby wings of the *Pericles* extended gradually, almost organically. They began to bite, and provide lift.

They were going very fast, and they weren't burning up. And no one was shooting at them. Nbaro checked; they were still in their very tight orbital insertion corridor, and the whole space-frame was vibrating now. Unlike space, air had flaws; nothing here could be taken for granted.

She used her lace to build in an alarm if her craft left the green corridor of safe orbital insertion, and then she looked back up into space. She was appalled to see how blind she was. She couldn't access much of anything, passively. Even the thin atmosphere of Medulla blocked her comms.

She hadn't seen that coming.

We won't know what's happening out in space for three hours.

She checked her instruments by eye, the old-fashioned way – instrument scan was too much of a habit to drop just because she could 'live' inside the plane's instruments – and they were coming to the end of the orbital insertion corridor, on course and on speed.

Now it was her turn. She would be flying for three hours, at low level, mostly by eye. Because Morosini had calculated that if they hadn't been caught on orbital insertion, the enemy ships probably didn't have look-down radars at all. And if they did, a stealthy craft a hundred metres off the deck...

The yoke came alive in her hands, and she was flying. But not with her hands. She dropped in to the datasphere of the *Pericles*, and she was the *Pericles*. She took in the data directly, and she responded with her metal and plastic body.

Time passed slowly, yet quickly, in the way of machines; there was a great deal of healthy detail, and not much else. In a very strange way, it was relaxing; for three hours, she felt no fear, worried about nothing, judged nothing. She *was* simply one with her machine, manoeuvring over the endless orange desert of iron-rich Medulla. She flew over canyons and valleys, and then, as she crossed an invisible shadow line – or information line – that let her see the station, came the hardest part of the mission for the pilot.

The part that required luck.

Her sensors, all passive, looked up at the station and the defending NDR destroyers, searching for traffic. Her antennas listened for spaceport chatter. Out there, above the atmosphere, they were still dealing with the clutter from the battle, orbiting the planet.

It was not Nbaro's day for luck. Nothing was leaving the planet; there was no NDR destroyer whose shadow she could use.

Neither she nor Morosini had really expected there would be. But it would have been nice.

They'd be naked for the last three thousand kilometres. Heavily stealthed, presenting the smallest possible radar and ladar cross-section. And out in space, if Morosini was still on plan, Pisani would present a new package of conditions simultaneously with a mass launch of two space wings, forming up for battle.

Every eye and lens and antenna should be focused that way.

Nbaro pointed her nose at the distant station and began to let air resistance slow her craft. She felt absolutely exposed. Anyone who had the means to look could see her craft, and she might as well have walked to the horrible showers at the Orphanage naked – that's how this felt. Daring the creeps and the bastards to come and hurt her.

It didn't help that they were decelerating all the way to their target.

It did help that Medulla Station, a Bernal sphere, had been built by the DHC, and maps of every metre of her hull and corridors were available for planning.

'Thirty minutes, folks,' she said to her passengers.

And if someone caught them here, they were dead, and no amount of brilliant piloting would save them.

Gunny Drun came forward to see her, and grinned.

'We're going to do it, ma'am. Even though Juarez just puked her guts out for three hours.'

'Almighty!' Nbaro said. They were high enough now that she could almost see space.

Drun smiled. 'I'm here to remind you that all you have to do is secure our retreat, ma'am.'

'I understand.'

'No, you don't, ma'am. I am not going to sugar-coat this. In every single exercise and sim we've run in the last five months, you've died every fucking time. You never learned, in any exercise we ran. You just can't stop yourself from taking a risk. But we ain't got a backup pilot if this goes pear-shaped, so please don't do anything that comes naturally to you. Do not rush the bad guys. Do not win more medals. Do not come and save me if my

465

arse is hanging in the wind. That is not your fucking job. *Your job is to save as many as you can if it all blows up*. Am I making myself clear, ma'am?'

Nbaro just looked at the Marine, her mouth slightly open.

Drun nodded. 'Ma'am, you have my absolute respect, but if it was up to me, I'd take your weapons and armour to ensure you couldn't leave the ship.'

Now she had to smile. 'Am I that bad, Gunny?'

He nodded. 'Yeah, you are. Now, did you hear what I just said?'

'Yes, Gunny, I did.'

'Good.' He grinned. 'I live for the moments when I get to ream officers.' His grin turned cold. 'Almost there. When we're down, just let us do it.'

'Roger that, Gunny.'

He nodded sharply and turned away.

Qaqqaq raised her eyebrows. 'You know you outrank him, right?'

'Not really,' Nbaro replied.

Locran laughed aloud. 'I was going to say the same to you,' he put in 'Morosini sent me to restrain you. Drun put it well.'

'That's me told,' Nbaro said.

They were seven minutes out. Her nerves were good.

At four minutes out they were interrogated by an automated IFF transponder. Locran had already provided a false ID code.

'Dirtside cargo hauler,' he said into the silence. 'Food for the station.'

It must have been accepted, because no one fired at them.

Station Control came up. '*Ibex*, this is Medulla Station, over?'

There was a very tricky piece of flying coming up, and they were forty seconds from passing into the shadow of the station and being almost undetectable.

Nbaro nodded to Locran.

He keyed his mic. 'Medulla Station, this is *Ibex*, over. Agricultural products for station consumption, ready to transmit lading.'

Nbaro dropped back into the *Pericles'* datasphere. She became her ship.

They'd slowed to match the orbit and rotation of the station-sphere. It was like a small moon floating in orbit over the major settlement, and it spun on its axis, providing different levels of gravity. The bridge was a magnificent xenoglas bubble at the station's north pole. She couldn't see it, because they were coming up from almost directly underneath, but it must have a superb view.

'Roger, *Ibex*,' Station Control said. 'Ready to receive.'

Locran smiled; Nbaro was aware of his almost feral grin as he jabbed a button on his console, and the contents of a very nasty piece of custom-built military software were dumped into the station's computers.

Nbaro had the exact temperature and pressure of the station atmosphere from data; she set their cabin pressure to match, and her ears popped.

'Ninety seconds,' she said.

'Hook up!' Drun called.

'Entry team ready.'

She was flying them along the surface of the station like an ant crawling over an orange. She suspected that they'd been seen now, if only by people looking out into space. But seeing them, and the transmission of that information to someone who could do something, were two different things.

'*Ibex*, you have left docking parameters? Please respond, over?' The station sounded calm despite losing them from radar.

Slower.

The bridge bubble appeared over the horizon of the station.

Nbaro was flying about two metres above the station at close to one hundred and fifty kilometres an hour relative to the surface.

Suddenly the spacecraft began to handle very badly.

'Thirty seconds,' she said. Everything read as green; the port-side engine showed a little extra thrust to maintain stability, and suddenly they were slewing…

She *was* the *Pericles*. With a thought, she shut down the port-side fusion engine and calculated the use of all her manoeuvring thrusters, cold and hot, to balance being on one engine. It was as instant as thought, like magic.

They weren't going for the apogee of the dome, because it was too high. They wanted a spot perhaps three metres up the side, where it projected above the metal surface of the station, at the base of the dome.

'Brace!' she roared, and flipped them end for end. She fired her thrusters, everything calculated by computer.

At exactly the planned speed and angle, her craft came to rest against the side of the sphere.

'Down!' she called.

The base of the Marine compartment locked to the sphere with a resin that was used in xenoglas industrial applications. It was given three seconds to cure, then the shaped charges inside the seal fired all together.

A six-metre circle of xenoglas blew inwards along fracture lines, and the atmosphere of the station mixed with the atmosphere aboard the *Pericles*.

'Go, go, go!' Darkstar called, and the Marines dropped straight through the roof and onto the bridge. The cargo pod containing the Marines was now sealed off from the rest of the *Pericles*. If Nbaro had to leave, those seals would hold, at least for a while.

'There's some fluctuation in the port-side fusion plant that I don't like,' Qaqqaq said. 'Is that why you killed it?'

Nbaro glanced at her. 'Yeah.' She was out of the *Pericles*' datasphere and now her hands were shaking.

'I'm going to check it out.' Qaqqaq slapped down her visor and went aft. Her boots sounded loud against the metal deck.

Below them, men and women fought and died. Nbaro hated it, but Drun's words were burning in her ears, and she knew he was right.

After several minutes of inaction, Locran put a hand to his ear. 'I think we have Da Costa,' he said. 'I have to go.'

Nbaro nodded. She popped the hatch and he dropped through into the command bridge of the station.

While she was dogging the hatch again, Qaqqaq appeared from the stern.

'I need to go outside,' she said.

Nbaro thought about it. They were in combat, perched atop a huge space station, and however lucky they'd been so far, soon someone was going to act against them.

'How bad is it?' she asked.

Qaqqaq looked harried. 'No idea until I look outside.'

Nbaro muttered something about a combat EVA, but she trusted Qaqqaq absolutely; the Inuit woman was like a rock – always reliable.

She thought about opening the airlock, and instead, checked her suit, closed her visor, vented all the cabin air into bottles, and opened the airlocks straight to hard vacuum.

Qaqqaq – small, compact and brilliant at EVA – slipped out. She wasn't wearing a harness and she took no precautions.

Nbaro checked comms, using low-power helmet radios.

Qaqqaq came right up. 'Got you,' she said.

After an agonising two minutes, Qaqqaq said, 'Something must have hit us. The insertion vanes…'

'Can you fix it?'

'Ask me in five minutes.'

After about one minute, Darkstar came up on their encrypted command channel. 'Phalanx, we have secured the command bridge and we have access to their encrypted comms. The counter-attack is inbound. I'm sending Locran and some prisoners for evac in case we lose the perimeter. Do you copy?'

'Roger, Miltiades, this is Phalanx, copy all. Be advised, we have some issues. We're working on them.'

'Copy that, Phalanx. Get it done. Out.'

Nbaro flipped back to helmet comms. 'Naisha?'

'We have a problem,' Qaqqaq said.

'Lost the engine?'

Qaqqaq took a shaky breath. 'Remember that lecture Drun gave you?'

Nbaro didn't laugh. She was already reaching for her carbine. 'Yeah?'

'We have two sticks of EVA-suited troopers moving along the outside base of the dome.'

Nbaro took a deep breath, and apologised to the absent Drun. Then she checked the boarding pistol at her waist and the energy pack in her gauss carbine.

'Where?' she asked Qaqqaq.

'On the port side, or I'd never have seen them.'

Qaqqaq didn't even have a pistol.

Nbaro tabbed the command channel. 'Miltiades, be advised, you are under attack from outside – two sticks, shaped charges.'

Darkstar's voice was calm and natural. 'Understand.'

'I am responding,' Nbaro said, and turned the channel off. In her head, she responded to her court martial. *My craft was inoperable. There were no other armed personnel.*

But in her head she heard Drun. *Do not rush the bad guys. Do not win more medals. Do not come and save me if my arse is hanging in the wind.*

'It's got to be me,' she said to no one. Or perhaps, to Drun, and Dorcas. She climbed through the open hatch to the surface of the ship on the starboard side, keeping the nose cone between her and the enemy. Her beautiful custom-made EVA suit made her graceful and fast. She used the bow of the *Pericles* for cover, moved forward along the starboard side, peeked out over the nose, about nine metres above the surface of the station.

The attackers were still fifty metres away, moving in bounds, with more caution than Nbaro would have used.

They are undertrained in EVA.

That's too bad.

Nbaro could barely breathe. Her heart was hammering. She was only going to get one chance at this.

She thought it over for perhaps one second and decided to use their caution against them. She leaned out, the surface of the station already very cold against her armoured chest, turned on the weapon's optics, picked her target, and shot him.

Gauss carbines have no muzzle flash. She took out the last trooper she could see. Then she shot the trooper in front, and then the next.

She got four before they realised they were under fire.

Number five dropped flat. She killed him despite the slight curvature of the hull. They still didn't know where the fire was coming from.

Another good lesson from all those exercises.

One of the remaining troopers guessed her location and threw a grenade. With her augment and her rifle and all its electronics, Nbaro shot it as it sailed through the vacuum.

Unfortunately, that gave away her position. She got another of them, and then a well-aimed EMP burst got her optics and her magnets, and the carbine was reduced to a complex club.

She turned on her reserve radio and turned the command channel back on.

'Militades, I have seven hostiles pinned on the hull. I believe I got the shaped-charge guy. They just EMP'd me.'

'On the way, Phalanx.'

Nbaro was now afraid to peek out. The aerodynamic antenna she'd used as part of her cover was being chewed away by slugs. She backed away again, deeper into the shadow of the hull.

She was in zero *g*, with no up or down, which gave her a crazy idea. She backed further along the hull, and radioed Qaqqaq. 'Bad guys incoming.'

'Shit,' Qaqqaq said. 'I'm not through here.'

Nbaro didn't have time to think it through. She bounced along the hull, switched her boots from *magnetic* to *sticky*, mentally thanking Mpono for showing her where to buy good EVA boots, and landed on the dome. Close up, she could see that it wasn't all xenoglas; it had crystal viewing panels set into the xenoglas. She got to one of the metal ribs, clicked her boots back to magnetic, and ran all the way to the apex. She almost overshot and just avoided hurtling off the top into space.

There was no room for hesitation. Nbaro guessed where the back of the enemy stick was, along the edge of the dome of which she was now at the top. She could only hope they were all watching the *Pericles*' hull for her. She chose a descending rib – one that she hoped came down a few metres behind the last enemy trooper – and drew her boarding pistol.

Then she ran down the rib. She no longer had her fancy optics, but the EMP hadn't got her neural lace, and she let it do the calculations as she crested the horizon of the hemisphere of the bridge dome.

She saw them, crouched against the dome, unmoving.

Too hesitant, she thought, but then, she was the one who had died in every exchange.

She shot the heavy pistol at a range of perhaps fifteen metres without thinking, without consciously aiming, and a trooper died messily, the top of his helmet exploding out with most of his head. Another step forward exposed the next and she shot the woman in the back. Bad luck, or bad tactics, sent her heavy bullet through the woman's EVA pack, through her back, out of her front and into the EVA pack of the man in front of her, so that her victim fell forward, spraying air and blood, and he turned...

They were very close, because Nbaro was still running down the dome, leaping, shooting on the bounce, so that the recoil drove her back into the dome, bouncing back into space with an outbound vector.

She took a round in the back that spun her around, but her armoured EVA pack shed the small-calibre round.

She wasted one of her own bullets driving herself back into the station, using it as a propellant to get a new vector. She'd never left the station by more than two metres, but floating was floating. She landed on her feet and her magnetic boots bit in, and she was hit again – a punch in the gut that meant her armour had held. She shot back, a range of perhaps three metres, as she'd been taught, a reflex honed in months of boarding exercises.

This time luck was with her; her shot didn't break the other man's armour, which was clearly better than his mates', but it drove him back, and three of them fell, bounced, rolled. She shot one without thought, and got hit again, spun, bounced, and lost her pistol.

On a positive note, she was now a few metres further around the sphere. She backed away, her hand reaching for her sword hilt. Her pistol was gone; she couldn't see it anywhere, and she had no time...

'Phalanx? This is Taxi?'

'Gunny? I'm behind them. They're all looking my way... I think.'

'Roger that,' Drun said.

Nbaro stood flat against the surface of the dome, presenting the smallest target she could manage, with her sword in her hand, for ten long seconds, and then ten more.

And then ten more.

And then Wilson Akunje was standing in front of her. 'Ma'am?' he said, helmet to helmet.'

'Very glad to see you, Wilson,' she managed.

'Might want to put the sword away, ma'am,' Akunje said. 'Is this your pistol?'

Twenty-six DHC Marines, no matter how well trained, could not hold a station designed for fifty thousand people, but Locran's best guess was that the NDR hadn't placed insurgents among the population, all of whom were locked down.

The more immediate problems were the four NDR destroyers in close orbit and the admiral's flagship physically docked to the station. Locran and Nbaro had the skills and the neural lace to make sure the ship's crew couldn't get back on to the controls; their cyber experts were locked out of all systems in seconds.

'Four hundred sailors aboard,' Darkstar opined.

'Just call for their surrender,' Nbaro said. 'We're perhaps nine hours from a general action, and they're doomed. All five of these are too far into the gravity well to survive battle.'

'My thoughts exactly, Lieutenant.' Darkstar didn't give away whether they approved or disapproved of Nbaro's contribution. They looked at Drun. 'Can Connelly do anything to interfere with their onboard systems?'

Connelly was the Marine data specialist. She was crouched over a terminal with Locran – a New Texan in the DHC Marines.

Wonder what's going on inside her head? Nbaro thought. They were facing New Texan sailors, mostly.

474

She looked back at her officer. 'I *think* we just shut down their environmental systems. Their supervisory control and data acquisition (SCADA) defences are pitiful, and I'm about to start flashing the lights.'

For the first time, Darkstar's lips formed a smile. 'Excellent,' they said. 'Comms?'

Locran pointed at someone, tapped his earpiece, gave a thumbs up.

Darkstar stood straight. 'All units of the New Democratic Republic, this is Major Darkstar of the DHC Marines. We are in full possession of Ultra Station and we request the immediate surrender of all military units in-system.' They looked at Nbaro and winked – something Nbaro had never seen the major do. 'We have possession of the station railguns, NDR. You have five minutes to surrender.'

'Station railguns?' Nbaro asked.

'Absolutely. You don't think we built a frontier station without teeth?' Darkstar shrugged. 'Apparently the NDR techs couldn't unlock them. Whereas Locran...'

Out on the hull of the station, pop-up turrets began to deploy.

37

Millions of kilometres away, the Starfish group powered in-system. There was movement almost everywhere in the system, but most of it was opaque to Nbaro and the Marines, and more than half the symbols on her laced VR screen were ellipses or unidentified blips.

What Nbaro could see was that the Hin ships continued to engage one another, but several had run, inserting in non-human directions and at non-human speeds. Three pods dashed towards a rendezvous with the *Beautiful War Dance*. As they came up, they formed a battle globe, a Hin formation of multiple ships that no human had seen before.

Some of the outer NDR ships had surrendered; it was clear from their manoeuvres. Others turned and ran.

Morosini surprised Nbaro and let them go. He didn't give chase, even though the DHC battlecruisers had the angle to do so. Instead, they passed the fleeing NDR ships, almost close enough for engagement, and ignored them as if they were annoying children. The battlecruisers continued on course.

The DHC battlegroup flipped end over end again, facing the Starfish. And then, using their big engines, the two greatships powered up, decelerating faster than the Hin as the Hin formed up. The human battlegroup passed through the Hin formation and expanded, interposing itself directly between them and the incoming Starfish.

Nbaro watched, her heart in her mouth, five minutes behind the action at relay speed. By then they had near-real-time communications with the *Athens* and the *Dubai*; someone thoughtful was posting some of the Hin communications.

Honourable Blood Wa-Kan Asinpal Las complained formally to Master Vettor Pisani that he was blocking her lines of fire to her enemies.

All four forces manoeuvred for another hour. Pisani kept the DHC ships between the Starfish and the Hin.

And then the *Athens* began to broadcast messages.

Feather Dancer appeared on vid, its words translated into Hin and Anglatin. Their Starfish was apparently using the correct data stream to transmit chemical codes.

In translation, it said, 'This space is human space. We welcome you to visit and trade, but your conflicts have no place here. If you attempt violence, we will retaliate.'

That's what the translation claimed it said. In fact, Feather Dancer went on for quite a long time.

The Hin was fluent, and Nbaro even understood a few words.

'These waters are ours to hunt. Come to trade, but hunt elsewhere.'

Locran surmised that these were the same Starfish they'd seen at Trade Point. The ones that Dorcas called the Pirates.

At a hundred thousand kilometres from the Hin formation, the Starfish flotilla began to slow, decelerating at their usual 17 *g*. Their formation spread, clearly looking for a line of engagement.

A lone NDR destroyer had actually *joined* the DHC formation, and she, like the other DHC ships, chose a line of action and manoeuvred there.

The Starfish continued to close.

The *Dubai* and the *Athens* had now deployed virtually every able spacecraft, a cloud of deadly attack craft behind literal clouds of reflectives that filled a vast volume of potential battle space.

Gradually, the Starfish coasted to a stop with a wall of sand and ablative clutter between them and their hereditary foes, punctuated by the DHC ships and their allies.

Another of the NDR destroyers left its brethren and joined the *Stealthy Change* on a vector. Otherwise, thirty-six ships from three races floated in space, watching one another, fingers or tentacles or rhinophores on triggers.

On the bridge of Medulla Station, no one spoke.

And then, as suddenly as they'd come, the Starfish began to leave, accelerating smoothly back to their insertion point. All except one ship, which tossed an object into orbit over the inner gas giant before accelerating to Insertion twelve hours later.

By the time the package had been retrieved and identified as a small cargo of xenoglas, Nbaro was back aboard the *Athens*, hugging Thea Drake.

38

New India was magnificent in every way: the beauty of the planet; the sheer opulence of her incredible station-side hotel; the food, and the unending work.

'You'd think we'd lost the battle,' Thea complained. Because New India was one of the DHC's most important, most valuable, and most highly populated planets, the cargo load there was as hard as it had been at Sahel. New India had an orbital elevator; in fact, it had two, because it was in many ways the hi-tech rival to Sahel, far out across DHC space to Spinward, and New India was happy to spend trillions of credits to show her advances.

But the planet had just spent almost a quarter of a year under a New Texan military government, and the New Democratic Republic had practised some very old-fashioned plundering, the marks of which could be seen in the corridors of the stations and dirtside.

Station-side liberty was complicated by the defection of three NDR destroyers to the DHC forces back at Medulla. They were now allies, and they had certainly held the line in the critical moments with the Starfish, but no one trusted them, and their spacers were not made to feel welcome on the docks or in the bars.

It was further complicated by the nine Hin ships that now, apparently, viewed themselves as close allies and trading partners. Fifteen degrees around the massive wheel of Simla Orbital, construction crews were showing off New India's economic and technological muscle by constructing a station area for the Hin. It was already flooded and under water pressure; Hin engineers had provided the chemical mix for the water, and humans and Hin were working together to install shops and hostels. Nbaro had supported Dorcas in this effort while flying four to six sorties a day, carrying delicate components all over the system, and down to the sprawling cities dirtside.

Thea Drake had worked around the clock for seven days. One unexpected consequence of her hunt for the hidden nuclear bomb, months before, was that she now had an unusual command of the lading lists and the locations of cargoes throughout the ship. She was in charge of collating battle damage to their cargo – a job that started with computerised lists and ended with Thea walking along dark corridors in the holds, looking with her helmet lights to ascertain the state of a cargo. A 30 mm iron round from a Hin gauss cannon did surprisingly little damage to sixty-four cubic metres of rice, and a great deal more damage to a two-metre cube of blown glass from Madagascar.

'There are hundreds of lawsuits already,' Thea said, throwing herself into the incredibly deep cushions of a massive chair. They had two, looking out over the planet. 'Only no one knows how to litigate against the NDR or the Hin.'

Nbaro was drinking a glass of something sticky and very alcoholic. 'Good luck to 'em,' she said.

Thea leaned out of her very comfortable chair to clink glasses. 'Are we going to have any ducats left after three days in this palace?'

Nbaro shrugged. 'You tell me. You're the brains of the outfit.'

Drake downed her drink and stretched her legs. 'I think just combat pay will cover it. We're not touching our capital or our xenoglas.'

Some of the spacers lucky enough to have bought into consortiums of xenoglas were already selling here at New India, at very high prices. Captain Hughes, the head of Cargo, had let it be known that he wanted the rest of the cargo to go to New London.

The news from New London was bleak. The DHC messenger service was down; the messenger pods had been taken out by NDR privateers until New London stopped sending them. But ships came through, some with the NDR's blessing and some covertly, and there was some news. Nbaro thought about it, savouring the sweet taste of her mixed drink, looking down at the blue and green and white magnificence of one of humanity's most successful colonising efforts. The news of their two-week long battle and its aftermath wouldn't reach New London for weeks – maybe months, if the messenger service couldn't be restored. But she could imagine the news moving through space with ripples of activity and change spreading in its wake.

And the news reaching them was mostly bad. Some said there'd been a coup against the DHC government; others said the coup had failed. No one could agree on who had backed the coup.

'How's Rick?' Nbaro asked. She'd meant to be more sensitive, but the booze hit hard, and so did the rumour that Eli Sagoyewatha, the chairman of the Directorate of Human Corporations, had been assassinated. Nbaro could remember him, speaking to everyone in the DHC sphere about the death of the *New York*.

'Better,' Thea said. The single clipped word indicated a great deal of worry and not enough news. Rick Hanna was badly burned and had radiation sickness; he was also sedated, so that Thea was denied even the kind of chatter that Nbaro and Dorcas had managed. And his condition was critical. 'Christ, Marca, I just want him to wake up. I don't give a fuck what he looks like.'

'I'm sorry.' Nbaro hated the hollowness of her words, but had learned they were better than nothing.

'Me too, honey,' Drake said. And then, with brittle humour, 'Let's just get drunk and not talk about it, OK?'

They sat, watching the planet turn beneath them, and drank too much. Nbaro thought Thea was right; it wasn't a bad way to spend an evening with a friend, and screw the universe.

She fell into the endless luxury of her station-side bed, with thick satin sheets and an apparently elastic mattress, but despite the bed – or perhaps because of it – she had some trouble sleeping; dead people, nuclear lightning, tentacles and the chapel at the Orphanage filled her dreams. And Dorcas...

For a few days after Operation Marathon, she'd taken Dorcas like a drug. But now he was working around the clock, and she was here...

...feeling sorry for herself.

The next day Dorcas was still working, so she and Thea cruised the station, visiting the shops, which were superb and disgustingly expensive, and met with Tad Dworkin and Storkel by chance. They ended up in a dockside wine bar with officers from DHCS *Lepanto*. Storkel brought a round of drinks.

'Here's to being alive.' Storkel's rich voice said it without disrespect to those who weren't alive. It was just a fact.

'Right you are,' Drake said. 'Alive and probably rich.'

'Except that the DHC is in the middle of a fucking civil war...' Dworkin said bitterly.

'It's not that bad...'

'There were riots!' Nbaro said. 'They used DHC Marines against rioters!'

Drake waved for more drinks. The exclusive wine bars all had human waitrons, an incredible display considering New India's degree of automation. 'The so-called rioters tried to assassinate the Doje. They may even have succeeded!'

Wrong target, Nbaro thought. *The Doje doesn't run the DHC – the AIs run us.*

Do I really believe that?

I should stop drinking.

The four of them looked at one another, raised their drinks and changed the subject.

An alarm went off, and Nbaro was groggy. Her mouth was like sandpaper, and she'd been snoring, and she was still in her flightsuit…

She rolled, felt a wave of nausea, and the opulence of her surroundings hit her. For a long minute she hadn't known where she was. *Medbay? Acceleration couch?*

She was on Simla Station, in the fabulous Star Mountain Hotel, and the alarm… was her tab, on the bedside table. It sounded like the shipboard collision alarm, and she wanted to swat at it, but she was still very fond of her tab and her sub-AI Sabina, who had saved her many times.

'Sabina?' she asked.

'Mr Dorcas has tried to reach you three times, and this time he said it was urgent.'

Nbaro touched the small ceramic weapon she wore under her arm, and tried to ignore the dull ache in her head. 'Call Mr Dorcas.'

'Marca!' Dorcas said. 'Where are you?'

'I'm station-side having a romantic tryst with Thea,' Nbaro said.

As usual, she watched Dorcas process this, first accepting it at face value and then registering the attempt at humour. She could already tell that his urgency was not life-threatening.

'All the better,' he said, deadpan. 'Nik'ri Put is asking for you, by name. We're a couple of hours from opening the station to the Hin, and Nik'ri Put insists on your presence. You might as well bring Ms Drake.'

'Er...' she began.

He smiled. 'Drink lots of water.' He sent her co-ordinates for meeting up. He waved and cut the connection.

She went to Drake's room, as opulent as her own. Drake had managed to get undressed, but hadn't made it into her sleeping robe. She was snoring. Nbaro grabbed an ankle and pulled.

'What the fuck!' Drake swore, snapping awake. 'Oh, God!' She put a hand to her head. 'Go the fuck away, Rick!'

'It's Marca,' Nbaro said. 'And we're needed to make some history.'

'I don't want to,' Thea said, rolling over and trying to hide her head under a pillow.

Nbaro retreated to the shower, stripped, and was surprised how much better she felt after a hot shower with beautiful soap. Then she poured a crystal glass full of cold water, went into Thea's room, and poured it over her friend.

'I'll *fucking* kill you,' Drake sputtered.

Two hours later, their hangovers hidden inside EVA suits, the two women joined political representatives from New India, as well as Master Pisani and Horatio Dorcas, as part of the official welcoming party.

'You realise that we're about to swim our way into a flood of your furry octopuses,' Thea said on a private channel.

'Almighty,' Nbaro said aloud. She hadn't really thought about it. But the space was huge this time, and the volume of water must have been vast; the engineering feat to make this possible might be unrivalled in human history, but then, the Hin were about to be the first aliens ever welcomed into a human habitation.

The docking iris opened, and they came in. There were more

than fifty, and they were in no sort of order. Seeing them gave Nbaro a queasy moment, but no one latched on to her suit or her mask, and after the much more agile Hin danced around them for a little, the speeches began.

Drake said, 'I *should* never forgive you for the cold water this morning, but I'm a nice girl, so ... set your helmet to pure oxygen. It'll blow your hangover away.'

And later, Nbaro swam through the enormous volume of red-orange water with Nik'ri Put by her side. Nik'ri Put was wearing a device that modulated her sound into the frequency of human hearing before putting it out as a radio signal.

'You are well, my *KePoja*?' Nik'ri Put asked.

'I am well, my dear *Tse-Tsu*,' Nbaro answered.

She didn't have to turn her head to see that they were being watched by dozens of pairs of eyes, both Hin and human.

'We are famous, you know,' Nik'ri Put said in Anglatin. 'I expect that there will be poetry about our meeting.'

Nbaro hadn't thought about that. She smiled. 'I think I like that,' she admitted.

'Me, too,' Nik'ri Put said. 'You know? Yes, and also yes. When you took me ... I was *afraid. Hyuk in te*! I could barely control myself. Dark ... everything so dry, instant death if my suit cracks ... and you ... You looked like a monster.'

Yes, Nbaro thought. *Yes, I'm definitely the monster here.*

'We learn about the old enemies, you know. And you *umani* look like *Venit* ... the old *Venit*, eh? Yes. And also yes.'

'The *Venit*?' she asked, but she knew the name. No one was allowed to forget information gleaned from aliens and passed to Intel. *Venit* was the Hin name for the Circles, or so Dorcas thought.

'You fought the *Venit*?'

'Everyone fought the *Venit*,' Nik'ri Put said with a tentacle

485

flick, dismissing the subject. 'But that was long ago, and *pffft*, thou art not the *Venit*, my good human.'

They entered a bar. That is, Nbaro knew it was a bar because she'd seen a mock-up before the ceremony. Everything had been fabricated in a hurry, but Nik'ri Put gave a bubble stream of pure pleasure, and moved to one of the dozens of elegant brass and xenoglas machines that looked like hookahs. The walls were a deep red plush that waved slightly in the currents, and there were several other Hin spacers, bodies orientated in every direction, sucking away at the hookahs and talking away in their dolphin squeaks. Nbaro was the only human.

'If we were home,' Nik'ri Put said, 'there'd be *osah* swimming in the water, so that we could take them and eat if we wanted. There's a game...' Tentacles flicked.

'I think we're a little short on *osah* fish,' Nbaro said. And then, 'You know, I was scared, too.'

'This is good, and also must be true,' Nik'ri Put said. 'And needs to be in my poem. I wish we could drink and take drugs together, like shipmates.'

Nbaro laughed. 'I had a little too much last night.'

'Ah!' Nik'ri Put said. 'This is also good.' She sucked greedily at her long, flexible straw. 'Ah! This is good. You *umani* are clever. A waterside port? Hin will *want* to come here. Your Fringers never offered us a port before.'

Nbaro laughed. 'They wanted military allies, not trading partners.'

Nik'ri Put jetted bubbles. 'Listen, I am being promoted. And I will go home. All the way home – a long way. My captain– mother's pod has been in space three lives-of-elders. We have much to report, yes and also yes?'

Nbaro noted Nik'ri Put's fluency; the alien had been speaking Anglatin, probably without pause, for weeks. She wondered if Dorcas could match her in her own language, and wondered, too, what the dangers were to only hold these conversations in human languages.

And she thought, *How far is it to your home? How many insertions?*

Nbaro hadn't been briefed on any of this, but she knew her lines. 'Will your people accept that we won't allow you to hunt Starfish in our space?'

Nik'ri Put took a long pull on her straw, and some coloured bubbles rose. Nbaro had time to note that Nik'ri Put used a sidelong glance in a very human way. *How similar are our brains?*

'You know now we have many ... groups. Factions. Nations. *Umani* have so many words to describe rival social entities. So do we, but ours all begin with family and relation–allies. Even then ...' Tentacles shifted restlessly. 'I lack the words. My mother–captain and her sisters and cousins, and the *Dodock-Geerlan* lineage are ...'

Another pull. More dark-coloured bubbles, rising ...

'We agree that we should treat your DHC' – she said DHC as if it was an Italian word, *dieci*: *dee-aych-ee* – 'as an ally. You and I ... we now have an honourable relationship. This is not binding like marriage or offspring shared, but it is binding. Please, do you understand?'

Nbaro tried to nod, but her helmet wasn't built for nodding.

'Yes,' she said. 'But to be fair, *Tse-Tsu*, we are not the same species and I'm not wired the way you are.'

'*Pfft!* We were the first breath of fresh water against the fur. Now there is the pull of a whole tide. We have hunted together, rescued each other, shared much. Is this so different from your people?'

'No,' Nbaro said. 'You are talking about loyalty.'

'Of course! A beautiful word. Something we share.'

Nbaro wished she had a drink. *Do AIs feel loyalty? Do human political entities feel loyalty? Do the Hin have a word for enlightened self-interest?*

But she let it go. She couldn't see anything to be gained by pursuing humanity's many failings. 'Will you come back?' she asked.

Nik'ri Put's tentacles rose and fell, the balletic movement that seemed to accompany happiness. 'This is what I am telling you, yes! And emphatically yes. I may even have my own ship. I will come with cargo, to trade.'

Nbaro felt a surge of affection for the tentacled little monster. 'I will look forward to that,' she said. 'What will you trade?'

Tentacle flick. 'That is my secret for now. We have many things that humans should want – you have things we will want.' She sounded smug, but Nbaro wasn't sure that was a human reading of an alien's words.

They talked for a while about promotion – something that seemed to cross all boundaries – and then each told the other a tale of their life before meeting. Nbaro talked about the Mombasa Orbital and their plan to raise a pod of whales, because it involved sea creatures; Nik'ri Put discussed visiting planets with various non-Hin life forms.

Finally, the humans were leaving, the ceremonies over. Nbaro took a deep breath and dared to ask the big question: the one that Darkstar and Morosini and the whole DHC would want to know the answer to.

'When will you return?'

Tentacle flick, as if it was a question of little importance. 'Wait while I calculate according to your somewhat odd reckoning.' Nbaro had spent enough time with Nik'ri Put and Dorcas to know that both Starfish and Hin calculated time based on a particular pulsar's millisecond rotational period. Terran years were incredibly irregular by comparison.

Nik'ri Put didn't use a tab or a calculator, either. She just did the maths.

'Perhaps as little as five years, four months, sixteen days, nine hours and some seconds. Perhaps twice that.'

'I may not be here,' Nbaro said, 'but I'll come when I hear you are inbound.'

'May I touch you?' Nik'ri Put said.

Nbaro hoped her hesitation didn't show. 'Yes,' she managed.

Nik'ri Put embraced her with eleven appendages. Gently, Nbaro squeezed back, trying not to shiver. The Hin's tentacles were very strong; Nbaro couldn't pretend it was a comfortable hug.

And yet...

39

'Rick tabbed me,' Thea said, and she wrapped her arms around Marca, and then they both hugged Dorcas. The three of them were sitting in their beautiful suite. They toasted Hanna's recovery, and Thea babbled for a while and then fell silent, a tribute to how much she had worried. The three of them sat in friendly silence for several minutes.

'I think Feather Dancer is preparing to replicate,' Dorcas said, as if that were the natural next step in the conversation.

Nbaro had drunk enough to become interested in the black marble floor with veins of something very green running through it; she was following the veins, trying to decide if the whole was a computer creation or real marble. It seemed to repeat, but then, perhaps they'd cut slices off a slab with a laser...

She sat up. 'What?'

She had been lying across Dorcas, and Thea was in one of the deep chairs, gazing out at the cosmos. The rotation of the station's wheel had taken the view of the planet away and replaced it with the infinite.

Dorcas swirled his amber liquid in a crystal tumbler and stared at it as if it was the result of a vital chemical experiment. 'I said—'

Nbaro cut in. 'Replicate how?'

Dorcas smiled. 'Ah ... Well, we were wrong about their reproductive systems, but then, we didn't have much to go on. The oddly shaped appendages? Apparently, they can bud a new Starfish.'

Thea Drake looked interested. 'Which oddly shaped appendages?'

'The rhinophores?' Nbaro asked.

'Rhino-whats?' Drake laughed.

'Actually, the cerata, although it is possible that the transmission of genetic-analogue material takes place through the rhinophores ...'

'I just love it when you talk science to me,' Drake said in an exaggerated purr.

'Cerata is a plural, from the ancient Greek *Keras* meaning a horn,' Nbaro said. She felt she had to, if only to prevent Dorcas from saying the same thing.

He smiled at her.

'I thought you turned your neural lace off when you were on the beach,' Drake said.

'I do,' Nbaro said. 'Some things you just learn,' she added, looking at Dorcas.

Drake giggled. 'Get a room!' she said. 'OK, they have horns. They're horny!'

Dorcas raised an eyebrow.

Nbaro giggled, and the two women, slightly the worse for drink, began to laugh uncontrollably.

Dorcas waited them out. 'It appears that small sacs of genetic-analogue material are forming at the tips of Feather Dancer's cerata. My intuition says it is replicating. My observation says it is about to produce about four hundred offspring.'

'Almighty,' Nbaro said, after a queasy moment. Then she thought about it.

It was not just a leap into the void, separated forever from its race. She was too drunk to think it through, but it looked as though...

'Have we promised Feather Dancer a home?' she asked. Dorcas drank off his amber liquid.

'Yes,' he said.

Nbaro winced. 'We live in interesting times.' She didn't have to use her neural lace to know that humanity had access to dozens, if not hundreds, of methane-ocean worlds. *Or would it be easier to just ruthlessly dispose of Feather Dancer now, rather than create... a subject population of Starfish.*

'Gack,' she said.

Thea looked at her. 'I'm not supposed to know any of this, right?'

Dorcas shrugged.

Drake sipped her drink. 'Fuck, just when you think everything is looking better.'

The cargo loading was every bit as hard as the unloading had been, and the suite of rooms on Simla Station became a fading memory. Nbaro was flying cargo runs around the clock as co-pilot, with Tatlah under instruction in the pilot's seat, a nice inversion of her own early days. New India's automated systems made her feel unnecessary, and she had time to consider the impact of all the technological change she'd seen in one cruise. It was only a matter of time before atmospheric cargo-haulers were... just robots.

New India had automated factories, automated space mining and automated exploration drones. She saw them on sortie after sortie, and when she ditched sleep for time with Dorcas, they went dirtside to see alien ruins between two six-hour flights. They had twelve hours together.

Dorcas hadn't booked them a room. Instead, he had a list of things he wanted to do.

492

She smiled, thinking of her first dirtside liberty with Rick Hanna. They were very different men.

One day of exploration dirtside revealed that New India had magnificent cities, a fabulously preserved section of Circle xenoarchaeology in what Dorcas thought was an ancient river delta, and sprawling shanty towns of desperately poor people who had neither DHC citizen rights nor any share of the riches being generated by automation.

'This isn't going to end well,' Dorcas commented.

'The poverty?' Nbaro was looking at a shanty town that ran right up to the security fence of the xenoarchaeology site.

Dorcas was looking at the interlocking circles. 'The *Venit* civilisation was destroyed,' he said. 'All of them died, I'd guess.'

She nodded.

He looked at her. 'Before this cruise, humanity had a cosy sense that we'd got past the Age of Chaos and we were home free. Maybe a couple of planets would fight a stupid war, but never the DHC or the PTX.' He shrugged. 'Now, it's like we're living through someone else's age of chaos, and we're not even important players.'

'But...' she began, and he shook his head.

'And the shanty town. No one in the DHC should be this poor. We tend to blame New Texas for everything, but look at this. Who let this happen?'

Nbaro wasn't ready to handle the DHC's many failings, because she was still working through the deaths: her shipmates, and the thousands of spacers she'd helped kill. But she did agree that the universe looked much more dangerous than it had on the day she'd climbed the boarding tube to the *Athens* airlock.

The Taj Mahal was tiny compared to the size of the city around it, but beautiful and stunning and remarkably *human*. She and Dorcas stood and looked at it for fifteen minutes, and Dorcas was silent.

'How did they ever get it here?' Nbaro asked.

'You could look that up on your tab.'

'It's more of a rhetorical question,' Nbaro put in. 'I've seen Qaqqaq at work. Engineers... they probably enjoyed the whole thing.'

They shared a meal – wonderful, fresh, complex, spicy food – with Captain Fraser and Captain Mpono, who they met by chance at the exit from the xenoarchaeology site. Mpono was on edge, clearly appalled by the poverty. Fraser was more phlegmatic.

'This isn't New London,' he said.

'They built a *second* sky hook to out-construct Sahel,' Mpono spat. 'They can fucking take care of their people.'

Heads turned.

'It's disgraceful,' Mpono said loudly.

There was a thick silence around them.

Dorcas said, 'I agree.'

They left through the silence and stares of the local elite. On the way back up to the ship, in Mpono's private barge, they turned to Nbaro. 'I wanted to talk to you, Marca. You have changes coming.'

'Changes?' Nbaro felt cold.

'I need you to fly the *Pericles* when we leave here. At least until Han is operational again, which is weeks away.' Mpono waved a hand, and Nbaro thought it was surprisingly like Nik'ri Put's tentacle flip, brushing objections away. 'I've already spoken to Truekner.'

'But—'

'But nothing. We have reason to believe there's bad guys several systems ahead. Someone took out all the messenger drones. Someone took down some passenger ships between here and Tamil Nadu.' Mpono leaned back.

494

Marca rubbed the bridge of her nose. 'Shit, I thought that part was done.'

'Welcome to the new world,' Mpono said. 'This won't be *done* for a generation.'

The last cargo was loaded, the last farewells said, the last hypocritical devotion to the DHC sworn. New India's puppet NDR government had fallen the instant the two greatships came in-system, but no one was fooled. There were people on New India who were very happy to be out of the DHC, but no one could say so with so much military force in-system.

Pisani, now the commander of the whole flotilla, ordered the *Lepanto* and both of the defector NDR destroyers to stay. He didn't even give a reason.

Nbaro had a farewell with her former captive. She swam in a wetsuit with just a respirator, and it was the bravest thing she'd ever done, because at the end of the swim they shared an embrace, and Nbaro *almost* relaxed.

And she thought, *The Starfish don't have a chance, if the Hin understand hugs. All of humanity will prefer the Hin.*

And in that moment, a thought hit her...

I wonder if Feather Dancer knows how to manufacture xenoglas?

40

They were three insertions from Tamil Nadu, but first they had to boost outwards to the insertion point and bid farewell to the PTX heavy cruiser *Stealthy Change*.

With commendable openness, Captain Jiang Shunfu informed Master Pisani that he knew about the route that allowed long-jump-capable DHC vessels to cross the middle of DHC space from Draconis to New India. From Captain Fraser's obvious consternation in the wardroom a few hours later, Nbaro gathered that it had been one of the great secrets of the DHC's commercial empire.

Captain Jiang was courteous enough to request permission to use the route. Pisani granted it with grace, and after some messaging back and forth, the *Stealthy Change* signalled her intention to depart and then took on a different vector, inserting two full days earlier than the *Athens* and the *Dubai*.

Nbaro was Tower for the extraction at Deng's Star and Lioness for the extraction five weeks later at HR 6426, a dull red dwarf in a system that looked like it had been stirred with a stick. All of the DHC navigation beacons had been destroyed, as if to remind them that they were still in something like a war. The two-greatship group deployed a heavy screen on system entry, every time; at HR 6426, Nbaro deployed her space wing in perfect synchronicity with the *Dubai*, thanks to practice and a neural lace. There followed four weeks of tedious searches and patrols, as the system offered a great many places to hide, but it was empty.

By the time they extracted at Li's Star, the glories of New India were a distant memory, and speculation was rife about the situation at Tamil Nadu, one of the most important systems in the DHC sphere. Would they find NDR resistance? Would they have to fight again?

Would there be shore leave? It was still almost a year to home.

They were transiting Li's system, deep in the boredom of the Deep Black, and Dorcas said, 'We should get married now.'

'Now?' Nbaro asked.

Dorcas shrugged. 'We could live in the same quarters, and Morosini would be forced by regulation to make our duty cycles match.'

Nbaro had been reading a manual on her tab, and Dorcas was reading somebody's xenoarchaeology paper, the two of them lying in opposite directions on Dorcas's acceleration couch. Practice had shown that if they lay in the same direction, eventually, someone gave in to temptation and no work got done.

She rolled over. 'That's very practical,' she said.

He shrugged. 'I could tell you that you're brilliant, and that you're properly snarky, and that your hair is fascinating...'

'What the fuck does that mean?' she shot back. But she was laughing.

'But mostly... I'd like to do it.'

She smiled, then frowned. 'You know that when we get back to New London, you'll be the husband of the Orphanage cadet who had sex in the chapel, right? Thornberg will have that vid everywhere.'

Dorcas spread his hands. It wasn't one of his usual arsenal of gestures. 'I thought we'd destroy Thornberg,' he said.

Her eyes widened. She could feel it. 'We will?'

Dorcas wore an expression she'd only seen a few times: once when he watched the video of the murder of the assassin on Madagascar; once when Feather Dancer described the treatment of its people by the pirate faction.

It wasn't anger or rage. It was a reptilian stillness. 'Yes,' he said. 'First, for our own interest. Second, because he and his faction have committed terrible crimes. And finally, I think you have proved to me that we are Morosini's tools, and that will be our task.'

'It doesn't sound so great, when you put it that way.'

Dorcas crawled to the other end of the acceleration couch and put his arms around her. 'One victory does not win a war.'

'Do *not* patronise me, Mr Dorcas, just because I intend to marry you.'

She felt him laughing.

'But my point remains. The other side, whether it's a group of AIs or a consortium of petty tyrants, were willing to kill millions and end the DHC to expand their own power. I guarantee that none of them were aboard any of the ships we destroyed. In many ways, nothing will have changed.'

'But *everything* has changed,' she said. 'We have our own Starfish. We will have a new trade deal with the Starfish and with the Hin. The PTX has the technology to go to Trade Point or anywhere else they want – in a decade, everyone will have it. And... I'm making a leap here, but surely Feather Dancer knows how to make—'

Dorcas's hand came over her mouth. 'Not even here.'

She nodded, and he nuzzled her neck.

She leaned back and then said, 'And you think we have to participate, instead of, say, buying a small ship and running off to New Shenzen to be independent traders.'

She felt his chuckle. 'I had the same thought.'

Nbaro smiled. 'It's Storkel,' she said. 'He's selling it as a retirement plan.'

Dorcas shrugged. 'Honestly? I will if you want. But I think I am enough of a patrician to believe it is my duty to stay and fight.'

'You will have to teach me all that,' Nbaro said. 'Any patrician I ever had in me got kicked out at the Orphanage. I'm not even sure that I think the patrician class is a good idea.'

'I can't wait until you're on the Great Council,' Dorcas said.

For the insertion to Tamil Nadu, Nbaro had the *Pericles* with Qaqqaq and a mostly recovered Gorshokov. She'd been flying quite a few missions with the *Pericles*, but not so many that she wasn't keeping in qualification with Flight Six, and Truekner never mentioned it.

No one opposed them, and the first ship to hail them was an armed DHC merchant, the *Cardinal Richelieu*.

At Tamil Nadu, the NDR had never taken control. A privateer fleet had swept through and destroyed some comms stations and the messenger relay, but a pair of armed DHC merchants had pursued and engaged them, and the war – if it had really been a war here – had moved out Fringeward to New Kyiv and never come back.

What was more, the messenger station had been repaired, and for the first time in more than two years, the *Athens* and the *Dubai* were back in the DHC information bubble. Tamil Nadu to New London was at least nine insertions – even for a long-jumper, a journey of a year. But the messenger ships were just engines and computers and a single human pilot; they would leap from system to system, transmitting the moment they were clear of their own extraction radiation. The next messenger would pick up the transmission, delete whatever elements weren't meant for its target system, and head for Insertion. There were never enough messenger ships to go around, so messages could be delayed, but when the system was working a message from New London could reach Tamil Nadu in as little as three weeks, and never took more than about ninety days. Old-timers called it the Pony Express and messenger pilots were a breed apart, flirting with the Flying Dutchman effect with every insertion.

At Tamil Nadu, the past and future caught up with them. Nbaro had quite a volume of correspondence from the City Investigative Branch of Special Services about the attack on her person (kidnapping, aggravated assault). The DHC promoted openness in its various civil services, and she was presented with details of the investigation, including the in-detention murder of the man apprehended for the attack.

'Almighty,' she muttered. She showed it all to Dorcas, and then, at his prompting, to Lieutenant Smith, who made clucking noises like a mother hen.

'Interesting,' he said. 'Someone didn't want him to talk, I'd say.'

And later that afternoon, as they fell in-system towards Tamil Nadu and its beautiful oceans, Nbaro was summoned to the Master's briefing room.

Everything had been restored. There was a magnificent table – perhaps it wasn't really wood, but something wood-like from New India – with beautiful matching chairs that were comfortable and yet severe in design. The landscape of the river and trees was gone forever, but in its place was another, of a sun setting over a nearly limitless plain. The artist had caught the vista, somehow making the savannah's extent nearly infinite even inside the frame. The tag said 'Sunset on the Serengeti'.

'Lieutenant Nbaro,' Pisani said.

She had reached out to touch the painting, and she snatched her hand back.

Morosini appeared on his throne.

'*This is a private conversation,*' Morosini said. '*I'm not recording it. The Master is here as the only witness, so that you will not feel this is some devious plot.*'

Nbaro felt as if a hand was choking her.

Morosini flicked his fingers and an image appeared: documents. He riffled through them, too fast for her to read. His cat raised its head.

'*Let me be brief. Working from within the Great Council and in alliance with at least one of the City bureaucratic AIs, either our adversaries discovered or Hakon Thornberg informed someone of your demerits. You were ordered dismissed from the Service.*'

Nbaro hadn't worried about this for so long that the blow came in under her armour.

She choked and fought tears. And made herself say, 'I understand.'

Pisani said, 'I told you this was the wrong way to go about this.'

Morosini was a blur, her eyes were so full of tears.

'*No, no,*' he was saying. '*You cannot imagine I would allow you to be dismissed from the Service.*'

Nbaro snuffled. She hated her weakness, but she felt as if her head would explode.

'*Your recommendations for a fistful of medals crossed with the orders for your dismissal. The recommendations were erased.*' Morosini shrugged. '*And then the conspirators attempted to seize the bureaucratic AI cores and made an attempt to kill the Doje. This will all be common knowledge soon enough.*'

She could see again, and Morosini looked *smug*.

'They did what you expected?' she managed.

Morosini laughed. '*You are too good to be believed, sometimes, Ms Nbaro.*' He patted Tom, who purred. '*Yes. They walked into a trap. In the very complex aftermath, your medals were re-evaluated by a less biased judge.'*

'Or perhaps differently biased...' she said with some bitterness.

'The point is that several prominent patricians were arrested for treason, and you, my good and loyal lieutenant, are confirmed in your rank and will receive the Starburst as soon as you pass your lieutenant's exam.'

'Pass the...'

Pisani was shaking his head. 'Morosini, you may be the kingpin of the DHC, but you still don't manipulate people as well as you think. Marca, Morosini set you up for rapid promotion, and he's using your level to leapfrog you *past* lieutenant, but you have to pass the exam so your promotion becomes permanent, and we can pin the medal on you and make you a lieutenant commander.'

Nbaro couldn't think of anything to say. She did realise that Truekner had tried to tell her this – not once, but twice, but not in so many words.

'So I'm in the Service?' she asked.

Morosini nodded. *'For now. I'm hoping you will agree to run for the Great Council in the spring elections.'*

'We won't be home for a year!' she said.

Morosini nodded. *'You are about to become the greatest DHC military hero of all time,'* he said. *'That fame will last about five months and then it will be forgotten.'*

Pisani laughed. It was a good laugh – the laugh of an old man who'd seen too much and survived it. 'Oh, Morosini, I find it very unlikely that anyone will forget Marca Nbaro.'

Nbaro passed her lieutenant's exam along with Andrei Gorshokov and Thea Drake, Tim Eyre and forty others, some of whom were still midshippers and some of whom were acting lieutenants.

One unexpected consequence of a three-year cruise full of heavy cargo movement and combat was that everyone passed; there wasn't a midshipper aboard who hadn't had to perform most of the testable scenarios in real life, and under pressure.

So when they finally had the long-awaited awards ceremony, the ship no longer had any midshippers, but some forty newly minted lieutenants. The list of awards meant that the ceremony would have lasted for seven hours if the Master hadn't elected to present them in batches. The messenger boat from home had held dispatches that should have reached them at Draconis.

Nineteen weeks later they did it all again as they entered HR 724 and received the next batch of dispatches, with awards confirmations and promotions following the actions at Trade Point and Ultra–Medulla. Then Nbaro heard the roll called of all their dead – heard the bravery of Ko and Suleimani extolled – and then was called forward herself to receive the DHC's highest honour. She really didn't hear the words as Pisani read off her citation; it all felt as if it was happening to someone else.

Afterwards she hugged Thea, and Dorcas, and even Rick Hanna, who was up and functioning, if still in pain. And Fuju Han, who was now a commander, set to be the executive officer of Flight Three; Cortez, who had medals of his own and was engaged to Klipac; Storkel and Dworkin; Mpono, now a full captain, and Musashi, now a commander, about to take command of Flight Five. Chu had been promoted to Chief Petty Officer, and so, in spite of his test-taking problems, had Patel; both were going to training commands. By the end of the cruise, most of her original back-seaters – those who had survived – were pilots and officers.

They still were weeks out from home, but in a way their cruise was already over, as people made plans for the future: commands, changes, resignations. Storkel was leaving the Service, going back to Terra. He was pulling strings and using his new fame to try to convince the DHC to sell him the *Single Star*, still strapped to the underside of the *Athens*, if slightly the worse for wear after several months of combat. He'd taken to eating with Nbaro since their shared liberty on New India; he and Qaqqaq had struck up a friendship that sometimes looked as if it might be romantic.

'You have a Starburst and a new promotion,' Nbaro said over pie. 'Why get out?'

Storkel rubbed his chin. 'I killed five hundred people,' he said. 'I don't really regret it. But I don't ever want to do it again.'

She accepted that. His ice-blue eyes said he meant it.

'Besides,' he said, 'I joined up to make enough to buy my own ship.' He shrugged. 'I got a piece of Hanna's piece of your xenoglas syndicate, so I'll do the DHC Merchant thing – get the government to pay a third, and I'll have a bird. Maybe I'll come out to the Fringe? Who knows?'

Qaqqaq shook her head. 'He wants the *Single Star*,' she said. 'She's riddled with dead systems, and she's taken hundreds of CIWS rounds from being strapped to our hull.'

Storkel spread his hands. 'She has big engines and lots of secrets,' he said. 'My ancestors were Vikings.'

Everyone laughed.

Mpono had already been selected to command the *Athens* as Master on their next mission. Mpono and Fraser joined their juniors at the usual table, and everyone congratulated them. Mpono looked strained. But they didn't say anything about their reservations until the others were clearing away their plates.

'I thought of saying "no",' Mpono said.

Nbaro nodded her understanding.

'Big patrician now, me,' Mpono said, aping their family's patois, and then, in a much primmer tone, 'I *really* cannot disappoint my mother.' They shrugged. 'Besides, there's never been a 'gyne Master before.'

'You are the best officer I've ever served with,' Nbaro said suddenly. It was spontaneous, and it shot out of her like a missile launch.

Mpono looked at her.

Nbaro grinned. 'It's true. You'll make everything better.'

Mpono looked at her. 'You are something else,' they said. 'Where did all the sharp edges go? You used to be such a little hard case.'

The changes rolled on. Truekner was promoted to Captain, but he was retiring; Thulile got permanent promotion to Commander and was taking the squadron, and all her spacers were being promoted, some to other flights. Nothing would ever be the same. Nbaro missed it already, and the last weeks had a curious air, as all of them felt nostalgia for a life they were still living.

The work was still hard, even as they all prepared for home. Everyone let their hair grow; cargo operations returned to the forefront of every decision, and by Montreal, it was half a year since Nbaro had flown any spaceframe with a weapons package uploaded.

Five insertions from New London, at Montreal, the DHC's third-largest system, she and Dorcas were married. There were dozens of marriages, and Montreal Wedding was a service euphemism for the relationships that had formed out in the Deep Black. It was somewhat anticlimactic, as they'd been together for almost two years by the time they were married.

It was odd, leaving the cabin she shared with Drake, and so she didn't, really. Many mornings in their dwindling store of precious ship days, she'd go to her old cabin and have coffee with Thea, and both of them would watch the interstellar DHC xenoglas markets. As the two greatships, loaded to the gills with fresh glas, headed towards New London, the prices went up and up.

But the work never stopped, and so, two days after her military wedding, for which she had worn a dress uniform and a sword, Nbaro was seated with Truekner, handling comms while he took re-entry and dived into an Earth-like atmosphere, through clouds, and then rain, to land on a water-slick runway on a vast ground starport outside New Quebec.

'Aren't you going to miss this?' she asked. They had to taxi forever; it took longer to reach their assigned loading hangar than it had to come down from orbit.

'What – taxiing?' Truekner said. 'No. I won't miss it.'

'Command?' she asked. 'Flying?'

He made a face. 'When I'm on the beach, and I've had a few drinks, I'll probably imagine that I miss it.' He turned his helmeted head and his eyes met hers, and she had a visceral memory of their first long flight together. His mouth twitched towards a smile. 'I liked being a glorified merchant officer. I think that's over, though. I think we're about to be a navy. The navy of an empire.'

Nbaro chewed on that while they unloaded cargo, and while she meticulously checked everything that was going into the belly of her spaceframe. Then they were taxiing out to their launch point with a full fuel load and cargo, and she said, 'Yes. Yeah, skipper, everything is going to change. But we need you.'

He smiled and started the preflight checks. 'Nope,' he said. 'I've done my turn. Anyway, Morosini asked me to run your campaign for the Great Council.'

She acknowledged to New Quebec Tower, got a launch window, and passed it to Truekner. He scanned his instruments; she adjusted the flow of hydrogen to her engines with her neural lace.

He sat back, allowing the full engagement of his acceleration couch, and she did the same.

'Now this part never gets old,' he said. 'Launching from a planet into space. This, I will miss.'

'Alpha Foxtrot 6–0–7, you are go for launch,' said New Quebec ATC.

'Roger, Tower,' she said, and they rose on a column of fire.

Epilogue

The Great Council chamber wasn't in the reconstruction of the Doge's palace, mostly because you couldn't fit three thousand patricians into a building constructed in the fourteenth century, no matter what anachronisms you allowed. The council chambers were in their own xenoglas bubble in one of City's two outer rings. Even though a great many councillors only attended by holocast, there were still more than a thousand attending in person, and many of them were there to see Lieutenant Commander Marca Nbaro-Dorcas, hero of what some politicians were already calling the Non-War.

She and her newly elected friend, Thea Drake, were in uniform, their midnight blue and gold especially striking in the chamber light. She wasn't as tall as people expected; Thea Drake was, but the taller woman didn't have quite the same air. Nbaro's husband came in behind her; all three of them were now great councillors, and he was dressed as a patrician, his hair in a queue, his brocaded long-coat almost brushing the ground.

As the foremost hero of the now-famous *Athens* voyage, Nbaro had been invited to speak. She gave quite a good speech, about unity, about the Hin and the Starfish, and the opportunities that the DHC had to be ready to grasp. She received a standing ovation, but then, as one wag put it, they'd have given her a standing ovation if she'd vomited on the podium, such was the power of fame.

At the end, she said what she wanted to say.

'Our society, and indeed, any society, depends on the faith of its people in the ideals of their social contract. When that faith is eroded, the ideals themselves wither, and the social contract is damaged. Those of us who fought the Non-War have seen the consequences of the greed and selfishness of a few. We will never forget our dead, nor the deaths we were forced to inflict to win a future for the DHC. It is my hope that, going forward, every citizen will look to the selfless sacrifice of hundreds of DHC merchant spacers, many of them my friends ... my hope that all of us will remember them, and keep faith with them. We who remain must polish our ideals and make the DHC better.'

Many seats were empty, because so many councillors had chosen to holocast in, and a thousand pairs of eyes watched the three new councillors walk up the main aisle, but Nbaro led the way and she seemed sure of where she wanted to sit.

'Hakon Thornberg,' she said. She made herself smile.

Thornberg had watched her come up the aisle. She knew that. But he was still surprised.

She sat at her new desk and smiled at the man who'd tried to ruin her life.

'If you attempt any kind of retaliatory action ...' he began.

Nbaro flicked her hand a fair copy of a Hin tentacle flick. 'Hakon,' she said, as if they were old friends.

He stopped talking.

She leaned over. 'Do whatever you like,' she said softly. 'Anything. See what happens.' She gave him her best wide grin. 'I thought it was best to say that in person. Save your threats. Just do ... whatever you want. And accept the consequences.'

She smiled.

Dorcas smiled.

Thea smiled.

Hakon Thornberg rose from his seat in the Great Council and left the hall.

Nbaro began to type on her tab.

Drake looked at her. 'That was fun. What are we doing next?'

'Next?' Nbaro said. 'I thought we'd get Mombasa Orbital a pod of whales.'

Credits

Miles Cameron and Gollancz would like to thank everyone at Orion who worked on the publication of *Deep Black*.

Editorial
Gillian Redfearn
Claire Ormsby-Potter
Millie Prestidge

Copy-editor
Steve O'Gorman

Proofreader
Patrick McConnell

Editorial Management
Jane Hughes
Charlie Panayiotou
Claire Boyle

Contracts
Dan Herron
Ellie Bowker

Audio
Paul Stark
Jake Alderson
Georgina Cutler

Design
Nick Shah
Tómas Almeida
Joanna Ridley
Helen Ewing
Rachael Lancaster

Finance
Nick Gibson
Jasdip Nandra
Elizabeth Beaumont
Ibukun Ademefun
Sue Baker
Tom Costello

Inventory
Jo Jacobs
Dan Stevens

Marketing
Hennah Sandhu

Production
Paul Hussey

Rights
Tara Hiatt
Marie Henkel
Alice Cottrell

Publicity
Jenna Petts

Operations
Sharon Willis

Sales
Jen Wilson
Victoria Laws
Esther Waters
Frances Doyle
Ben Goddard
Karin Burnik
Anne-Katrine Buch